The Blade's

The Sorrow-Song Trilogy

Part Three

By

Peter C. Whitaker

ISBN-13: 978-1977591630

ISBN-10: 1977591639

The Blade's Fell Blow

Copyright: 2017 Peter C. Whitaker

First Edition 2017

The right of Peter C. Whitaker to be identified as author of this Work has been asserted by him in accordance with sections 77 and 78 of the Copyright, Designs and Patents Act 1988.

All rights reserved. No part of this publication may be reproduced, stored in a retrieval system, copied in any form or by any means, electronic, mechanical, photocopying, recording or otherwise transmitted without written permission from the publisher. You must not circulate this book in any format.

Cover: The Blade's Fell Blow.
Copyright: 2017 Peter C. Whitaker

Acknowledgements:

For my wife, Donna, as always,

My children, Chloe and Oliver, for remaining underwhelmed,

My parents, Eddie and Beryl for having me,

David Moody who, at the time of writing is fighting his own battle with courage and dignity,

Paul Burnett and Patrick Gladstone for being friends for life.

And for Roy.

Table of Contents

Thursday, 28th September 1066 1
   Romney Marsh, Kent. 1
   Pevensey Bay, Kent 13
Sunday, 1st October 1066 16
   The City of York 16
   The Norman Encampment at Hastings 38
   The City of York 44
Monday, 2nd October 1066 74
   The City of York 74
   Norman Encampment at Hastings 80
Tuesday, 3rd October 1066 86
   The City of York 86
Wednesday, 4th October 1066 94
   The City of York 94
   The Village of Bexelei, Kent 102
   Coenred's Estate in the Isle of Holderness 107
   Ermine Street, the Road to London 124
   Coenred's Estate in the Isle of Holderness 133
Friday, 6th Octobre 1066 145
   London 145
Saturday, 7th October 1066 164
   The Palace of Westminster, London 164
   The Norman Encampment at Hastings 174
   Westminster Palace, London 178

Sunday, 8th October 1066	185
Coenred's Estate in the Isle of Holderness	185
Monday 9th October 1066	191
The Palace of Westminster, London	191
The Village of Lamberhurst, Kent	195
Tuesday, 10th October 1066	200
The Town of Hastings, Kent	200
Coenred's Estate in the Isle of Holderness	211
The Norman Encampment at Hastings	216
Wednesday, 11th October 1066	221
Near to Sentlache Ridge, north of Hastings, Kent	221
Thursday, 12th October 1066	229
The Norman Castle at Hastings	229
Near to Sentlache Ridge, north of Hastings, Kent	233
Friday, 13th October 1066	237
Between Sentlache Ridge and Hastings, Kent	237
Saturday, 14th October 1066	247
At Sentlache Ridge, north of Hastings, Kent	247
Thursday, 25th October 1066	365
Coenred's Estate in the Isle of Holderness	365
Rome, Italy. 1087	371
Author's Notes	375
Historical Personages	I
Anglo-Saxon and Viking Lexicon	i

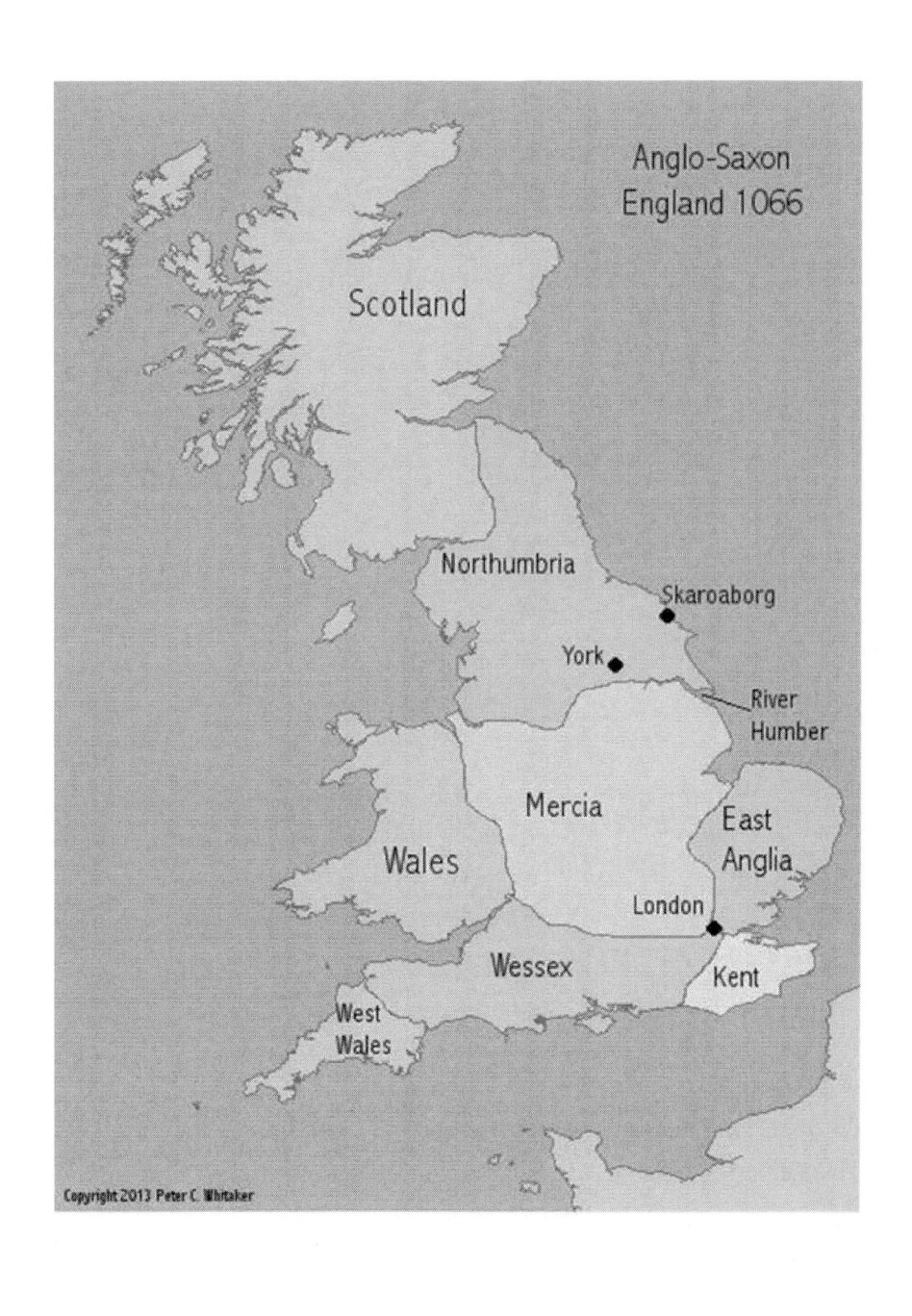

Anglo-Saxon England 1066

Scotland

Northumbria

Skaroaborg

York

River Humber

Wales

Mercia

East Anglia

London

Wessex

Kent

West Wales

Copyright 2013 Peter C. Whitaker

The Blade's Fell Blow

Thursday, 28th September 1066

Romney Marsh, Kent.

"Hence Heardred's end. For shelter he gave them, sword-death came, the blade's fell blow, to bairn of Hygelac." – Beowulf.

The dawn had broken upon a desolate spectacle. The surf was a distant sigh, no louder than the last breath to leave a man's body. It was a scene of isolation. Nature was raw here. The animals lived their lives on a knife's edge, or so it seemed to the men who looked upon this foreign landscape.

Robert of Saon stood on the English shore, breathing in the salty morning air, and wishing that he was back at sea again. Once more he turned on his heel and looked out to the far horizon. It was a desperate and pointless act, he understood that, but he could not resist the urge. He wanted to see the sails of the lost fleet. He wanted to feel, once again, that he was part of something great and terrible. He did not want to feel alone. All he saw, however, was the one ship that had accompanied his own and, like him, become separated from all the other Norman vessels of war.

"We should put back to sea!" Wadward insisted again. "We cannot beach the vessels here. We know not where the duke will be."

"But we already have," Hubert responded from a few paces away, "beached the ships that is."

He was right, of course. The tide had washed them in and they had, in their ignorance of their real situation, rowed the vessels up onto the beach in the dark of the early morning. The two vessels listed on the wet sand, stranded like whales after a storm. The Norman soldiers had quickly disembarked, many of them professing that they would rather stand on damp English sand than reside another hour cramped in the confines of the transport ships.

Robert sympathised with them. He was not a natural sailor and, like many of them, he could not even swim. He was not a natural soldier for that matter. Robert of Saon was a just a minor noble. He was a man who owned a small estate and owed fealty to Duke Guillaume, the master of the Duchy of Normandy. Outfitting these two vessels and most of the soldiers that they carried had almost bankrupted him. The several weeks spent paying for their inactivity as the storms raged through the channel between Normandy and England effectively had. Robert of Saon was made prisoner to the promises of Duke Guillaume by that nobleman's demands for servitude and loyalty. It was the assurances of land and titles that offered him the only hope of escaping the ruin that now faced his family. The barren sea coast of England did not offer much support to him in realising that escape, however.

"Robert, we must decide!" Wadward pressed him.

"I say we march south-west along the coast," Hubert advised.

"And leave the ships here for the Saxons to claim?" Wadward countered.

"The tide is out man, it will be hours before it returns."

"The duke was making for a point south-west of here, once the tide has turned and raised the ships from the sandbank we can follow the coastline and find the body of the host again."

"We sailed the channel last night in view of the fleet and your sailors still lost them, even by the light of a full moon!" Hubert replied derisively.

Robert of Saon wished that they would stop their arguing. He wished also that he could come upon a decision. He was unable to resolve for himself what course of action to follow. He could see merit in Wadward's suggestion to wait the turn of the tide and put out to sea once again. Indeed, despite the confines of the ship's timbers, that option appealed greatly to him. It suggested safety and less chance of being surprised by the enemy. His mind was frozen, however, by the knowledge that most of the soldiers were now camped on the sand. Many had built fires and were set about enjoying breaking their fast. He knew that they would resent being told to board the ships once more. Their voices would be raised against him in anger. Robert of Saon was only a minor nobleman; he had never wanted to be a leader of armed men. He did not deal well with confrontation, even from people beneath his station in this life.

"Robert!" Wadward snapped at him again.

"I think..." his voice trailed off as he continued to battle with his indecision. He mused for a moment more. "I see benefits to both sides of the argument." He chose to ignore Hubert's loud sigh and rolling eyes. "However, I am decided."

"Hurrah!" Hubert failed to keep his derision out of his tone.

"We are too few in number to march the land of our enemies; we will fortify our position and await the return of the tide. Wadward will then steer us to where he believes the fleet to be anchored. Once there we will rejoin the main army." Robert's voice had moved from a high uncertain pitch to end on a more decisive note. He nodded to emphasise that he was convinced of his own decision. "Yes, this is the right course of action."

"I agree!"

"It matters not," Hubert said. He was looking inland again, but only because he did not want to gaze at either of his companions at that particular moment.

"Your arguments, directed against Wadward here, would suggest otherwise," Robert answered him. He felt a little more confident now and he knew that he would have the mariner's support in this.

"Aye, you were set against my plan from the start." Wadward insisted.

"It matters not, I say," Hubert returned again. He looked down at the sand beneath his feet and spat. "I mark thee as my dying place, cursed land of the Angles!"

"What means this?" Robert asked with a touch of apprehension. He had thought that the confrontation was over now, a wave of relief had swept through him at the prospect of a decision reached and made, but now it seemed that Hubert was intent on starting another argument.

"What means this? I am abroad with children!" Hubert snapped back. His hands were now on his hips and he stood with his feet apart. It was a challenging stance. "If you had had any experience in the army of the duke you would know that we have wasted too much time. Whether Wadward was right or wrong matters not, a decision should have been made. It should have been made quickly. Instead, we have wasted close upon an hour trying to decide what we should do. Your vacillation, Robert, has doomed us all to die on a foreign shore."

"What mean you?"

"By my Lord Jesu, he means them!" Wadward pointed inland. Robert followed the mariner's extended arm.

"No!" He shook his head in disbelief.

"Call the men to arms," Hubert urged him.

"No!"

"CALL THE MEN TO ARMS!" Hubert shouted as he spun on his heel.

"No!"

"EVERYONE TO ARMS!" Wadward yelled as if he were competing against the roar of a storm.

"No," Robert repeated himself yet again, but he was not speaking to his companions. He had not spoken to them since finally realising what it was that Hubert had seen.

He was almost whimpering.

The armed soldiers quickly roused themselves. They were trained men. They had spent a long time training as there had been precious little else to do when the army had been camped on the shores of Normandy waiting for the unseasonal storms to abate. They formed into three ranks with those at the front presenting their kite-shaped shields as a defence. All of the men wore the typical conical steel helmets with the extended nose guard so favoured by the Norman fighting man. None of them, however, wore the expensive chain mail vests as their lord could ill afford to equip them with such expensive armour. Instead, they wore humble padded jackets. In some instances these had patches of hardened leather or metal plates fixed to key areas to improve personal protection.

The sailors were urged to join their fellows on the beach. Many brought spears with them, a typical weapon amongst the common soldiery. Some elected to use bows, however. They formed a loose line behind the practised soldiers.

"No," Robert said again in a plaintive voice.

"Robert, come!" Hubert took hold of the nobleman's arm and steered him back to the safety of the lines drawn up by their men.

"We must parley for peace," Robert now insisted. Hubert hated the sound of fear in the other's voice.

"There can be no peace between us and them. Duke Guillaume has invaded the land of the Angles, their King Harold warned him that such would be met by the cold steel of Saxon spears, this will be their only answer."

"But we can try?"

"Grip thy courage if you have any man!" Hubert snapped angrily. "You cannot appear thus before the men, not before they meet the enemy. You are a lord, act the part!"

They retired behind the small formation of Norman soldiers. Their horses had not been brought ashore as yet so the knights present, a mere handful, would have to fight on foot. They all wore heavy chain mail armour and helmets of steel, but then they were richer than Robert of Saon. It would give them better protection than their fellows would enjoy, mayhap, but it would also mark them out as the lords of these men and Hubert knew that the Saxons would press to kill them first. The knights had boarded their ships simply because there had been space in the holds of these vessels to carry them and their horses. It may prove to be a decision that they would come to rue. He glanced at Robert and saw the naked fear in the man's eyes.

"Ready thee men," Hubert called out in a loud voice. As Robert could not take the lead he would, if only to give these men that they commanded some semblance of hope. "They are Saxons only, peasants, farmers of the land with shit on their heels and wood-axes in their hands. They are not warriors! They are not a match for thee. Today, we will give the poets cause to sing songs about our deeds. Today, we will be the first Normans to spill Saxon blood!"

Hubert wished that he felt as confident as his words suggested. He had served in the army of Duke Guillaume previously. Indeed he was the only minor noble present, with the exception of the knights, who had any experience of actual combat. It was because of that fact that he was able to muster the scant power that they had, some sixty men, into a semblance of a defence. It was also because of that experience that he knew that their cause was lost even before the first blow was struck. He would die this day, along with every other Norman soul that stood upon this desolate beach.

Advancing towards them was a formation of men that outnumbered the Normans some four to one. It was not a loose band of peasants armed with farming implements, however. These Saxons were warriors ranged in three long rows, marching in good order and under the command of a leader who knew what he was about. The men at the front had their large round shields presented forward, loosely interlocked. Those warriors wore the best armour. Their role was to hold the shield wall intact and suffer what blows the Normans could land upon their defence. Behind them, other Saxons would reach over the shoulders of their comrades with long fighting spears to stab at the enemy. Theigns would also lash out with vicious Dane-axes or gold embellished swords to cut down the opposition. This was not a rabble, as he had suggested, but a practised fyrd, an army of trained ceorls and theigns. They existed to defend the people and their villages from marauders, more commonly the Vikings, but today it would be the Normans to test their mettle. They were coming to put their skills to the test against a new enemy.

"Stand thee firm!" Hubert shouted out as several of the sailors glanced longingly back at the safety that the stout boards of their ships seemed to offer. He knew that it was an illusion. The ships were too heavily ladened to be moved off this beach easily. Their holds were stuffed with the victuals and other necessary supplies for a campaign abroad. Re-floating them without the help of the tide was an impossible task. Even more so with blood thirsty Saxons at your back.

"We should have put to sea," Wadward said again. Hubert glanced at him and saw that the man wore a grim smile that was also somewhat mocking.

"One of us should have made a decision."

"Robert! Draw your sword!" Wadward shouted at their titular commander.

The Saxon fyrd halted, just short of a spear's throw from the Normans. For a moment the two forces faced each other in silence. There was a movement in the ranks of the Saxons and a man appeared before the shield wall. He was well built and wore a long coat of mail. His face was obscured by a steel helmet but his voice rang out loud and true.

"Normans, we know thee for what thou art, enemies of our land. King Harold bade thee not to set foot here upon pain of death. You have chosen death." The Saxon spoke with a heavy accent but his words were clear enough to be understood by all those who heard them.

"Our duke has brought a great host to thy land," Hubert answered him, but he chose to remain behind the protection of his men's shields. "Know that to oppose us is to bring death upon thy heads."

"We will deal with your duke after we have dealt with thee, if, that is, our king has not dealt with him first and cast his head into the sea." The theign was clearly unmoved.

"Draw thee back and leave us unmolested here, you will do well for such a course of action!" Hubert tried once more.

"Normans!" The word was spat out with disdain. "You come to our land unbidden and tell us how to act and what to do here. No one born beyond our shores tells a Saxon what to do. Prepare, now, to die!" With that, the theign turned and disappeared back into the Saxon ranks. The time for talking was done.

"They will press us hard," Wadward observed.

"They will press us to the earth and then they will press our bones beneath their heels," Hubert predicted grimly.

He opened and closed his grip on his sword once more and thought of his wife, Mary. She seemed to have made a life out of his long and frequent absences from their home. Theirs had never been a passionate romance, more a marriage of convenience really, between two people of similar station, but they had honoured each other in their own way. He felt a moment of sadness at the realisation that he would never see her or their children again.

If he felt any anger at his fate it was perhaps inspired by the thought that a man like Robert stood higher in society than he did and yet clearly lacked the same kind of ability that Hubert possessed. This was not mere envy on his part, he did not dislike Robert personally; he just felt that if the nobleman's advantages had been his own then he would have done far better in life, both for himself and for his family.

The air was suddenly rent by the noise of battle-horns. Men visibly flinched at the awful sound that assaulted their ears. After several loud blasts, the Saxons took up a rhythmic chant. It was accompanied by the tapping of spear and axe shafts against the metal rims of their circular shields. Continuing this liturgy they started forward with impressive precision. Their shields were drawn closer together, presenting an apparently impenetrable defence.

The only warning that the march had given way to the attack came with a sudden movement behind the front rank. The chant died on the air as a volley of throwing spears was hurled at the Normans. The heavy missiles were aimed at the tall shields presented to them. Spearheads impacted on wood and where they pierced, as many did, they made those shields heavy and cumbersome. More than one Norman found his defence dragged down by the weight of the stout shaft of the angon, combined with the heavy iron shank and head.

With a sudden rush, the Saxons closed on the Normans. Their shields clashed together and long spears licking forward with vicious intent. Anyone who had lowered their shield was vulnerable to this assault and their blood was quickly spilt. The Normans offered their defence with spirit, however. They fought back with spears of their own and also with flashing swords. Weapons forged with foreign steel that also drew blood.

The impetus lay with the Saxon's greater numbers, however, and they would not surrender it. To meet the longer line of the Saxon shield wall the Norman sailors, neither well-armed nor armoured, had placed themselves on the flanks of the soldiers. They could not hold against the heavy infantry that they faced, however. Saxon archers, moving independently of the shield wall, ranged around the sides of the Normans and sent well-aimed darts into their ranks. When the press of men came too close to clearly mark an enemy from a friend the archers slung their bows and drew their langseaxes, single edged knives as long as swords, and charged into the unprotected flanks.

The weight of the Saxons bore down upon the Norman lines and shattered them. The sand beneath their feet turned red and quickly became a mire to trap feet and limit movement. The Normans could neither retreat nor advance. Assailed on every side their men were cut down by axes, by glittering swords, by long reaching spears, and also by the langseaxes of the peasant soldiers.

After what seemed like only moments the violent struggle was suddenly over. The Saxons stood in the warm morning sun, breathing heavily after their exertions. Not a single Norman took a breath with them.

Pevensey Bay, Kent

The Norman fleet had sailed through the night heading roughly north-west out of St Valéry-sur-Somme. The wind had held true and the much feared Saxon ships had not attempted to intercept them. As Guillaume, Duke of Normandy, stood at the stern of his ship, Mora, he thanked God that the Saxons had not yet been encountered. His army would never be more vulnerable than it was now, crammed into the ships making the vessels difficult to manoeuvre. Skilled crews in swift Saxon warships could have dispersed his fleet at will and then picked them off one at a time. This invasion of England was a most dangerous enterprise and the crossing of the channel was probably the most perilous part of it. Now, it was complete, but yet new dangers were to present themselves. Those were, however, the kinds of danger that he, a seasoned warrior, could deal with. With his feet upon solid ground, Guillaume possessed the confidence to deal with any foe that challenged him.

Harold Godwinson must still be in London, he reasoned. Today it really did feel as if God was smiling down upon him and the Duke of Normandy acted the part. He was effusive with the crew, entering into their banter, complementing their seamanship. He encouraged the soldiers as they nervously awaited the command to disembark the cramped vessel.

The fleet crowded into the bay on the southern coast of England but there was an ordered discipline about their formation. The ships had first assembled back in July at the port of Dives, a time that now seemed like a distant memory. The sailors had had the opportunity, at least before the persistent storms had arrived, to be trained in marshalling their ships in such close quarters. They did so with little trouble. As also had been practised the archers were the first to disembark. They went with one arrow nocked at the ready and quivers full. Cautiously the bowmen made their way up the beach, spreading to the west and east as they went. They fanned out in a crescent shape all the time scanning the horizon for adversaries. None were to be seen.

Once the landing site was declared safe the general disembarkation commenced. Foot soldiers quickly alighted to set up a perimeter. Once they were ashore the knights followed with their horses. The sailors began to prepare their various cargoes to be moved from the ships' holds onto the beach.

Duke Guillaume watched with growing anticipation. No one could understand where the English might be or why they had not yet attacked. Convinced that all was safe Guillaume made his mind up to step onto the shore. As he came off the gangplank, acknowledging shouts from his soldiers with a wave of his hand, he lost his footing and fell. The men near to the duke watched in horror as he stumbled and came down hard upon his hands and knees. They were superstitious and the fall of their leader in such an ignoble manner would not sit well with them.

For a moment no one spoke nor moved.

"Look!" Guillaume cried suddenly. He clenched the damp sand in his fists and then raised his arms into the air. "I seize the soil of my rightful kingdom with my own hands!"

"That was close," Robert, Count of Mortain, commented dryly as he walked over to his half-brother. "And quick thinking on your part." He helped Guillaume to his feet. The Duke was weighed down by his armour and not as young as he used to be.

"I tell thee brother, God is with us this day!" Guillaume asserted. "Was not your crossing as smooth as you could wish for? No alarms! No sight of the enemy! Does this not go against all that those who opposed our plans counselled?"

"Providence is with us, brother, I agree with you there," Robert admitted. "There is yet much to do before I'll feel safe in this foreign land, however."

"Then let's to it. We are here now and I mean for us to stay!"

Sunday, 1st October 1066

The City of York

The great mead-hall of York had never been so full. High-Theign Aethelwine, as the feast-giver, had entered into the organisation of the event with a rare passion. After the first eve of the Battle at Stamford Bridge had passed Aethelwine had begun his preparations to honour both the victorious king and all of their fallen heroes.

His days had been spent in purchasing the necessary victuals and drinks, organising the menu, arranging the seating plans, contracting entertainers. The hall itself was being used to house the court of King Harold of England, but each evening afterwards the High-Theign emptied the long hall of everyone and decided what was to be done. Over the next seven days, his servants scrubbed it clean. The wall hangings were taken down; those deemed worthy enough to go back up were taken outside and beaten free of the dust that had accumulated on them. Some of the hangings were banished to the storage cabinets and were replaced by more expensive examples, those deemed more befitting for entertaining royalty. New straw covered the clean floorboards, scented with herbs. Tallow candles filled the place with warm light and lamps bedecked the tables. Four new trestle tables and accompanying benches had been ordered, along with fine goblets of silver for the nobles, of kiln-fired clay for the theign-worthy, and of artfully turned wood for the ceorls, the peasant class of Saxon society.

During the week leading up to the celebration feast, a selection of the captured Viking weapons and armour taken, from the field at Stamford Bridge, were fixed to the rafters of the roof. It was intended that all might see them and be reminded of the great feat of arms that the Saxons had inflicted upon their ancient enemy. The best quality arms and armour were to be awarded by the king to those deemed to have excelled on the field of battle, as a public display of gratitude. The rest were reserved for use by his army. Any metal armour was highly prized and even the King of England could not afford to outfit every fyrdman with a steel byrnie. The captured Viking armour would give many more Saxon warriors the protection that they deserved should they ever need to fight again.

The feast was being held at the king's command to honour the fallen. It was also an opportunity for him to introduce himself to his people in the north. It would obviously serve to remind everyone present that Harold of Wessex was the greatest of all Saxon aethelings. Therefore, on the day before the bread was to be broken, Harold suspended his court and went hunting instead.

At last, Aethelwine, his face still bandaged from the wound he had suffered at the Battle of Fulford Gate, got to lay out the hall. He had lost his eye due to that hurt but it did not hinder him from his duty as a Royal Theign. The trestle tables were bedecked with tablecloths and napkins made from fine linen. Eating in public demanded a certain set of manners and it would not reflect well on the feast-giver if he neglected to set a proper table for his guests.

Lamps had to be positioned around the hall to ensure that everyone would be able to see properly too.

Aethelwine even took an uncharacteristic interest in the choice of food to be presented to the guests. There would be beef from freshly butchered oxen, the quality of each cut reflecting the station of the guest. Pork was to be served in pies with their crusts moulded into clever designs. That which was intended for the table of King Harold would have the Wyvern of Wessex to adorn it. Unfortunately, the recent battles had meant a scarcity of game animals, but there would be poultry and fish to whet the appetite. The latter would be served as a pate, once again decorated to compliment both the guests of honour and the feast-giver himself.

All of the meats would be accompanied with rich sauces, fresh salads, and cooked vegetables. Mature cheeses would be provided too, along with various types of bread, some of which would be enriched with added milk or eggs. Late summer fruits would also be on every table.

Of no less importance would be the drink. The High-Theign of York was determined to impress his royal guests with a fine array of wines, ales, and mead. Weak-beer would be made available for the guests of lower standing. Indeed, it was of some relief to both him and the cooks that the best of everything would be reserved for the eorldermen. Those of lower rank would still be offered a fine selection but less time and energy would be spent in the presentation of those dishes. Even less again for the food intended for those of the lowest class who would be formally invited. Of course, the very poor would receive the leftovers after the feast, anything that could not be stored against the coming winter at least, and they would be grateful for it. The poor may go hungry through necessity but there would be many a guest who would fast before the feast. It would be deemed an insult to the feast-giver if they were not able to eat their share of what he offered.

There were many who looked to be seated with the king, of course, and it was not possible that they could all be accommodated. Eorl Gyrth, the king's brother, proved of great help in deciding who was worthy and who could be relegated to the benches. Nevertheless, the demand for just being present at the feast itself was unprecedented and Aethelwine had to appoint door-wardens to ensure that only the invited passed over the threshold.

Coenred was not disappointed to find that he and his men were sent to the benches. The presence of so many eorldermen and Royal Companions filled the top table to overflowing. He had no need to be seen in such company, although he noted that both Edwin and Morcar had been included. It was proper that they should be, as the Eorl of Mercia and the Eorl of Northumbria respectively, and it pleased him somewhat that they displayed the good sense to attend, with the appropriate humour as well it seemed. Coenred had not spoken to them since the day he had been called to attend upon King Harold at the makeshift court. At that audience, he had been offered, and declined, a place in the Royal Companions. The young eorls had not been happy to hear that the son of Eorl Godwin now coveted their captain of huscarls.

For her part, Mildryth preferred their allotted seat as well. She would not be on display to everyone else in the hall down here, as she had been at the previous feast to be held in this hall. She also hoped that they would not attract any undue attention. Mildryth had experienced more than enough of that recently. Their table was situated close to the top table, however, and it would give them a good view of the entertainment, but not so close that they would be mistaken for aethelings. Of greater concern to her was the immediate company that they would keep.

Sigbert was present with his wife, Hilda, a stout woman with a kind face and an easy manner. She chatted freely and seemed totally unimpressed by her surroundings. Nevertheless, she wore a fine dress of cobalt blue, with accessories of yellow. Around her neck hung a thick gold chain suspending a crucifix made from the same precious metal. Mildryth noted that Sigbert and Hilda were uncommonly devoted to each other, even in public. They sat close together, touched each other's arms frequently, and leaned close one to the other when they spoke. Without his armour, and in a clean tunic of earth brown, Sigbert looked more like a theign-farmer than a victorious warrior.

Young Aethelmaer joined them with a very fair companion, a young girl who looked to be terrified by the occasion. She barely spoke and sat as close as possible to Aethelmaer, an occurrence that he did not seem to mind at all. It was possible that she was actually uninvited and that Aethelmaer had somehow smuggled her past the door-wardens, or, mayhap, she was merely shy and overawed by the experience. Coenred did not seem concerned by her presence. Indeed he appeared to revel in the company at the table. Mildryth had never seen him like this before, relaxed and good humoured when in company, and it pleased her greatly. Not that she would have complained about the girl's presence herself anyway, whether she was invited or not, though she knew of some that would.

Another veteran of both the Battle of Fulford Gate and the Battle of Stamford Bridge also joined them; Thrydwulf. Although the rules of the feast usually restricted the presence of women as guests to those of a certain station he too was not alone. His companion seemed more of the world, a woman of confidence if not necessarily good character. In that, she seemed to reflect Thrydwulf's own personality. Her name was Osthryd and she spoke politely enough, but she also laughed readily at Thrydwulf's coarse humour. There was no doubting that their union was contracted for one night only. Again, Coenred turned a blind eye to Thrydwulf. As far as he was concerned his brother huscarl had hazarded his life twice to help bring about the cause of this feast and he was not going to chide him for a minor flouting of the rules of etiquette. Mildryth did not need to discuss the matter to settle her own opinion. She was grateful for what these men had done, for the hazarding of their very lives, and believed that they had a right to celebrate the victory in a manner that seemed best to each and every one of them.

Only young Hengist sat without a companion. Aldfrid had been his close friend, the two were of similar age, but Aldfrid was gone from this turning world now, killed at Stamford Bridge. Hengist smiled readily when anyone noticed him but the light would fade just as quickly from his face. He was a huscarl and he would bear his loss but the pain was still fresh within him and he was young. He did not know it and they did not reveal their concern to anyone else but both Coenred and Thrydwulf were keeping an eye on Hengist. They would not let him slip from grief into despair. Huscarls did not just claim a brotherhood, they lived and acted as brothers.

Others were of much happier moods than the young warrior. On such an evening as this, all the guests presented themselves in their finest. Gold, silver, and rare jewels adorned them and each item glinted in the torch light. The women had spent hours bathing, anointing themselves, having their hair dressed, and their best clothes cleaned. There were men present who also seemed to have spent just as much time in indulging their own vanity, but then this was a special occasion. It had been some years since the King of England had last ventured north and everyone wanted to see the event and, mayhap just as importantly, to be seen as part of it.

Minstrels played on harps and lyres whilst everyone found their seats or a place to stand at the rear of the hall if that was their lot. The musicians would reserve their more lively refrains for after the largest portion of food was eaten. Then there would be dancing to music played on drums, trumpets, flutes, and even bagpipes. Each musician would look to entertain the guests as best as they were able to. In the presence of the king, they could expect a fine reward. They each hoped for more than just the traditional horn of beer that Aethelwine was known to distribute. A ring of gold, a cup of silver, a precious jewel, this was the way of true ring-giving. Saxons liked to see people of merit and ability duly rewarded.

Everyone stood for the arrival of the eorldermen led by the king himself. If the guests thought that they themselves shone in the warm torchlight then the nobles simply glittered. Circlets of gold were on every head and jewelled rings on clean fingers. Broaches of the finest workmanship held light linen cloaks in place at the shoulder, many of such decorated with cloth of gold hems. Even the Archbishop of York himself was not above a demonstration of his wealth, he wore a fine gold crucifix decorated with rubies.

Once the guests of honour had taken their seats a minstrel stepped into the clear space before their table and sung a brief song of welcome on behalf of High-Theign Aethelwine. He extolled the theign's virtues as a loyal servant and a brave warrior, to which Aethelwine modestly pretended a degree of embarrassment. Everyone knew, but no one mentioned, that he had paid in advance for the song to be sung, as tradition demanded.

The food was then brought in. Servants entered carrying the first dishes, moving from the top table down through the hall. They struggled somewhat as they came to the far end where more people than were expected seemed to have managed their way past the door-wardens, or, more likely, dropped a few coins into their grateful hands to pass over the threshold unobstructed.

Edwin, son of Octa, stood near the back of the hall. He was the shield bearer to Coenred the Huscarl, but the feast was so well attended that there was no room for servants at the tables of their lords. Edwin did not mind, however. He was the son of a ceorl, a man who had been a farmer and one of the free peasant classes. This was only the second time that he had attended such a feast as this in his young life. Previously he had been commanded by Coenred to work in the kitchens. Tonight he took his place as a free man and he was happy with that, even if he did have to stand at the back and wait for the food to come to him.

As the servants worked to bring out the courses a scop, the very man who had performed in this hall before Eorl Edwin and Eorl Morcar on the eve of the ill-fated Battle of Fulford Gate, appeared. It seemed that the passage of the many days of toil and trouble had left him untouched. His tunic was still a bright shade of summer yellow, his trousers dark red, and his hair tinged with grey, but his face retained the vitality it had shown then when he had sung *The Wanderer* to the assembled warriors on that fateful night. This evening, however, he was here to sing the praises of a king following a victorious battle, rather than for the vanity of young noblemen before their imminent defeat.

He held his customary staff in his left hand and, turning on the spot, he bowed to each corner of the hall in turn. A silence began to fall on the gathering as they recognised that a poet of renown was about to entertain them. Once more his deep voiced boomed out beneath the rafters of the long hall of High-Theign Aethelwine of York.

If any living man longeth for glory,

And fame without gain would fain have for his own,

Then with my words would I beseech him,
On all sides about him far out to spy,
Clearly to look, south, east, and west,
And consider how broad with the clouds all about,
Is the vault of the sky. So may the wise man,
Easily deem this earth of ours.
By the side of that other wondrously small,
Though to the witless wide it seemeth,
To straying men strong in its place.
Yet may the sage deep in his spirit,
Feel great shame for the lust of glory,
When the thirst for fame fiercely presseth,
Although he may not make it to spread,
In no wise whatever, over these narrow,
Quarters of earth. How idle is glory!
Why ever, O proud ones, take ye pleasure,
To bow your own necks beneath the yoke,
Heavy and grievous, glad that ye may?
Why do ye labour so long in vain?
Aim to possess fame in the world,
Over the nations, more than ye need?
Though it befell that southward and north,
The uttermost denizens, dwellers of earth,
In many a tongue intoned your praises;
Though you were known for noblest birth,
Worshipped for wealth, waxing in splendour,

Dear for your valour; Death heedeth these not,
When heaven's Governor giveth him leave.
But the wealthy man, and the wanting in goods,
Death maketh equal, in all things alike.
Where now are the wise ones, Weland's bones,
The worker in gold, once greatest in glory?
I ask where the bones of Weland are buried,
For never any that on earth liveth,
May lose any virtue lent him by Christ;
Nor may one poor wretch be robbed with more ease,
Of his soul's virtue, then may the sun,
Be swung from his path, or the swift heavens,
Moved from their courses by the might of a man.
Who now is aware of wise Weland's bones,
In what barrow lying they litter the ground?
Where is the senator so mighty of Rome,
The bold champion of whom we chant,
Head of their army, he that the name,
Amid the burghers, of Brutus bore?
Where is the wise one that wished for fame,
The people's shepherd, steadfast of purpose,
That was a sage in each thing several,
Keen and the cunning, Cato was hight?
Many long days ago these men departed;
No man knoweth now where they be.
What is left of them but their fame alone?

Too slight is the glory of such teachers.
For they were worthy, were those heroes,
Of more in the world. But worse it is now,
When over the earth, in every quarter,
They and those like them are little spoken of,
And some not a few are clean forgotten,
And their fame cannot keep them longer,
Known to all men, noble heroes.
Though ye now deem, desire strongly,
That long in the land your life may last,
However, the better can ye be or seem?
For Death no man leaveth, though long it seem,
His life-days told, if the Lord it alloweth.
But what profit doth a mortal possess,
In this world's glory, if he be gripped,
By death everlasting after this life?
There is one Creator, we cannot doubt,
And He controlleth every creature,
Of heaven and of earth, and of the high seas,
And all the things that therein dwell,
Of those unseen, and likewise of such
As with our eyes, we are able to see,
Of all creation; Almighty is He.
Him humbly court all things created,
That of their service have any knowledge,
And none the less of those that know not,

That they minister unto the Master.

In us, He created ways and customs,

And for all His creatures peace unaltered,

Never ceasing in its nature,

When that He wished whatever pleased Him,

As long as He liked should live and last.

So it shall be, and for ever abide.

The scop bowed dramatically towards King Harold as he finished his recital. For his turn the monarch remained still and quiet a moment, apparently unmoved, his chin resting upon the heel of his palm, but his eyes were bright.

It was but a segment of the *Lay of Boethius*, a portion that dealt with the vanity of seeking glory when death would bring the same end to everyone, in line with Almighty God's will. Some might take it for a rebuke, some, like Eorl Edwin of Mercia mayhap, but wiser minds would find a lesson in the words of old King Alfred, for a lesson it was meant to be.

"You speak bravely," Harold eventually said. His posture remained unchanged.

"I speak as God inspires me, My Lord," the scop replied with his right hand over his heart.

"I do not doubt it and, therefore, I thank you for your lesson." Harold stood up suddenly and raised a golden cup in salute. "You speak bravely, I say, and rightly also. A fine performance I deem it. Fine indeed." He drank from the cup and when finished he tossed it freely to the scop who caught the priceless vessel deftly. "The first of many gifts this night.

"We won a mighty battle against the presuming Norse but this fight was not sought for glory. Nor was it fought for the fame of my crown, nor for that of my house. We raised our shields and brought down our spears upon the enemy for you, the people of the north. If old Hardrada were the Wolf of War then I am the Shepherd of Peace. God's will is for peace to reign in this land and He directed that the War Wolf be laid low and made food for the rapture of ravens. So often does the shepherd deal with the wolf when his flock is threatened. My good scop, thank you for reminding us, one and all, that it is to God that we must look for our deliverance. All glory that rises from this act belongs to Him alone."

The audience cheered the words of Harold, who seemed at that moment more one of them than a king upon a dais. Fists pounded the boards, almost deafeningly. In his turn, Harold of Wessex bowed to his people. He beckoned the poet closer and removed a large gold ring from his finger. He held the gem aloft for all to see and, with a smile, deposited it into the golden cup already given to the poet as a due reward. The sound of gold on gold brought another cheer from the assembled crowd.

Harold Godwinson was a ring-giver like the chiefs of old and the people liked what they saw.

High-Theign Aethelwine rose from his seat next to that of his honoured guest and raised both hands into the air to call for quiet.

Eventually, the guests obeyed him, or rather, ultimately responded in the manner that he wished them to.

"I can find no better suited moment, or words of greater wisdom, with which to open this feast. Break ye the bread upon the boards, drink the wine, one and all, for this feast is begun!"

They needed no further urging. Cups were raised and emptied in one draft and then everyone fell upon the food that was being served to them. As the feast progressed the noble lords took turns in praising their king. As the drink flowed ever more freely their compliments became less accomplished and often gave rise to unlooked for laughter from the benches. As this went on dishes were cleared away and replaced by new servings from the hard working kitchens. Some of the Royal Companions were eloquent, some were clumsy, but the best was brief. Harold seemed to take the praise in good spirits, even making fun of a few of the speakers. Finally, he rose to his feet to speak to the assembly once more before they were too merry themselves, and also so as to allow the rest of the evening to be occupied with dancing, singing, games, and ring-giving.

"Good people of York. Friends. This day is not for me; this day is for all of us. There are many here tonight who can trace their bloodline back to the Danes, and some of us might turn an unfriendly face upon such as them, but I hold them dear to me for when Harold Hardrada set foot on English soil and called for those of Viking blood to come to his banner, none did!

"England takes those of once foreign blood and makes them English. So it was with the Saxon, so it is with the Viking. It is because we become of one mind, one kingdom, one blood, that we have proved stronger than the Norse. Our shield wall is firmer, our spears longer, our warriors bolder.

"But we should remember the blood that has been spilt upon English soil to make this day a happy one. At Fulford Gate, many brave Saxons stood their ground and looked to turn back the threat of the Land Ravager. Those firm warriors have left this mead-hall, never more to raise a cup to their lips in our company. Do not let them be forgotten. Of those that survived that fateful day I give you gracious thanks for doing your duty!" Harold turned and raised his replacement golden cup to Edwin and Morcar, and then again to the general assembly of people before him. A murmur of approval passed through the throng. The young eorls nodded back their own acknowledgement in return.

"Still more brave companions we lost at Stamford Bridge; men of Sussex, men of Kent, men of Essex, men of East Anglia, men of Wessex, men of Mercia, and men of Northumbria. But think on, Saxons from the length and breadth of this Kingdom of England stood together at Stamford Bridge and their combined might was greater than the Vikings, great enough to destroy the enemy!" A roar of approval followed this declaration.

"When the men of England stand shoulder to shoulder what enemy can defy us? Gone are the days of the warriors of one burgh fighting to defend only their own land. Gone are the days when the people of Wessex care not what befalls the people of Northumbria. We are one now. One land. One Kingdom. One people!"

The ovation that the king's speech received was like nothing that anyone had heard before. Gyrth smiled at his brother as he stood there, toasting the crowd with a golden cup that had been placed within his reach and filled with more wine by a keen servant as soon as the previous one had been thrown to the poet. Perhaps it was all true. Certainly, there had been no exaggeration in what Harold had said. There had indeed been men from each of the great eorldoms of England in the shield wall at Stamford Bridge, but what Harold had not mentioned was just how hard it had been to get those men to come north in the first place. However, Harold had done it. He had broken tradition and moved men from the south to defend the north and Gyrth could see the value behind this accomplishment. If warriors would now move further than their traditional burghs to fight and defend the homes of other Saxons in other parts of the kingdom the king's army would become a much more formidable force.

The entertainment resumed once more as the king re-took his seat. They enjoyed a series of wrestling matches between men fighting for a ring of gold. Others tested their strength in lifting heavy stones. At more than one table a drinking game ensued and it was not long before people were falling from their benches or being heaved out of the door to avoid retching and staining the newly cleaned floorboards.

Coenred leant back from his table and smiled to himself. His fellows were being as rowdy as everyone else present. He did not resent them a moment of it. They were warriors one and all, huscarls, men who had sworn an oath to defend their lord with their own lives. The also defended all the people for whom their lord was responsible for and in that defence they might often die. At Fulford Gate over a thousand huscarls had stood firm before the spears of the Vikings and paid the fateful price of their courage; hacked down mercilessly. Brave Hereric had mustered five hundred huscarls to him as the battle went against the Saxons. He had won a respite that had given Eorl Morcar the chance to escape the Norse and flee to the safe custody of Coenred and his small band of warriors who had already rescued his brother, Eorl Edwin. From the edge of the marsh, they had watched as Hereric had turned his men to face the advancing horde of Vikings. In honour of their death-oath, they had flung themselves at their hated enemy to buy Morcar the time he needed to escape the field of battle.

Coenred would never forget the sacrifice of Hereric and his brave five hundred huscarls. They had died as warriors, with honour and the blood of their enemy upon their swords.

And then there had been Alfrid; the youngest of his band. Brave beyond his years, young Aldfrid had been cut down from behind while maintaining the shield wall at Stamford Bridge. The promise of his youth was gone, lost in a single moment, to a Norse sword stabbed into his back. The daughter of the Theign of Tadcaster would even now be weeping over his memory. They had stood in a field, hard by the wooden walls of the town. Believing themselves unseen their declaration of love had been made and witnessed all the same. Following the age old ritual of a young man and a young woman, they had plighted their troth, one to another, but with no chance to realise the love that had grown between them. Theirs was a bright but short lived flame extinguished by war. War was their work after all.

Thoughts of young Alfrid and his lover, Eawyn, inevitably brought the older warrior's mind back to the woman who sat next to him. He turned his head slightly so as to look at her unobtrusively. Mildryth was a Saxon woman of Nordic descent. A representative of the people that King Harold had alluded to in his speech. Her long blond hair was plaited and bound with a braid. Her blue eyes sparkled in the flickering light and a carefree smile graced her lips. It had been many months since she had enjoyed such a moment, free from the threat of danger. She was not a girl, like Eawyn of Tadcaster, she was a woman experienced in the ways of the world. Mildryth had been a wife to a middle theign and a mother to his child. She had lived and lost more than most people who had yet to see their thirtieth year. She was beautiful, it was true, but the shadows of sorrow haunted her as well. The acts of cruel men like Tostig Godwinson, the king's own brother, had marked her with the heartache of the loss of her only child and plunged her into the grief of widowhood.

It came to Coenred's mind then that she, like him, was practised in carrying the sorrows of this world. Like a warrior, she stood before that world and unflinchingly she braved the trials it sent her. The cold murder of her husband and son. The loss of their wealth and lands. Even falling again under the shadow of the very man who had done so much to destroy her life. She had also endured the Vikings in York once more. It was not that she had experienced so much that impressed him, it was that throughout it all, she had never surrendered, not once, to despair, nor sought pity from anyone. Mildryth had fallen into grief but she had survived it and still clung to life with a tenacious grip not suggested by those slender hands. She had a warrior's soul.

He began then to understand why he had been drawn to her. It was not her beauty alone, which was sufficient to attract the eye of many a man, he had perceived something more beneath that shallow veneer. He understood her pain and respected her stoicism as only another warrior could. They had both suffered wounds. Their battles may be different, like the weapons they wielded and the foes that they faced, but their fight was the same; to survive with honour. They were kindred spirits cast in different guises it was true, one a man and one a woman, but perfectly suited to each other all the same.

"I love you!" The words slipped out before he realised what he had said.

Her head turned and her eyes fastened upon him. The warmest smile he had ever seen broke over her face. Gently she laid her hand on top of his, her soft skin caressing his tough, battle hardened leathery hide, and she squeezed it affectionately.

"And I thee."

He had hardly heard his own words, the noise about them was so raucous, but with her feminine wiles, she had understood him. In the past, he might have been alarmed or embarrassed to hear himself talking to a woman in such a way. He had chosen the path of the sword and forsworn that of the husband. He had used women as men do when not looking for a wife. They had been just company for a short while. Thrydwulf was doing much the same with his companion this evening. His life had been one of sacrifice and the lasting love of a woman had been one of those sacrifices. Now, however, he sat in the company of one whom he intended never to leave again.

They sat in the mead hall of York, in the presence of the King of England, surrounded by eorldermen and theigns and proud warriors, but it was Coenred's dream of another place that filled his vision then. He saw not the stout timbers of the hall but rather the more humble walls of his house at Holderness. Mildryth sat not as a guest but rather as the lady of the manor; his wife. They would know peace there, in the Isle of Holderness, and he would be in her company never fearing the call of his lord to come again.

The blast of the horn was totally unexpected. It came from the main doors, which few noticed had been flung wide open in a most uncustomary manner. The general noise continued, however, as people failed to realise the significance of the interruption so the horn was blown again and again until the music stopped and the noise of drunken voices ebbed away. Once this had been achieved a warrior in full armour strode forward, towards the raised table of the king and his aethelings.

People strained to see, many of them rising from their seats. Coenred rose also and his men unconsciously followed his example. It was not to show due respect to a visitor, rather it was to ascertain whether or not the new arrival brought with him a threat of danger to the king. They saw a man in rich but travelled stained armour. He walked with a dread determination, looking both weary and distraught. Harold also slowly rose to his feet, his brother Gyrth joining him.

"Speak!" Harold commanded gravely.

"My King-" the man began.

"Speak!" Harold's voice rose and for a moment he looked most unforgiving. The warrior licked his parched lips nervously. "Alric, please, tell me your tale. You bring me woes but not by your own doing." The king's voice was calmer and his face softened.

"My Lord, the Normans are come!"

The Norman Encampment at Hastings

"Why do you stand here?" Odo, Bishop of Bayeux, enquired. Guillaume sighed heavily and did not turn from looking out into the darkness, beyond the castle's wooden walls. "Does something vex thee? Are you weighed down in your heart?" Odo persisted.

"No, brother, I am just enjoying a moment of solace."

"Ah!"

"Is there something that you want of me?" Guillaume did turn to face Odo now. He knew that such moments of peace and isolation were inevitably few for a duke, and usually as short lived as this one had proved to be as well.

"No, I just saw you stood here on the wall, in a place better suited for a sentry, and I thought that you might want for company. I realise now that I was wrong."

"Yes, you were, but I will not chide you for it." He managed a smile but Odo could not help noticing how tired his older brother looked. "I take what moments of solitude I can find and meditate."

"And I have spoilt this moment for you."

"Odo, if you had spoilt it I would have told you so." A more rueful smile crossed his face this time. "If it had not been you then I am sure that it would have been someone else, and I am glad to see you all the same."

"What were you contemplating?"

"That this might have all been a great mistake!"

"My Lord?!"

"Oh, come now, Odo, you cannot tell me that you have not thought so also, in your private chambers or when you were communicating with God?"

It was Odo's turn to smile now. In public, before the usual ducal audience, he would have had to measure his words carefully, but in private, like here, standing on this makeshift defensive wall, the bishop could afford to be far more sincere in the words that he spoke to his half-brother.

"If I have doubted this enterprise it is only in consideration of the fact that you might have overreached yourself."

"There is nothing new in that."

"Mayhap, but it is what I thought."

"And you did not concern yourself as to whether or not I am right to do this thing?"

"You have the pope's blessing, signalled by the giving of his banner. He has excommunicated Harold for the breaking of his holy oath to support your claim to King Edward's throne. The pope is the Vicar of Christ and through him, God's voice speaks to us. He chose you to be King of England."

Guillaume became pensive again. Odo was not saying anything new. They had had this conversation many times previously, in one form or another, and always his brother rested on his religious certainty. In a way, Guillaume envied Odo's unquestioning devotion to the church and, mayhap more particularly, to the authority of the pope. Like all Normans, Guillaume was also a Catholic, but his faith was far more practical for he was a soldier also. And yet he had found himself wondering, more than once as a matter of fact, if he possessed the right in this matter.

"We tricked Harold into his holy oath." The words invoked a look of surprise on the bishop's face. "You know this to be true, Odo."

"He swore to support your cause."

"He was my prisoner at the time, to all intents and purposes, and he was ignorant of the fact that you had placed holy relics for him to swear over."

"This is immaterial."

"No, it isn't, but it was expedient. Do you know what impressed me when I met Harold Godwinson that first time after his ship had been wrecked upon our coast?"

"That he was an able man."

"Yes, but more than that, that he had the potential to become an able enemy."

"You said that you liked him, personally at least."

"And I did, and I still do. He would have made the best of allies, which is the one reason why I wanted him to swear his oath; I genuinely wanted him to be my friend."

"He is foresworn now."

"He failed to keep a promise into which he was forced by circumstance and also misled by us two concerning the severity of the making of it."

"Still you excuse him!" Odo became somewhat incredulous.

"No, Odo, I do not excuse Harold Godwinson. I understand him and give a far more honest account of what happened as a matter of consequence. Because I knew that Harold would make a formidable friend or foe I feared him. I wish now that I had been far more honest with him, won him over to my side with true words rather than attempt it with deception and coercion. Indeed, I think now that our deceit is the cause of the violence that is to come."

"The pope was not wrong to excommunicate Harold."

"Had he known everything then I think he might not have been so willing; we tricked the pope too, Odo."

"God is on our side!"

"If he is then why did he keep us in Normandy for so many weeks with unseasonal storms? Why did he bring us here to England with so short a time for this matter to be settled? Where is Harold? Why hasn't he descended upon us with his army and thrown our corpses back into the sea?"

"You cannot gainsay God!"

"Because he moves in mysterious ways?" He spoke with a sarcastic tone.

"Guillaume!" Odo's face was turning red, even in the flickering torch light, the Duke could see the darkening of his skin. It only amused him, however. "It is not given for us to know God's plans. They are revealed to us only when the time is meet."

"Have you not thought, Odo, that all of this is indeed God's plan, to bring us here to a foreign land, far from Normandy, and make an end of us on the points of Saxon spears?"

"Never!"

"I have done many bad things, Odo, as the Duke of Normandy. I have had men killed and I have killed them myself. Do you remember that Pope Leo IX forbade my marriage to Matilda on the grounds of consanguinity?"

"Pope Nicholas II gave you both a papal dispensation."

"But what if Leo had been right? What if our blood was too close to allow us to form a marriage acceptable in the eyes of God?"

"The pope-"

"Was Nicholas right and Leo wrong?"

"The pope-"

"Is never wrong! Even when one pope appears to contradict the opinion of another."

"Guillaume, you are uttering blasphemies!" Like the sky, at the passing of the sun, the Bishop's face was once again changing colour. "I do not understand why you say such things?"

"You asked what was on my mind, Odo."

"Such thoughts should never be held, let alone spoken."

"Should we deceive both God and ourselves? In such a case how can we be true to ourselves or to God?"

"By following his teachings."

"But we don't though do we, Odo, except when it suits us."

"I don't know what you mean."

"Thou shalt not kill, but I do, I have killed many times."

"At Mount Sinai, God entered into a covenant with the Israelites. They were to obey His law by the letter and in it, the killing of people was permitted, in the right circumstances. Their holy book is part of our Holy Book."

"I admire your learning, brother."

"Now you are playing false with me!"

"Mayhap. What all my meditations bring me to, Odo is that nothing is decided." Odo opened his mouth to speak, probably to insist on a point concerning God's will, but Guillaume denied him the opportunity. "It is a gamble and nothing more. My army is not as large as I would like it to be and my landing in England happened much later than I would have wished it to do as well. The town of Hastings fell to us easily enough but then why wouldn't it? Their fighting men were few in number compared to ours, but one town is not a kingdom and when Harold comes it will be with a power that can at least match our own. I do not believe that anything is decided, Odo, at least not until I meet Harold on the field of battle and one of us is left lying there, dead and bloody."

The City of York

"We must move!" Harold said simply. "Gyrth, prepare the army."

"Yes, My Lord." Gyrth walked quickly for the door, his captains following in his wake, not waiting to be called by their lord.

"People of York, I must rudely take my leave of you before this splendid feast is even completed. More rude is this intrusion into our southern lands by a foreign enemy." Harold told them. "Those of you with a mind to aid your king may join me on the journey south." With that, he turned and followed in the wake of his younger brother, his Royal Companions abandoning the feast in a similar manner to the Eorl of Anglia's followers.

In an instant, all merriment was gone.

Coenred glanced at the men around him, saw their faces turned expectantly his way, and knew from the look in their eyes that their minds were already made up. Even young Hengist was looking forcefully at him. Coenred could and would, speak for them. He saw Mildryth's face also, read instantly the disappointment revealed there, knew that it collided with his own determination, but he could not allow himself to be deflected. He opened his mouth to speak.

"No words." She said simply. She squeezed his rough hand again.

In the sudden quiet it was no longer difficult to hear her voice. She wanted to cry, the tears were welling up inside of her, but she would not. In truth, she had known that his moment would come, even when Coenred had turned down the king's offer of becoming a Royal Companion. She knew also, deep in her heart, that he had not looked for this forced parting. Indeed, she believed in his intention to stay with her, always. He had not spoken falsely, but a warrior does not turn from war overnight. The emergency was too great and no man of character could spurn the king's call. She had fallen in love with him because of the strength of his character; she must learn to live with the consequences of that quality in these times of danger.

Coenred realised then the ferocity of his conflicted heart. He had indeed said that he would not leave her again and yet here he was, at the first suggestion of danger, up on his feet and itching to tighten his hand around the hilt of his sword. He was not yet a husband then. Again he looked into her eyes and saw emotions there that he was ill-equipped to understand, but, mayhap, more importantly, he saw no reproach. It seemed that she understood him better than he understood himself. Leaving the table he pushed through the excited throng. Voices were being raised again but now they were talking excitedly about what the messenger's news might import. He made directly for where Edwin and Morcar still sat at the table on the raised platform. The two brothers were in conversation as he approached but for once he did not wait on ceremony before them.

"Will you go?" Coenred demanded.

"What?" Edwin asked in surprise.

"The king asks for you, will you go?" Coenred almost glowered at them.

"We cannot," Edwin insisted. "Our power is broken. We have no men to take-"

"Then take yourselves." Coenred interrupted him. "There are still men, of both Mercia and Northumbria, who will make up the numbers and they will gladly follow you."

"We are decided." Morcar asserted.

"Did you not hear the king's words?"

"Oh, fine words indeed!" Edwin sneered. "But fine words won't win a battle."

"This is not about a battle, this is about the kingdom. This is about England!"

"And we are about Mercia and Northumbria!" Edwin retorted.

"Then it is done!" Coenred said with finality.

"What is done?" Morcar demanded.

"I leave your service, as does every man that follows me south." He turned and started to walk away.

"If you go south with the king you will not return north again!" Edwin declared to the huscarl's back.

"I would rather die under the banner of a real man than spend a lifetime with two boys who refuse to grow up and take their stations in this world!" Coenred spat back at them.

Morcar rose furiously and drew his scramseax, the jewelled knife that he had worn more as an adornment than carried as a weapon. Edwin reached out and grabbed his arm, holding him back.

"I should kill you!" Morcar raged.

Coenred turned to face him. Edwin rose to his feet then, tightening his hold on his younger brother, expecting violence to erupt immediately.

"I am a free man, Morcar of Northumbria, the choice to end my service with you is my right. You, however, have neither the right nor the ability to kill me in return; unless you attack when my back is turned, but that would be the action of a nithing!" Morcar pulled angrily against his brother's restraining hold but Edwin fought harder, genuinely afraid for his brother's life.

Although Morcar had a temper it would not compare to the huscarl's fighting ability. Coenred would have no trouble in killing the young eorl and in doing so with Morcar's own knife. As Morcar would be seen as the attacker, many a face was turned already in their direction as the argument grew, there would be no complaint to be answered for by an unarmed man defending himself.

"Go!" Edwin told Coenred. "Your time with us is done. Take what fools will follow you, we can do without them. I doubt that we will see each other again. I hope to never see your face again!"

Without another word, Coenred left the two brothers alone at their table.

***

Wulfhere had not been able to attend the great feast on this occasion, but he had loitered outside the mead hall nevertheless. He had learnt long ago that things happened in the presence of great personages and that those closest placed to learn of those happenings first often stood a good chance to profit by them. His plans for the immediate future were still unsure. It had seemed that, following the great victory, the king would stay in the north to reaffirm his governance of the shires. That had raised the prospect of employment in the royal household, but not as a fighting man. Wulfhere did not delude himself into thinking that he possessed the qualities necessary to become a Royal Companion, but there were other tasks that were required of lesser men. All he wanted was security and an easy life.

Outside the walls of York a hloth, a gang of outlaws, waited to hear from him. He had formed a loose association with them in order to stop them from slitting his throat when they had chanced upon each other in the forest after the ill-fated Battle of Fulford. He had been fleeing the lost battle then, they had been fleeing the law. He had led them to some little wealth, modest pickings to be honest, but it suited him because his was the role to find the mark, the one to be robbed, and theirs was to do the robbing; with violence if necessary. Wulfhere was quick witted enough to know that there was not much of a future to be had with such people, however. The war had seemed to be over and the pickings that a hloth enjoyed during times of unrest were likely to disappear once the fyrd returned from the field again. The tithingmen would soon be out hunting down the outlaws.

Even with the appearance of the Normans in the south, it was likely that many a warrior would remain here in the north to defend his lord's land and property. There might prove to be opportunities that would increase his lot, however, something less dangerous than running with outlaws, and in this life that was always Wulfhere's prime motivation.

His thoughts flitted to the woman, Mildryth; he had not forgotten her. Everyone knew everyone else's business in this world and the news of her compensation, awarded by the king himself, had reached his ears through the chatter heard on the streets. So had the news of her apparent union with that Captain of the Huscarls of Mercia and Northumbria also. Wulfhere had been around enough of those kind of men to know that it would be folly to challenge this Coenred in any physical encounter. Stealth would be his way if he were to exact the revenge that he contemplated.

And now the world changed again, as the poet fancied.

The Normans had landed in the south and the king must hurry to save his crown, yet again. All the great fighting men would go with him of course. That would leave her alone and unprotected, but what other opportunities might be lost to him if he were too rash. Many had died in these perilous days; lords still needed men to do their work. He could wait for his revenge. His main objective was to secure another post, best it be one that did not require him to hazard his life in these dangerous times.

Inside the great hall, the music had died and those stood without could hear clearly the voices of the guests talking excitedly within. The feast was ended early. Some were making their way home, their conversation dominated by the dire news of a second invasion. Others were calling their servants to them, beginning their preparations for following the king. Now might be a good time to listen out for an opportunity to volunteer his services.

Wulfhere passed through the doorway, no longer guarded by its' wardens, and into the hall. Although many had left there were still a fair number remaining inside and they communicated a frenzied air about the place. Men dashed past him with serious faces, going to do some lord's bidding with a determined attitude. With agile hands the former buttescarl lifted choice morsels of food from the abandoned tables, all the time listening as he wended his way through the confusion.

"I need more men!" A theign complained. Wulfhere's attention was immediately caught and he drifted over to where the man stood with several of his retainers. Wulfhere was careful not to attract the theign's attention yet, this might prove to be an opportunity to let slip just as much as one to seize. "There must be men of character left in York who cannot travel south but can guard all that I leave behind!"

"The battles have taken their toll." One of his companions pointed out.

"But even a warrior carrying a hurt can still do a lord's bidding." Another countered.

Wulfhere brightened at what he heard. This sounded like just the thing he wanted. He preferred the idea of going south, back to familiar surroundings, but with the enemy now present there staying in the north had become attractive to him once again. He knew that he could feign a wound as he had a ready one upon his face, a knife cut given to him by that whore, Mildryth. He could claim to have received it at Stamford Bridge, mayhap, and he still had some of his war-gear to impress upon them his martial experience and training.

Yes, this would do. Wulfhere closed in on the group and began to raise his hand to attract the theign's attention. He was barely a pace or two away when someone grabbed his arm and spun him around.

"YOU!" Edwin, son of Octa, declared angrily. Wulfhere was taken by surprise. For a moment all he could do was stare back at the young ceorl. "What mean you here?" Edwin demanded. He had been on his way to the stable to help his master when he had spotted the nithing who had once attempted to abduct the Lady Mildryth.

"Go thy way boy! My business has nothing to do with thee!" Wulfhere responded and pulled his arm free.

"But I still have business with thee!" Edwin insisted.

His hand fell to his side but his langseax was not there; weapons were not welcome at a feast. Wulfhere's eyes followed the movement of Edwin's hand and he knew immediately what had been intended. He drew his own scramseax. He had not been a guest at the feast, unlike Edwin, and therefore openly carried his knife in his belt.

"You would draw on me, eh?!" He shouted angrily and stabbed at Edwin.

People turned to see what the altercation was about. They drew back at the sight of the flashing blade. Edwin also stepped backwards and the knife missed him, but Wulfhere gave him no chance to grab his arm again, bringing the weapon quickly back out of his opponents reach.

They began to circle each other. Edwin looked concerned but unafraid. Wulfhere knew that he had to end this fight quickly. He would then claim that the ceorl had drawn against him first so as to be seen to be acting in self-defence. He tried to close the distance with Edwin, feinting with the knife repeatedly, trying to tempt Edwin into making a move.

When it happened it happened quickly. Wulfhere stabbed out and let his arm linger just a fraction longer than necessary. Edwin grabbed at it with both hands and Wulfhere crashed his left fist into the side of the young man's face. There was a pained look of surprise on Edwin's countenance. The fist hit him again but still, Edwin clung to the knife arm, fearing the danger that it held. Another blow and this time Edwin's legs began to buckle. Wulfhere used his weight to bear him down to the floor. He fell on top of Edwin, knees each side of his ribcage, and pulled his knife arm back and out of the other's desperate grasp. Edwin could see his death in the buttescarl's eyes as the knife lingered momentarily before beginning its' plunge.

"PEADA!" A voice roared from the crowd that had gathered to watch the fight with morbid fascination. Wulfhere froze. His eyes left the defenceless Edwin and searched the faces of the gathering. "PEADA, THOU CUR!"

A theign burst through the ranks of spectators. He looked to be almost fifty years old but he moved with strength and vitality. With surprising agility, he drew his foot up and crashed it into Wulfhere's disbelieving face. The impact sent the buttescarl rolling to the floor and allowed Edwin to scramble away.

"WHAT MEANS THIS IN MY HALL?!" Aethelwine now appeared, looking furious. He glared at the fallen Wulfhere and then at the theign who had kicked him, demanding an answer.

"This Peada, this disowned son of Amleth, is wanted for the murder of his own brother!" Explained the noble theign to his peer.

"I know you not!" Wulfhere declared, holding a hand to the injured side of his face. "I am not this Peada!"

Aethelwine nodded to his own people and two men stepped forward. They picked Wolfhere up from the floor and relieved him of his scramseax. They held his arms tightly.

"Who are you?" Aethelwine asked the theign.

"I am Ceadda, a theign of East Anglia, a follower of Eorl Gyrth. This dog's family live on my lands. He was caught stealing from his own kith and kin by his elder brother." The theign stabbed a finger at Wulfhere with each pronouncement. "This animal attacked his brother from behind to stop him from revealing the crime. Though sorely injured Peada's brother lived long enough to declare this nithing to their father. Peada fled before he could be brought before the court and then he roamed East Anglia as an outlaw. We thought him dead. His father wished him dead!"

"This is not true!" Wulfhere whimpered.

"On my honour as theign-worthy, I accuse you!" Ceadda growled. "I will drag you back to the Hundred Court in East Anglia and accuse you there and then we'll see how many oath-makers thou can command to speak for you."

Wulfhere had fear in his eyes. He knew the truth of what was being said but even more so he knew already the sentence of the court. No one would speak for him and there was no compensation to be paid to his own father for the death of his first son, Peada's brother, only one death for another.

"Eadgar was alive!" Wulfhere protested.

"He was alive when they found him!" Ceadda agreed. "He was alive after thee fled, but he died of the wound that you inflicted upon him. Your own brother!"

"This sickens me!" Aethelwine declared. "Ceadda, you go to fight under the king's banner?"

"Aye, I do."

"Then you don't need the duty of guarding this nithing when your thoughts should be on other matters. Leave him here in York until after you have met with the Normans." Aethelwine suggested. "My people will guard him well until then. He will face your Hundred Court, whole and hearty and ready to suffer their doom."

Ceadda grunted his agreement. He scowled one more time at Wulfhere and then left the scene. Aethelwine's men took a firmer hold of their charge and began to lead him out of the hall.

"Peada the brother killer; that tells me much about mine enemy!" Edwin hissed at him as Peada, once known as Wolfhere, was dragged away.

***

They had never made a march quite like this before. Of course, the eorls had made journeys around their earldoms, and, as huscarls, they had been required to accompany them, but the pace was often unhurried and there were people employed by the household to make sure that there would be places to rest and to eat along the way. Even Eorl Aelfgar's exile to Ireland and eventual march on Hereford did not compare to this adventure. That had been a means to change the mind of old King Edward concerning Aelfgar's exile, conducted in alliance with the Welsh who had scores of their own to settle. Even the occasional dash to respond to some danger did not measure up to what they were about to undertake.

The thrill of the journey had captured the imagination of the men of York, aided by the words of King Harold that dripped like wassail into their souls. He had filled them with a fire to fight once again. In truth, many of them knew little about what they were getting themselves into. For most of the city folk, a journey of a few miles would be considered a great feat of travelling. The thought of returning south with these southern warriors who had come to their rescue blurred the lines of reality. Most of them did not even own a horse; they would travel on foot all the way to London.

Coenred concentrated on the men that he knew, men like Sigbert, Thrydwulf, Aethelmaer, and even young Hengist. They were huscarls who could be counted upon. They knew what it was to be prepared and equipped for the coming encounter. There were many would be warriors who came to offer their service, wanting to be in the company of such great fighters as the huscarls, but Coenred sent them on to see the king's own captains, men better placed to decide who was to come and who was to be thanked but left behind.

He worked in the stables preparing his horses, glad that he had bought a replacement for Eanfrid's mount prior to today before the need had suddenly become urgent. Edwin worked alongside him and they kept their conversation business like. The young man seemed happy enough, quick to learn how to look after the animals even though his father had only ever owned one horse, and that was an animal that had always seemed old. It had been good enough for him to use when learning how to ride, however. He remembered it fondly and it showed in the care he took with his own mount and the new pack horse.

Coenred had noted the bruise on the side of the boy's face but as Edwin had not volunteered to explain it, and no one had come to complain about him, the huscarl decided to leave the matter well alone. Instead, he toyed with the idea of leaving Edwin behind with Mildryth, as a form of protection as he had done before the battle at Fulford Gate, but the lad had let slip enough comments to leave his master in no doubt that he had every intention of participating in this adventure. If he was honest about it, Coenred knew that such an act as leaving Edwin to watch over Mildryth would have been nothing but a peace offering only. It was something designed to alleviate his own sense of guilt inspired by Mildryth's disappointment in his quick decision to abandon her.

In turning down the king's offer to become a Royal Companion Coenred had been quite sincere in his reasoning, but he also knew that such a decision would have been welcomed by Mildryth as well. Indeed, the life of a huscarl had become less attractive to him anyway, and it was not just because of the young eorls. Holderness was a place of only fond memories and the thought of settling there with such a fine woman, as he held Mildryth to be, had led him to seriously contemplate leaving his service as a huscarl in the very near future. Mildryth's receipt of the king's compensation even made that decision more practical.

He could not, however, turn his back on his king and his friends in this time of danger, not in the same manner as Edwin and Morcar had. The eorls were honour bound to defend their king, to bring whatever forces they could muster. They were bound by blood also; their older sister was now married to Harold. He was their brother and their king.

My king.

That was a new thought. He had on occasion travelled to London with Eorl Aelfgar, father to Edwin and Morcar, to visit the court of King Edward. He had not been impressed. There was money and there was power at the court, but the king had seemed shallow, always keen to display his piety, constantly reminding the court as to the alms that he dispensed to the poor, as well as the building of the abbey at Westminster; dedicated to the glory of God. In matters of state, he seemed weak and indecisive, and far too reliant upon the counsel of his Norman advisors. Edward was then King of England but he had not been Coenred's king. In this Harold was different. In this Edwin and Morcar were wrong.

Mayhap, they may be right in that to fight under the king's banner might lead only to death and defeat, but huscarls did not stop to consider such eventualities. Death was a part of their life as warriors. Even so, he knew that this turn of events would cause Mildryth pain. He did not know what to do about that, except to try and recall how they had felt and acted before the battle at Stamford Bridge. If only that had been his last such fight.

His duty had seemed clear then, without any other considerations, the way it had been before she had given him her knife as a token of her faith in him. He remembered now why he had not gone looking for a wife before. He had never had this conflict to deal with previously; always his lord had come first. Always there had been nothing to deflect him from that determination. But now he had two duties, one to his lord and one to his woman, and they were in opposition.

He was too long the warrior to even think of abandoning the king, and too soon a lover to be able to place Mildryth above him in his loyalties. They were the same in many respects, but that did not ease the pain that he felt. He thought that he had been right in the past, that to have this distraction was not good for a man who lived by the sword, and yet he knew for certain that he could not surrender Mildryth either. She had become necessary to him.

"The dawn will soon be breaking," Sigbert commented. "You must go speak to her." Coenred glanced at his friend from where he worked on the horse.

"You have taken your leave of Hilda?" He asked.

"That is something of which I wish to speak to you, come over here a ways, Coenred." The man looked grave. Coenred did not understand and looked more acutely at the warrior. He realised then that Sigbert had not donned his armour.

"What is this?"

"Away from the others, if you please!" Sigbert insisted. He went through a door that led from the stable into a small alley outside. Coenred followed, looking bemused. Sigbert turned to face his friend. "There's no easy way to say this, Coenred, so I will just up and be done with it; I am hanging up my sword!" Sigbert looked away quickly.

Coenred stared at him again and then nodded. "I see."

"Rail at me if you want to, you have every right, but-"

"But you have made your choice."

"Yes, I have." Sigbert was still not looking him in the face. "Nothing you can say, no raised voice or deserved oaths of anger will make me change my mind."

"How long have we been friends, Sigbert?"

"Many years indeed."

"And yet you were afeared to tell me this?"

"I was."

"Do you remember when we sailed to Ireland with Eorl Aelfgar?"

"I do."

"And of our adventure in Harlech when we fought the demon that we found there?"

"A demon in a cleric's habit!" Sigbert risked a glance at his captain's face and was surprised by the expression that he saw there. The man was not angry, which is what he had expected.

"We have been brother huscarls for many years, you and I, fought many battles together, I will miss you."

"Is that it?" A note of disbelief coloured Sigbert's voice.

"Aye, that's it. You know I am not a man of many words."

"You should be angry!"

"Would it help you to know that but days before the news of the coming of the War Wolf broke I also dreamed of following the same path as you?"

"Mayhap."

"It's true. I contemplated retiring to Holderness. It was why Eanfrid and I came to York. I volunteered to carry messages to Aethelwine from the young eorls, but I had hoped to have the time to visit my family and tell them of my plans. Instead, the Vikings came and I pensioned Eanfrid off and sent him to live at Holderness."

"I see."

"Not all of it, you don't. On that same day, I met Mildryth for the first time and she asked protection of me. I thought it was wyrd at work, that I should be thinking of hanging up this sword and becoming a theign and then there should come this woman of quality, a good match in every respect, asking me to protect her."

"That sounds like the work of wyrd."

Coenred smiled. "I know it troubled you deeply to have your family here in York after the Vikings had taken the city."

"I knew them to be safe."

"No, you didn't. No one did. It was to everyone's good fortune though that old King Hardrada dreamed of making this city his capital in the north, and that he would not give leave to any of his kind to pillage it. Your family went unscathed and were there for you when we took the city back."

"God be thanked for that mercy!"

"Was it then that you thought your days as a huscarl were done?"

"No, well, not straight on anyway. Know thee that Hilda has worked at me to put up my sword. We have plenty of money. Her shop does well and offers a future to our children, one more certain than the life that we have led." Coenred nodded his agreement. "Over the past few days we have talked the old talk, touched time and again on what my being an eorl's man really means to my family, with each passing day I found it harder to justify."

"That is good."

"Is it? What about honour?"

"You have honour."

"Some would say not. Edwin and Morcar refuse to follow the king and they are roundly criticised for it, some would call them cowards."

"They are men who cling too tightly to still being boys, they lack your years of service and they lack the guiding hand of their father. I was supposed to be that guiding hand but they turned from me some years ago. All that said, they are aethelings, their lives have great privilege, great power, but with that comes the responsibility of an eorl as well. They have a duty to perform and some would say that they have been sadly lacking in that department, especially since Fulford Gate."

"Do I also not have a duty and a responsibility, like you?"

"If you were a sworn huscarl then I would say yes."

"IF?!" A pained expression crossed the warrior's face.

"Sigbert, Edwin and Morcar broke faith with us the moment they turned their horses and fled to the safety of Durham after we lost the battle at Fulford Gate, do you not see?"

"Yes, but they are only boys, you said so yourself."

"No, they act like boys but they are of the age of men. Their station demands of them better behaviour, but they fail to give it. Edwin and Morcar should have led us to Tadcaster to meet the king's army, but they did not, they gave that duty to me."

"And you did it well."

"But it was not mine to do, I am not an eorlderman. The moment that they surrendered their responsibility to their people was the moment that they broke their pact with us. A huscarl cannot serve with honour one who lacks honour himself."

"You declined the king claiming that you still served Edwin."

"I did because at that time I still had a hope of Edwin becoming the man he should be. Today he convinced me that that is something that will never be realised. It would cause his father much pain if he were alive to see it."

"Aye, it would."

"So, in my eyes, when you decided to hang up your sword you were a huscarl without a lord. Your service to the House of Aelfgar was ended before then. You are a free man and the choice was yours to make, as it is for every huscarl."

"But I leave you in a time of need."

"You have good reason, you have your family. No one will believe you to be anything but honourable."

"Some might say I am a coward?"

"Not to my face!" A small smile appeared on Sigbert's countenance but he still looked troubled. "I am not a man who claims great wisdom, Sigbert, but I have learnt a few lessons in my time, one of them is this; the only opinions I care about are those held by the people I care about."

"Coenred, thy be a scholar!" Sigbert managed a short laugh.

"I would rather have thee at my side than any other man, but my claim on you is less than Hilda's. Truth to tell, if I had come to a similar mind several weeks instead of several days ago then I too would no longer wear the huscarl's raiment. Go thee in peace, Sigbert; know only good days my friend." Coenred held out his hand. Sigbert glanced at it and then down at his leather shoes. He was embarrassed. Finally, he reached out and they grasped forearms.

"Let me do thee a good turn." Sigbert suddenly enthused.

"How do you mean?"

"Have you taken your leave of Mildryth yet?"

"No."

"Do you plan to?"

"I don't know."

"You should!"

"I don't think that she wants that of me."

"Men lack the wit to guess a woman's mind," Sigbert told him with sincerity. "If you leave without speaking to her it will plague you the whole journey and your life won't be worth living when you return." Coenred laughed awkwardly. "With all seriousness, Coenred, if you go without taking leave of her and, God forbid, you do not return, you will plunge her into a world of guilt and grief once again, and I reckon that that woman has suffered enough for one lifetime."

"I know."

"Then consider this my parting gift, go to her and hold not back one word that expresses what you feel in your heart. She will not hate you but love you all the more for it."

"You said that we men lack the wit to know a woman's mind."

"Aye, and it's true as well. These words I speak are not entirely my own, some, if not all, were put there by Hilda!"

"Fare thee well friend, when I call on thee again I will be a theign looking to buy his wife a new cloak."

"May it be so, and I will stand you a drink so that we may talk over our memories like old men. Fare thee well."

***

Coenred returned to the stable while Sigbert made his way home; he could not bring himself to face the rest of the men who had been his brother huscarls for so many years.

"Where's Sigbert?" Thrydwulf asked in his gruff voice.

"He comes not," Coenred answered.

"What?" Hengist looked shocked.

"Sigbert has hung up his sword. His war-work is done."

Thrydwulf nodded with a grunt and returned to preparing his gear. Hengist was not so easily answered, however. "How can Sigbert not answer the king's call?" He demanded.

"Because he is no longer a huscarl," Coenred told him easily.

"How can that be?"

"We are free men," Thrydwul interjected. "We give our oath freely and we can take our service back freely."

"But the enemy is in the south."

"And Sigbert is a man of the north. Like many another, he has decided to stay here and defend his family."

"There is honour in this?"

"Of us all here Sigbert is the only one to have a family," Thrydwul spoke up again, something that he was not always given to do.

"Hereric had a family." Hengist pointed out, his young face colouring.

"And Hereric is dead and his family without his protection. It is a hard decision to make, Hengist, but some of us, well, make it we must. The eorls broke faith with us, abandoned us, our oath to them no longer held us."

"But we joined the king to fight again."

"That was the right thing to do!" Thrydwul asserted.

"And it suited Sigbert because in defeating the Vikings he was protecting his family. He fought well that day, as did you all. Another day will come, Hengist, when your war-work is done as well. When that day comes to me I hope to be more like Sigbert, alive to know that I made the right decision, rather than dead like Hereric and to know, as my last breath leaves my body, that my family no longer has anyone to protect them."

"You are young and the day of which Coenred speaks seems lost in the future to you, but he's right, it will come to us all."

"And how do you hope it will find you, Thrydwulf?" Hengist asked earnestly.

"As a cure to my sore head after my best night of drinking and wenching, lad!" He replied with a grin. "If I am free to make that choice then I think Sigbert is free to make his and it sits ill with any who blame him for making it. The man has stood and fought in the shield wall longer than you have been in this world, young Hengist, he's earned the right to choose for himself."

"I suppose so." Hengist looked far from convinced.

"There will be time to talk more of this on the road," Coenred told him, "rather we should be looking to make ready for the journey before us."

They heard running footsteps and suddenly Aethelmaer entered the stable in a flurry of noise and activity.

"You're late!" Thrydwulf snapped at him.

"I had to take Sunngifu home and she had to say good bye to me!" He defended himself. He made a show of how heavy his gear was as he dropped it to the floor, perhaps hoping that that would explain the redness in his young face.

"Then if she were saying goodbye to me I would have tarried a while more!" Thrydwulf declared. "But then mayhap my spear is a little longer than yours!" Aethelmaer reddened even more and scowled back at him, not able to think of a rejoinder.

"Edwin, can you finish here?" Coenred asked, knowing full well that the animals were now prepared for the journey. He left the men to make some more lewd jokes at Aethelmaer's expense, of which there would be many.

The night was coming to an end but it was unlike most other nights that Coenred had ever known here in York. People thronged the streets, most of them on errands of one kind or another. Traders had opened up their stores to supply the army with everything that it might need. Excitement filled York again and the city responded with unusual nocturnal activity.

Within minutes he was at the door of Mildryth's small house. He had suggested previously to her that she use some of her new found wealth to move to a better quality area, but she had refused. Mildryth had claimed that she had grown fond of the place and that the money was only to be used for their new life beyond the city walls. As a

Saxon woman that was her right, to own and dispense her money as she saw fit, and she did not need a man's agreement to do so. He hesitated on the threshold, knocked lightly and stepped in.

Mildryth glanced up at him from the hearth and smiled; it melted his heart. He had partly expected a frosty welcome, even feared it to be honest, but her face betrayed no duplicity. Indeed, she rose and came around the hearth to embrace him gently, but enthusiastically.

"How goes it?" She asked.

"Mildryth-"

"There's no need!" She insisted.

"But there is," he told her. "I know how this news must have pained you."

"It did, but that is past now." She reassured him. "The pain of one woman is of little matter in this world. I should know that better than most."

"It is everything that I believe you feared, even when the King of Norway lay dead upon the field at Stamford Bridge. If this were not for King Harold then I would not go!" He tried to explain.

"I know." She looked more serious. "I will not deny that I feared that you would be taken by the king once you had won his favour. It seemed the most likely thing to happen. Some would look for it too. When they brought you home from the battle, all bloodied and pierced by the weapons of the enemy, I prayed to God so many times, asking Him that that would be your last fight. But what are our concerns against those of kings and their kingdoms? Your calling has ever been in the shield wall and if I thought otherwise then I was only deceiving myself. But this threat is not just to King Harold is it? These foreigners who come look not just to take his life; they will take our whole world if we let them. The king needs fine men like you under his banner. His words made it clear to me that this fight is so much more than just one man looking to take the life of another, and King Harold spoke such fine words at the feast didn't he?"

"Yes, I've never heard better," He agreed. He felt his anxiety easing at the sound of her voice.

"I feel that he is chosen by wyrd to lead us, Coenred. I know that some tongues scorn him for breaking with Ealdgyth Swannesha, the mother of his children, and any other man would deserve such disdain, but he is a king and he acts not just for himself, but for everyone."

"I spoke with him on the matter of his former wife, Ealdgyth Swannesha, when we were at Tadcaster. He knows how people see it but he needed to marry Ealdgyth of Mercia to try and bring her brothers to him as friends. That they spurn his offer of friendship is now, mayhap, of no surprise to we who know them well."

"And that is where my pain died." He looked at her quizzically. "When you went before the eorls at the feast I saw them for what they are, noble in name but not in nature; unlike you." She caressed his arm and looked up into his face. "You stood before them a proud man, but not arrogant; you were honest. I saw your courage and your loyalty. I saw that you were better than they were because you responded to the king's call as only truly noble men can. I do not want you to go south with King Harold, my Coenred, but I will not stop you. I will not have you leave me here today with a heavy heart and I will not pine for you while you are gone. I will do everything to help you leave York with a brave heart, fit to fight for our king. And you will know that, when you face the Normans in the south, I will wait for you in Holderness. You will fight for Harold and you will fight for me, I know it, but when this fight is over it will be your last battle and you will never leave me again." She rose up and kissed him. He could say nothing in return, although there was much that he wanted to say. He knew not the words to express his emotions so he simply embraced her and returned her affection with all the passion that he felt in his heart.

"This will be my last battle." He said eventually. "After this, I will hang up my shield and stay at your side forever."

"And I ask nothing more of you. May God protect you, your friends, and the king. In the past you have taken your leave of me quickly, forced by circumstance, I think that it is better that way. I'm not sure that I am as strong as I would wish to appear to you."

"You are telling me to go!" He tried to look stern but his face was too honest. He could not master his true emotions in that way.

Mildryth returned to the hearth where she had been working. She finished wrapping the food that she had prepared, packing it into small bundles. She wrapped these in a larger piece of Hessian.

"This moment will always be precious to me, but it is bittersweet also. I long for the day when it will only ever be sweet." She told him.

"Then do not come to see the army leave York for you will only see me lost amongst their number." He took the bundle from her. They looked at each other for a moment. She raised her hand up to the side of his face, the side with the old scar and the new bruise that was only just beginning to fade.

"I only wanted a protector." She spoke softly.

"I never wanted a wife." He replied.

They kissed again and she felt as if her heart had broken once more, like it had when her husband had died, only the cause of her pain was still here, holding her, returning her love. She could not let him go while she felt like this and yet the moment came. He pulled away and looked down into her face and she smiled.

How did she smile?

Where the strength came from to smile she did not know. He stroked her cheek with a strong finger, he caressed her so softly. The texture of her skin never ceased to amaze him.

"I will come to you in Holderness. You should know that I have already sent to my brother, Osred, asking that he send my friend, Eanfrid, to come and take you there. He was a fighting man and he will protect you on the journey. In these days there will be danger on the road, but I trust him and know that you will be safe."

"If only I could do as much for you."

"War is not the work for women and neither should it be, though you often bear the greatest weight of it. I will trust to my arms and armour, to my skill, and to the skill of my friends. In the king, I think we have found a leader worth following. I can ask for no more."

"But you will have my prayers all the same."

"I am not a religious man but I will hold that sacred."

A moment passed them in which neither felt compelled to say anything more. They enjoyed the silence as they enjoyed each other's company. Together they were attempting to delay the departure that both knew was inevitable and also heavy with a promise of pain.

Finally, Mildryth spoke. "Our time of parting has come."

"I know." He gave her a quick kiss and then turned and moved to the door. He reached for the latch and glanced back for one more look at her. There she stood, next to the hearth, bathed by the warm light, still dressed in her finest clothes that she had worn for the feast. He did not know if the angels that the Christian priests talked about really existed, but if they did he felt that he was looking upon one now.

In her turn, she saw him framed in the doorway, a man of tremendous physical power governed by a noble heart and a quiet mind. The light glinted on his steel byrnie, the sword hanging at his left hip in its' leather scabbard. The red cloak hung from his shoulders, making him seem all the more upright and martial. They represented the exact opposite in human strength, one physical and powerfully violent, the other, enduring, resisting, deeply feminine, but no weaker for being that. In this moment they understood each other perfectly in that respect and each took what solace they could from that understanding.

They both captured the moment as they saw it, enshrined it in their hearts, and then it was gone.

Monday, 2nd October 1066

The City of York

At the break of day, the first elements of the army began to leave the City of York. Royal Companions headed south on their horses. They would follow the old Roman road of Ermine Street all the way to London. Other horsemen were sent before them to scout out the country. At this distance, King Harold did not fear to come across any enemies but food and places to rest would be needed for the army itself.

Groups of men began to leave the safety of the walls of the city. The largest number of them were on foot and they would have to march throughout the day to reach a safe haven before the sun set.

The excitement of the people of York seemed to abate. They lined the south wall and palisade, as well as the road that led through Fulford Gate and Water Fulford. Some eight days previously Fulford Gate had been the scene of the dreadful battle between the eorls, Edwin and Morcar, and the wily War Wolf, Harald Hardrada, King of Norway. The Saxons had been slaughtered out there on the land between the marsh and the river. There were few signs of that struggle having taken place now. Brave Hereric and his five hundred huscarls were but ghosts in the land and in the memory of the people that they had fought to defend.

Those same people cheered the kings' army today. They waved bits of rag and the children ran alongside shouting. Hounds barked and chased the children, excited but not knowing why, their tongues lolling, their tails wagging. On the surface, it seemed a happy enough scene but there was no disguising the sorrow that lay in the eyes of the people, especially the women. It lay just below the surface of their brave faces. War had come again just when many had thought that it might have been defeated for all time, or at least for this year. The men talked of glory and the clash of arms but the women knew the truth of what was to come and it haunted them.

Not all those who had volunteered had been accepted. Some were still carrying injuries from the earlier battles, wounds considered too serious to allow them to make the long march and stand before the new enemy. The experienced warriors knew that such men would not be hale, hearty, and fit to fight. Some were simply too old or too young. It was surprising that of those that did leave York with the king's army their numbers were quite small; the Vikings had taken too great a toll.

There was also a rumour that the Eorls of Northumbria and Mercia had forbidden their people to follow the king. Coenred's decision to leave their service was public knowledge now and it surprised no one that the best of the eorls' fighting men, huscarl and fyrdmen alike, followed his example. It was something but many wondered if it was enough. Better that the eorls had done their duty and accompanied the man who was both their king and their cousin. Despite their defeat at Fulford they could still have raised a power to supplement the Southern Army and won some glory for themselves.

That they chose to ride to Mercia instead did little to restore their reputations.

The world had slipped into October and autumn now began to dress the land in shades of brown, red, orange, and gold as the army passed through it. The days were still warm but the nights became a little colder, a little sooner, and for a little longer. The farmers worked to finish the harvest and store up the food against the coming winter. The summer had been kind to them this year, the harvest was good. Excess food would be taken to the nearest markets and sold for a profit. Only the march of the fighting men suggested any prospect of hardship as the moon entered its last quarter.

"I enjoy this time of year more than any other," Aethelmaer declared as they followed the Roman road through the heart of the forest that had grown up around it. "It is as if God blesses us before the coming of winter."

"My father always said autumn was the season when God gave the most to show that we would not be forgotten in the winter," Edwin added.

"This is the time when the warmth of the hearth becomes something to treasure. To sit in the glow of the embers with a full stomach and good company. This is what I like about autumn." Aethelmaer said.

"And what of you?" Thrydwulf asked of Coenred. "Does not your newly softened heart rise to the changes of the season?" Coenred knew that he was trying to bait him but he did not feel the need to bite. He looked around at the beautiful scenery with an appreciative eye.

"I feel the change of the seasons like any man," he replied simply.

"Does God not touch you at this most bountiful time of year?" Edwin pressed the conversation with a good nature.

"I do not go to church," Coenred answered.

"Sigbert said that you believe in God; you once told him such when you were exiled in Ireland with Eorl Aelfgar." Thrydwulf recounted with a sly smile.

"Aye, I do." Coenred moved with the rhythm of his horse's gait, enjoying the expectant silence maintained by his comrades.

"So?!" Thrydwul demanded, somewhat out of character. He did not normally contribute so willingly to conversations himself but today the need to talk seemed great with him.

Normally Thrydwulf was something of a hawk when it came to talking, watching and waiting and then pouncing on words spoken by another, usually with a sarcastic retort. He had always enjoyed sparring with the younger warriors in just such a manner.

"Religion should be between a man and himself," Coenred told him.

"The bishops don't think so," Aetherlmaer observed. "The pope in Rome doesn't think so. They brushed away the old gods and sent us the God of the Christ to worship instead, and a strong religion it seems to me. Fair conquered this land and that's a truth!"

"You believe something different?" Edwin enquired with obvious interest.

"I don't believe in a heaven or a hell. I don't believe in a God sat upon a throne passing judgements upon us." Coenred realised that this conversation was not going to be dropped.

"What do you believe?" Aethelmaer demanded.

"I believe that God lives in the earth, in the sky, and in everything else that lives in the land, and in us also."

"Thee believes in pagan worship?!" Hengist declared.

"Mayhap. I have seen much of this land in my travels and nowhere do I find a lack of beauty, except, mayhap, where men turn their hands to make hovels for others to live in. I have witnessed both heaven and hell made by people for people. We are both cruel and kind at the same time."

"This is true!" Thrydwulf agreed. "I prefer to be out here, under the sky, than inside a cold church. Out here I sometimes feel that I can look God in the eye!" He glanced at his comrades, embarrassed at his own moment of candour. Coenred only smiled.

"This is like the talk of the old gods," Aethelmaer observed.

"No," Coenred countered. "The old gods were fashioned in the likeness of men. God is nothing like a man."

"What is he like then?" Edwin enquired.

"God is everything!" Coenred replied with a confident smile.

"*God is everything!*" Hengist repeated in a disbelieving tone. "What kind of answer is that?"

"The truth, as it seems to me."

"A truth that will get you excommunicated!" Hengist observed.

Coenred merely shrugged. "I don't think that I can be banned from a church that I don't belong to. Besides, I don't need another man to tell me that I am closer to, or removed from, God simply because of some words in a book that most cannot read. I rest easy with my own conscience, all the same, doing no hurt to man nor beast unless one looks to hurt either me or mine."

"You should have told me this before offering me service," Edwin complained. "I knew not that you were a heathen!"

"It matters to you?" Coenred turned in his saddle to look at his retainer. Edwin sat and thought for a while.

"In truth not. No priest came to aid me when I was thrown upon the fate of the world. 'Twas a heathen who saved me!" He grinned as he spoke the last.

Norman Encampment at Hastings

The room was dark as there were no windows to allow for natural light to enter. The feeble flames of tallow lamps fought to hold back the shadows but their jittering only reminded him of when he had been holed up at St. Valery Castle. The wind there had seemed to force its way through the solid stone of the ramparts to torment him even then. The location had changed but their situation had apparently not.

Guillaume sat in a chair, alone except for the two door wardens. He glowered at no one in particular. His breakfast, set out on a trestle table, remained untouched. He knew that he should eat to maintain his strength even if the campaign fare was not likely to stimulate his palette. Guillaume liked food, it had become one of his joys in this life, a fact evidenced by his expanding girth, but he was still a stout man, a capable warrior. He mused that, mayhap, his palette had become too refined for the rations that the army now subsisted upon, and he ate only what they ate, but he knew that this was a lie. It was certain that he was just fooling himself and, he hoped, others as well. There was another reason as to why he had lost his appetite of late.

Worry gnawed at his guts.

Even as he pondered sending for his favourite brother, the Count of Mortain, the man entered, but he was not alone. Guillaume grunted absently to himself. Robert's company he longed for, but he did not feel disposed to entertaining. He saw then that the fellow following his brother was Eustace, Count of Boulogne, and he resolved to make an effort to at least be civil. Eustace was one of his most important allies.

"Morning, Your Grace!" Robert saluted him formerly. "I hope I find you in good humour this day?"

"Robert, have you broken your fast?"

"As meanly as becomes us."

"Eustace, it is good to see you, my friend."

"Likewise, Your Grace."

"Please, we are but three here, let us dispense with the formalities of court when amongst friends." Guillaume rose from the chair that served as a substitute to his ducal throne and approached the trestle-table. He sat down and began to tear a loaf of bread apart. Robert and Eustace joined him but showed no interest in the meagre repast.

"It has been but three days and yet I sense that your mood has soured," Robert observed.

"Soured? No, not soured. I am bemused, Robert. I came here looking for a fight and we have had little to whet our swords by."

"We have the town." Eustace offered.

"The town is not the country," Guillaume countered. He saw Eustace's face darken and cursed himself for too sharp a tongue this morning. "My friend, talk to me, help me dispel these foul humours that beset me." He smiled vainly.

"Guillaume, I will do my best, as always."

"Verily, you curse talking too much and yet I believe it is how you come to set your world to rights." Robert smiled more naturally.

"Verily, you speak true."

"Well, we are here, in England, with little accident."

"Only a handful of ships were lost in the crossing," Eustace added.

"For that, I am grateful unto God!"

"This town of Hastings that lies hard by has been taken with little bloodshed. The castle was erected without mishap or intervention, our troops are billeted much more comfortable than they were in Normandy, we have rations, and we have security. The fleet is safely anchored in the harbour. We are here!"

"We are here," Guillaume nodded to himself, "but Harold is not!"

"I would expect him any day now."

"And why would you do that, Eustace?"

"Why because he has a kingdom to protect of course."

"Is this what galls you?" Robert asked his brother. "Is it Harold's failure to appear before our spears that so confounds you?"

"You make it sound like a matter light."

"Guillaume, I know your purpose but we have fought many enemies enough times to know that they seldom do what we would wish. It has been but three days since we arrived here and everything has gone as we would hope. The Saxons of Hastings put up a spirited fight, but we overwhelmed them, killed a few hundred, and beat the rest into submission. This castle is made of wood, its many parts built and sectioned by your carpenters back in Normandy, and put together again here in England as protection against the backstabbing knives of the locals. It is, as I said, made of wood rather than stone, yes, but the peasants have not the means to destroy it. That Harold of Wessex chooses not yet to appear before us is, I think, something of a blessing."

"Do you?"

"Yes. The men only grow in surety that this enterprise can be achieved."

"I agree!" Eustace enthused.

Guillaume glanced at him and then back to his brother. He sat a little straighter before the board. "You think that I worry without cause?"

"No, I think that you detest inactivity."

"And why not, it has plagued us this very summer with unseasonal storms that kept us in Normandy well past the day we were want to come here." The Count of Boulogne added.

The Duke of Normandy mused for a moment. He knew that they were both right, that was the easy part anyway, but he wondered if they understood the true gravity of their situation.

"I accept what you say, the both of you, but you must then know why I have cause to worry?"

"We have been stalled too long," Eustace said easily, "and because of this delay, we sail too close to winter. Soon the season for campaigning will close and there will be no fighting. The Saxons will withdraw to their hearths, the winter storms will hazard our supply vessels, the men will grow indolent again, food may become scarce and a bad winter will surely thin our numbers."

Guillaume was admittedly surprised by how concise Eustace was in his assessment. "Then you can see that we must bring Harold to the field sooner rather than later?"

"I agree, so I would suggest that we should take steps to ensure that he does just that."

"And how would you do it?"

"How would I provoke a fight?" Eustace looked amused. "I would set him a slight from which he cannot, as a man of honour, a so called king at least, turn his back."

"Which would be?"

"Attack his people!"

"Attack his people?"

"Yes, Guillaume, attack his people. I know that I did not spend the whole of summer in your presence, as you requested, but that does not mean that my absence made me ignorant. I listened not only to what you had to say about this Harold of Wessex but I set my people to learn something about him also. It seems that even the Saxons have some sense of honour. Their king is their shepherd, as it were, his role is to protect his people, if he is found wanting in this then he may well be found wanting in other ways as well."

"This notion has merit," Robert agreed.

Guillaume nodded to himself. It was hardly an original proposition, attacking the local populace had been used by many others to initiate a full conflict previously, but it did, as Robert pointed out, have merit.

"Do it!" Guillaume rapped the table before him for emphasis. "Send out men to scour the area and inflict outrages on the people hereabouts."

"To what degree?" Robert asked as he rose from the table.

"To whatever degree it takes to bring Harold from London!"

Tuesday, 3rd October 1066

The City of York

Aethelwine looked like a tired man. Mildryth had never seen him like this. His eye had been lost to the wound he had suffered at Fulford Gate, but it was not this injury that had worn him down. The king had gone south and rejected the High-theign of York's request to travel with him. In truth, there was a good argument for this decision. Northumbria had been unsettled by the recent troubles and the king needed his representatives to exercise their authority on his behalf. Morcar had withdrawn to Mercia, his brother's earldom, leaving Aetherlwine to do his work for him and it did not sit well with the theign.

Despite his own disappointment, Aethelwine remained courteous as ever. He had sent for Mildryth and she had attended his summons to the great hall promptly. A Saxon fighting man stood talking to Aethelwine when she entered. He looked old, a little worn even, but he stood straight and proud before the theign.

"My Lady!" Aethelwine greeted her warmly. "I understand that Lord Coenred has made provision for you?"

"Yes, My Lord." She bowed to him. "He has sent to Holderness for a friend of his to escort me there."

"Then this is he who has come to fetch you." Aethelwine waved to the older man. "This is Eanfrid, one-time shield carrier to Lord Coenred, now a servant at his holding in the Isle of Holderness."

"My Lady!" Eanfrid smiled warmly and bowed deeply. Mildryth was somewhat surprised.

"You come so soon?" She observed.

"I was trained to war, My Lady, those who move slowly when called suffer accordingly." Eanfrid returned.

Despite his apparent age, his eyes looked bright and his demeanour was courteous without fault. Mildryth wondered for a moment why she now felt a pang of sadness, a feeling of resistance even, at the arrival of Coenred's friend.

"I have known Eanfrid for as long as I've known Lord Coenred," Aethelwine declared, misunderstanding the conflicting expressions on her face. "He is trustworthy and will guide you safely to Holderness; of that, I have no doubt."

"My apologies, good Eanfrid, I do not doubt you, it is just...so sudden!" She tried to explain. Eanfrid smiled warmly.

"There is no hurry, My Lady. We will not leave until you are ready. Upon the morrow is best, mayhap, as the nights are drawing in and it is not wise to travel lightly on the roads at the darkest hour. As I say, when you are ready we will set out but only when everything is in order." He assured her. "I will stay here-"

"As my guest!" Aethelwine insisted. "We can talk of the old days eh?"

"As usual, My Lord," Eanfrid agreed with resignation. "When you have your affairs in order then we shall leave York for Holderness, My Lady."

Leave York!

Leave Branda!

And there it was. The truth. Leaving York for a new life in Holderness would mean leaving her truest friend, the one who had never judged her, never turned her back on her. The ceorl who had proven herself theign-worthy through the strength of her loyalty and kindness to Mildryth. And now they would say goodbye, probably forever.

"I understand." She said at length.

"'Tis but that the seasons draw on and the nights close around us a little earlier with each day. I would not like you to be upon the open road when it grows dark." Eanfrid insisted. "But I come early so that you may still have time to take your leave. We depart upon the morrow if you wish it, and the day will last a little longer with us on our journey, but if not then mayhap the day after, or the day after that?"

"Then this will be my last courtesy to you, Mildryth, as the wife of my dead friend, Aethelheard," Aethelwine spoke. "Whatever servants you need to prepare your baggage they will be yours. Whatever time you need to take your leave, it will be yours. I am glad to see thee go to a better life than the one I could give you here."

"My Lord!" Instinctively she went to him and embraced the theign. "You have kept faith with Aethelheard, my husband and your friend. You kept me safe and secure when others spurned me. I thank you for my own sake and for Aethelheard's. He was proud to call you friend in life. Now he would know that he was right to call you friend indeed."

"Then so be it!" Aethelwine spoke loudly as if to hide his emotions. "Eanfrid, make yourself a lodger in my hall and, My Lady Mildryth, begin to make yourself ready to leave us."

***

Wulfhere, once called Peada, lay curled in the meagre straw like a dog seeking warmth in a kennel. The room was dark and had only an earthen floor. The chill of the approaching winter was creeping up through the hard packed soil beneath him. The only light came from beyond the wooden door that did not fit the frame very well. This was an outbuilding, a storeroom made into a temporary prison. It was not fit for keeping a man alive in.

He could see the shadow of the warrior tasked with guarding him. It was not an onerous duty. People had been curious at first, their small lives excited by the detaining of a declared outlaw and a murderer. All the guard had to do was ensure that no one approached the gaol too closely, a task made easier by the loss of interest soon evinced by the people. At regular intervals, the guard was changed and shortly they took to sitting on a stool or walking to and fro to while away the time.

Wulfhere was left to thinking. The guard who took the evening watch became his target. When this man took up his station

Wulfhere sidled up to the door and pressed his face to the crack through which fresh air whistled.

"Man! Man!" He called quietly.

"Shut thy mouth or I'll shut it for thee!" The guard responded aggressively.

"There's no call to talk like that," Wulfhere suggested in an appeasing tone. "I merely wonder after your welfare?" The guard did not reply.

"'Twill be cold again tonight and thee out there with only a cloak. At least I'm undercover though I lack a hearth. Do you have a warm hearth at home, tended by your woman? Every man deserves that don't he? You go not with the king's army, were thee wounded? I fought at Fulford Gate and Stamford Bridge-"

"They say thee be a murderer and a coward!" The guard interrupted.

"Aye, they would, and who is it that does the saying I ask thee? The theigns and eorldermen, thee knows. Aye, they command us to the battle and spill our blood but 'tis we who come home with the greatest hurts and the least to show for it. I stood my ground at Fulford Gate until the great Eorl Edwin ran from the field. What shame is it that I, seeing his desertion, should look to save my own skin? Others did the same, as thee knows. And is it a bad thing to save your life in one battle to hazard it in another. I fought again for King Harold at Stamford Bridge. Look thee! Look what I took from the battlefield! Look beneath the door!" Peada crouched down and took a large silver crucifix from inside his byrnie and slid it beneath the door, but he kept hold of the chain.

On the other side of the door, the guard looked down and saw the cross. Even in the failing light, he knew it was made of silver and worth more than he made in several months.

"I would buy my freedom with this!" Wulfhere declared. He let the silence drag out knowing that if he broke it first then he was a lost man, at least as far as this individual was concerned.

"They would know I had failed my duty and I would be punished, cast out at worst!" The guard declared but he kept looking at the cross as it lay in the dirt.

"I have more," Wulfhere assured him. He took out some coins and jingled them in his hand. The sound was unmistakable. "They will not cast thee out in these times of trouble when weapons men are needed. They will fine you but the coins in my hand will more than cover that."

The guard bent down to look more closely at the cross, his tongue moving over his lips as he weighed up the consequences with the likely rewards. Wulfhere drew the cross slowly back under the door with his foot.

"How came you by this treasure?" The guard suddenly insisted.

"From the bodies of dead Vikings!" Wulfhere replied without hesitation. "There were many of them at Stamford Bridge, did you not see?"

"I did not fight at Stamford Bridge." The guard admitted straightening up but still looking at the place where the cross had been. "I took a hurt at Fulford and retired early...as My Lord commanded!" He added the last urgently.

"Here," Wulfhere pushed a coin under the door, "for the wound thy suffered. I doubt your lord did as much but we are brother warriors." The guard looked fervently at the coin. Wulfhere watched him through the crack in the door knowing that if the man took this one coin then he would more than likely take more. His freedom and escape from death were but an indecisive second away.

The guard took the coin.

"And the silver cross?" Wulfhere offered. "T'is but the price of you raising the latch and turning your back."

"And the compensation?" The guard insisted. Wulfhere let the coins jingle again in reply. "I must raise a hue and cry!"

"Yes, but not until I have had time to get clear of the city."

"You mean to leave?"

"Of course. I am of the south and there will I return. I have no business here in York or in Northumbria. You will raise a hue and cry, as you say, but they will not search for me, a southerner, beyond the city limits. None will know what passed between us. You will have the cross and the money both; I will have my freedom and escape from false prosecution by a man who is not theign-worthy!"

"The cross first!"

"I will trust you." Wulfhere pushed the crucifix back under the door with his foot. The guard bent down eagerly and picked it up. He held it before his face, watching the weak light of the evening reflected in the pure silver. Wulfhere jangled the coins again.

"Your compensation!" He reminded him.

"Get thee gone, quickly!" The guard instructed him as he raised the latch.

"If you turn your back and not see me leave, you will not be forsworn before God!" Wufhere pointed out. "They will require you to make such a vow."

The guard understood and turned his back on the doorway. Wulfhere stepped out stealthily. He was loath to leave without the silver cross and looked around quickly for some means of recovering it.

"I will put the money on this stool," he said and bent down unhurriedly. The guard wore no armour. A langseax hung at his side and a tall fighting spear leaned in the crook of his right arm. Wulfhere caught up the stool and crashed it heavily against the other man's head. The guard fell to the floor. Wulfhere rained down several more blows until blood stained the seat of the stool. He dropped his makeshift weapon and then recovered the silver cross followed by the dead man's langseax.

He glanced around to see if anyone had noticed the commotion but there was no one else around. Hurriedly he dragged the man's body into the gaol and dumped him, face turned away from the door, in the centre where he could be seen by anyone looking in. He put the stool inside also, over to one side where it might not be seen from outside. Then he closed the door and dropped the latch. Wulfhere, once called Peada, disappeared into the night.

Wednesday, 4th October 1066
The City of York

The morning air was a little colder than yesterday, or so it felt. Mildryth chose to wear a woollen cloak instead of the linen that better-suited summer. Outside the small house that had been Aethelwine's gift of sanctuary a cart waited. Eanfrid stood patiently next to the horse. All of her belongings sat in the back of the cart, covered over by a travelling cloth. The hearth had burnt out now and it saddened Mildryth to see that there were no more glowing coals there. This small house had been the place from which she had rebuilt her life. It had become her home and in its own way it had grown upon her, but now it was empty. It was time to leave.

If leave I must it was best done quickly!

As she made her way to the cart Branda appeared bearing a bundle in her arms. They had spoken last night, far into the dark hours, but it had not been enough. The ceorl still needed to take a public and proper leave of her theign-worthy friend.

"For thy new life!" Branda declared with a forced smile. She proffered her bundle and Mildryth took it from her. "There's bread that thee might have food on arrival. Wine that thee won't go thirsty, and grain that thee might plant a crop in the spring to see thee through next winter."

"Branda, as always, you're a true friend." Mildryth smiled at her. Eanfrid took the bundle and placed it in the back of the cart. "I will miss thee most of all that I have known in York."

"Ah, my lamb!" They embraced warmly but both were aware of observers and so fought to control their emotions.

"I will see thee again in the spring!" Mildryth asserted. "I will command Coenred to come buy grain from Caelin and I will come with him to make sure that he does."

"And I will suggest to Caelin that we take to buying and selling wool, the finest that the Isle of Holderness has to offer, and, mayhap, I will join him on a visit to see your flock?" Branda returned.

"Goodbye, my friend!"

"Fare thee well!"

They embraced once more and then Mildryth climbed into the cart with Eanfrid's discreet assistance. He then took his place, caught up the reins, and motioned the horse forward. Slowly they left behind them the small house and Branda who stood watching their departure. Soon they were on the main road and heading for the city's eastern gate and the road to Holderness. One life was ending but another was beginning. That thought raised her spirits somewhat.

"Will the journey be a long one?" She asked at length.

"Longer than most but shorter than my master's" Eanfrid replied in an easy manner. He turned to look at her and smiled gently. "Thee has nothing to fear. I am armed and trained in weapons, and I know the road well. Lord Osred has prepared for your coming and we will be safe and secure before the night touches the sky."

Slowly the cart headed eastwards to become lost in the countryside.

***

Wulfhere sat upon a stolen horse behind a makeshift shop that a peasant had erected near the eastern gate of York. There were many such structures placed around the gates to the city. They belonged to the very poor, peasants without masters and, obviously, without land to grow their own food. They sold tat, cheap rubbish, to more well-to-do people coming and going through York. All of these ceorls had fled before the coming of the Vikings and their stalls, if they had been left behind, had been used for firewood by the same. That constituted no great loss, however. Such structures were quickly and easily raised again, once the enemy had been driven away. Life was surprisingly quick to return to normal after such events.

Usually, Wulfhere would have despised being so close to this, the lowest class of free ceorl, but on this day he was grateful for their mean ways of scraping a living. They hid his presence from the one he hated most in this world; Mildryth!

Upon his escaping his crude prison Wulfhere had thought to leave the city for the forest, to search out his hloth, but then it occurred to him that that would be the first place the tithingmen would look once they discovered the body of the guard. He sought then to be more like Reynard the Fox. In the forest, hunters would track his spoor, follow his trail, but in a city where many feet walked every hour of every day, there was little to mark his passing. The prison had been located close to the western gate, one of the several buildings owned by the High-Theign of York. Wulfhere chose to head back towards the centre of the city. He found another outbuilding, it was not difficult, and spent the night in there, hidden from view.

Sleep did not come immediately to him; his mind was occupied by many thoughts. Now that he had escaped execution, the fate he knew surely awaited him if he had been sent back down south to his family's lands, he had time to ponder the course his life had taken. Once again, almost inevitably, he considered the harlot, Mildryth, and how his chance meeting with her had so vexed his wyrd that he had been dealt a poor hand at every turn.

At first, he had coveted her and the wealth that she seemingly had to come to her after laying a complaint at the Shire Court against Tostig Godwinson, the king's own brother. In truth, it was the money more than her body that attracted him, although her beauty was still something a man should enjoy. She had seemed like an easy mark but then she had given her charms freely to that brute of a huscarl. This he had learnt the hard way when he had fled the field at Fulford Gate as the battle went against the Saxons. He had thought to carry her and her monies away but the huscarl had sent his servant to protect her. It was that same peasant who had provoked the fight in the long hall that had led to him being taken into custody. There was another who deserved paying back.

Mildryth, it was she who commanded his attention for the moment, however. She would be dealt with first. The peasant boy could wait his turn. Absently his finger traced the line of the fresh scar on his face, put there by her hand in an unguarded moment on his part. The woman was a witch. She had cast a curse upon him, one that had robbed him of his senses. Like a child, he had staggered through the forest after she had spilt his blood on the road. He remembered then the man that he had inadvertently met, the one with the girl-child that he was taking to a convent. This remembrance brought him more pain. He had not liked that man with his strange eyes who seemed to be able to read the soul of another so easily. In truth, he had been afraid of the stranger because his understanding gave him a power over Wulfhere. They had parted company quickly and it was in a reflection afterwards that Wulfhere realised that, mayhap, it was not so much that the man could read his soul so readily but rather that the witch Mildryth's curse had made it so plain for all to see. He had known then that the only way to rid himself of this curse that put him under the power of others was to kill the witch.

When a witch is killed all of her dark magic dies with her.

He could never thrive whilst Mildryth lived. He had wanted revenge upon her, to despoil her beauty and use her body against her will, but that was now forgotten. Death would be her fate, to die under his hand. Only then would he be free.

It was said of this middle-earth that no one lived a life without another knowing of it. Wulfhere had used this truth to come by information of other people's good fortune, a fortune that, when able to, he had freed them of. In the early morning, he had risen and broken his fast, paying like an honest man. Stealing would only attract more unwanted attention upon himself and besides, stealing small had no attraction for him. Slinking carefully through the early risers he had stepped with ears wide open and discovered much. The widow Mildryth was to go to Holderness in the company of the Captain of Huscarl's retainer.

So it was that Wulfhere made his way to the gate that would lead to Holderness while the sun was still climbing and the church bells had not yet rung the ninth hour of the day. Stealing the horse had been child's play for one such as he. Murdering the owner had taken a little more work but he was capable of that as well when in need.

He watched the cart trundle by with serious eyes. He could see her sat next to the driver, a cloak pulled close around and the hood covering her fair hair. The man looked old but not weak. Underneath his own cloak, he wore a byrnie of toughened leather reinforced with steel plates. On his head, he sported a steel helmet, an expensive piece of armour. The word was that he had been Coenred's shield bearer in another life. Some might weigh the threat he posed as light but Wulfhere knew different. Huscarls trained their servants in the very use of the weapons that they carried. This man, as old as he seemed, had much knowledge of the arts of war about him.

Wulfhere had once sought to pass himself off as a buttescarl, a mercenary, and he had worn the war-gear of a warrior. Like many other things that he had once seemed to be Wulfhere was not a weapons-man, however.

He was cautious though.

As the cart headed into the distance Wulfhere came out onto the road a league or two behind it. He had never been to the Isle of Holderness before, his wanderings had never taken him in that direction, but his mind had begun to form a plan that might lead to his revenge and the securing of considerable wealth also. This Coenred was said to be the owner of a large estate and his woman, Mildryth, had been paid a great sum of money by the king by way of compensation for the murder of her husband and son, a crime enacted by his brother when Tostig had been the Eorl of Northumbria. That money was probably even now travelling in the back of the cart. Wulfhere determined to follow them to Holderness and spy out the land, as he was his normal way, and then return in the dark of night with his hloth; his own gang of cutthroats. They would do most of the killing. A man like him, one who lived by his wits, need not take to knife-work unless either the moment or the intended victim demanded it of him. The killing of Mildryth would demand it of him, though. Only if he killed her with his own hand, marked himself in her warm blood, would the witch's stain be lifted from his head.

He smiled to himself as he relaxed into the rhythmic motion of the horse, plodding down the well-worn road. Mayhap wyrd had turned once more and now favoured him above and beyond what it had ever done before. He could see in this plan how he would put the woman to death under his own knife while his men butchered the tenants of Holderness. Having a huscarl for a lover would avail her not. Mildryth would die and Wulfhere would be both rich with her money and free of her curse.

The Village of Bexelei, Kent

Richard the Beast was so named for one reason only; he knew no limit of behaviour when cruelty was required. Men said of him that he was as dangerous to a friend as he was to a foe when the red mist of the fight descended upon him. It seemed that in the madness of battle Richard was the maddest of all. The scent of blood appeared to inspire his foul humour like no other drug. The screams of men and women were music to his ears. Richard the Beast lived only for one thing; the persecution of torment, pain, and death to others.

In the early morning light Richard had led his men, or rather the men he had been given to command, west of Hastings and followed the coastline. His commission was simple, to create havoc in the local area. His lord knew well the abilities of his man and feared him like everyone else, but the order had come from Duke Guillaume himself. Indeed, there was no better sword in the camp of the Normans for this act and besides, it was something of a relief to many to have this madman walk out beyond the walls of the castle and so spare them his disreputable company.

They had marched for some two hours before they came upon the Saxon village of Bexelei, although its name would forever remain unknown to them. It was surrounded by a palisade, which in its turn was encompassed by ploughed fields, the crops newly harvested. This was no real obstacle to the Norman soldiers, however. Quietly they approached the village and found that a watch had not been posted. A handful of the agilest of the men scaled the wooden wall near the gate, dropped to the other side and drew back the bolts without raising an alarm. The fate of the village was then sealed.

With a cry, the Normans raced into the settlement with weapons drawn and began the killing of the inhabitants. It did not matter who they encountered, man or woman, peasant of theign, armed or not, they were all put to the sword. Children and animals as well.

The fight was brief, barely half an hour, and Robert the Beast's bloodlust was far from sated when he realised that there were precious few Saxons left to stain his bright sword.

"We hold these as prisoners!" Ralph announced. He was of equal rank to Richard and, his lord hoped, something of a steadying influence on the other.

"There are to be no prisoners!"

"Yes, there are. The duke wants word to spread of what we have done here. He wants all the Saxons to know what it is we do."

"Why?"

"To provoke Harold to the fight."

"We have hardly killed but a score of them." That was an underestimate but no one looked to correct Richard.

"The number matters not, that they fear us is what matters."

"You want to spread fear?"

"The duke wants to spread fear."

"So I do this for the duke then?"

"As do we all."

"Then let us give them something to talk about." He marched over to the small group of survivors who stood cowering before a ring of

Normans. All of the men were either old or just boys, the rest, the greatest number, were female. He grabbed an old man and dragged him out of the huddle, throwing him to the ground just beyond the ring formed by the soldiers. "Are you a warrior, old man?"

The Saxon did not understand him as Richard did not speak English and the peasant had never heard French spoken in his village before. He remained cowed on his knees, looking only at the earth immediately before him. It did not matter that neither knew what the other said, this was to be a demonstration of why the Saxons should fear the Normans.

"Hold him!" Richard commanded. A Norman soldier dragged the old man to his feet and held him by his upper arms from behind.

Richard sheathed his sword and withdrew a knife. He cut the man's tunic away, exposing a gaunt and aged body. He glanced at the other Saxons to make sure that they were watching and was satisfied to see the morbid fascination etched upon their several faces. Taking the knife Richard cut carefully across the man's abdomen. The Saxon screamed out in sudden pain and several women cried in horror also. Delivering a cut of the desired size Richard sheathed his bloodied knife and with two hands reached into the opening and proceeded to withdraw the man's entrails. The soldier suddenly found that he had to hold the aged Saxon up as his legs gave way. He felt fortunate that his position meant that he did not have to witness exactly what was being done.

Richard the Beast stepped back, his hands dripping blood and a pile of viscera at the feet of the Saxon who was no longer screaming but whimpering. He nodded to the soldier who released his captive. The old man fell where he stood, lying in his own entrails. He might take hours to die or, if he were lucky, the shock of his ordeal combined with his age might kill him quickly. It did not matter, the point had been made.

"This is how we should deal with Saxons!" Richard grinned.

Ralph looked shocked. Like the others present he had seen many a man die violently, both on the battlefield and as an act of capital punishment, but he had rarely seen the killing performed with such relish. Nevertheless, he counselled himself, it was an effective means of achieving their aim.

"Release the others so that they can go and put fear in the hearts of their neighbours with stories of what they have seen here this day!" Ralph commanded.

"Wait!" Richard countered. "This is not enough."

"Richard, enough blood has been spilt."

"Fear is what the duke wants to bring to these people so let's instil some fear in all of them!" He raised his voice.

With an unnerving determination, he returned to the prisoners once again. He found a woman who stood with two girls clinging to her. With his left hand, he grabbed the woman's hair and pulled her head back violently.

"Ugly!" He snarled.

Whether she understood his words or not she spat into his face. Mayhap it was just an act of defiance, the result was the same, Richard cut her throat with his knife. Her daughters began to cry out even as the body of their mother fell to the floor and the arterial blood pumped out of the savage wound. Richard the Beast grabbed both of them in the same manner that he had treated their mother. He looked around and saw a small Saxon house. Some of them were on fire but not all the dwellings had yet been put to the torch. The Norman dragged the two young girls towards the building.

"They are but children!" Ralph protested.

"They are Saxons and I am not yet satisfied. You want these others to live, to spread the word and put a fear in the heart of all Saxons? Well, this is the price of it."

Ralph watched as the trio disappeared into the hut. Like everyone else there he heard the door slam and just like everyone else he did not move. He was a married man who had children of his own and this act did not sit well with him. Indeed, the disembowelment alone was not what he considered soldiering. That act, the killing of a man, he could put into context, however, considering the orders that they had been given, but the children were another matter.

A young girl screamed. Ralph turned and walked away knowing that if he stayed he would have to hear the cries of the two sisters for some time yet.

Coenred's Estate in the Isle of Holderness

"I am Godgifu, wife to Osred, and soon to be your sister," the woman smiled. She was, mayhap, a year or two younger than Mildryth. Her hair was a dark chestnut, worn long and plaited, and her eyes a warm brown. She had a feeling of autumn about her as if this were her season and it suited her well.

"I am Mildryth, though I doubt not that my coming was already known to you."

"Indeed, we have prepared the house for you. It is to be yours to make into a home."

"In this, I have no happiness. I had no intent to take your home from you."

"You have not." Again Godgifu smiled with such warmth. "Coenred has a house of his own here at Holderness, although he seldom spends any time in it. Come, let me show you."

"My things?"

"Worry thee not, My Lady, I will bring the cart over by your ways," Eanfrid assured her.

Godgifu took hold of Mildryth's arm and gently walked her towards two large houses. Both of them faced south, towards the broad river that separated Holderness from Lindsey. Each house stood two stories high and had shuttered windows.

"Mine is on the east, yours on the west," Godgifu told her. "I have had the hearth lit, the floors dusted and strewn fresh straw. I hope that you don't mind?"

"No, of course not, that is very thoughtful of you."

"I know some like to light their own hearths."

"Indeed they do, but I have been without a home of my own for some time now, just to be here is a blessing."

"Your story sounds sorrowful. I hope that it is not, you must spin the yarn one evening before the hearth."

Mildryth knew that Godgifu was referring to the common custom of gathering around the hearth at night and telling stories. Some of these tales would be of battles, others of heroes and monsters. There would be happy tales of the family's members, including events that some of them might be embarrassed to remember. Some tales would be one person's story of how they came to be there as a means of an introduction. Her story would be both sorrowful and happy.

They entered the western house through a large and heavy wooden door that swung silently on steel hinges. Inside they immediately entered a large room warmed by a fine fire in the stone hearth positioned in the centre.

"I always think that a house is not a home without a lit hearth," Godgifu asserted. She released Mildryth's arm and went to the fire, taking a metal poker to move the burning wood about and so improve the flame. "Look at me, I take charge in your own home, you must chide me!"

"Never!" Mildryth smiled in her turn. The room was well appointed with quality furnishings, chairs, small tables, pots and pans, and even wall hangings of bright colours and good taste. She especially liked the fact that there was not a single item on view that referred to Coenred's occupation as a warrior. "In York, I was befriended by a good woman by the name of Branda, my home was her home and hers likewise with me. I would be the same with you, Godgifu."

"It is passing strange, I find, that Coenred has spent so much of his life away from this place and yet when he visits he and my husband, Osred, are as close as any two brothers can be. I think that it would please them both if we could be the same." Her smile seemed totally natural, a true expression of her own happiness. "For this reason, I call you sister."

"Then so shall we be. I have few friends in this turning world, but all that claim to be so are people of proven quality. I would be honoured to count you as one of them, Godgifu, even more so if we were indeed to become sisters through marriage to brothers."

"We begin so well, might it continue long into our lives yet. You must come eat with us this evening. You will meet Osred, who sends his apologies for being busy on the estate this day, and there will be his mother, Abbe, who will appear stern to you but in time she will mellow; I promise thee."

"I would not wish to impose on you."

"Family never imposes upon family and I cannot let you eat your first meal here on your own."

"I have eaten many meals on my own but that was in the past, I will embrace the present, I will embrace my new family." Mildryth suddenly felt a wave of happiness that had been for so long absent from her life that she did not know what to do or to say. The noisy arrival of Eanfrid with one of her trunks distracted Godgifu, however.

"And here are your possessions. I will leave you now to sort them as you would wish."

"Watch the cart, milady, Aesc is tending to more of the lady's portage," Eanfrid warned her kindly. Godgifu departed without incident.

"She is a warm and friendly lady," Mildryth commented.

"She is a fine lady of the manor," Eanfrid enthused, straightening up after lowering the heavy trunk to the floor. "Her family own an estate not far from here, good people they are too. I am glad that Lord Coenred is to settle here now as well, it will be good to have the family together after so long apart."

"Coenred called you his friend but had little time to tell me much more about you, good Eanfrid, or his brother, or even of the estate."

"Did he now?" The older man's face reddened somewhat. "Well, I served him many a year, carried his shield and weapons I did, in such times as those a master and a servant might grow something that others would take for friendship."

"Indeed, they might and if you be a friend to Coenred then mayhap you will also be a friend to me?"

"But you are theign-worthy?"

"My closest and truest friend in York was a geneatas lady. She did not hold my station against me. You were a huscarl's servant; you fought with Coenred when required."

"Many times."

"When two men hazard their lives together the lines of master and servant rightly blur, they will not be redrawn when Coenred returns to us and I will not be a reason for why you should think otherwise. If you think me theign-worthy then I would be truly unworthy of such an estimation if I came between two men who were rightly friends."

"You do me a great honour!" Eanfrid suddenly bowed to her in a very formal manner.

"No!" She raised a hand but then smiled. "It is not I but you and yours who do me the honour of taking me into your family here in Holderness. Never have I been made to feel so welcomed. If I am happy here then let all who reside on this estate be happy also. I would not want it any other way."

"I think that we will be good friends, My Lady."

"Then help me?"

"How so?"

"Tell me about them, about Coenred's family."

"Well," a cloud seemed to cross his face, "it don't seem right for a servant to be talking about his masters."

"Don't play coy, all servants talk before the hearth!" She accused him, but with no severity. Mildryth was merely giving voice to a truth everyone knew but few ever expressed.

"Aye, we do." He smiled at her.

"And you would not want me going before his mother unarmed, would you?"

"No, I would not. Not that the Lady Abbe is too severe, mind you."

"I am glad to hear it."

"Just appears so is all!" He smiled again. "I'll tell thee this, Coenred's father, Aethelred, was a huscarl also. He served old Eorl Leofric of Mercia, and then his son, Eorl Aelfgar. Coenred was Aethelred's first born and trained to be a huscarl from the moment he could walk. Aethelred was a mighty warrior, like his own father before him, and won great renown by the strength of his sword arm. The old eorl was a ring-giver in the ancient tradition, proud to honour men of ability, and Aethelred spent his money wisely, buying land and sheep here in the Isle of Holderness. Coenred inherited his grandfather's sword, the one he carries to this day, and he continued the tradition of being a weapons-man with Eorl Aelfgar."

"Did he die in battle, Aethelred I mean?"

"No, that is not the way of it with this family. 'Tis a strange wyrd, but with three generations of hearth-companions, not one of them has died in battle. Aethelred's father was first a theign here, not a huscarl, but proved himself in single combat against invading Danes. He died on this estate a proud and happy man, hale and hearty up to his last day. Aethelred hung up his sword when he took an arrow to the knee and could not walk without discomfort. Hard it is for a warrior to fight rightly when he cannot move freely. He became a theign once more and also died here, at Holderness. Coenred was man enough in years to take his father's place at the eorl's side by then and so he did. Aethelred spent many a good year as a theign, teaching his second son, Osred, the ways of the land and of sheep. He died happy, like his father before him."

"Is Osred not resentful of Coenred that he works the land for him and has little claim upon the product of his labour?"

"Osred? There's no bad blood in that boy!"

"I'm sorry! I did not mean to suggest that there was!"

"No, My Lady, I am sorry, I mistook you. I should know better for I have seen the jealousy to which you refer. It happens with other brothers, don't it? Well, mayhap it do and mayhap it don't, but not with Osred. He be Coenred's junior by two years but they have never had a cross word between them. In all things are they equal, neither has a better house than the other. Osred loves the estate, loves working the land and raising the sheep. He wastes no time on thinking about being a huscarl. He has no time for poems about warriors and glory, but he marks every piece of good fortune that Coenred sends their way through his service to the eorls. Aye, he marks it well. 'Tis a matter of honour with him that Holderness thrives while Coenred is away."

"Then he is a good steward?"

"The best!"

"And his wife, Godgifu?"

"She is of good family, as I said, and devoted to Osred. The Lady Abbe was not minded to like her, even spoke against the wedding, but Coenred would not hear of it. He said that she possessed a noble soul and would bring only goodness to Holderness, which is what she has done. They have three children, two boys and a girl. Lady

Godgifu had a small chapel built and gives alms to the poor. No one at Holderness goes without unless they prove themselves undeserving, and I know no one so foolish as to do that."

"She sounds like a saint."

"She is a woman if you pardon me for saying so."

"I prefer that she be a woman, like myself, and not a saint."

"Sometimes people who are just good of heart can be mistaken for the wrong thing."

"For weak, mayhap?"

"Aye, for weak is one, or a saint is another, but it is a mistake all the same. Her kindness is a strength that has helped many round here through dark days."

"Now of that, I know a little something. So, tell me of Coenred's mother."

"The Lady Abbe, she would seem more of a mastiff than is really in her heart." Eanfrid grinned to himself. "You see, when Aethelred died abed, she deemed Osred not yet man enough to run Holderness in Coenred's absence; what mother ever thinks her son old enough eh? As he seemed to her to lack the iron of the master she became stern in herself and fair terrified the ceorls. I think in time she forgot that she had ever been any different and now it's just a habit with her, to be always grumpy and dissatisfied, but she is loyal and fierce in the defence of her own, her family, her servants, her estate."

"You make her sound formidable!"

"And she can be, but in all truth, it is a show. The ceorls here know already that they have a good life. The work is no harder than it should be, the wages are good, and, as I said before, no one but they who deserves to goes without. Osred is a good master, well liked and always obeyed. We don't really need lady Abbe to bite our heels, but it seems to give her some small enjoyment all the same."

"So her bark is worse than her bite?"

"Aye, I reckon so. She did not take to me bringing Cynwise here, we being unmarried, and won't speak to her until we are, but it did not stop the Lady Abbe from sending my love a gift of bread and wine to warm our house, though it came by our door late at night and unannounced." Eanfrid laughed to himself.

"Do you think that she will take to me?"

"Aye, I reckon so."

"Even though I and Coenred are also unmarried and are to share this house?"

Eanfrid frowned. "Then I reckon you will also receive a gift at your door late at night and unannounced."

"Then we will be much the same, you and I!"

"Aye, I reckon we will!" He laughed.

***

"'Tis too large, you overreach yoursen!" Imminric declared.

They stood just within the treeline of the nearest wood in the Isle of Holderness, some 10 rods from the settlement owned by Coenred. They could see the two large houses possessed by the brothers and which stood close by each other. There were several smaller dwellings, all single storey but with windows protected by shutters. The thatch on the roofs came no lower than the top of the window frames, just as with the current building trends seen in cities like York and London. There was also a stable, a barn, and what seemed to be several storehouses.

To the south good pasture land reached down to the wide estuary. On the east and west, the ground had been ploughed, at least as many as eight hides. Further to the east, a smaller river ran as a tributary into the slow moving but powerful Humber. A beaten path wide enough for a large cart wended its way down from the north and led into the heart of the settlement, which appeared undefended by either ditch or wooden walls. Children played between the buildings, chasing each other or being chased by playful hounds. Men and women worked the fields, finishing the harvesting. A man on a horse was dragging a fallen tree in from the very wood in which the spies lurked. A boy of about thirteen walked alongside the trunk and carried a wood axe. Obviously, the tree was going to be turned into fuel for the many hearths that burnt on this estate.

"How much gold be there 'ere?" One of the hloth asked of no one in particular.

"Matters not," Imminric insisted, "'tis too large an undertaking."

"You are large yourself, Imminric, this is meat and bone to the likes of thee," Wulfhere spoke at last. He had travelled back to York, not without a little trepidation considering his most recent crime, but he had stayed clear of the walled city and headed for the homestead that his men had violently taken from its rightful owners. As he had expected, without him to suggest a course of action, they had stayed put, enjoying the spoils of their last haul. "Let not the apparent size of the place put you off, there is a genuine king's ransom in there."

"And many men with many langseaxes." Imminric continued to oppose him.

"Peasants!" Wulfhere responded with a scowl.

"It be us ceorls who make up the fyrd when called, peasants can be weapons-men too." There was some general assent to this statement from the others. Like all robbers, they were greedy but essentially lazy. A few days ago Wulfhere had led them to a clothes-seller who had hidden a stash of coins in the forest, it had been easy to relieve him of both the monies and his life, but the takings had not gone far.

"I promised you riches when I joined you," Wulfhere reminded them, "and here I bring you to them. Know you not that the woman who has come to abide here received from the hand of the king himself compensation for the death of her husband and son, murdered by the king's own brother, Tostig, when he was the Eorl of Northumbria?"

"Aye, that word has been spoken and heard by even the likes of us," a cutthroat agreed. "They say also that her lover is a mighty warrior, a huscarl even. They are dangerous men, trained only to war. I would not cross swords with their like even for a king's ransom."

"And where have all the huscarls gone?" Wulfhere demanded to know.

"Either out of this middle-earth on the point of a spear or south with the king!"

"Aye, that's right. She is here but her lover is not."

"But many men are. There be many hides for tilling, many 'ouses, many hands to fight us off." Imminric remained unsure and as the titular leader of the gang, he had the last say.

Wulfhere continued to stare at the estate but he did not see the buildings or the people that inhabited them, he only saw the face of Mildryth. Nevertheless, his mind worked to find a way to turn the opposition in his favour; he wanted the woman dead. He wanted her gold too, but that was another matter. If he spent time pondering it he might have been surprised to find that, for once in his life, he valued something more than treasure; revenge.

"Like all ceorls, they will retire for the night. Mayhap they will post a watch but if they do it will only be one or two such men. We will wait until a goodly hour when all are asleep and dreaming not of what is going to befall them, then we strike."

"In the night?"

"It will be our cloak. Look, there is no palisade to overcome; the place is open to the four winds. If we come at it from each of those four directions we will take them on all sides. We will have them before they know that we are even there." Wulfhere smiled to himself. He had acquired some knowledge of tactics in his time as a rich theign's buttescarl.

"That has merit!" A conspirator's voice said from the darkness behind him.

"There be hounds," Imminric observed.

"We catch some meat and feed it t' hounds, their bellies always overrules their heads."

"What meat?"

"Sheep! There be plenty of sheep 'ereabouts."

"Aye, Imminric, there are plenty of sheep. This place be rich in them, but it contains greater riches yet. I was in the long hall at York when this Mildryth was paid by the king to withdraw her suit from the shire court. I saw the gold and silver that was paid out of the king's treasury and into her hand. Her lover has gone south with that same king, taking his weapons-men with him. All are gone now. There are only peasants here, and a treasure the like of which none of thee has ever seen. Do any of you want to continue this wretched life that you cling to or do you want to quit this place, go to lands new and start again with gold and silver in your purse? Enough money to set thee all up as well to do ceorls or better!"

The evening grew quiet as the peasants on the estate began their final chores for the day. They did these mostly with good cheer for they knew that the evening meal was cooking over a warm hearth and that their lord was happy with their work this day. The outlaws mused on the words of Wulfhere. They had begun their lives outside the company of law abiding men for one reason or another, but there was one thing that they all had in common; they had been hungry and in want of money. Imminric had become their leader because none could match his strength, but he had not led them to better times. It was Wulfhere who had done that. In a few short days, he had given them more coin than most had ever seen in their lifetime. Their thoughts of tomorrow had been occupied with food and shelter, things that they already had thanks to Wulfhere. These were things that they knew they would lose now that peace had come to the north. The tithingmen would set forth soon, once more to impose the rule of law. The duller of them might not comprehend what Wulfhere was suggesting but the brighter knew that there was a chance of a new start in the offing, in a place where none would know their past.

"This be beyond us." Imminric broke the silence.

"No, it isn't." Wulfhere insisted. The two turned to face each other, the large Saxon's face beginning to crease into an angry mask, the buttescarl appearing unmoved.

"Winter be coming soon an' such as us will suffer in t' cold." A robber dared to raise his voice.

"We have a place to stay, warm and food in t' larder," Imminric answered the speaker without taking his eyes off Wulfhere.

"That be true now, but not maybe tomorrow." It was the lad who spoke for the first time. He was the youngest of them, barely thirteen, but well-practised in the art of living wild. He was a feral child by appearance also. "T' Vikings be put t' sword, gone from this world now, peace will come and wit' it the king's law. T' owners of the farm that we took will be missed one day, sooner or later, and som'un'll come lookin' fer 'em. We'll 'ave to run or fight if we don't move on afore then."

"The lad's right!"

"I told you it would be this way at the start," Wulfhere spoke in a reasonable tone, "always is it going to ground somewhere safe, resting a night or two and then moving on. Such as we who tarry too long get caught and dragged before the court, punished we are in wicked ways. Painful ways. The brand burns hot and long and some have died from the boils it can give rise to. I have always avoided that fate. Came I from the south to stay one step ahead of it. Mind thee, always have I looked for wyrd to throw a pearl like this my way. Many cold nights under the stars have I spent dreaming of a chance like this; a king's ransom almost within our reach. All we have to do is lift a blade and take it."

"There are too many to kill." Imminric looked as if he were struggling with some great philosophical question.

"No, there isn't, there's never enough!" The man who spoke played with knives for sport. He was generally disliked for his morbid fascination with the slow killing of things, like the clothes-seller in the woods, whom he had pierced many times with the blade that he now used to clean under the nails of his left-hand. That man had died slowly, bled out like a pig at the butchering. "We have more than this knife as well."

"Aye, we do now."

"Us have weapons, I grant thee, but so do they."

"But they have to be awake to use them. My plan is that we take their lives while they still yet sleep." Wulfhere smiled in a friendly fashion but his eyes were cold.

"Imminric, we want this!" Someone declared from the shadows, the others seemed to give their assent as well.

"All of you?" The large man demanded. No one raised their voice against the proposal.

He was not the cleverest of men, even he knew that, and he had always harboured doubts about Wulfhere. He was afraid that the buttescarl would conspire to take his leadership away from him in some clever way for there was no doubting that he was a clever man. The leadership of this gang was the one thing of note that he had in this life. He had looked forward, at least as far as his limited powers allowed him to, and seen a time when he would no longer be the leader of it. At first, he had feared losing the leadership to Wulfhere, but now he could see that success could rob him of his position just as surely. No one would want to stay and live this hard life if they had a purse full of gold and silver. He understood that much. As to the money he had no idea what to do with a king's ransom beyond spending it on food and drink and women; what else was there in life? What would he be in this turning world without his hloth?

Imminric did not know the answers to these questions. In the past, his great strength had always been enough but then he had spent little time on pondering anything but the most basic of priorities. Slowly, it occurred to him that if he continued to oppose this plan then the men, his men, might freely support Wulfhere anyway and follow that man into the settlement under the cloak of night and recover the treasure for themselves. Even for all his strength, he knew that he could not force any of them, not even the boy, to follow him if they did not wish to. They wished to have the treasure.

It dawned on Imminric that his standing in the group might rise higher if they were indeed successful and he was the leader who made that success happen. Aye, they might each of them hold more coins than any of them had ever seen before. It would not be so much, however, that they would not have to get some more, one day or another.

"If this be what thee want, this be where I will lead thee," he announced at last. "Rest up lads, there be some 'ours betwixt now and when we strike, let's rest up an' be ready."

"Do as our leader says." Wulfhere smiled, glancing around himself. "The better rested the man, the keener the blade."

Ermine Street, the Road to London

"We met once before in a similar situation," King Harold of England said. They sat at a table reasonably close to a good fire that warmly dispelled the chills of early autumn. A flask of wine and two silver cups sat on top of a clean tablecloth. Bread and cheese lay on a board.

"That was the longhouse at Tadcaster then," Coenred replied. He was feeling uncomfortable, having been summoned once more into the king's company and not knowing the reason why. "Is this your lodge?"

Harold glanced around the interior of the room before answering. It had been hastily prepared to receive him by his men who had travelled on before the royal party for just that very reason.

"I do not know in all honesty." He shrugged. "I cannot say that I have been here before, but when I became king I inherited all that had been King Edward's and time has not been given to me to carry out an inventory of all my holdings. Mayhap, this is mine, mayhap, it belongs to an eorlderman who does me the favour of allowing us to spend the night here."

"My men, such as they are, will not have the same benefit."

"Your men, such as they are, which is to say, men that I highly value, are used to such little hardships, I am sure. I would sleep under the stars as they do, but my companions would not allow it of me."

"You are the king, you could command it."

Harold laughed quietly. "Like many another, you believe the king is unfettered, free to do anything that pleaseth him, the truth, however, is very different; every king is a slave to his throne."

"You make kingship sound like, well, a hardship."

"It is," Harold nodded to himself. "The throne is a golden cage."

"Then I am glad that I never desired it."

"What is it that you *do* desire, Coenred?"

"To know thy mind." The huscarl looked more closely at his host. Harold looked tired but not weary. His eyes were alive and his manner friendly, confident as always, which suggested to Coenred that this audience was, as he had first suspected, being carefully orchestrated.

"Is that all? I seem to remember in York that you told me that it was to settle in Holderness with the Lady Mildryth."

"So I said and so it is with me, but I had not expected to have another audience with you, My Lord."

"Because you turned down my offer to become a Royal Companion! You think me so petty?"

"To become a Royal Companion is a great honour; some would call me a fool for spurning such an opportunity."

"Aye, they would, but not me. I know many men who would snatch that prize from my hand, men who hunger for it, think of nothing else; but they are not the men that I look to promote. Their very desire makes them unworthy for it reveals a self-interest that is, to my mind, belittling."

"People seek advancement all the same."

"Yes, but the best do it through their labour. The good ceorl is he who works hard, obeys his theign, and profits from the opportunities given to him. Rightly is such a man promoted up a class and rewarded for his ability. So on and so on from theign to eorl. However, there are those born to a position for whom labour is not attractive, they demand rather than earn, they expect what in truth they have no more right to expect than anyone else, but they will lay their petitions before me all the same."

"I know of what you speak, though I be but a huscarl. There are some who think it is enough to have a full purse to make themselves one of us."

"Yes, those who would dress seemingly like a warrior, but of whom no man can trust in the shield wall when it comes to blows with the enemy. Such is it on the field of battle; such is it in the court of a king. It is for this reason that I must choose wisely who I put in positions of power over my people, for some would sooner bite the hand that feeds them than do my bidding."

Coenred ate a slice of bread with some cheese, as he had been bidden to do when he first arrived at the king's request. He was not satisfying his appetite, however, but rather avoiding making any reply to Harold's words. He knew, like many did, that the Godwins had pursued advancement on their own terms and that this had, on more than one occasion, brought them into violent conflict with old King Edward. It would be easy to point out the similarity between the actions that the Godwins had once taken to advance themselves and those that Harold was now complaining about. To remain silent seemed the better option.

"I am glad that you can find the time to spend with me, Coenred, I miss the opportunity to talk to people who are not always in my presence and distracted by the ways of the court." Harold sipped his wine and relaxed a little more.

"And I am glad that my refusal of your initial kindness did not anger you."

"You acted in honour and, I may say, with honesty. Quite rightly you pointed out to me your obligation to Edwin and Morcar. In some respects it was wrong of me to make you that offer at that particular time, knowing as I did that you were a huscarl to the sons of Eorl Aelfgar."

"My service with them is finished now."

"Because they would not follow me south?"

"Yes."

"My father always taught us to value loyalty and I do, Coenred. I value it more than gold. Any man can possess gold; very few can inspire loyalty in others. How did Aelfgar bring you to such loyalty?"

"My father also taught me a similar lesson. He told me that loyalty to one's lord is important, but no more important than one man's loyalty to another, especially when their lives depend upon it."

"What do you think is the particular quality of loyalty that makes it so valuable?"

"That it works both ways, servant to master, master to servant."

"Yes." Harold nodded absently. "And when the master breaks that bond?"

"He loses all claim to the men who gave him their loyalty."

"All claim?"

"To my mind, yes."

"Loyalty imposes an obligation upon us, you are right. No master can demand of another what they are unwilling to give of themselves. Acknowledging loyalty is not just about playing the ring-giver when times are good, it is about sharing the burden when times are hard. It is playing honest with your people at all times and not using them in a way that you would not want to be used yourself. I make no claim to be a man of wisdom, but I know few men who acknowledge the true bond of loyalty."

"I do not wish to speak ill of them, their father was a great lord to me, but I think both Edwin and Morcar have failed to grasp an understanding of the role of loyalty."

"I agree. In York I made a mistake with you, Coenred, I was selfish."

"How so, My Lord?"

"I wanted to take you away to my court, but there is no place for you there."

"Mildryth would be pleased to hear you say such."

"I doubt not and, mayhap, even more so with what else I have to say." Harold smiled.

"My Lord?" Coenred could not keep the sudden wave of concern from his tone. Harold knew much about both Coenred and Mildryth; that was understood between them. Such knowledge could prove a boon or a hurt, depending on how it was used.

"There is no man in this kingdom who knows Edwin and Morcar better than you, most certainly true since their father died."

"Mayhap?"

"I have no doubt. I have sought to strengthen the bonds between our families, of Wessex and of Mercia, since taking their sister to wife, but they have disappointed me at every turn."

"They are moved by a jealousy of your success, My Lord, they would be like the Godwins."

"I know. It was their ambition that brought about the fall of York to Hardrada, after the battle at Fulford Gate. It was that poor judgment that drove me to march north and rescue my kingdom from the Norse, a feat that they might have made unnecessary if they had followed wiser counsel."

Coenred stared at the board before him. Not so long ago he would have leapt to the defence of the two brothers, even before the king, but now he found that he lacked the compunction to do so. He was no longer an eorl's man, not even a huscarl properly as he had no lord to give service to. He did not realise it but his silence was telling as far as King Harold was concerned.

"You spoke previously to me and explained Edwin and Morcar's thinking, what made them choose to give battle as they did, there is no need to go over this again. I am thinking instead of the days to come. The sons of Aelfgar will not respect me, I admit that, and so I need to put someone in the north who can exert some form of influence over them."

"Mayhap, only their sister could do that." Coenred was almost dismissive.

"Or you?"

"My Lord?"

"Eorl Aelfgar set you to be the teacher to his sons, did he not?"

"Aye."

"They outgrew you as their teacher, but they could not dismiss you as their equal."

"I am but a theign, at best, my estate is sufficient for that, I am not equal to an eorl."

"Unless you were made one, Coenred." The king smiled as the warrior gave way to surprise. "If I make you the Eorl of Holderness you would be the equal of the Eorl of Mercia and the Eorl of Northumbria. You would be my man in the north, set to steady the young eorldermen and rightly rewarded for such a task."

"You would make me the Eorl of Holderness?" There was no mask on Coenred's face, which was probably why the king laughed in response. He had not expected this weapon's man to betray his emotions in such an unguarded fashion.

"Aye, I would. To counter Edwin and Morcar, as I say."

"They may still resent me."

"At their own peril! Coenred, I do not sit idly on my throne, I make it my business to know my kingdom. In both Mercia and

Northumbria your name is spoken with respect and your men show you loyalty. You are known to be a man of quality. Excepting yourself, mayhap, no one would be surprised to see you raised to the station of an eorl. For myself there would be only advantages on all sides, the people would see me as the ring-giver of old, rewarding a good man's ability, and I would have a man that I could trust to oversee that part of the kingdom to which you cling so obstinately." Harold swept up his silver cup as if he were sealing a bargain. "What say you?"

"I did not look for this boon, My Lord, but I will not refuse you a second time."

"Good, now drink with me!" Together they emptied their cups and Harold quickly refilled the vessels again. "There is but one requirement, my Eorl of Holderness!"

"Requirement, My Lord?"

"Aye, Half-foot, my secretary, has drawn your papers and my decree is already upon the road to London. You are invested without ceremony, I am sorry to relate, but that is because that while you now hold the rank and title of eorl you will not be able to take your seat until after we have defeated Guillaume the Bastard!"

"I understand that, as do all men here."

"Then understand that this requirement that I speak of is simply this; that you stand beside me as the Eorl of Holderness in this coming battle. You, a man stout and true, a man to be relied upon in the shield wall, at my right-hand upon the field of battle and then my right-hand in the north of the kingdom. I will put my very life in your hands, Coenred. My requirement of you is that you safeguard it."

"With all my strength, My Lord!"

Coenred's Estate in the Isle of Holderness

The October night closed in and, before the longest hour, the hloth had split into three parties. One, led by Imminric, sat and waited north of the estate, another headed east in a wide circle so as to avoid discovery, and the third, led by Wulfhere himself, had a shorter journey going to the west but staying within the shadows of the trees. There were no means to tell the passage of time, no church bell to ring out the hour, so the attack was coordinated on instinct alone. Wulfhere had impressed upon them all that they were to remain quiet for as long as possible. No battle cries were to shatter the silence of the night. A sheep had been caught and butchered by two of the lads, its meat cut to give every man something to throw to any watch-hounds that they might encounter. Once the guard animal was distracted they were to cut its throat.

Wulfhere rested against the bole of a tree, his langseax hanging listlessly from his hand. He was impatient to begin the work but his eagerness was tempered by his desire to see the woman dead before him at last. Mildryth had become almost like a wight to him; a supernatural creature. She had escaped him twice previously; he could not allow her to do so for a third time. He felt the mark of the witch upon him and knew that he would enjoy no success in this life while she still lived.

The night sky was a patchwork of clouds and openings through which the stars shone. It was difficult to tell what hour it might be but the settlement had grown quiet and one by one the lights had been extinguished behind the shutters. They waited a little longer but saw no movement nor heard any sounds. Sleep had claimed them all at last.

"We go now!" Wulfhere commanded.

"What about the others?"

"If they be not moving yet they will when they see us in the settlement. Remember, walk like a fox, make no sound unless pressed to do so. The more we kill in the quiet of the night the less we will have to fight after the alarm has gone out."

Their shadows flitted across the fields under the slow moving clouds. They came quickly upon the first of the peasant houses, which, although smaller than the grand structures built for the two brothers, were still of a generous size in and of themselves. Two of the hloth went to try the door but found it barred against them. They glanced at Wulfhere but he had continued moving into the centre of the estate. He had no designs on the peasants whatsoever.

"What do we do?"

"I know not."

"Break it down?"

"I have no axe."

"We'll try the next one then, mayhap they be not so careful!"

Wulfhere left his men behind and closed on the most western of the two large houses. He reached the main entrance, two wide wooden doors, strongly crafted. Like his companions, he found that it was barred against him. All the shutters were closed also and it was difficult to tell if anyone actually lived in the building. It occurred to him that mayhap Mildryth lodged this night with her man's family, all together around one hearth, but then he saw the orange light seeping out of a chink in the shutter to the right of the door. He put his eye to the gap and could see a dull glow from beyond, but little else. It mattered not. More important was that it confirmed to him there was someone residing in there. Mildryth, alone he hoped.

Imminric led his followers out from the trees when he thought he saw movement to the west. He lumbered forward on heavy legs. The langseax in his hand looked more like a knife than a single bladed sword. They came upon a house that was larger than all the other peasant dwellings. A hound snarled at them.

"Throw the meat!" Imminric commanded.

One of his men did just that and advanced on the animal as its head went down to sniff at the raw mutton that fell just before it. The others continued forward, looking to come at the house from the south where its main door seemed to be placed. The robber who had thrown the meat drew his knife and reached out to grab the hound by the scruff of its neck. The animal growled at him, its lips curling back and showing yellow fangs. For a moment the two simply stared at each other. The man took a step forward and tried to grab hold of the beast. Whether it thought he was trying to steal its food did not matter, the hound reacted with sudden violence. It lurched forward, twisting its large head and buried its teeth into the exposed right arm.

The man screamed in both fear and pain. The knife fell from his hand. From somewhere else, another dog started barking and then another. The hound engaged in the fight shook its head as it pushed forward, knocking its quarry to the dusty ground. Imminric turned to see the commotion and saw his fellow laid on his back with the large hound stood over him, rending his forearm into a bloody mess. He thought of going back to help but then decided better of it. If the man were worth his salt he should be able to fight off a watch-hound, he reckoned.

The door of the house nearest to him was suddenly flung open and a man appeared. He was partly dressed, wearing linen trousers but no shirt. His body looked emaciated and yet he carried a fine two bladed sword in his right hand.

"That would make a fine weapon for me, give it over!" Imminric demanded of him.

"Nithings! You would attack in the night! This alone is what I will give thee!" Eanfrid spat back at him.

His instincts as a weapons-man were still acute, despite the ravages that his recent illness had inflicted upon his once strong and hearty body. In the dim light, he sensed rather than saw the langseax swing down at him. He parried it easily and took a step back. There were four of them, he realised. The giant before him was by far the most dangerous, but the other three were not to be discounted. He took another step, leading them away from his house and his wife of common-law.

Wulfhere cursed in a whisper. The sound of the man's screams and the barking of the hounds had awoken everyone on the estate, he reckoned. He could not countenance that wyrd had turned against him once again. More fool him for trusting in the abilities of men hardly any wiser than sheep. He thought to flee but then, still being close by the shutter, he heard movement from within. Quickly he retreated to the western corner of the house where there was dark shelter to be found. From his vantage spot, he watched as a pool of light appeared in front of the house and a person appeared.

It was a woman.

He could tell immediately from her shadow and so risked leaning out from around the corner of the house.

It was her!

She stood alone in her nightclothes, her eyes desperately trying to see what the disturbance might be. Wyrd had not tricked him. Indeed, it had led him right to her and she was alone and defenceless now. With sudden vigour, he surged forward. At the last moment, Mildryth sensed a presence and turned towards him but too late, his hand was over her mouth and he was pushing her back over the threshold before she could make a sound.

Eanfrid stepped towards a dirty looking man who was on his right, the fellow backtracked cautiously away. He had in his hands a wood axe but he clearly lacked the confidence to use it as a weapon. The giant swung at him again but the old warrior dodged the blow easily. He had another assailant on his left and the final one behind him. He appeared trapped, surrounded, but he knew that he was now in control of them. Again he moved, this time stepping backwards, and the ring moved with him, keeping their distance from his sharp looking sword.

"Are we going to dance all night or is one of you going to make a cut?" Eanfrid goaded them.

"Get 'im!" Imminric bellowed.

The one on the right moved, holding the axe in two hands across his body, it was not a very efficient attacking posture. Eanfrid closed the distance to him but it was a feint. The man on his left, armed with a long knife, lunged forward a second after Eanfrid moved, not realising that he had been drawn into making a mistake. The Saxon warrior changed direction with admirable speed and his sword flashed out, the tip of the blade disappearing into the knifeman's stomach, cutting through muscle and organ. With a deft twist, Eanfrid retrieved the weapon and deflected another attack from Imminric. The man on his left fell to the earth with a groan, his hands clutching at the wound that would give him a slow death.

Now there were only three.

Somehow Mildryth broke free from Wulfhere's grasp and scuttled away from him, putting the hearth between them. He glared at her but then smiled, looking sinister in the weak light from the fire. He half turned, closed and barred the door, and then returned his whole attention to her once more.

"You'll not escape me this time," he told her in a voice that sounded strangely normal.

"Escape you?" Her chin came up and she could not have looked less afraid. "As I recall it was you who escaped from my knife the last we met." Unconsciously his hand went up to the fresh scar on his face. "'Twas on the road north from York, if I remember rightly."

"Wyrd favoured you last time, but not this." Wulfhere insisted, his eyes narrowing.

"What did I ever do to make you haunt my heels like you do?"

"You put your mark on me."

"Afterwards, fool, after you tried to steal me from the city and after you came at me on that same road. I never gave you leave to come to me, I never invited you into my home, why did you make such a presumption."

"I would be what you are."

"You will never be theign-worthy, you are a murderer; the killer of your own brother!"

So she knew. It was no great surprise. This was a small world and it was easy enough to discover another's business. He remembered that she had worked in the long hall in York, the high-theign was a friend of hers. She would know what occurred under that roof.

"It matters not what you know, not after this night. I will kill you and lift your mark from my head." He told her, his voice even and sure.

"It was not me but God who put that mark there for all to see."

"I don't believe in your god!"

"It matters not, as long as I do."

"He will not help you, neither will your man. I know that he's gone to war with the king."

"Coenred is my protector against men like Tostig of Wessex, but God is my protector against men like you!"

"Think you so? Where then is your guardian now?"

The man with the axe finally committed himself. He stepped towards Eanfrid and swung his weapon with all of his might. He was not, however, practised in the art of fighting with such a blade. A Saxon warrior knew that timing was everything in combat. Raising the axe made his abdomen vulnerable and it was all the invitation that Eanfrid needed. He could move quickly even when wearing heavy armour, he moved even more quickly wearing only his linen trousers. Once again his bright steel was sullied by unworthy blood. The keen steel ripping into the man's stomach cavity and causing fatal damage. The axe-man's legs buckled and he fell to the dirt with a groan.

The giant came at him again, hoping to catch his opponent off guard, but Eanfrid had read him now. He knew exactly what the big man would do, the angle of the downward stroke of the sword, the pace, the swing, everything. He moved quickly into the arc of the weapon, a dangerous move for anyone who lacked training. His sword came up and met the langseax, pushing it further up and away. Eanfrid moved again, towards his enemy and under the reach of his weapon. His arm drew back and then lunged forward as he put all of his strength into the stroke. The keen steel severed the large thigh muscles in the exposed leg.

Again Eanfrid twisted the weapon to stop it becoming stuck in his opponent's flesh. Somehow Imminric continued his attack, bringing his sword down once more. He had formidable strength but lacked training. Eanfrid stepped aside and backwards, easily avoiding the blow. Imminric took a step forward to close the distance once more but his left leg suddenly gave way. He became aware of the pain and howled in distress. As he fell to the ground he released his weapon and clutched instead at the damaged limb.

For a moment Eanfrid just stood and looked down at his opponent. The man was alternately cursing and crying out in pain. He reminded Eanfrid of the great Viking warrior who had held the bridge at Stamford against the advancing Saxon army. It had become a popular tale how that giant had been cut to the ground in just a similar manner as this. The Viking titan had died before the eyes of his king and his enemies, hewn by many bright blades where he fell. Eanfrid had only one sword; he used it to put the nithing out of his misery with only one stroke.

The fourth assailant departed like his courage, quickly, turning tail and running away into the night.

All around torches were burning, people shouting, hounds barking. The estate was fully awake now and putting their attackers to the sword. He had trained them well in the ways of war, at Coenred's command of course.

"God may help those who help themselves," Mildryth said in a firm voice.

"But you cannot help yourself now," Wulfhere told her. He hefted his heavy langseax. "You have no defence against this." She did not reply but just looked at him from the other side of the low burning hearth. "Even this fire will not keep you from me."

"The fire is to warm a home, to make it welcoming for my man, it is not meant for the likes of thee either in hospitality or defence." Again that haughty look that made his blood boil.

"Enough!" He shouted at her. "Time now to end this matter. I grant you some mercy, I will make this quick, which was not my intent before. On your knees and die, wench!"

"I, kneel to the likes of thee?" She fixed him with a cold look that only served to inflame Wulfhere further.

His lunge came quickly. He threw himself across the hearth, his left hand reaching out for her and his right raising the heavy weapon, making it ready to swing down upon the woman. Mildryth moved only at the last moment. She did not know where her resolve had come from but it fortified her heart. There was no fear inspired by this man that she knew to be a coward and a murderer; a true nithing. There was only contempt for him now.

There was no fear.

Against her initial wishes, her husband had taught her how to fight with a knife. He had told her that her station might make her the target for men such as this Wulfhere, this Peada. When she had mastered the way of the small blade he had presented her with a beautiful scramseax, embellished with her name. She lacked that weapon now, it hung from Coenred's belt, but since the last time that she and Wulfhere and encountered each other such a weapon, in style if not in quality, had not been far from her hand.

Mildryth let Wulfhere grasp her with his left hand. Just as she presumed he pulled her closer to him, it added momentum to her thrust. The knife slipped between the lower ribs on his left side. The man's face, initially angry and afire with bile, turned pale and the eyes widened. Mildryth withdrew the blade and stabbed again, aiming for his stomach. Wulfhere tried to push her away from him even as his right arm collapsed and the heavy sword fell to the boards beneath their feet. The knife bit again and again. Wulfhere's hand tightened its hold on her but his knees began to buckle. She felt his warm blood on her hand, saw it stain her nightclothes. All the colour left his face and his speechless mouth formed an 'O'. Slowly she pushed him from her and he collapsed backwards onto the hearth.

For a cold moment, Mildryth simply stood and looked down on her fallen enemy. She felt neither remorse nor elation. In fact, she felt nothing. A loud banging at the door suddenly caught her attention. It might have been going on longer than she realised. She moved quickly and unbarred the door. Eanfrid and several ceorls pushed their way in, weapons still drawn.

"My Lady?!" Eanfrid cried urgently, looking at the bright blood that stained her clothes.

Before Mildryth could respond the voice of a demon cut the air. A scream the like of which few had heard before. The light from the hearth flared up and they saw the body of the buttescarl suddenly become consumed by the flames.

"He still lives" A peasant gasped.

"No, he does not!" Eanfrid stepped forward and swung down at the man's head. Wulfhere's hair was on fire, as were most of his clothes. His face was terrible to behold. The screaming stopped when the steel cut through the bone of his skull. Quickly Eanfrid withdrew the weapon and then grabbed hold of the man's right hand, mercifully untouched as yet by the flames, and dragged the body from the hearth. "Now men, get him outside."

Already they could smell the stench of burning flesh. Mildryth raised a hand to her face. The peasants unceremoniously pulled the dead thief outside and dumped him onto the dusty ground.

"'Tis well done except for him falling onto the fire," Eanfrid told Mildryth.

"I thought that he was dead already."

"He is now, My Lady. He is now."

Friday, 6th Octobre 1066

London

"And this is London!" Remarked Thrydwulf, seemingly unimpressed by what he saw.

The straight line of Ermine Street led their eyes down to the city that sat on the north bank of the great River Thames. Woodland bordered them on both the east and west but there was a large cleared area all around the city in which sat small settlements, tilled land and livestock, all to feed the city.

"It looks like York," Aethelmaer observed.

"Only larger," Coenred agreed. "The walls are Roman, just like York, but both longer and taller. There's also a river that cuts the city into two, east and west, and of course, the Thames protects the whole of the south of the city."

"We could get lost in a city that big!" Edwin remarked.

"No fires burn and no warriors clamour around the gates; the Normans have not yet attacked then!" Thrydwulf pointed out. "I hope that this is a good sign."

Coenred glanced at his friend. Signs and portents, they had been a chief subject of conversation during the last six days of travelling. Thrydwulf's comment might have been meant harmlessly but Coenred knew all too well how the minds of the more superstitious worked.

"More's the pity," he announced in a loud voice to his companions. "Imagine, if we came upon the Normans now, camped before London, with the king at our head and the Saxons of the north and south united into one fyrd, and all with swords and spears to whet?"

"We'd repay our southern friends the courtesy they showed us at Stamford Bridge!" Hengist agreed.

At that thought, the weary spirits of the warriors seemed to lift and they spurred their horses forward, down the rolling countryside to King Harold's capital city.

To many a northern man, York seemed like a sprawling place that was hemmed in by tall, dark walls, and yet it was half the size of London. The buildings here were much the same as in the north, although there did seem to be many larger structures, rising to two and even three stories. As in York some of the churches were built in stone and even more were also being rebuilt accordingly, although several examples in wood still remained.

In truth, London was a city recovering from abandonment. To the west, where the Thames made a sharp turn southwards, stood the remains of a purely Anglo-Saxon habitation, Lundenwic as it had been called. The local people had preferred to live there than within the Roman walls in an earlier time and much of the old city had fallen into ruin as a result. Violent times had driven them back behind the protection of the stout walls, however, and slowly the old city was being reborn.

Although riders had been sent ahead to warn the city men of the return of the king and his army there seemed little preparation for their reception. The streets were thronged with people, a large number looking to get a glimpse of King Harold, who was clearly liked in these parts, but most were simply going about their daily activities without any concern for other events.

Coenred and his companions moved to the side of Ermine Street and watched portions the army arrive in straggling lines, passing through one of the seven gates of London. The mounted troops had pushed on ahead, riding their horses hard, but the largest part of the army had journeyed on foot. Everyone looked tired. Everyone was tired.

The sun was beginning to descend into the west. Each night seemed to begin a little earlier as they marched into October. Autumn had hold of the countryside now, bleaching green from the trees, the bushes, the fields, and replacing it with burning browns and red that flared into beauty but then faded all too quickly. As they had made their way south they had also watched the first migration of birds heading the same way but on much longer journeys than the war weary men beneath them. Coenred wondered if spring would find him back in familiar haunts, particularly Holderness where he now longed to be more than anywhere else. More so even than in the great city of London.

Edwin had endured the march with better humour than anyone else. It was all a great adventure to him and he lived to experience it to the full. Thrydwulf often told him to stop his chatter, in his typical grumpy manner, but in truth, they had all been comforted by the young man's presence. It was good to have a companion whose mind was not shadowed in foreboding born from the experience of war and the thought of facing an enemy largely unknown to them. Aethelmaer and Hengist had accepted the young servant well as he was closer to their age than either of the two older huscarls.

The future remained hidden from them. They wondered if it would be a long campaign or a single encounter that would decide the fate of the kingdom. Their constant talk on the subject had led to the agreement that only wyrd knew what the outcome would be. Everyman thought of wyrd as being unreliable and, mayhap, even unknowable. That may well be why so many looked for signs and portents with regards to their future. Many would put their trust in Jesu Christ for that faith was strong within the land of England. Many would also acknowledge a much older faith, even if not openly, and call on their illustrious ancestors to protect them in the fight to come.

Coenred turned his horse away from the weary troops and led the way into the city. They had been told to find lodgings on arriving in the city but eorldermen, which Coenred had to remind himself he was now one, were to go to the mead hall where they had been informed King Harold would be settling in.

There was always an energy around the king. It was in the air of his military court, in the busy movement of men pacing quickly to do his bidding, in his brothers, the princes, and of course encompassed by the man himself. It was even there in the seriously faced servants fulfilling the most menial of tasks. This energy seemed to fight against the weariness of everyone inside the building and, as if close proximity to the king gave it strength, it always seemed to win. Coenred felt his own tiredness slip from him like a discarded cloak as they arrived at the Hall of the Godwins in London. Climbing down from his horse he passed the reins to Edwin.

"We'll stable the beasts and find somewhere to lodge," Thrydwulf told him. "I will send the boy to find you."

"But who will you send to find me when I get lost in this place?" Edwin wanted to know."

"Mayhap I will accompany you?" Hengist offered. "My legs are stiff and a walk would ease my seat."

"Note the name of the lodge you take and on your way to me, if you should wander from the path, just ask for the Hall of the Godwins, someone will point it out to you," Coenred told them.

Thrydwulf led the huscarls and Edwin away, the latter towing his master's horse. Coenred turned and looked up at the impressive building before him. He knew that the Godwins were fabulously wealthy of course, but the site of this great house, complete with glass in the window frames that looked out onto the street, brought home just how powerful the Godwin clan really had become.

He stepped through the open doorway and into a passage that led into the heart of the building. Rooms opened up on either side. Where the door was open he could see large amounts of stores, food, wine, beer, cloth, and such. At the end of the passage, a large and impressive hall opened up. It was two stories high with an open balcony on each side. Rich hangings, weapons, shields, and pieces of armour decorated the walls. The place was thronged with people, lords and servants alike. Their voices merged together as they spoke creating an unintelligible drone. For a moment Coenred just stood there and looked around, reminding himself that this was only the house of the Godwin family in London and not the court of the king; that was at Westminster Palace.

"Eorl Coenred, you have arrived?" Half-foot emerged from the throng. For a moment Coenred simply stared at him.

"We have met before?" He said after a moment.

"That's right, first in Tadcaster and then in York." Half-foot reminded him.

"Yes, you are a servant of the king."

"His secretary." It was a small point but it mattered to Half-foot.

"Then may I tell you something?"

"Of course."

"I know not what to do!" Coenred felt sheepish at such a confession, but it was true and he felt that he could trust Half-foot with this admission of ignorance.

"Well, I suppose that is understandable, what with you only recently having been made an eorl and still a stranger to the court," Half-foot returned with a friendly smile. "As an eorlderman, you are necessarily a companion of the king, different to a Royal Companion, but important at court all the same. This is not the royal court, however, so you are not required to present yourself formerly to King Harold, but I would advise greeting him all the same."

"Thank you."

"I am not here by accident, however."

"You aren't?"

"No, I was commanded to look for you on your arrival. There is someone who wants to speak to you. Follow me, My Lord." Half-foot turned away and started to make his way through the throng, favouring his left leg as he went and leaning on this gold decorated staff. It was as much his badge of office as a double edged sword was for a huscarl.

Coenred obediently followed. They came close to King Harold and the Eorl of Holderness bowed in his direction. Harold acknowledged the pleasantry with a nod but did not halt his conversation, or indicate for Coenred to join him, so he continued to follow the secretary.

"Lord Coenred, or should I say Eorl of Holderness, I'm glad to see that you've made it this far with us!" Eorl Gyrth declared as he appeared from what seemed to be a sea of bodies. Retainers trailed in his wake, some trying to get his attention, but Gyrth appeared to have a detached air about him. He ignored the commotion that surrounded them.

"My Lord Eorl." Coenred bowed in acknowledgement.

"How now, we are brother eorls, you do not need to bow to me." He laughed. Half-foot, his task accomplished disappeared once more.

"I am sorry, a force of habit."

"Of course, I understand. You are new to your station, and well deserved it is too, and I presume no one has yet instructed you in the etiquette of being an eorlderman?"

"No, indeed they have not, but then there was little opportunity on the road to London."

"Quite. How do the men of Northumbria?" Gyrth asked as he took the former huscarl's arm and directed him to the side of the hall.

"No better and no worse than the men of other shires," Coenred told him. They came to a trestle table and Gyrth motioned him to sit. He waved away his retainers but demanded drinks to be brought before they were beyond earshot.

"That's as much as we can expect I suppose. Thank you for this much-needed diversion."

"My Lord?"

"I have no doubt that for you and your men this march has been a toilsome affair, but for those of us who are Royal Companions it has been a long session of constant talking, debating, and counselling. Everything has been discussed with regards to the Normans and how to best them. The truth is, I need some relief, some conversation that is not to do with the morrow. I seek the company of one who is not privy to the king every hour of every day." Gyrth smiled good-naturedly but there was no hiding the tiredness in his eyes. He was weary, both physically and mentally. "In other words, I am being selfish and using you as a means of escaping my duties as a prince."

"Even princes enjoy time for leisure," Coenred offered.

"Agreed!" A servant deposited a bottle of wine and two wooden cups on the table, he then disappeared wordlessly. "I know not what quality this may be but I hope it will meet our needs." He opened the bottle and poured the contents into the two cups. "Drink with me?"

"What to, My Lord?" Coenred raised the cup from the table.

"To the simple pleasures of life."

"That I can do so, happily!" They emptied their cups and Gyrth refilled them, but he did not raise his drink to his lips so quickly this time.

"Despite the days of travel I found no time on the road to congratulate you on your promotion, but it was one of the good things to come out of the seemingly endless days of talking." Gyrth leant forward in a conspiratorial manner.

"I thought that it was the king's decision?"

"So it was, but the king rarely makes a decision without first discussing it with his council. Seeing as you were too loyal to leave the service of Edwin and Morcar, when first asked, raising you to their level seemed like a good course of action."

"I have left their service all the same. Some might deem this a reward for doing so."

"They might, people often do mistake their opinions for fact, but it was not so. I proposed the idea to Harold on the road and it was discussed at length; many could see the virtue of having such a stalwart man as yourself in the north to support the king."

"Then I thank you, My Lord, for your good opinion of myself, but still it came as a surprise to me."

"Why did you follow the king south, even after you were a free man no longer beholden to Edwin and Morcar?"

"I came because my king called for weapons men to come to his banner. I ended my service with Edwin of Mercia because he chose not to follow what I considered to be the right path."

"And that is the measure of your worth as we saw it," Gyrth told him emphatically. "My father, Eorl Godwin, always impressed upon us the value of loyalty. You are a man of loyalty, Coenred, we saw that in Tadcaster, and again in York. You were highly valued even then."

"Even when I declined becoming a Royal Companion?"

"Even more so, as I know my brother explained to you when he made you an eorl. You put your service to your lord before your personal ambition, that is true loyalty, and if Edwin of Mercia neither sees it for what it is nor values it, then more the pity for him. You told me previously that Edwin and Morcar are jealous of our success and wish to emulate us, they will fail if they cannot keep hold of men of quality like yourself."

"You flatter me with too many compliments, My Lord." Gyrth laughed at Coenred's embarrassment and drank some more.

"You must call me Gyrth now, we are both eorls."

"But you are an aetheling, a prince of the realm."

"Aye and short of true friends, but surrounded by men who want me to do something for them. They show me precious little reason as to why I should. I remember still when we first met, before the gate of Tadcaster. You drew your men up in a shield wall, not knowing us to be either friends or foe. You met me then with brave words and I was wise to halt my steed short of your throwing arm. I believe you would have fixed me with one of your angons."

"Only if you had proven to be a Norseman, as the watch feared you to be."

"I do not doubt it. It was your actions though, not your words, that earned our admiration. You did what an aetheling should have done, even if that then was not your station. It was you, Coenred, who proved yourself worthy of reward. There is much to be doubted in this changing world and so it seems meet that when we come across something that inspires a little faith in us then we should grasp it tightly. I would have you as my friend, Coenred, and titles do not come between such as I would have us be."

"I would be honoured to count you as a friend, My-" Coenred laughed at his own instinctive response, "Gyrth."

"And what of the Lady Mildryth, she waits for you I presume, but in ignorance of your good fortune?"

"Yes, I have sent her to my estate in the Isle of Holderness, on the understanding that I will hang up my shield, no more to be the huscarl, when I return. She thinks that she will marry a theign, not an eorl."

"I cannot fault you," Gyrth admitted with sincerity. "Although you are now counted eorl-worthy with us I do not doubt you would still be but one of many retainers at the king's court. In Northumbria you have the opportunity of making your own kingdom and with a goodly queen. I understand your thinking and in part I envy you."

"You envy me?" Coenred.

"I am brother to the king, whether I will it or not, my time is not my own. My presence is demanded wherever he is. The affairs of the state are now mine to deal with also, by blood relation as well as by rank, even though I have matters to look to in my own shire. I have a family there and I miss them greatly." A shadow passed over his face as he uttered the last. "I have wealth, power, and rank, but I do not have the freedom to decide where I will live my life or with whom. You have that choice, even as an eorl, and so yes, I envy you, Coenred."

"But you would not surrender these things to be in my place?"

"I could not, my father saw to that. I sometimes think that he bred us to rule this kingdom. Certainly, he made us love Wessex beyond measure. My eorldom is East Anglia, which makes my attachment to Wessex an awkward bind, but I am coming to favour Anglia. I will remain an aetheling and you an eorl, and each of us will take what happiness we can find, eh?"

"Aye, life is too fleeting to spend staring into a pool of dismay. This night will pass and so too the morrow. Whatever it brings we will meet it as men, as best prepared as the life we've lived will allow us to be."

"Wise words, my friend." A silence settled between them but it was comfortable and they sipped their wine without making eye contact.

"What plans are there for us in London?" Coenred asked eventually. Gyrth smiled weakly.

"You return us to the subject I longed to get away from," he observed. Coenred began to apologise but Gyrth only raised a hand to stop him. "You are a fighting man brought south to fight; of course you wonder what the king has in mind for you and your men. In truth, we know not yet, which is what makes all the talking on the road so laborious. We do not know exactly where the Normans are or what they are about. Once in London, the army will be quartered and we will discover what it is that the enemy intend and then, I hope, we will best know how to meet them."

"Have you fought the Normans before?"

"No, but my brother has fought with them, over in Brittany after his ill-advised trip to Normandy foundered on the rocks. He went then to recover our youngest brother, Wulfnoth, taken as a hostage by the Normans and held captive by them for most of his life now. Harold was taken captive also, but in the manner of a nobleman of course. Harold tells us that the Normans do not fight like we do. Their army is split into three. First, there are the spearmen, much like our fyrdmen, but they do not stand in a shield wall, rather in a much looser fashion. Then there are the archers, men with bows formed into bodies."

"As we saw at Stamford Bridge!"

"Yes, that's an idea my brother is trying out, borrowed from the Normans. Unfortunately, the man who commanded those archers of ours fell at Stamford Bridge and we have yet to find a replacement. Finally, we come to the strangest part of their Norman power; knights, men who fight from horseback."

"I have heard that said before but never thought to see it."

"It is a thing that is true. King Edward had a small body of them drawn from his more active Norman advisors, though he was never active enough himself to adopt their martial ways. King Harold advises that these knights are dangerous to footmen such as ourselves and that we must be wary of them on the battlefield."

"I have never killed a man fighting with me from on top of a horse," Coenred admitted. "I look forward to killing a knight in combat."

"Harold was himself knighted by Guillaume," Gyrth commented. "How strange that our leader should be made of the same class as the greatest enemy that we are likely to meet on the field when arms decide this issue between them, someday soon now I think it will be."

"I am not given to omens," Coenred admitted although he accepted that the greatest part of their people most certainly were. "I need only know where our enemy is. I doubt that they look so much like we that I will mistake friend for foe, even if he be a king made a knight."

"At Stamford Bridge, Harold used a horse to show himself to the men so that they would see that he was unafraid and so take heart. The Normans lead from the rear it is said, in a like manner."

"Is that then a measure of their bravery?"

"Mayhap, but their dukes seem to survive many battles and that, they deem, is more important."

"Will your brother be a Saxon king or a Norman duke on the field of battle then?"

"That remains to be seen, but I don't look to unsettle you with this matter. Indeed, I wish you to know, and through you, the men also, that the enemy is not completely unknown to us as some would have it said." Coenred nodded as he pondered what Gyrth had revealed to him.

"Many fear what they do not know. No doubt there are those who, in their ignorance, have talked the Normans into being taller and darker shadows of things than what they really are. They are only men. And a Norman can be defeated in battle and killed, just like any other man. We must go into this war believing that we can win and that our enemy has no superiority over us." Gyrth asserted.

"I do not doubt that!" Coenred declared.

"Then do not let your men doubt it!" Gyrth insisted. "There will be time in London for them to rest. They may find themselves with little to do and I fear that the idle minds of some may find much to fear in what they think is to come, but do not have the wit to see it for what it is."

"Men from across the sea who look different to us, speak different to us, but are men just the same as us. The proof of this lies in the fact that they can be pierced by a bright spear point, just like us!"

"That you have this sense about you, Coenred, is why my brother wants you under his banner. He wants only men of quality to help him throw the enemy back into the sea that so unfriendly bore them to our shore. Drink one more time with me!" They raised and drained their cups.

"Now, I must go and carry out this task you've given me," Coenred said as he rose from his seat. "But I would say that there are many out there, sat around their dismal campfires, who will not need much in the way of persuading."

"Go with my best wishes, friend, and I hope all their fears are so easily laid to rest when we eventually get to meet the Normans on the battlefield."

***

"You have no time for me!" Eadgyth, Queen of England, complained.

"This is not true," Harold replied with a warm smile. He stood by her bed in the Palace of Westminster. It was very late but he had decided to move his court from the family house in London to this, the more genuine seat of his authority. Tomorrow he would be the King of England proper again. "I had thought that you might have been delivered of your child by now?"

"Our child," she corrected him. "It is true, I have gone by the expected time but the midwives say that the birth is imminent. I will be confined from you." She lay propped up on pillows, her distended stomach obvious beneath the bedclothes.

"I know and that is why I came to see you, despite the hour. Affairs will confine me as well."

"Guillaume of Normandy?"

"Yes, he is come."

"Do you think God hates us so that he sends one murdering invader after the other?"

"No, God loves us."

"I used to think so, but I find this world often cruel. How harsh must it be for the ceorls if it is hard for the likes of us?"

"I think your maternity colours your thoughts."

"Mayhap, I know of nothing but discomfort lately."

"You have been through childbirth previously."

"Indeed, three times. It does not seem to get any easier for me but they tell me the ceorls find it so."

"If I can, I will come to you after the delivery, may God keep you well."

"Harold, I have missed you these many days that you have been in the north. Indeed, I thought that I might not see you ever again. Dark thoughts have laid like a veil over my mind. I would not have you go from me again."

"I went north and slew the War Wolf, a feat no other man could match, how great can the danger be from this presuming Norman? My army has returned with me and we bring many men from the north also. They are grateful for what we did at York and come to repay a debt that they freely acknowledge. Our spears are keen and many."

"You talk of spears before your unborn child?"

"Boy or girl it will be a Godwin and battle will always be spoken of before its face."

"Such is the way with eorldermen and aethelings."

"And who would know better than you, a queen to two kings in your own lifetime?"

"Edwin and Morcar did not come did they?" She looked sad all of a sudden.

"No, they did not. I told them of your condition, hoping that the news might provoke them to a degree of brotherly love, but they are still lost in their bad humour after losing York to the Vikings. I could not sway them."

"Neither to come south with you in your hour of need nor to be friends also with us?"

"No."

"I had thought my brothers more loving than that."

"I will give them time to think on it. Winter draws ever nearer. We will defeat the Normans and then rest up until spring. Mayhap, the two of us will return then to Mercia and encourage Edwin and Morcar to be more like family to us?"

"Mayhap, but now you must take your leave of me as I feel unwell and I will not have you here to see me in this disposition."

He did not know if she were telling the truth or merely giving him an excuse to leave her again, but Harold stepped forward and gently kissed her on the forehead. She smiled at him, a genuine affection in her eyes, and he wished, in that instance, that he could be a proper husband to her. The pull of the crown, however, was too strong for him to ignore. He returned her smile and then left the chamber without another word.

Saturday, 7th October 1066

The Palace of Westminster, London

"Friends, we are gathered here to meet another danger. Guillaume of Normandy has landed to make good his threat to take the crown of England. Fortunately, he has been contained within the area of Hastings, but already he has begun to attack our people." King Harold looked grimly at his war council.

They were gathered now, within the halls of the Palace of Westminster. He had called together all of his brothers, the princes of the realm, along with his Royal Companions, and all those eorldermen and high-theigns who were, for whatever reason, present in London. All those who had responded to his request for support. They were a goodly number, but there were also faces well known to him who were noticeably absent as well. Eorl Edwin and Eorl Morcar were not the only ones who had chosen not to respond. Harold Godwinson of Wessex had the popular support of the people, but not every eorlderman felt the same about the rise of the Godwins. Theirs was a personal opposition to him, however, and one that existed in spite of the threat to all of them. Harold hoped that word of this council, the existence of which was not kept secret, might reach the ears of those lords who put their personal dislike of him, based on such petty grounds as it were, before the welfare of the kingdom. He hoped it might lead them to put aside such differences for the greater good of Saxon England.

"We have news from our people who are suffering the unlooked for attentions of the enemy. Half-foot, please make your report." Harold looked at his secretary.

"My Lord, this will make for painful hearing, but I will do as you command. My lords, I have gathered this news from proven sources. I do not exaggerate the contents for they make for bitter reading as they stand. Our people suffer and you should know it.

"The Normans remain at Hastings, having captured the town. The people put up a fight but were overwhelmed. Some fled afterwards and they have brought news that Hastings itself is intact; clearly, the Normans intend for it to become their base. It gives them a port through which they can receive supplies from Normandy. The people suffered but no more than to be expected when a settlement falls into the hands of the enemy. What comes next is not what one might expect from the Normans who claim to march with the pope's banner.

"The Normans have reached out into the lands around them, sending men in armour to terrify the villagers immediately hard-by. They have succeeded. I have witness accounts of unarmed men being put to the sword, just ceorls, harmless villagers, butchered before their families. Old men, young men, lower theigns, clergymen, and women too!"

Many voices suddenly erupted at this news. Harold commanded them to be quiet and indicated for Half-foot to continue.

"Houses were burnt, stores, stables, and churches too. What livestock could not be carried off back to Hastings was slaughtered where it stood. Food taken so that those left alive must leave the area or starve before the coming winter. Many have now reached London and brought this news with them. They have told it to my scribes many times over and the accounts vary little. They tell of cruel acts, of murder, mutilation and rape, enacted not only against the mothers but also against their girl-children. These men, these Normans, claim to be Christians, their actions reveal them to be monsters."

"What kind of enemy is this?" Osfrid, Captain of the Royal Companions demanded. "This bastard claims the crown of England and puts the people he would lord over to these outrages!"

"He looks to provoke a fight," Gyrth answered sullenly.

"And he'll get one," Harold promised with barely disguised anger.

"But at a time of your choosing when all paths have been explored." Gyrth insisted.

"You expect me to sit here and wait until he has laid waste to the country around Hastings, my holdings included?" High-Theign Esegar asked angrily.

"It is the fate of the people that concerns me," King Harold told him. "Lodges and houses can be rebuilt, fields re-sown, but the people cannot be replaced so easily."

"There are always more ceorls." Another High-Theign insisted. He received a few scowls from those stood around him in response

"Think you so? Then you do not have the right of authority over them!" Harold raised his voice angrily. "A lord who commands over ceorls, be he a theign or an eorl, is put there, first and foremost, to be a shield to his people. Always has this been the Saxon way. The ring-givers of old rewarded their stout warriors who fought well against the enemy. Great was the chieftain who could protect his people against any danger, for what is a chieftain without his people, nothing but a man alone."

"But our wealth is measured by our holdings." A theign suggested.

"Your wealth, mayhap, but not your worthiness," Harold replied. "I promote those that I find worthy. Know some of you this man, Coenred, once a huscarl to Eorl Aelfgar of Mercia?" Harold pointed directly at the person he now talked about and Coenred, in his turn, understood now why Gyrth had insisted that he stand in the front row.

Clearly, this had been planned, which led him to wonder how much else of this public council had also been arranged before it had even begun. He guessed that Osfrid, Harold's most loyal companion, was very much a part of it as well, expressing an outrage designed to raise tempers and to provoke an angry response against Guillaume of Normandy.

"Coenred served also as Captain of Huscarl's to Aelfgar's sons, Edwin and Morcar. He fought bravely at Fulford Gate and brought both the survivors and important news to Tadcaster where he waited for me to come. This man proved his worthiness then, and again on the field at Stamford Bridge, where we slew together Harald Hardrada, the King of Norway.

"More than that, Coenred followed me south from York when news of the Normans came to us there. He is a loyal man, a proven warrior, and now he is made Eorl of Holderness in recognition of his accomplishments and qualities. A chieftain of old would have done no less."

The hall was filled with voices that sounded their approval for what they heard. They appreciated their king's words, just as Harold had expected that they would.

Gyrth, Eorl of East Anglia, stepped forward a pace so as to be better seen by all. "Men have been sent for from the west, the south, and the east; they will come. The army is tired, they have walked many miles, and their numbers have been depleted for the Vikings were not an easy enemy to overcome. Our warriors need to rest, to recover from their journey and their wounds, but time stands in our favour, not Guillaume's."

"These outrages are not new to our people," Osfrid asserted. "We have seen them before. Even the cruelty suffered by our children is not so new to us. In past times the foes that did these things were barbarians, not men of the cross. Then we called them Viking, now we know them as Norman. That is the only difference."

"And you think that we should do nothing?" High-Theign Esegar pushed his concern once again.

"No, I mean to act, but we must decide carefully on what to do. Our actions should be decided through deliberation, not provocation." Harold asserted.

"It is October, autumn has taken hold and winter is not far behind. Guillaume will be holed up in Hastings with little food and scant chance of resupply from Normandy. Our fleet, ranging along the

Whale-road, will see to that. Storms also will come to hazard any ships that dare put to sea when the sky turns dark and Thunor sends his thunder. The English winter will thin out his men; eat away at their strength and their resolve. Come the spring we will march against them with a host well fed and well rested. A mighty fyrd that will push their broken bodies back from Hastings and into the sea, to wash up upon the shores from whence they came." Gyrth suggested.

"It is not in my mind to wait so long!" Harold declared.

"Why not?" Gyrth appeared surprised by his brother's response.

"I did not wait to meet the threat of Hardrada in the north, why wait to defeat Guillaume in the south? I intend to move as soon as possible. Once the food has run out at Hastings I expect the Normans to move camp and ruin more of our countryside. They may head for Dover. If they capture that port they could open a more secure line of supply with Normandy. They would also have the Roman road to London down which to move when they are ready."

"Our fleet could cut any such supply route, once it has been refitted," Osfrid observed. "Also, Dover might not prove so easily taken, it has its' stout walls and the Normans will require siege engines."

"In truth, I see the recall of the fleet as a mistake now," Harold admitted. "I trusted too much to the strength of the weather and the weakness of Guillaume's resolve. If we had caught them at sea then nary a Norman foot would have touched English soil."

"The milk has been spilt," Gyrth observed, "there's little to be gained from regretting such actions now. We must proceed along a path that will bring us to victory."

"Aye, brother, and I propose to move to the offensive." Harold insisted.

"We could pen them in for the winter with a chain of burghs around Hastings!" Eorl Thurkill suggested.

"We have not the time for such an undertaking. I doubt that they will sit in Hastings and let us build such a fence around them? It would be an incitement to battle that we may not be prepared to meet." Harold opposed the suggestion.

"The army is numerous already; it would take but days to build the burghs!" Thurkill countered.

"But they would need manning and supplying throughout the winter. Each burgh would need to be strong enough to throw back a determined attack by the enemy, should they sally forth from Hastings." Osfrid pointed out.

"If the one were built close enough to the other then they could give support in time of trial." Coenred surprised himself by suddenly feeling the need to voice his opinion. "Their closeness would rob the Normans of any chance of a surprise attack also, against any single burgh."

"This is a worthy plan, my friends, but I believe it to be beyond our ability to undertake," Harold interrupted the discussion. "The expense alone would be too great. The fyrd is not meant to carry out such a task, so far from their own homes, and there are not enough huscarls left to man the burghs alone."

"Have lesser kings not performed so great a feat?" Gyrth asked. "Offa built a dyke to keep out the Welsh."

"That took years to build!" Harold countered. "We have not the luxury of that much time. Indeed, I fear that if we give the Normans any time at all then they will use it against us. Their fighting men are such by trade, they kill for money. As long as Guillaume retains the means to pay them then they will stay under his banner. For these men, a winter in Hastings will be a time to relax and keep warm, burning Saxon wood in Saxon homes."

"Can there be no words between thee and the bastard?" A theign enquired.

"Such has been attempted already, but the Duke of Normandy is resolved to take the crown by force. Indeed, I do not think that Guillaume went to all this effort merely to talk the crown out of my hands." Harold replied in a reasonable tone.

"Mayhap, My Lord, but, if the Normans do love gold as much as is said of them, then could not a price be set upon their withdrawal from our lands? King Alfred once did the same with the Danes."

"Aye, he did, but then few lust after gold like the Vikings."

"'Tis said that the Normans are descended from Viking stock, settled in Normandy by the French to protect them from the Norse men's ravages, and this Guillaume is rumoured to love his gold as much as any Viking we have ever known."

"There is merit in this," Gyrth observed. "Brother, you said that Guillaume was beset on all sides of his duchy by enemies, a gift of gold might help turn his mind to his defences at home and make a campaign in foreign lands that much less necessary?"

"We should have provoked the bastard's enemies to worry his borders like wolves earlier then. He might never have left his blasted duchy in the first place." Osfrid grumbled

"I was crowned in January, what chance has there been to make such schemes come to fruition?" Harold asked of his council. "Nevertheless, I take the point. Indeed, an embassy to the young King of France, and maybe even to other lesser, but also noble enemies of Guillaume, may create a danger on his borders that would demand his withdrawal from our kingdom. We will think upon it for when the weather along the whale-road improves and a successful voyage to France can be assured."

"And of having a discourse with Guillaume in the meantime?" Gyrth prompted.

"Mayhap, it would distract him somewhat, but I doubt that he would indulge us," Harold replied. "However, if one day's worth of talking would reduce the number of Saxon lives lost then I would be willing to listen to his lies once more. Too many of us have already died this year. I would countenance anything short of giving up my crown to avoid the loss of even one more hearth-companion. Select an embassy to go to Guillaume, let us see if he can be talked to."

"In the meantime, the army must be allowed to rest and grow in strength." Gyrth asserted.

"And there are the preparations for winter to be made."

"So let it be done!"

The Norman Encampment at Hastings

"You seem troubled?" Guillaume observed as Odo joined him at the table where he was consuming a bowl of thin soup. It was a meagre repast for a duke, but he shared it with his soldiers and he would not take anything more than they were allowed.

"I have heard news of what your men are about, particularly one by the name of Richard." Odo did not sit down.

"Also known as 'the Beast'!"

"If what I have heard said about him is only half true then that is an appellation well earned."

"Please, sit."

"Very well, but I am not happy."

"Hmm, I know."

"Well, what would you say about this Richard the Beast?"

"That he is a soldier carrying out his orders." There was no suggestion of sarcasm in either Guillaume's voice or expression.

"Who would give such orders?" Odo demanded to know, his voice tinged with anger. "Do you know what it is said that he has done?"

"No, and I don't want to. I gave an order that the Saxons are to be provoked to the fight. I am frustrated by my ignorance of Harold's whereabouts; I had expected him here by now. That he keeps himself distant from me serves his needs better than my own, I believe, so I reach out to bring him a little nearer."

"By the wilful murder of women and the rape of children?" Guillaume shrugged his response. "Are we not Christians?" The bishop's voice grew hotter.

"Odo, you are a clergyman, yes, but you are not wholly ignorant of the ways of the world. Since the first warrior drew his sword women have suffered the burden of war. Often they are amongst the first casualties and often they are outraged before their deaths. That is the way of it with men who have the scent of blood in their nostrils. Children die also."

"You condone his actions then, this Richard the Beast?"

"No, I do not."

"But you allow them to happen?"

"Only in the hope that it will bring about my intended purpose, which is to have Harold draw his army up before me."

"And this villain, this dog that you have unleashed, he is to be rewarded for his acts of depravity with a title and lands when the battle is done and Harold lies dead at your feet?"

"By God no!" Guillaume's face darkened. "Understand me, Odo, I know this man to be a beast by name because he is a beast by nature. In this instance, he is useful to me and I will use him, but afterwards, when this quarrel is settled, I will see that he pays for his crimes."

"I am not sure that that will absolve you."

"Neither am I. I have done many questionable things in my time, Odo, and no doubt there are many who believe that I will pay for those acts when I go before God myself, but I did what I believed I needed to do then, just as I do what I believe I need to do now. There is nothing about this Richard that would stay my hand when the fight is done. Indeed, it would not surprise me if he did not suffer a mortal wound in the battle against the Saxons."

"You cannot know such a thing!" Guillaume sighed at what he presumed to be his brother's naivety.

"I can if I have already arranged for it."

"Surely, he should go before a court, like those other two that you had hanged for a similar crime before we sailed for England?"

"Those two were made an example of to maintain the discipline of the army, the woman that they raped was of age and due compensation was paid, from my own pocket I remind you. This man, this Richard, has carried out orders that I gave, if I bring him to trial for that then I will lose all authority with the army. If a man may fear condemnation for carrying out my orders then why would any man obey me?"

"I see your logic, Guillaume, but I like it none the less."

"I understand, Odo, but you are a bishop and I'm a duke, you care for a kingdom spiritual and I seek a kingdom temporal. I am pressed to do things that you would not countenance."

"Like a barbarian?" Odo scowled. His words stung his half-brother, but rather than respond Guillaume returned to eating his tasteless soup.

If he had been talking with another man then mayhap Guillaume would have vented the anger that Odo's words first inspired in him, but he was also aware of a sense of guilt that shadowed his thinking.

In this he was glad that it was Odo who had spoken so honestly; he could, and would, forgive him for it. The whole thing was tainted, however, and he now silently admitted it to himself. He detested what Richard had done in the act of carrying out his orders, which was why he had arranged for the man to be stabbed in the back when his face was lost in the press of bodies before the Saxon spears. It was an admission of his own guilt in this thing, he understood that now.

"I will seek absolution from you brother," Guillaume finally said. "After this matter is settled, you may set my contrition at whatever you think best."

"I worry only for your soul, brother."

"And I love you for it!"

Westminster Palace, London

"I was not expecting to have to send an embassy to Guillaume!" Harold insisted angrily. They had retired to the king's chambers at the Palace of Westminster.

"We could not control the whole of the council meeting once it was begun," Gyrth told him.

"I thought it went well," Leofwine added. He had been forbidden to speak at the council by his elder brothers and, for once, he had obeyed them.

"Aye, it went well, except the question of the embassy," Harold conceded. "I did not mention it before but I have received a letter from your brother, Wolfnoth." Harold went over to a decorated box that stood on a large chest placed against the wall; from this, he withdrew a folded piece of paper. He handed it to Gyrth.

"When did this arrive?" The Eorl of East Anglia asked as he began to open it.

"After you went north, I kept it against your return," Leofwine told him.

"In this, you did well," Harold complimented his younger brother, "I would not have this letter known to the court."

"Wulfnoth believes that Guillaume will play fair by you, should you surrender the crown," Gyrth observed as he read the missive.

"We know that to be untrue," Harold replied with a little heat.

"Why?" Leofwine asked with genuine curiosity.

"The Duke of Normandy is not known for allowing his enemies to live long when once they are in his power. If I lived after he was crowned then I would always be judged a threat, if not an actual enemy. Any move on my part that might be construed as treason would end with my immediate execution, of that I am sure."

"Wolfnoth has been so long a Norman prisoner that I doubt he knows anything of how things stand here in England," Gyrth said as he handed the letter back to Harold. "This will not sway you?"

"No, it will not, but mayhap it opens a door to Guillaume."

"How so?"

"This letter reached me because Guillaume willed it to. He would not be surprised if I were to answer it, therefore."

"And how would you answer it?" Gyrth sensed that his brother had a design already in mind.

"With an embassy!"

***

"I don't understand!" Edwin confessed with a look of confusion on his face.

"Neither do I!" Coenred agreed with him.

"Then that makes three of us," Thrydwulf added.

They stood in Coenred's room in the lodgings that Thrydwulf had managed to procure for them. It was not an establishment befitting of an eorl, but it seemed that in London suitable lodgings were always scarce, and even more so when the army was camped within the walls.

"This is the matter as it was explained to me by the king." Coenred took a breath before beginning his explanation. "The Duke of Normandy has sent to King Harold a message from the youngest Godwin, taken prisoner by the Normans when he was just a boy. In the letter, this Wulfnoth Godwinson suggests that Guillaume is open to talks to avert any further bloodshed. Some of the theigns, whether they knew of this letter or not, suggested a similar course of action at the council of war. The king has decided to send an embassy to Guillaume, in Hastings, to discover the truth of this matter."

"And you are the embassy?" Edwin asked.

"Me and some others, a small number."

"You will be killed out of hand!" Thrydwulf decided.

"We travel under truce."

"You should travel with a fyrd and nothing less!" The huscarl insisted.

"Am I to go with you?" Edwin enquired.

"Yes, I think I will take you."

"That much is fitting," Thrydwul conceded, "but I like this not."

"Neither do I!" Coenred agreed.

"Are we both to get our throats slit?" Edwin asked with a worried expression.

"Well, if a master is to be murdered then it's most certain that his servant will also!" Thrydwulf told him with a humourless smile.

"The Normans will respect the truce," Coenred asserted, but he lacked conviction even for himself.

A strange thought then entered his head. He remembered again how Mildryth's husband had gone to the court of Tostig Godwinson, then Eorl of Northumbria, to answer a summons, along with other theigns, and to supposedly talk over longs standing grievances. It had been a trick, however, a ruse by which the eorl was able to murder the high-theigns Gamal and Ulf and, of course, a number of their lower theigns, their supporters, with them. Aetherlhead had been one of those lower theigns and he had taken his son, Aelle, to give him the experience of the court of an eorl. Instead, they had been murdered by Tostig's men. The eorl had chosen to ignore the rules of the truce in order to be rid of some whom he counted as his enemies. Was he, Coenred, about to go to the same fate as Aethelheard?

Unconsciously his right hand dropped to the handle of the fine scramseax that he wore in his belt; Mildryth's knife. It was now a symbol of the agreement made between them, her request for protection from Tostig Godwinson, and his acceptance of that responsibility towards her. It was an obligation that had since grown into a genuine love for the woman, which had brought other responsibilities to her with it. Tostig now lay dead in his turn, killed on the field at Stamford Bridge by Coenred himself. The feat had been achieved but Mildryth had not asked for the return of the knife and he had not thought of surrendering it. It was a fine blade with a worked antler handle, but that was not why he still kept it. The value of the scramseax in coin meant nothing to him, it was the fact that it had been given to him by her. The knife, made to defend Mildryth from the dangers of this world, had become a token of their love. Mayhap, not the most likely token, but somehow fitting between a man, for whom fighting was a way of life, and a woman who had fallen under the shadow of violent danger.

"Who else is to go with you?" Thrydwulf inspected his nails as if disinterested.

"The King's Secretary, a man popularly known as Half-foot, also a Royal Companion that I do not know, a priest also unknown to me, and some fyrdmen as an honour guard."

"A priest?" The huscarl was surprised.

"It seems the Normans have brought with them a large body of priests headed by a bishop. King Harold thinks that having at least one of our own might win some sympathy from them."

"I put scant trust in priests!"

"I know, but they are all men of God and, in that, even I may have to put some trust."

"Even though you're a heathen?" Edwin asked. Thrydwulf cuffed him heavily.

"You're the servant to an eorlderman now, don't thee forget it!"

"Thrydwulf, you will prepare the men as best as you can against my return. If the fyrd moves before I come back to London again then you are to follow the king's orders. Wherever he sends you, I will find you."

"As your huscarl, I should go with you!"

"Mayhap, but too many warriors would make our embassy look more like a war-band."

"Mayhap, but I will keep your life in your body all the same."

"And probably pick a fight with a Norman or two just to test your mettle, and break a few of their skulls!" Aethelmaer broke his silence.

"Only if I had some beer in me; do the Normans drink beer?!" Thydwulf laughed.

"I will stand guard over you, My Lord!" Edwin enthused.

"That will be all the guard that I need. Edwin, prepare the horses, we leave within the hour."

"There is something else of which we must speak!" Aethelmaer suddenly said. "Thrydwulf mentioned it, though I think he did it in passing and without forethought."

"Which is?" Coenred prompted him.

"Are we your huscarls? That is, is the Eorl of Holderness our lord?"

"Aye, that is something of which we must talk!" Thrydwulf agreed.

"You are right, Aethelmaer, but now is not the right time, for I have precious little it to spare. I am not looking to avoid this subject, I wish only to talk to you as men and as my friends when the moment is right and our minds clear. At the moment, I find mine beset by thoughts as to this meeting with the Normans in Hastings."

"I Understand." Aethelmaer looked disappointed but did not press the matter.

"Then go your way, Coenred, this will wait and we will wait," Thrydulf said with certainty.

Sunday, 8th October 1066

Coenred's Estate in the Isle of Holderness

"My story is not an interesting one," Mildryth insisted, "I fear it will drive thee to boredom."

They had gathered in Osred and Godgifu's house and sat now around the hearth, having eaten their evening meal together. It was only the adults who now formed the company as the children had been sent to bed and slept in a separate room.

Mildryth had secretly dreaded this event, her being formally presented to Coenred's family, but she had also known that it was unavoidable and would happen anyway. Also, the stench of burnt human flesh still lingered in her own house. She had left it with the doors and shutters open to the air, as it had been since Wulfhere's death, in the hope that the awful smell would soon be gone. That fact alone had given Godgifu an excellent reason to invite Mildryth into her own home. Reluctantly she had decided to get it over and done with. The meal had gone well with plenty of chatter. Mayhap the presence of the children had encouraged just such a friendly atmosphere. Throughout the meal, Godgifu had been smiling at one and all, a charming hostess.

The one person that caused Mildryth the most trepidation was Abbe, Coenred and Osred's mother. There were many tales of such women, recounting how they ruled the house while the menfolk ruled beyond its walls. Harridans they were with awful tempers and spiteful words and who made the lives of the other women in the family as uncomfortable as possible. Certainly, Abbe had the countenance for such a domestic monster, her face was lined and her hair had turned grey. She had no qualms in admonishing anyone who attracted her attention for the wrong reason, and yet she seemed quite forgiving with her grandchildren. Indeed, their welfare appeared to be her chief concern and throughout the meal, Abbe could be heard asking the children continuously if they had had enough to eat and drink. This demonstration of maternal instinct encouraged Mildryth somewhat.

When they had first gathered around the hearth there had been more idle chatter as Godgifu handed out drinks, which did not take long as there were only the four of them present. The ceorls who worked the estate were only invited into the house on special occasions and although the arrival of the woman intent upon marrying their lord was a noteworthy event it did not result in even Eanfrid being invited to attend. It had been Godgifu who suggested that Mildryth recounted her life story to them.

"We tend to hear more about my brother than see of him ourselves," Osred told her with a friendly face, "so a few words on how the two of you met would be a good way to pass some of the hours still left to us this evening."

"Then let me begin by telling you that I was once married to a good man by the name of Aethelheard, a theign, and that we had a son, Aelle. Both were taken from me by Tostig Godwinson when he was the Eorl of Northumbria."

"Murdered you mean?!" Abbe spoke up. Her voice was surprisingly strong, despite her age, and her eyes sparkled with interest.

"Yes, yes they were." Mildryth glanced down into the cup of wine that she held in two hands and balanced on her knees. "I was a widow when I met Coenred in York, at the hall of the high-theign. I went before him seeking protection against the rumoured return of Tostig."

"Those rumours were proven true," Osred observed.

"Indeed. I should tell you that I sought but a protector then. I knew Coenred only by reputation, as a huscarl and an eorl's man. I was living much in the shadow of fear. My husband was still dear to me and I was not looking to replace him, my grief was still strong, but Aethelheard had always believed in going on with life, in making the best of any situation."

"Wise words," Abbe muttered.

"Coenred would not refuse you," Godgifu said with certainty.

"No, he did not. He took me under his protection, though, as the world turned, he was driven far from me after the fall of York. You should know that after the battle, even as the Vikings took possession of the city, he came to me there." Mildryth looked directly at Abbe and raised her chin for the first time. "There is so much honour in your son's heart that he hazarded his life to ensure that mine, someone little more than a stranger to him, was safe." The old woman only nodded. "We hardly knew each other then but it touched me deeply that he would so honour his word to me. I think that was when my love for him, despite my sore grief, truly began to grow."

"And you survived the retaking of York." Osred prompted her.

"Yes, though that was not so hard a task as it might seem. King Hardrada wanted York for his capital in the north and placed a watch to keep the peace while his army camped at Riccall. Coenred went with King Harold to fight at Stamford Bridge and there he put an end to Tostig Godwinson with his own sword. He returned to me, however, sorely wounded. I nursed him to the best of my abilities and he recovered his strength, only to be taken from me, from all of us, by the king, to fight once again in the south. By then we were lovers for we obeyed our hearts and did so with honesty." She coloured a little at speaking the last sentence. Of course, everyone knew that such things happened, it was not considered polite, however, to openly speak of it.

"You have told us nothing of this nithing that attacked you in your own home?" Abbe pointed out sternly.

"The buttescarl? There is little to say. He came to me in York pretending friendship. He had seen me at the Hundred-Court in Ripon and knew that I had a complaint laid against Tostig Godwinson for the murder of my husband and son, and the loss of our lands and possessions. I think that he hoped to profit by currying favour with me, but I would have nothing of him. He has been like an evil shadow over me ever since."

"Did you tell Coenred of this man?" Osred asked.

"No, he had greater battles to fight. I deemed that I could rebuff the fool myself and I had friends to call upon." Mildryth suddenly laughed gently. "My friend Branda attacked the nithing with a broom once and drove him away. Another time I cut his face for him with my knife. That seemed to turn his mind to believe that I was some kind of witch who had cursed him. He told me that much before he died." Her face dropped at the awful remembrance.

"Then this nithing has haunted your steps for some time?" Osred asked.

"Yes, more's the pity."

"But you overcame him, relying on your own strength, your own courage. That was a brave thing to do." He complimented her.

"A very brave thing to do!" Godgifu agreed.

"I would speak no more about him," Mildryth told them sincerely." He is gone now and I will think no more upon him. I would wish only that you not mention any of this to Coenred upon his return, it is a matter that need not concern him."

"But he would be proud of you," Godgifu insisted.

"As I said, the nithing is gone."

"Good riddance to bad rubbish!" Abbe suddenly said loudly. She looked slowly around at their faces. "Women are too often weak and lean too readily upon the strength of a man, this world is not kind to such unless the man is rich and foolish. Women can be strong like men. They should be strong, for only a woman can bring new life into this turning world. Only a woman knows how to raise well a child in a home that is good and strong. The bonds of love give strength to such a home and they are woven by woman; the stronger the woman the stronger the bonds. Know this, Mildryth, once a widow and a mother, that I hold you worthy of my son."

No one said anything else but Godgifu beamed directly at Mildryth and Osred stared into the fire with a smile upon his face.

Monday 9th October 1066

The Palace of Westminster, London

When Gyrth entered the king's chamber he was somewhat surprised to see that his younger brother, Leofwine, was already in attendance. A warden closed the door behind him as he walked forwards.

"You are somewhat tardy this day, Gyrth," Harold observed.

"I was tending to matters within my own earldom, My Lord," Gyrth responded tersely. "It is difficult when one spends so much time away from it!"

"Mayhap I will allow you to return to Anglia after this last battle is over then." Harold smiled back. He neither knew nor cared if Gyrth had indeed been tending to concerns in Anglia or pursuing more personal pleasures. "First we have Guillaume to deal with."

"I presumed as much when I received your summons."

"Are you put out, brother?" Leofwine asked, almost with a hint of scorn.

"I have spent many days on the road of late, fought in a battle, done your bidding without complaint, is a few hours to myself too much to ask for in return?" Gyrth was becoming irritable.

"I was commanded to remain here in London!" The younger brother felt a need to go on the defensive.

"And sired another bastard no doubt!"

"I have been a man these past eleven years, it is time for you to stop treating me like a child, just because I am the youngest of us here!" Leofwine retorted angrily.

"ENOUGH!" Harold commanded. "Gyrth, I am sorry if I have torn you away from what little time you get to yourself, but my need is pressing. Leofwine, you are correct, too often we forget your age and treat you as if you lack your one score and ten years. This is one of the reasons why I wanted you here, to hear what I will next command, but first I want my brothers at peace with one another."

Gyrth took a deep breath and exhaled slowly. He looked at Leofwine, who was really only two years younger than himself, but who appeared much more youthful than that.

"I am sorry, brother, it is not you who inspires my foul mood. I spoke in heat and my words were unbecoming."

"I understand, brother. I take no ill-feeling from you."

"Good. Now listen to me." Harold stepped towards them and put a hand on each of their shoulders. He looked warmly into their faces. "As King of England, I have decided, the army moves towards Hastings this day. As your brother, I want the two of you stood with me on the fateful day that we cross swords with Guillaume. Leofwine, so often have you been left behind to do a watchman's duty over our holdings, but not this time. I will give you my right hand to hold and defend. Gyrth, you have been ever loyal to me and I know that I have sometimes overused that loyalty. I ask only that you give me the best of yourself one more time and then I will return the favour by granting you a leave of absence from the court for a year and a day. Does this suit you both?"

"Yes, My Lord!" Leofwine replied enthusiastically.

"What of the embassy?" Gyrth asked.

"The embassy is of no consequence."

"Then why indulge it?"

"Because it gives me an opportunity to inform Guillaume of how things really stand with us. The fame of the old War Wolf extends to Normandy and far beyond it. He was a formidable foe. The report that Half-foot will deliver of his defeat will be unwelcome news to the Normans."

"They will know that it was by your hand," Leofwine observed.

"You give them cause to fear you."

"Exactly, Gyrth, anything more than that will be a blessing."

"And what of the men that you have sent to deliver this news?"

"I hope to see them again, but I trust the Normans to honour the truce that they travel under."

"And if they do not?"

"It is a risk that we must take." Harold looked momentarily uncomfortable and turned away from them. "Will you come with me to face the Normans, Gyrth?"

"Of course, and I am glad that Leofwine will fight with us also. When do we march?"

"Today. I have already given the order. The army will assemble in the neighbourhood of the hoary apple tree. By Wednesday at the earliest, but the soonest after most likely."

"If only Wulfnoth could stand with us!" Leofwine smiled.

"If we win this battle then our youngest brother will be free and we can welcome him home," Harold told them with a grin.

"Then you mean to fight and press the battle sooner rather than later?" Gyrth asked.

"This stratagem worked against old Hardarada, I see no reason why it will not work against Guillaume." Harold looked more serious. "Do you oppose it?"

"We have talked enough on the matter," Gyrth told him sincerely, "and a decision has been reached. I will be commanded by it. We go to the hoary apple tree!"

The Village of Lamberhurst, Kent

"We will be at Hastings by noon tomorrow, if we push ourselves somewhat," Half-foot told them. They sat at a trestle table close to the hearth. The evenings were beginning to get chilly now, even if the days themselves were still mild.

They had arrived in the village of Lamberhurst and requested hospitality of the local theign. It had been grudgingly given to them. No ceorls were at hand to administer to their needs, however, but the small party had some servants of its own, including Edwin son of Octa, so the hearth was soon lit and the food was in the making.

"Is this the usual reception in these parts for the king's men?" Coenred enquired with a rueful smile.

"Somewhat lacking compared to your northern halls, eh?" Half-foot conceded.

"I have travelled the lands of the kingdom many times and hospitality tends to be short only when the visitors are not well liked."

"True enough and it is to be said that King Harold is not liked in all the parts of his kingdom." Half-foot nodded sagely.

"If there weren't more pressing matters ruling us I'd have these nithings beaten!" The Royal Companion, Sweyn, grumbled. "They have no right to slight the king so!"

"They don't slight the king, they slight us." Half-foot corrected him.

"We are the king's men, they slight us, they sleight him!"

"We are all the king's men, including these people. If you beat them then you beat him, and so you would have to beat yourself in punishment for beating the king!"

Sweyn opened his mouth the make a retort but then thought better of it. He returned to glaring at his beer again.

"I wonder at our purpose?" Coenred changed the subject.

"We will sway the Duke of Normandy to leave our lands. I have prayed both night and day for this. I will pray when we reach Hastings, and, once there, I will beseech the Norman priests to pray with me for a peaceful outcome. They are men of God also, they will not deny me." The priest Leofric spoke for the first time in many an hour.

Half-foot scowled. "Pray if you will, but it will be the steel of Saxon spears and swords that will dissuade Guillaume, if such a thing were possible, from taking another step into our kingdom." Sweyn smiled at the words that were better suited to his ear.

"The Lord is mightier than any host!" Leofric's voice rose.

"I will bow down to your lord in heaven if he does indeed turn the Normans back!" Half-foot responded with some sarcasm.

Coenred glanced at the secretary. They had met on several occasions now, but always it had been to do with the court of the King of England. This was the first time that they had been together away from the presence of Harold Godwinson. For some reason, Coenred had not expected Half-foot to show such hostility towards the church. Harold was known to be a great supporter of that institution. That Half-foot did so openly surprised Coenred but informed him also.

"Praying cannot hurt," the Eorl of Holderness suggested. He did so more to calm the atmosphere than to express a personal belief. "I would rather that the Normans withdrew and no blood was shed, by any means whatsoever, be that prayer or the use of clever words."

"Where's the glory in that?" Sweyn suddenly demanded to know.

"The glory is in the saving of life." The Eorl of Holderness told him.

"The saving of life? It's said around the campfire that you were a huscarl afore the king made you an eorl, such as we don't live to save lives, we live to kill."

"I have fought three times already this year, Sweyn. The first was in repulsing Tostig's marauders from Lyndsey. The second was at Fulford Gate, where we pitched ourselves for glory against the War Wolf. The third was Stamford Bridge, a battle fought because the War Wolf won all the glory to be had at Fulford. I saw over a thousand of my brother huscarls killed in that second fight, some I counted as friends. There was no glory in their passing, only the smell of blood and the sound of Saxon women bewailing the deaths of their men."

"God will take them unto heaven!"

"The fight is what makes us strong," Sweyn insisted. "Warriors prove themselves, chieftains are made great. Our enemies die so that we may live in peace."

"If you ever achieved that goal you would no longer have any reason to live yourself," Half-foot pointed out. Sweyn did not comprehend his meaning, however. "When a warrior has killed all of his lord's enemies of what purpose is he?"

"There are always more enemies!"

"Then you set yourself a task that can never be accomplished," Half-foot smiled knowingly. "Where's the wisdom in that?"

"In part, I agree with Sweyn, but my thoughts are a little different," Coenred added. "I see an eorl, or a chieftain if you will, as the shield of his people. His obligation is to protect them, yes, and to do this he calls warriors to his hall, but they are there to repulse the attacks of the enemy."

"What better way to repulse the enemy than to attack them first and put them all to the sword?" Sweyn demanded to know.

"He who does the attacking is the enemy," Coenred told him. "You said that our enemies die so that we may live in peace, that would be achieved if no chieftain ever attacked another and without a drop of blood being spilt."

"I think that in days long gone by that may well have been the way of it, but once a host is gathered together, once a chieftain has felt the power at his command, the urge to attack another people for the land or the animals or the gold or the women they hold becomes irresistible. They attack and, as you say, Coenred, they become the enemy. The chieftain becomes an eorl, his host grows bigger. He then becomes a king and no longer looks to raid a neighbouring chieftain; he looks for another king to attack."

"So have the Normans done with us!" Sweyn asserted, banging his cup onto the boards of the table.

"So have all chieftains and all kings through the countless days of men," Half-foot observed. "I am sorry, Coenred, but it would seem we are destined to fight the Normans on another bloody field. Guillaume may be called a duke and Harold a king, but they are both chieftains all the same and our talk suggests that one chieftain must indeed attack another for they know no other way."

"Then what really is the point of this thing that we are about?" Coenred demanded with a hint of frustration.

"To learn about our enemy."

"Not to persuade them to return to Normandy?"

"I will attempt that but I do not expect Guillaume, after all he has done to get this close to the crown, to turn back now. Whilst I am talking I will test his resolve, however. I will probe for a weakness, and whilst I am about that you and Sweyn will look over the Norman power, assess its might. Brother Leofric will urge the Norman priests to pray for peace. Together we will return to King Harold and give him what news we can so that he might better form a plan to push our enemy back into the sea."

Tuesday, 10th October 1066

The Town of Hastings, Kent

"What manner of thing is this?" Sweyn demanded.

They sat upon their horses looking down into the valley that lay between both the east and west hills. From here they could see the town and port of Hastings, but it was not the settlement itself that attracted the Royal Companion's attention, it was the large structure that had been placed close by in open land.

"It looks like a burgh," Coenred said.

"What sorcery can bring such a thing to our shores in so short a length of time?" Leofric the priest asked of no one in particular.

"The Normans are known to be as ruthless and as efficient as the legions of Rome were in their day," Half-foot replied. "The castle is small, made of wood, and erected quickly to give the Normans somewhere to reside, safe from Saxon knives."

"If that is where the Normans have their army then that is where we will find the duke," Coenred surmised.

He spurred his horse forward, the others following his example. Together they descended into the valley and followed it towards the castle. It was not too long before they arrived at the Norman stronghold and realised that it was indeed made entirely from wood, not freshly sawn logs but planed and seasoned timbers. From their position, they could not discern, however, that the whole building, walls included, had been made in sections prior to arriving in

England. The castle had been carried across the sea in numerous ships. When Hastings had been secured the soldiers had turned to putting it together to make a defensive position as strong as possible and certainly beyond the ability of the local Saxons to overcome.

A ditch had been dug to a depth of six feet around the circumference of the walls, the earth excavated had been used to form a mound that raised the wooden walls even higher. A simple and precarious wooden bridge spanned the ditch at the single point of entry, fronted by a large double gateway. On reaching this point they stopped short of the bridge itself.

Two Norman sentries were on duty on the wall above the gate. They called out to the party but seemed more curious than alarmed. Half-foot spoke to them in French. After the brief conversation, he turned to his companions.

"It seems that we're not entirely unexpected, they have gone to fetch a lord to admit us."

"Then we are to go before the Duke?" Sweyn asked.

"So it would appear. Remember, we represent King Harold, be on your best behaviour. Do not let them rile you."

"You think that they will try?" Coenred asked.

"This is diplomacy, my friend, anything will be tried if one party thinks that it will give them an advantage over the other, or something else that they want badly enough and they think violence is the means to get it."

"What point would there be in provoking us to a fight?"

"A test of your mettle as individual warriors, something to be taken as an assault against the duke, an excuse to make an example of us; you know of the outrages that these people have already committed in this land?"

"And you call this civilised!" Sweyn swore spiritedly.

"No, I call this diplomacy; it is as civilised as the level to which either party is willing to sink."

"It is unchristian!" The priest insisted.

"It is the way of the world," Coenred told him, "and as this is the business that we are about then, methinks, it is best done now and not avoided."

"I agree," Half-foot said. "Sweyn, would you stay with the horses in the courtyard and look about you, measure their spears, the quality of their men; learn their strength?"

"I would not be a horsbegen," Sweyn replied. Half-foot opened his mouth to speak but the Royal Companion gave him no opportunity. "Excepting to get the lay of the land!" He grinned ruefully.

"There are days when you surprise me, Sweyn."

"I live for such, and killing of course."

"And what part shall I play in this?" Coenred wanted to know.

"If you would be so good as to leave your attendant with Sweyn I would have you stand with me before the duke."

"So be it. Edwin, you will stay with Lord Sweyn and watch over the horses."

"Yes, My Lord," Edwin responded with a troubled face. He had fancied seeing the famous Duke of Normandy for himself, but now that he was here, in the very presence of these invaders, remaining in the relative freedom of the courtyard, close to their only means of a swift escape, appealed to him much more.

"I will seek out my brother priests and hold conversation with them," Leofric the priest declared but no one cared to acknowledge his intent.

The double doors of the gate opened and a man in good quality armour but without a helmet and with his sword sheathed appeared before them. They could not help but notice that his hair was cut short in a manner that suggested that someone had put a bowl on his head and followed around it with their shears. He called out in French.

"We are to follow him," Half-foot translated the speech, "and dismount once inside."

The small embassy made its way over the bridge and into the wooden castle. The two large doors were shut and barred after them. Edwin could not help but look backwards over his shoulder as the outside world disappeared from his view.

Once inside the fortress, they understood better the method of its construction and Coenred was impressed by their forward thinking. Saxons knew well how to build with wood but he doubted that even Kind Harold would have thought to construct a burgh in quite this manner.

"If we knew how to build like this then placing the burghs in a ring around Hastings might not have been so unlikely a task?" He spoke softly to Half-foot.

They were following the Norman officer across the bailey and into the single large building to the south. It was a large square tower that stood at a height of three stories. Inside they found the place dark and shadowy, lit only by tallow lamps.

"It is right to learn, even from the enemy," Half-foot replied in a low voice. "Those are the words of Ovid, a Roman poet."

"And a wise soldier."

They moved down a narrow passageway with rooms opening off it on both sides and came to a narrow staircase. They climbed up to the next floor and came to the chambers of the Duke of Normandy, such as they were. Other members of the nobility had a room each up here and on the next floor, but only those most senior in rank. A warden opened a rough cut wooden door and the officer led the Saxons into a low, dark room where stood Guillaume, Duke of Normandy, and his brother Robert, Count of Mortain. The officer spoke in French, the Duke responded by dismissing him. Behind the backs of the Saxons, the door closed once more.

"Good day to you, emissaries from my friend, Harold Godwinson, Eorl of Wessex!" Guillaume spoke English with a passable accent. He held his arms apart in greeting and smiled warmly at them.

"I bring greetings from King Harold of England," Half-foot returned in French. He had heard the officer inform his superiors that he could speak their language but he wanted to make a demonstration to that effect all the same and correcting the duke with regards to Harold's proper title and rank was a perfect opportunity. "He hopes that I find you in good health?"

"Your French is good," Guillaume complimented the secretary in the same language, "but I think that your companion does not understand us, for his sake shall we proceed in English? I would not want there to be any misunderstandings."

"As you wish, Your Grace."

"I am, as you have realised, Guillaume, Duke of Normandy, and this is Robert, Count of Mortain."

"I am Grendel of Wessex, popularly known as Half-foot, Court Secretary to King Harold of England."

"Your body is lame but your mind is sharp," Guillaume observed.

"I have some learning, Latin is not beyond me." He turned to Coenred. "This is Coenred, Eorl of Holderness."

"Eorl Coenred!" Guillaume inclined his head, not exactly a full bow but most definitely a formal acknowledgement. Coenred responded with the kind of formality that he was accustomed to demonstrate, having been an eorl's man for much of his life. "Now the introductions are completed would you drink with me?"

"We would be honoured, Your Grace."

Robert, without ceremony, removed the stopper from a flask of wine and poured the contents into four clay goblets. He turned from the tall chest on which the tray holding the wine had been placed and handed a cup each to Half-foot and Coenred, he then retrieved the companion cups for himself and his brother.

Coenred was a little bemused by the opening of this audience. He had been to the court of King Edward previously, many years now gone by, and understood that there was a certain etiquette that must be followed, but drinking socially with the enemy did not seem quite the right thing to do.

"To your health!" Robert raised his cup in salute and then took a drink. Both Guillaume and Half-foot followed his example. Coenred was a little hesitant.

"Now, tell me, what does Harold propose?" Guillaume held his wine absently.

"He asks you to leave."

"So simple?" Guillaume raised an eyebrow as if surprised.

"Yes, he invites you to leave, as you were uninvited to these lands, and then return in peace next spring at his warmest invitation." The Duke of Normandy smiled. "He does not wish to cross swords with you in this matter and believes that a more peaceful settlement can be reached."

"Does he now?"

"Indeed, a settlement that will prove of benefit to you, Your Grace, and one that will allow the people of England to live and flourish under the rule of the king that they have chosen for themselves."

"And how would that benefit me?"

"King Harold offers you ten thousand pounds of gold."

"We are not Vikings to be bought by mere gold!" Robert suddenly insisted.

"No, we aren't," Guillaume agreed. The offer interested him, however, as money always did, and he wished to learn more.

"No one is in the business of purchasing anyone. King Harold believes that this sum would ease your way to victory in your contest with Duke Conan of Brittany. My king is aware of Duke Conan's advances into Anjou, looking to turn lands friendly to Normandy more towards his own duchy, all in your absence of course." The two brothers exchanged a quick and telling glance. They had not believed that this news would be known to the Saxons.

"You are well informed," Guillaume conceded. "Very well informed indeed!" Half-foot nodded his appreciation. "That said, the power that I have left to safeguard my duchy is sufficient to the task. I do not fear Brittany."

"Would Brittany then fear Normandy if you were to lose the planned encounter with England?" It was a very pertinent question and it raised Half-foot, if not Harold himself, in the estimation of Guillaume.

"I thought that you were here to avoid any such encounter?" Robert intervened.

"Avoid, yes, but not at the cost of King Harold surrendering his crown to you peacefully. He sees no benefit to himself in that course."

"We have the pope's blessing in this matter!" Guillaume asserted with some vigour. He realised a little late that he had already lost the initiative in this meeting.

"Then you should know that neither of us are men of the cross and not swayed by the opinions of your priests." Half-foot inclined his head towards Coenred, who remained unmoved and still holding his goblet of wine from which he had taken but a sip.

"You dare insult the pope?!" Robert demanded.

"No insult was intended, nor should one be looked for," Coenred spoke up suddenly. "As Grendel said, we are not Christians. We would not hold you to respect our priests' opinions in this matter, do not look to hold us to yours'."

"Fair enough." Guillaume was disappointed, he had hoped to use the papal banner that his army carried to have some influence, but if neither of these emissaries considered themselves to be Christian then he was clearly outmanoeuvred in that respect. It was quite clear now that he had badly underestimated his adversaries in this matter and so he looked to gain some other kind of advantage. "Has Harold received a letter from his brother, Wulfnoth?"

"He has."

"And did it not sway him?"

"My Lord was much moved by the words that he read there, it touched him deeply to have in his hand a missive written by his younger brother, long separated from the family hearth. He commends you for having had the letter delivered to him."

"Wulfnoth would have us settle this matter peacefully."

"King Harold would have you leave this land peacefully, you, Your Grace, would have the crown of England peacefully, clearly, in this turning world, we cannot all have what we want; compromises have to be made somewhere."

"Compromises?" Guillaume looked disdainful.

"Compromise is the essence of diplomacy."

"And war is its execution by other means."

"War is not unknown to us," Coenred said firmly. "Know you the War Wolf?"

"You mean King Hardrada of Norway?" Robert returned.

"Yes, the King of Norway. He fell before our spears in Northumbria and lies buried now in the ground there, his army shattered, his son sent home having first sworn a vow never to set foot in England again."

"Harold was in the north when we landed!" Robert surmised.

"King Harold fought a great battle against the Norse and has brought that victorious army south to meet you in the field if you so choose to do so. His offer of gold to you is not an admission of weakness, it is a well-meant act to save the spilling of more blood, but do not be presuming. The Saxons have whetted their swords this year in the blood of their ancient enemy. We bore them down to the earth and trampled their bones into the dust. King Hardrada is no more, his saga ended in England where he was defeated for the first and last time. Your end will not be dissimilar if you press us the same."

Again the two Normans looked at each other. This was news unknown to them previously and explained much with regards to their questions as to why no Saxon power had presented itself to stop them from taking Hastings. It was a subject that required further debate, however, but not with the Saxon emissaries present.

"I will not leave England without the crown!" Guillaume insisted, breaking a silence that had been building since Coenred last spoke.

"King Harold will not meekly surrender it to you." Half-foot pointed out.

"Then it is war." The Duke of Normandy said simply.

"You wish me to convey this decision to King Harold?"

"You came under truce, you will leave under truce. Go with my good favour."

"I will see you to your horses," Robert made for the door behind them.

Coenred glanced one last time at the Duke of Normandy and was surprised to catch him in an unguarded moment; he looked worried. Guillaume suddenly became aware of the other's gaze and took command of himself again.

"Farewell, Eorl of Holderness. I hope that we do not meet on the field of battle for you seem a mighty warrior for your people."

"Farewell, Duke of Normandy. I, for my part, hope that we do meet once more upon that fateful field, but only as I am indeed a warrior and that is where I might best achieve the protection of my people."

"Nobly said."

Coenred's Estate in the Isle of Holderness

Men moved like the shades of the things that they were or even seemingly appeared to be. They wore armour and carried large round shields. The sky behind them was dark, a broiling mass of twisting snakes of grey, and yet an unseen sun caught the cold steel of sword blades, spear points, and axes. The reflected light was almost too bright to bear.

All sound was indistinct. Words, like well-known birds, flew close, so close as to be almost clear and vibrant, but before the moment of understanding, they were lost again. There were voices, many voices, all speaking but none of them being understood.

Something hissed through the sky, like rain when a sudden heavy shower erupts from the heavens. Dark rain, long and thin and when it touched someone it pierced their body. A man stumbled into view and turned his head towards the moving sky. He screamed. His head turned round again and his eye was transfixed by an arrow. The long dark rain was arrows, thousands of arrows, falling from out of the sky.

And then he was there; Coenred. He moved like a titan, sweeping all of the enemies before him away with his glittering sword. They fell like insubstantial shadow creatures to the burning edge of his grandfather's heirloom. They died before the blade's fell blow.

He turned to look upon something unexpected. A dark shape reared before him. It was huge. A beast on four legs made unfamiliar by the body of an armoured man sprouting from its back. The soldier struck out with a spear but Coenred deftly knocked the gleaming point away before it could reach his heart. The beast reared, its forelimbs kicking out at him. The wily huscarl ducked under the flailing hooves and struck with his sword into the chest of the monster. Still higher it raised itself, growing to an impossible height and all the time screaming as a shower of blood splattered the Saxon warrior.

"NO!" Her voice rang out into the darkness like a clap of thunder but it was too late.

Coenred appeared transfixed before his nemesis. The great shadow beast began to descend. Faster and faster it came, growing larger and heavier all the time. Falling down like a mountain on top of the man who stood there and waited for his doom.

And then he was gone and all was black.

Mildryth screamed as she flung herself up from the bed. Her eyes were open, almost as wide as her mouth. All she saw was the final scenes of her dream; Coenred being crushed beneath the body of a horse that he had killed with his sword.

A great sob escaped her. Mildryth's head fell forward and she clutched her hands to her breast. Her eyes closed again and tears sprang out to fall down her cheeks.

Her bed was near the low burning hearth, wrapped in the soft comfort of the orange glow, but she did not feel its warmth. She shivered.

It was only a dream!

She knew that it was just a dream. Never in her life had she experienced the gift of prophecy, this could not be the time when she first did. Her body shook with her sobs as she slowly laid down, facing the hearth.

Mildryth believed more strongly in the old ways of her people, both the Saxons and the Danes than she did in the Church of the Christ. Divination was a way of life to many. A part of her had never believed that one could tell the future by sighting a hawk in a particular portion of the sky at a particular hour. Even dreams had never seemed so clear to her that they could be used to predict the future. She had not dreampt of Aehtelheard and Aelle's deaths at the hand of Tostig Godwinson, but they had died all the same. Had she really dreampt of Coenred's death before a mounted Norman knight?

She clutched her hands more tightly. Why would she dream such a thing now? Her mind flew back to the night of September when the Saxons had lost the field at Fulford Gate. Coenred had come to her then, despite the great danger in which he stood. He had escaped unscathed from that awful slaughter after having killed a Viking champion, a good friend of old Harald Hardrada's. He had seemed indomitable to her then.

Another memory followed and it was painfully opposite to the image of a strong and whole Coenred that she was trying to cling to. This was also the remembrance of a night after a battle, this time it was Stamford Bridge where Coenred had slain Tostig. He had come home to her then wounded, bruised and bleeding. Laying himself out on a blanket on the floor of her little house he had succumbed to weariness as she had washed and dressed his wounds as best as she could. Then she had lain next to him and wrapped her arms around that strong chest, crying in fear that every breath he took might prove to be his last, but he had survived.

Wyrd had never played well in her life when it had really mattered. Yes, she had known the love of a good man and they had been blessed with a fine boy, but both of them had been cruelly taken away from her. The loss of their house, their lands, their wealth even, had not even measured in the depth of pain and grief that had consumed her then.

Is wyrd to punish me again for seeking to be happy?

It was a cruel thought but she reminded herself of an apprehension that had never truly left her after Coenred had fought at Stamford Bridge, 'wyrd had spared him in two battles, in a third they might not prove so lucky'. That was the fear that had motivated her to softly try and convince Coenred to put up his shield and sword and he had seemingly been willing to do so. Indeed, she had believed it to be so. Even when he had stood up to go before the young eorls her heart still believed that he would stay with her, but the pull of fate was too strong for even one such as he to resist.

No one can escape wyrd.

And so it seemed. The king had taken him one way or another. He had gone south to fight the Normans and she had let him. Another sob wracked her. She had made his going all the easier thinking that that was the right thing to do.

She had let him go to his death.

Outside the sky was dark and heavy without so much as a pin prick of starlight. Inside the fine house in Holderness, a woman found herself slipping into a hole at least as dark as the sky above her. Her descent was accompanied by the sound of her tears.

The Norman Encampment at Hastings

"So, you have met with the Saxon emissaries," Rufus said almost dismissively, "when do they surrender the crown?"

"They will not," Robert spoke most emphatically.

"Then we will take it as we originally planned!" Rufus leant back against the wooden wall, looking relaxed.

"Really, Your Grace, this can have been little more than what you expected?" Eustace suggested.

"Think you so?" Guillaume was the only one of them seated. Even within his rooms, there was not enough space for sufficient furniture. The goblet into which Robert had first poured the wine at the commencement of the embassy was still in his hand, but he had not touched it since Half-foot and Coenred had left. "I wish that you had been present when they spoke, their words might have raised them in your opinion to the station that they should occupy."

"What means Your Grace?"

"They did not come to plead, Rufus, they offered us a safe passage home instead."

"A safe passage?"

"And ten thousand pounds in gold to make our withdrawal more acceptable," added Robert.

"Ten thousand pounds?!"

"They knew more about our situation than we do about theirs," Guillaume told them with a rueful smile.

"Such as what?"

"That Duke Conan invades Anjou and stirs up lands we had thought at least neutral to us to invade our duchy."

"Harold of Wessex suggests we use this money to resist Brittany," the Count of Mortain added.

"Well, mayhap they got this information from some loose lipped Norman merchant trading in their ports?" Rufus did not sound too convinced himself.

"There's more," Guillaume said. "Harold and his army were not here to stop us landing because he was away in the north of his kingdom making war on old King Hardrada; the King of Norway is dead!"

"Hardrada followed up his claim to the crown then?" Eustace looked impressed. "Mayhap his army proved as weak as that claim?"

"We cannot know for certain if what the emissaries said about this matter is the truth, but then I can see no reason for them to lie. It explains Harold's absence, however." The Duke pointed out.

"It also means that Harold now has a veteran army on which to call." Robert felt that he should make everyone aware of this fact. "The emissaries said that they were victorious at a place they called Stamford Bridge and that Hardrada was killed there. His son sailed back to Norway having sworn never to return to England again."

"This means little," Rufus insisted. "If their army fought the Norwegians in the north then most likely they will have suffered a hurt or two and be tired from the long walk back to London. There is nothing for us to fear in this matter, I tell you!"

"Do you?" Guillaume looked directly at Rufus. "I underestimated the Saxons during the parley, that is no real matter, but to do so on the field of battle would be a different thing altogether. A Saxon axe would probably separate my head from my body in such a situation. I do not intend to make that mistake! Defeating a Norwegian army led by their own king is no small matter, it will fill Harold's men with the spirit necessary to face us and, mayhap, with the belief that they can defeat us as well."

"You have always spoken of Harold in the highest regard, if he has killed Hardrada of Norway in battle, a war-chief about whom they say had never lost a battle previously, then, mayhap, we should take our enemy more seriously?" Eustace offered.

"I would have you do so as I have told you many times before. I enforced upon the emissaries that we would not leave willingly, but that we come to take the crown, Harold will respond accordingly. There is some good cheer from this occurrence, however."

"What is that?" Rufus wanted to know.

"We now know that Harold is in London with his army hard by. I know where my enemy is and so I can make plans to bring him to battle in a field that suits us."

"We must do this thing before the winter comes then."

"Exactly!" Guillaume rose to his feet. "Send scouts up the road to London. I want to know how the land lies in that direction."

"If we move towards London Harold must respond." Robert conceded.

"I do not want him sitting behind his walls waiting to see out the winter, we must bring him to the fight." The Duke of Normandy insisted.

"Then we should continue to ravage the land and the people, but now we must point our men in the direction of Harold to goad him," Rufus spoke enthusiastically.

For a moment Guillaume was preoccupied remembering his conversation with Odo about the very topic of the outrages committed against the Saxon people. He hesitated, even feeling a tinge of remorse at allowing someone like Richard the Beast to slip his leash again, but then mastered his doubt. This thing had to be done, he told himself, and the sooner it was achieved the better for everyone, except the Beast, mayhap. He told himself then that he would indeed atone for using these methods of warfare; to his brother at least.

Odo was his conscience. Often he had listened without paying too much attention to what his brother, the bishop, had to say. Expediency was a necessity in war and Normandy had been at war for much of its existence. In war, Guillaume found that he could lose himself, but he was minded that at the end of the fight, when the dust settled and the screams turned to wails of misery, that he became a duke again and that he must rule with God's good grace.

In the moment of violence much could be excused, but, in the moment of cold decision making, there could be no appeal to a sudden rush of blood to the head.

Did God's good grace extend to such decisions as loosing animals to provoke a fight with another man?

"Have it done. Let's prick Harold's honour and mayhap he will prove rash enough to move on us all the sooner!"

Wednesday, 11th October 1066

Near to Sentlache Ridge, north of Hastings, Kent

"You did well," Harold, King of England, told them warmly. He met with his emissaries under the open sky, still some miles north of Sentlache Ridge. Around them, the Saxon army was encamped. Gyrth was the only other person present. "Sweyn, what can you tell me about their fyrd; their army?"

"I did not see all of it, but what was there was well equipped and they knew how to carry their weapons. In number, I would say that they do not overmatch us, but they are paid men, not fyrdmen."

"That is the Norman way, they conscript only when necessary, otherwise their soldiers are all paid for by the duke himself." Harold nodded as he spoke. He knew very well how a Norman army was constituted having spent time with Guillaume not so long ago and even having ridden with him in the field. "Their numbers interest me most, however, and if it is true that they cannot outmatch us then that is a good sign."

"There will be a battle, the only question of import is as to when and where." Half-foot told him.

"Guillaume will want to initiate it; he will look for a place most favourable to himself," Gyrth interjected. "You have already discounted waiting until spring, brother, therefore you must not allow him this choice."

"I agree!" Coenred spoke up. He was becoming more accustomed and, as a result, more at ease with speaking in the presence of the king. "The Normans are using each day to practice their fighting skills, much as we did in Tadcaster. They will be ready to meet us, the only choice before you, Your Majesty, is the question of when and where?"

"I understand," Harold assured them, "and on this matter, I am already purposed to move the army towards Hastings, there is a place in-between that will give us an advantage."

"You did not consider staying within the walls of London, My Lord?" Coenred asked.

"I did, but I do not find it to my liking. It will not meet with the purpose that we are about."

"You berated Edwin and Morcar for not doing the same."

"That was a different matter, Eorl Coenred. Edwin and Morcar have not our experience of war and they faced a foe too wily for them. Do not doubt that the Normans know how to take a stronghold from an enemy, they will know how to sunder the walls of London."

"Like the Romans they can build castles out of wood," Half-foot told them.

"Is the castle strong?" Harold asked.

"Strong enough," Coenred conceded. "The walls are tall and it is surrounded by a deep ditch. If the Normans chose to stay within it the castle would be a formidable burgh against which we may not have the strength to bring to ruin. Fighting in the field is the best course for we Saxons, I think. Having seen them now I believe, My Lord, that you have chosen the wiser path by meeting them openly."

"So be it." Harold looked determined now. "We will not wait for the Normans, but we will go out and meet them. As I said, I have a memory of a place to the north of Hastings that may well prove a good place for a shield wall to stand and it is not that far from here."

***

"What of the Normans?" Thrydwulf said by way of greeting.

"They are numerous, well-armed and armoured, and a fitting foe for the likes of thee!" Coenred returned.

His men, such few as he possessed, a handful of huscarls and maybe three scores of ceorls who felt a stronger loyalty to the new Eorl of Holderness than they did to their former masters, Edwin and Morcar, were camped not too far from the Royal Companions. They had been easy to find as a result.

"I like this news," Thrydulf enthused, "almost as much as seeing that you return unscathed."

"They honoured the truce, as the king said they would. What news here?"

"We marched out of London not long after you," Aethelmaer told him. "The pace was good and the men are not overtired. More spears have joined us here but, I fancy, not as many as the king was expecting or hoping for."

"It is not numbers that confer the advantage, it is quality," Coenred observed. "The Normans have many men, it is true, but most are forced to it, either by owing service to their lords, who in turn owe service to the duke or for payment, like buttescarls."

"Do they match us for numbers?" The young huscarl wanted to know.

"I would say closely, but they have many warriors who are mounted on horses from which they will fight."

"That seems unmanly." Thrydwulf scowled at the thought.

"Mayhap, but it is their way of doing battle and we must meet it."

"And how do you weigh our chances?" The elder huscarl remained direct in his questioning.

"Good, if we hold true to our way of fighting. In truth, I do not think that the Normans are in a strong position. Hastings gives them some protection, it is true, but our fleet can barricade the port and I believe our lithesmen are better sailors than theirs are. Winter will press them hard, the duke knows this, he will look to meet us on the field sooner rather than later."

"Then the king moving from London meets with the enemies plans for us?" Aethelmaer noted.

"Yes and no both. Guillaume wants to provoke a fight, you know this, but he also wants to choose where it is fought. King Harold may seemingly appear to be falling in with the Norman's wishes, but rather he is stealing the initiative. It is he who will decide when and where the battle will be fought and I think that he already has a place in mind."

"That is good," Thrydwulf told them. "A chieftain who knows his place of stand always has the advantage over his foes."

For a moment a silence descended upon the group and it seemed that no one knew what to do next. Eventually, the growing tension was broken, however.

"There is a small matter that we need to discuss," Aethelmaer said with a surprising degree of hesitation.

Coenred noted that Thrydwulf, Aethelmaer, and Hengist all looked equally uncomfortable.

"Shall we gather around the campfire?" Coenred almost spoke in jest.

"Aye, let's hunker down," Thrydwulf insisted.

He retreated to the huscarls' fire and squatted down next to it. The others followed his example. No one spoke. Coenred let the silence extend onwards, curious as to what had provoked this most unusual behaviour in his friends.

"The thing of it is…" Aethelmaer started but then lost his resolve.

"Yes!" Coenred prompted, looking bemused.

"The thing of it is they know the words better than I," Thrydwulf barked, "but it seems I'm the only one with the mettle to speak them anyway."

"It was Aethelmaer who talked of it first!" Hengist insisted.

"Do you have some complaint to lay before me?" Coenred asked in a reasonable tone of voice.

"No, nothing like that," Aethelmaer answered forcefully, his face reddening. "My Lord, we must speak of this!"

"And so we shall if one of you can tell me of what we are to speak of?"

"Our oath!" Thrydwul thundered.

"Your oath?" Coenred glanced at the earnest faces and an understanding dawned upon him. "This is the thing that we began to speak of in London, but I was called away for the embassy to the Normans. My friends, you are all huscarls, but you are not my huscarls."

"A huscarl without a lord is no huscarl, barely even a buttescarl!" Thrydwul insisted.

"What he means is, like you, we withdrew our service from Edwin and Morcar and, like you, we followed the king to this place with every intent to fight and defeat his enemies. No one commanded this of us, least of all you, but Thrydwulf is right, a huscarl without a lord is not a huscarl, he is just another weapons man."

"And we would be huscarls again!" Hengist added quickly.

"Aye, if we are to fight and face death for the third time this late summer let us do it as huscarls." The elder of the three nodded his head sagely.

"I am but newly made an eorl, there may well be better opportunities for men of your quality amongst the established eorldermen here, you should consider carefully where your service will lie."

"We were once all men of Mercia until the old eorl died, then we became Edwin's huscarls and he shared us with his brother, Morcar, when the lad was promoted to be the Eorl of Northumberland. Together have we stood many times before the spears of our enemies, in defeat and in victory, many are those of our brothers who have been snatched away on the points of those spears of wyrd. Though few of us now remain those that stand should stand together, always."

No one spoke after Aethelmaer, but all looked into the small fire that flickered before them, warming their bodies if not their spirits. His words had touched them all. He had at the last moment found the way to express what he felt; the same feeling that he knew the other two also shared with him.

"I will not bind any man in this moment," Coenred finally told them, "for words are sometimes spoken in haste, even though the time might feel meet to do so. That said, I know you all speak truly. If this act will please you each then I will accept your oath of fealty to me, as Eorl of Holderness, but I will have my way when I say that no man will be held to that oath beyond the last day of December. If any of you should then wish to continue in my service you may renew your oath as we huscarls are want to do each year. Is this meet?" Thrydwulf, Aethelmear, and Hengist all agreed in their turn. "Very well, I accept this honour that you do me and count each and every one of you as Huscarls of Holderness."

"My Death Oath to you, Coenred, as my lord, I will stand by thy side before your enemies and fight for your victory. If death should come for you then I will remain on the field of battle and defend your fallen body until either our enemies are slain or fled or I lay bleeding atop of you." Thrydwul pronounced with a face as grim as his tone. The other two repeated the oath but lacked the gravitas of the older warrior, nevertheless Coenred accepted them with equal consideration.

They sat together a long moment before the small fire, each lost in their own thoughts. Coenred understood the need within them to count himself a huscarl, a man of duty, loyalty, and honour. Although he had been their captain for some years now he was also aware that his new position as an eorlderman put an unfamiliar distance between himself and his comrades. It was he who they would be fighting to protect when the two armies met on the field of blood. He was now the object of their loyalty, which was something new to him. It was one thing to be a brother huscarl to the men stood on either side of you in the shield wall, it was quite another to be the reason why they stood there and hazarded their lives in the first place.

Coenred recalled what King Harold had said about the throne being something like a golden cage and he felt that suddenly he had had a glimpse of just such a reality. He was now responsible for these men as their lord, not as their friend, and he held their lives in his hand. It was an obligation that weighed down on him heavier than all of his war-gear. He was not sure that he liked the feeling.

Thursday, 12th October 1066

The Norman Castle at Hastings

"Harold has moved south!" Guillaume told his war council.

"Good!" Rufus declared.

"Where is he?" Robert asked with less enthusiasm.

"Some ten miles north of here."

"Then we have lost the initiative," Robert mused.

"Mayhap, but at least we have drawn him from behind the walls of London." Guillaume countered.

"Are these reports to be trusted?" Eustace asked.

"Yes, they have been corroborated. Several scouts have seen the Saxon encampment to the north. They reckon Harold's power to be the equal of our own. He sits between us and London now, out in the open."

"How will you proceed?" The Count of Mortain asked.

"Cautiously." Guillaume looked pensive.

"Cautiously? Why not march out now and meet him in the field before he can call more spears to his banner?" Rufus demanded to know.

"Have you forgotten what the Saxon emissaries told us?" Guillaume was almost derisive.

"No, Your Grace, I have not and neither do I care for it. We have no way of knowing if anything that they said was the truth. They may have been just words designed to instil fear in our men, this talk of slaying old Hardrada in the north. As I say, there is no way that we can know the truth of it!"

"Only, I see no reason for Harold to weave this tale as a falsehood for it explains his absence and we know that Hardrada did make a claim to the same English crown," Robert observed.

"We also know that Tostig Godwinson, Harold's own brother, left our court, as I was somewhat cool with him, and sailed to Norway. Tostig was seeking vengeance against his brother, his temper was hot, which is why I would have nothing to do with his plans. He was so blinded by his lust for blood that I would countenance that the former Eorl of Northumbria would make a deal with the devil to attain his satisfaction against Harold." Guillaume spoke in a measured way. "He may well have done just that."

"So Harold has an army that is tired and carries wounds, we should not give them time to heal and recover their breath!" Rufus insisted.

"Harold has an army that has recently been victorious against an ancient enemy led by a famous chieftain!" Robert retorted with some heat of his own. "We have one that has spent months sat on its arse doing nothing!"

"Will the Saxons lay siege to us?" Eustace wanted to know.

"Often they have been put under siege by the Vikings, but they have also placed towns under a siege of their own when so minded. I think, however, that Harold would avoid being caught outside with winter pressing upon us." Guillaume mused.

"We should avoid such a situation ourselves," Eustace told them. "As the Count of Mortain has pointed out already, indolence has been a chief feature of our activities to date. More time spent in such a fashion, even throughout an English winter, would do us no good whatsoever. The Saxons have veterans of recent battles within their host; we have to look much further back in our ranks for such experience."

"This is what it is to be a captain of men. Mine is the decision that will decide the fate of many, Norman and Saxon alike. I will think on it."

"There is time yet." Eustace agreed.

"Leave us now, except you, Robert."

The Count of Mortain remained where he sat within the confining room in which the council had met. He looked only at the flickering torch on the far wall until the others had all left and the door had been shut.

"Something vexes thee?" He said when he knew them to be alone and not likely to be overheard.

"Mayhap. I have a notion to do unto Harold as he did unto me."

"By which you mean?" Robert looked interested.

"He sent me an embassy in response to his brother's letter, I may do the same."

"To what purpose?"

"Rufus is impulsive, Eustace is supportive, and you are cautious."

"A council that gives only one flavour of advice is of little use."

"True. I intend to march forth on Saturday, but I would have Harold occupied, even if only in mind, until that time. I would meet with him once more."

"My Lord! You cannot hope to meet with Harold and come away with your life?!"

"I can and I do."

Near to Sentlache Ridge, north of Hastings, Kent

A knight and a priest stood on the periphery of the area in which King Harold of England had set up his camp. Harold had retreated several paces so as to stand nearer to his own tent after having spoken to the visitors. Gyrth approached him, responding to an unexpected summons. He glanced at the strangers and recognised them for Normans. Behind the foreigners' backs stood several huscarls, both as a guard to ensure that none should harm the visitors but also as a watch over them to ensure that they would do no harm to the king.

"What is this?" Gyrth asked.

"Read!" Harold handed him a parchment. Gyrth held it up in the failing light and quickly read the words written in passable English.

"A meeting, now?" He sounded surprised.

"Indeed. Guillaume would settle the matter peacefully, or so it would seem."

"Do you think that this is in response to your embassy?"

"I don't know. Half-foot was of the opinion that Guillaume was uninterested in our offer."

"Mayhap he felt that he could give no other response in front of his own people?"

"Only his brother was present at the time. Nevertheless, mayhap something else has occurred and our offer seems more attractive to him now?"

"Mayhap. What will you do?"

"I will meet with him."

"This could be a trap!"

"I doubt that. I know him and Guillaume would not stoop to assassinating me under the banner of a truce. He carries the pope's pennant before him, remember?" Harold smiled ruefully to himself.

"I would not trust him."

"I will not walk blindly into the lion's den. I have my Royal Companions and a pick of eorldermen. You look doubtful."

"I am. I say again, I do not trust him."

"Which is probably wise, but if I can avoid the death of just one more Saxon this year then it behoves me, as king, to take that action."

"You will not surrender the crown to him?"

"No."

"You will not go alone?"

"No."

"I still suspect some mischief, but I also think that you are right. There may be good reasons for the Normans to want to delay the battle, but it benefits us also; more men yet come."

Harold nodded and walked back to the two Norman emissaries. He spoke to them in French, agreeing to their proposal. Then he told the huscarls to see the two men safely to the limits of the Saxon encampment.

"The time is fixed for tomorrow evening. I will talk with Guillaume one last time."

"May I be of service to you in this?" Half-foot asked. He had been waiting both silently and patiently throughout the impromptu embassy.

"You may well be of service to me but not in this matter." He turned to face the others. "Leave us." The nobles began to disperse, leaving King Harold and his secretary. His bodyguard was in sight but not close enough to listen to what the king might say. "Half-foot, it is time for you to quit this place."

"Your Majesty, no!" His face betrayed a pained expression.

"The battle will be begun, it is no place for you."

"I would that it were! I would that you would give me leave to prove myself to you!" He spoke with some passion.

"You have done that many times but with a pen and a clever thought, not with a sword or a spear. That is not your way, my friend."

"For I am lame!"

"You knew that I would command this of you."

"Yet still I had hope."

"Of what, me letting you stand beside me?"

"You know my vanity."

"Alas, that is all it is. I wish that I had several thousand with your heart for then we would prove indomitable, but your heart is countered by your legs that cannot carry the weight of arms and armour." Half-foot looked crestfallen. Harold placed a friendly hand on his shoulder. "Be not sad, I send you from a place of danger out of both respect and consideration, not because I count you unworthy.

You are of more value to me at my court in London than waiting here in the rear of the fyrd."

"Wyrd plays a contrary game with me."

"Mayhap, but it has not masked your many talents from me and when I return to London I will promote you because of them, I will make you an eorl in reward for your constant loyalty."

"An eorl?"

"You are eorl-worthy, none may doubt that," Harold smiled at the other's disbelief. "Go now, take what you need and an escort to see you safe on the road to London, Osfrid will arrange matters. "

"As you wish, My Lord."

Friday, 13ᵗʰ October 1066
Between Sentlache Ridge and Hastings, Kent

The sun was dipping in the west. Long shadows began to march over the land. The road fell into a natural dip so that there was some high ground on either side of it. A ring of torches had been placed at the bottom of the incline to mark the place where the talks between King Harold of England and the Duke of Normandy were to be held. To the north, some one hundred heavily armed and armoured men sat on their small Saxon horses. They looked down into the ring of firelight with unfriendly eyes but kept their thoughts to themselves.

Directly opposite to them a similar number of Norman knights also waited. They rode taller and better quality steeds, but then their animals were bred to war, unlike the Saxon's.

"No one will enter the ring of torches but I and Guillaume," Harold told them. "No one is to leave this spot unless the enemy makes a hostile move against me. Gyrth, you are to command in my absence. I trust you to maintain the terms of the truce."

"Yes, My Lord."

"Eorl of Holderness!"

"Yes, My Lord." Coenred acknowledged the king.

"Will you be my horsgeben this one time?"

"It is my honour, My Lord."

"Stand thee outside the ring but keep an eager eye open. I would have you and my horse close to hand should the Eorl of Anglia's fear of mischief be proven true." Harold smiled at the both of them. "I will say again, I will not break the terms of the truce and I will have no man of mine do so either. No matter what the provocation, short of all of his men approaching the ring to slay me, you will keep your place of stand. This is between me and him only. No other will interfere."

Harold motioned his horse forward at the walk, Coenred followed in his wake. He wondered why King Harold had chosen him out of all of his followers to perform this duty. There was no immediate answer. Every one of the Royal Companions was an accomplished rider and, it went without saying, a warrior. It did not occur to him that as an eorl's man, an occupation that had taken up most of his life so far, Coenred was experienced in doing exactly as his lord commanded, without question and without fail. In that, he was a man to be relied upon.

They descended into the hollow as the sky darkened overhead. Harold dismounted just before the ring of torches and turned to hand his horse's reins to Coenred.

"Remain mounted where they can see you," he told him. "Keep a cool head and a sharp eye."

"I will, My Lord."

Harold gave him a quick smile and a nod, and then he turned to face the ring itself. Guillaume had descended from the other side in exactly the same manner as Harold, bringing only one knight with him. He too dismounted but he spoke no words to his companion. Together they passed the boundary and approached each other.

"Well met cousin!" Guillaume opened the discourse.

"I had hoped to have met you under better circumstances, mayhap in Westminster, where you would have been a welcomed visitor to my court."

"Straight to the point then," Guillaume gave him a knowing smile.

"It is October, the evening air grows chill. Winter approaches."

"I would avoid bloodshed if I could."

"But you won't."

"And neither will you."

"My crown is not on offer."

"Your crown?"

"Yes, my crown."

"That crown was bequeathed to me by King Edward. He made me his heir. The world knows this to be true. You know it to be true."

"I know the story that you have told the world, but it is without witness. King Edward failed to name his heir. My sister, Queen Eadgyth, has confirmed that King Edward looked to make Edward Aetheling his named heir. He brought him back from the Holy Roman Empire for that purpose, but Edward Aetheling died before this was realised. On his deathbed, King Edward passed the crown to me."

"So say you and without witness also."

"You would doubt the world of Queen Eadgyth?"

"No, for I honour her, but, as you say, she is your sister, and I know how tightly the binds of your father tie the Godwin family together. So tight that some of your siblings turned to treachery to break those bonds in order to be free."

"I could denigrate your family also, you had fighting of your own to do just to survive it, but of what value would this be?"

Guillaume nodded his acknowledgement of this point. "We are not here to talk over the past; we are here to decide the future. I will not withdraw my claim and you will not surrender the crown."

"That is it, in a nut shell, as we say here."

"Then, if we are both true to our word, which is the path forward from here that will avoid the greater bloodshed and resolve this conflict."

"It is said in older times war-chiefs would sometimes meet in single combat to decide the issue and spare the blood of their own men."

"In the words of poets, mayhap." Guillaume scoffed.

He glanced at Harold. The Saxon was the older of them by six years. He stood a little taller than the Duke and had a lighter build but there was no doubting that he was in the prime of his life. His limbs were well muscled, built up by constant activity, which would include training with various heavy weapons.

For his part, Guillaume was robust, strong, and possessed good health. If they were to meet in combat then they would most likely be judged a fair match, one for the other. There was a significant difference between the two, however. Saxon lords led from the front. They dressed in fine armour and stood in the front rank of their shield wall. These ancient chieftains referred to themselves as the shields of their people and they embodied that claim, literally, upon the field of battle.

Normans led from on horseback. Guillaume had fought in battles but it was his way to remain behind the ranks of his men and watch the development of the battle. He was brave enough to throw himself into the heat of the fight when necessary, and he had killed many men upon the bloody field, but it was not his way to seek out single combat, champion against champion. Indeed, it was not the Norman way of doing things.

"I will not stand toe to toe with you, swapping blows for the amusement of the common soldiery."

"Name another then. One to fight in your stead and I will do likewise."

"I have no other on whom I could lay such a heavy burden."

"Then withdraw!"

"Honour your sacred vow!" Guillaume's voice rose in frustration.

"No vow is sacred when forced."

"You were fairly treated at my court. I made you my friend."

"And when we were friends you did treat me fairly, up to, but not including, that moment when you forced me to swear an oath that you purposed and I could not avoid. If I had given my word freely, and in full knowledge of the holy relics hidden beneath my hand, then that oath would bind me now, but you tricked me, Guillaume. Friends do not trick one another, they speak openly, one to the other."

"Then you will not honour it?"

"I cannot honour what was done dishonourably, and an honourable man would not ask it of me."

"You know that I have placed everything upon this venture? The whole world knows that I am here and why."

"I offered you the means to return in peace to your duchy and defeat your enemies there."

"I can defeat them without your money!"

"Then it is a matter of pride with you?"

"If you were a real king then you would understand the value of reputation!" He was becoming angry.

"I understand it well enough; I just choose not to become a slave to the opinions of others."

"It is the opinions of others that force our hands to actions that otherwise we might avoid, like the taking of many lives."

"Like the taking of things that do not belong to us! You use a thief's way of thinking, Guillaume."

"The pope does not agree."

"The pope would do well to occupy himself with matters spiritual. When it comes to matters secular it is we princes who are looked to, for such is our provenance."

"You care not that you are excommunicated?"

"I care more about how God sees me as I am. I acknowledge the Pope in Rome as the head of the church. He has suspended me from that church, but his mind on this particular issue is also open to change. Next year, when this same issue has been decided, I will make a pilgrimage to Rome with my priests and make representations to have the pope's censure removed from me. He will see an England united under the rule of a king chosen for the Saxons by the Saxons. Many churches will have been rebuilt in stone by then, a more permanent expression of the zeal with which we Saxons have embraced the faith of Jesu Christ. England will be a bastion of Christianity and I its head. The pope will not refuse me then."

Guillaume fumed in silence for a moment. He had always known of Harold's piety, indeed, that was one of the reasons why he had sued Rome for support, hoping to bring religious pressure to bear, but he now realised that he had misjudged the importance of that approach on a personal level with Harold. The Saxon was playing a longer game on that front. Everything that he said concerning his censure from Rome was true; he would not be the first monarch to be forgiven after doing due penance.

So far, it seemed, Guillaume had achieved little. He had even failed to refute Harold's accusation of him being a thief. Desperately, he cast about for another means of influencing his enemy, but it was Harold who spoke first.

"There is a rumour abroad that you have broken up your ships and taken their boards to make hovels for your men to live in while you await the coming of winter. Fuel, mayhap, for their fires when the frost paints their shoulders white."

"Mayhap I did it to show them that there is no swift return home? We will not leave until this matter is decided, one way or the other."

"Mayhap you did it because you feared desertion from amongst their ranks? That would be the act of a desperate man though, one who was not entirely sure of the men who supposedly stand with him."

"Enough of this! We talk to no end."

"We talk because you willed it. If you see no return in this then why did you ask me here?"

"I suppose to confirm that you are still obstinate and will not listen to reason."

"The reason that you appeal to is simply ambition. It concerns no one but yourself."

"And yours doesn't?"

"I was chosen by the witan to rule after King Edward. If my sister had been blessed by God with a male child then all of this would be unnecessary, but she was not. Edward favoured me, at the end of his days, over you and the witan agreed with him. That is my reason for being here, wearing the crown of England."

"Harold, I once held you in fair esteem. I see in you a noble man who would make a noble ally. Can we not be friends once more? I would make you the greatest eorlderman in the kingdom, second only to myself, as your king."

"We can be friends again when you are returned to Normandy. As a friend, I would support you against Brittany and France. We cannot be friends, however, when it is me that you look to fight and not your enemies at home. We cannot be friends when you would rob me of my right to rule."

"Then I find that I have no more words to say. I will march north from Hastings."

"And I will stop you."

"Then you commit your men to die upon some nameless field."

"As do you."

They looked at each other over the several yards of open space between them. Each wore full armour but each was of their own particular design. They were marked out as leaders and men of war, but there were subtle differences between them.

"When I first met you, two years ago now, I had great hopes for our friendship. That it should come to this saddens me." Guillaume told him.

"As it does me, but know that it was not I who ventured to cross the whale road and into another's land with a host at my command. Time will not paint me as the aggressor nor as the murderer of common folk and despoiler of girl-children. Those things will stay with you for all the days that men can remember, they will always be numbered amongst the deeds that came to pass here."

"They will remember my greater glory."

"If you are indeed victorious when the final encounter is made then the weak minds of men may well be swayed to forget the uglier actions that you are responsible for, but God will not. If you are victorious, Guillaume, you will still have to answer to Him for all the heinous acts you commanded be done in your name, all committed so as to allow you to take that which does not belong to you. If you are victorious, but I pray to God that you will not be."

"You are not without stain yourself, Harold."

"I know, but I beg forgiveness and my sins do not approach those that you have committed to the people in and around Hastings. Think upon it, Guillaume, win or lose, you still have to answer to God."

"I am prepared."

"So am I." Having spoken what he intended to be his final words Harold turned from Guillaume and made his way back to his horse.

Coenred thought to ask Harold about the meeting but he saw in his face a strange expression and felt in his presence a heaviness that moved him to remain silent. They turned their horses and began to walk them back towards the rest of the company.

"You are not curious?" Harold said eventually while they were still some way from the others.

"I am, My Lord, but you have spoken so much, I think, that is, I believe silence might make a better companion for you in this moment."

"You are wiser than you know, my Eorl of Holderness, which is why I chose you to be my companion on this fool's errand. Enough to say that it is war then."

Saturday, 14th October 1066
At Sentlache Ridge, north of Hastings, Kent

"We will go no further!" King Harold declared.

"The way is open to us." Leofwine countered.

"There are Normans on the road," Gyrth observed, knowing full well that they all could see this for themselves.

"Nothing but scouts, we can brush them to one side or fix them with our spears," the younger of the three royal brothers insisted.

"They stay to watch what we do next, but they are not the sum total of those who have perceived our move from the apple tree," Harold commented. "Their fellows have already gone to forewarn Guillaume. We will not be taking him by surprise this day."

"But Harold-"

"Leofwine, give yourself to learning from those who know better than thee!" Gyrth interrupted him. "And have the measure to use a kingly title when it is required of you." Gyrth glared at his younger brother.

The young eorl opened his mouth to speak, his face reddening at the rebuke, but then he thought better of it and turned away from Gyrth.

"This is a good place to make our stand, I know for I had it in my mind always since the news of Guillaume's coming broke. We have the high ground and the Normans cannot bypass us without exposing their flank. Form the shield wall here!" Harold commanded. His

Royal Companions began to set about the business of putting the army into good order on the ground selected.

"My Lord, I would speak with you." Gyrth looked earnest.

"Step over here." Harold turned his back on the distant Norman scouts and rode away from his companions for a little ways, his brother following in the king's horse's footsteps. The army stretched away to the north, momentarily halted but already the order to form their defence was beginning to make its way down the column. With admirable discipline, the fyrd began to take its' position along the top of the ridge.

"Do you still intend for Leofwine to command on the right flank?" Gyrth asked once Harold had stopped his horse. They were away from most of the others now, including their brother.

"I do."

"He is not seasoned."

"And neither will he be if all we do is keep him in London to act as my surrogate when I am away from the court. He needs to learn his trade, brother, and I mean to teach him it."

"But is this the right time?"

"Is there ever a right time?"

"So much of import weighs upon this encounter I mean."

"I know, Gyrth. A lesser man would rail against me for handing authority over him to one who is, in many respects, a lesser lord, but you worry for me and not for yourself in what others might think of you in the light of this decision."

"I have a title, lands, and wealth; I care for nothing more than what I already own."

"Over Leofwine you have age and experience also, those are not things that even a king can give. All I can do is to give him the opportunity to acquire what we already have in that way, as our father did for us."

"But if he should fail you, if the right flank should give? There would be a disaster."

"I agree and, for that reason, I would set you to oversee Leofwine."

"I had expected to be on your left."

"Quite rightly, but you do have an influence over our brother, you can rein him in if necessary. I would have you steady my right flank so that I can be free of worry on that point."

"He never pays me heed!"

"Yes, he does, it just seems that he never pays anyone older than himself heed. We know all too well the weaknesses of his character, Gyrth, but I would discover his strengths. I believe that he has many."

"As you wish."

"You are not put out by this, brother?"

"For myself, no, I will obey whatever you command." The smile that formed on his face seemed somewhat forced and Harold saw not so much doubt but rather worry in his eyes.

"Fear not, my plan is simple, I know I suggested that we might move and take the Normans unaware, but that was always a vain hope. Guillaume is too seasoned in combat for such a stratagem to have worked. Always it was in my mind that fixing our shield wall here, on top of this ridge, would lessen the impact of those Norman knights that so many fear. We will hold this line and hold it well."

"And that is my duty, to ensure that Leofwine holds his place and nothing more?"

"That he does nothing more."

"As you will it, so shall it be."

"Have faith in our bloodline, Gyrth, we are all Godwins after all."

***

"Where shall I stand?" Edwin son of Octa asked eagerly.

"Edwin, between ourselves I ask nothing of you but what becomes a master and a servant, now that I am an eorlderman, however, you must use my title before the others," Coenred reminded him.

"Or I will cuff you for your insolence and ignorance!" Thrydwul growled.

"I am sorry, My Lord." The boy looked crestfallen.

"It is not a rebuke, Edwin, just a reminder. We are both new to this are we not?"

"Yes, My Lord." His smile came more naturally.

"I have a mind to leave you at the rear."

"My Lord?!" Now he looked pained.

"But you did well at Stamford Bridge."

"Aye, he did, or so Sigbert told me," Thrydwulf added.

"Haven't you had enough of killing yet though?"

"Yes, I have, but it seems to me that I did my better war-work guarding you from behind. I followed you into the enemy's ranks and thrust with my spear when that Tostig's eyes were on you and not me. I am not looking for a fight this time; I just want to be of use to you."

"Then you are showing some wisdom beyond your age, Edwin." Coenred smiled affectionately. "You are my shield-bearer and while such as Eanfrid found it necessary to kill now and again his real purpose was to carry my extra weapons, recover those that I was forced to discard, give me water to slake my thirst in the heat of the battle, and to help me away if I should take an injury. This will be your duty to me today. Stand behind me, never wandering, and mark my words so that I can rely upon you being always there for me."

"I will, My Lord."

"We will stand on the king's right hand. Mark you now where that is. His bannermen are already there, see?" Coenred pointed a little to their left where two heavily armoured Royal Companions stood. They each held a large pole, the butt of the heavy timbers currently resting on the ground. Canvas bags covered the top third of these tall flagpoles and beneath them, the famous fighting man banner and the equally famous Wyvern of Wessex banner resided.

"I see them, My Lord."

"Good. Now, take our horses and stable them at the spot that will already have been marked for them. There will be lads there ready and waiting to look after our beasts. Once done, replenish your flask and come back to me.

"I will!" Edwin grinned back.

The huscarls dismounted and passed their reins to Edwin who, once he had collected all of the horses from their small party, turned and headed back down the north side of the ridge.

"He's a good lad," Thrydwulf commented.

"Aye, I hope I have done him a good turn in bringing him here?" Coenred mused.

"He's your servant, it is right that he should be where you are. Eanfrid never thought anything other."

"Eanfrid has many years on the boy."

"This is true also, but then Eanfrid never fought in a battle quite like this one. When we win that is something that the boy will have over your old shield-bearer."

"We are not many," Aethelmaer observed as he joined them.

"By which he means the huscarls of Holderness!" Hengist offered in a bright voice.

"And the fyrd of Holderness!" Added Cudberct, the head ceorl of the fyrdmen.

"I would not be the first lord of men to wish that he had a thousand more spears at his back, but then numbers alone never guaranteed a victory." Coenred turned to face his small war-band. "Know thee this, you are all proven men. Though our numbers have dwindled through too many fights, not enough time to rest, and the desertion of those who should have led us better, still, I doubt none of you. There are not ten men here that could take the place of anyone of you, not twenty or fifty more. There is none amongst all the aethelings that I would accept in place of thee.

"Today we stand and fight by the side of Harold Godwinson, King of England, but that is not what fills my heart with pride, it is knowing that I stand and fight with thee."

Coenred was not normally given to the making of speeches; it was the moment that had caught him. The small group of some sixty warriors stood silently weighing up his words. It was young Aethelmaer who chose to speak for all of them.

"Coenred, I have known you for a shorter time than Sigbert or Thrydwul here, a little longer than Hengist, mayhap, but I deem it a lucky day when Eorl Edwin appointed me to you to learn my trade. I would not change my place now to fight with any other lord." His words provoked many echoes of agreement.

"My Lord!" Cudberct stepped forward. "We fyrdmen that followed you to Tadcaster and Stamford Bridge did so because we knew our duty. We followed you here because that seemed our duty also. We are but peasants and mayhap Lord Edwin and Lord Morcar might take the whip to us when we return home, but then mayhap they should be here with us as well."

"I will not allow for you to be whipped and neither, I believe, will the king," Coenred told them.

"There's but one more thing," Hengist said. He glanced at Cudbect meaningfully.

"Aye, there is." The fyrdman looked over his shoulder and there was some movement in the ranks behind him. Eventually, another fyrdman stepped forward holding a seasoned pole cut from an ash tree. He raised the tall staff into the air and shook it vigorously so that the length of cloth affixed to the top unfurled. "We have made a banner for the Eorl of Holderness so that our enemies might know who it is that fights them hard and slays so many of their numbers."

Their eyes were taken upwards to view the simple rectangle of cloth dyed a deep green and onto which someone had painted a representation of a huscarl in white holding a spear aloft.

"This will mark the place of our stand," Coenred told them with sincerity, "and let no man move from it unless either I or the king so commands it!"

***

"I like not this position!" Robert, Count of Mortain, announced in a quiet but decided voice. He sat beside his brother, Duke Guillaume, their horses moving restlessly. There was a definite tension in the air. "The land gives them all the advantages."

"I agree," Guillaume said morosely.

They followed with their eyes the road towards the large hill before them where they could see the Saxons building their shield wall. Men in heavy armour and carrying large round shields were forming up just below the ridgeline itself, allowing others to assemble behind them to a depth of four or five rows. The steep ground gave them a secure position and the Duke of Normandy knew well that the Saxon army was skilled in holding such ground. Indeed, it was a favoured tactic of the Saxons to build their shield wall and simply stand their chosen place, resisting all attempts to move them.

"How many do you reckon?"

"My scouts estimate at least an equal number to our own, but almost all infantry," Robert replied.

"I was expecting more."

"So was I, but mayhap the reason why Harold wasn't in the south when we landed might have something do with that?"

"Mayhap."

"We could return to the castle?"

"Castle?" Guillaume favoured his brother with a sneer. "It is made of wood and it will not stand a determined siege."

"I know."

"The place was meant to shelter our troops, not defend us against a vicious enemy in a foreign land!"

"I know."

"If we retreat now we forfeit this enterprise. We'll be lucky to return to Normandy with our lives. Even if we managed that the French would fall on us in our weakness."

"I know." Robert weathered his brother's temper stoically. Guillaume glanced sideways at him, saw the stern but resigned expression and felt a surprising surge of emotion for the count.

"I know that you know and I appreciate your intent to remind me of what few alternatives we have."

"Withdrawing in the hope of making the circumstances of the encounter more favourable is a wise move, one we have followed previously."

"I know," Guillaume smiled. The air between the two lightened appreciably. "The truth is, Robert, that winter nips our heels. We talked not so long ago about what a long winter in that wooden castle would do to us."

"We have the town under our control."

"But for how long? If we holed up inside the castle and Harold set his men to ring us in, they fed by their bumper harvest, we scratching for food from hidden caches, our supply ships raided by the Saxon's fleet; we would be in no fit state to fight come spring. There are no reserves back home for us to call upon. Hunger and disease would thin our numbers more surely than Saxon spears. My whole plan has hinged upon bringing Harold to the fight, but I wanted it on my terms, not his."

"And he thwarted you by disappearing like a trail of smoke."

"I thought that landing unopposed was good fortune, but it has been more than two weeks since we came ashore and all we have done is capture a small town. Harold has moved like a fox into a strong position to hold us in check. If your scouts had not been keeping a keen eye on him then verily he might have penned us up in Hastings."

"I'll say this for the Saxon, he's a better commander than I gave him credit for." Robert nodded to add weight to his statement. He was aware that in the past he had been dismissive of Harold and all the Saxons for that matter, particularly when it came to military concerns, but he was beginning to see that he might have been wrong in this regard.

"Have you ever broken a Saxon shield wall before?"

"The Saxons fight the same as the Norse and we have crossed swords with them in the past when they came to Normandy in quest of plunder."

"They were raiders only, this is an army led by a king."

"Harold is not a king!"

"He wears a crown and, in truth, that is all that one man needs to be called a king, but enough of that. It is all that matters that his men consider him their king. They will fight and die for him."

"If all of this country thought the same then we would be badly outnumbered!"

Guillaume smiled. "And there you give me hope, Robert. I think thee correct, all of England does not follow Harold or else they would send their warriors to strengthen his power. Yes, that gives me hope."

Robert of Mortain glanced around him at the Norman soldiers who were gathering into their own formations even as the nobles conversed. They were divided into three groups of equal size. Each group was fronted by archers and men armed with crossbows, behind which stood spearmen and behind them the mounted knights.

They had roughly eight thousand men to call upon, two thousand knights, two thousand archers and the rest all infantry. It was not a small number for such a force but Robert would have preferred more.

Up on the hill, it was difficult to see exactly how many men Harold had standing under his famous 'Fighting Man' banner. The front rank would be filled by heavily armoured eorldermen, theigns, and huscarls, and their task was to hold their shields together to form an impenetrable barrier. Behind them, more men of quality stood with bright swords and those fearsome Dane-axes that they swung two handed. And then behind them stood the fyrdmen, the peasant soldiery, armed with long fighting spears that they thrust over the shoulders of the men in front. Robert was a soldier of experience and his instincts were telling him that this battle would be hard fought and that the outcome was far from sure.

"'Tis said that the Saxon is a hardy fellow, as stubborn as an ox, and, once riled, as violent as a bear. The Bretons, on the other hand, on our left as it so happens today, are not so well renowned."

"I use them because I must, Robert."

"Men used out of necessity, rather than loyalty, are not so well honed."

"Alan Rufus will lead them well."

"Rufus, I have no qualms about, it is his men that I doubt. Bretons mixed with French adventurers from Anjou and Poitou."

"The right flank is no different, they hail from Picardy and Boulogne, led by Count Eustace is himself."

"He is a noble and a friend, he will do his duty by you and, I dare say, so will the men loyal to him, but, in this, we lack another of Harold's advantages."

"Which is?"

"He has only Saxons in his ranks, all men of one land, one lord, and one purpose. Our men, the nobles included, are here to sate their appetite for wealth."

"Of course they are, we stoked that hunger in their bellies to get them to undertake this journey in the first place." The Duke laughed a little. "Robert, waiting does not sit easily with you does it?"

"Brother, I find waiting for a battle only gives me leave to think and it is the thinking that puts bile in my gut." This time Guillaume did allow himself to laugh a little more heartily.

"So it is for all of us who have experienced war. In this time before the first blow is struck we have too much leisure to think on things that disappear in the heat of the battle. Each man knows best what distracts his mind from this useless rumination. You worry, Robert, because you have the time to do so."

"Again, I know. My men are well trained, their commanders know what they are about, there is little for me to do other than prepare to lead them when you call, so I look for things to worry about."

Duke Guillaume fell silent in his own turn. He had enjoyed the conversation with his brother as it had occupied his mind also, but he shared the count's misgivings as well. In some respects, it was even worse for the duke because he could not give voice to them, unlike

Robert. It would not do for the Duke of Normandy to question the abilities of the men he had put in charge of the various formations of archers and infantry and cavalry, even if he held misgivings about them privately. The fact that many of them were indeed motivated by greed rather than loyalty to him, or even fear of him, meant that the degree to which he could rely upon them in battle was limited also. Not one of those possessed of a mercenary soul would risk his life to either save Guillaume's own or to hazard a danger that might win them the battle. He knew this to be true, but he also knew that his Norman soldiers were indeed to be relied upon. They were tried and trusted men and they would follow where their duke led.

This was a role of the die, mayhap the most dangerous gamble that he had ever undertaken. In the eyes of others, even his own half-brother, Guillaume may look calm and confident, but, in truth, his stomach churned just as much as any other man's and his sleep had not been restful. There would be plenty of time to sleep, he told himself, either as a king or as a corpse.

***

"What manner of combat is this?" Young Hengist asked of no one in particular. He stood in the front rank of the shield wall, his head protected by a polished steel helmet, a mail vest covering his body, and a large, round, wooden shield held in place before him. He looked down the hill at the unfamiliar formation of troops facing them. They were an enemy that he had never experienced before.

"It matters not," Thrydwulf asserted. He stood next to the younger huscarl, equipped in exactly the same fashion. "They will die on our spears all the same."

"They are Normans. They say that they are of Norse blood but they have been exposed to the ways of the French for many a year. Mayhap this is the French way of fighting?" Aethelmaer mused.

"As Thrydwulf says, it matters not." Coenred joined the conversation from his position to the right of Aethelmaer. His small warband was positioned in its turn to the right of the king who properly took the centre. "What matters is that we keep the wall intact and we are well versed in that."

"Do they use horses in war?" Thrydwulf wondered aloud.

"How can a man use a beast in war?" Hengist added.

"I know not, but I expect we will learn the way of it," Coenred told them.

He turned and looked back at Edwin. The boy was dressed in his armour. He wore a steel helmet and a coat of mail over his padded jacket in the same manner as the huscarls. This war-gear had come from a dead Viking who fell at Stamford Bridge. There had been many such items for sale within York and Coenred had taken advantage of the surplus. As a huscarl, he had the means to do so. For weapons Edwin had a langseax in a leather scabbard and a scramseax, a smaller knife, hanging from his thick belt. He also carried a typical round wooden shield, several throwing spears, and a long fighting spear.

"How does the day find you?" Coenred asked.

"Warm and bound to be warmer still!" Edwin returned with his effortless smile.

"Remember, stay behind me so that you can be of use in the moment when I need it."

"Yes, My Lord."

Below their position, the last of the Norman troops were forming up. They were far enough away so as to be out of arrow shot, but close enough that the Saxons on the hill could clearly see the manner in which their enemy had drawn up his strength. The English were used to fighting in the compact formation of the shield wall, a tactic that called upon discipline, practice, determination, and the will to stand no matter what the enemy threw at them. All of the warriors knew both the strength and the weakness of the shield wall. In defence, it was practically immovable when held by experienced warriors. In attack, it was almost irresistible when the will of many became one, but it was slow moving, easy to outflank if the terrain permitted, and slow to respond to changes in the flow of battle.

Recently, Coenred and his men had seen all of those aspects of their favoured manner of fighting. At Fulford Gate, they had felt the shield wall turned and then splintered by the Vikings and their clever manoeuvres. At Stamford Bridge, they had seen those self-same Vikings collapse before the tremendous pressure that the Saxon shield wall had brought to bear upon them, even as it had marched up the hill. The truth was that the Saxons knew of no other way to fight. Their horses were not bred to war. They were used to carry warriors to and from the battlefield, never were they ridden in the midst of the fight.

Coenred glanced along the line of warriors. They followed the curve of the hill so that they stood in the shape of a bow, the tips some feet behind the centre. Each flank was protected by a river but the left hand straddled the road from Hastings. Over the days of their march from London and their assembly at the apple tree, the huscarl had cast an experienced eye over the fyrd. There was quality within its ranks, no one could deny that, and even the fyrdmen themselves, the peasant soldiery, seemed hardened and willing to fight, but there were not as many as he had expected. At Fulford Gate he had been the captain of one thousand five hundred huscarls, there seemed fewer than that number of elite warriors here today. King Harold had led some ten thousand men into battle at Stamford Bridge, but he had not been able to call as many to his banner down here in the south, where Coenred had expected him to enjoy considerable support.

The newly made eorl was not a man given to politics. The life of a huscarl had always been his main concern and in that he had excelled. That there may be reasons as to why local Saxons might not wish to support their king did not escape him, he just struggled to understand why, when a foreign invader took the field against them, those Saxons could not put aside their differences with the House of Wessex until after this danger was settled. In his own mind, he deemed that there was no better man than Harold Godwinson to wear the crown, which was why he was here to fight for him. King

Harold had proven his quality in marching north to save York and Northumbria from King Hardrada of Norway; it was a debt fit to be repaid, but so few seemingly agreed.

There had been talk around the campfire that King Harold had purposefully left Eorl Edwin of Mercia and his younger brother, Eorl Morcar of Northumbria, behind, that he had chosen not to press them to follow him south because he did not trust them. This thought grieved Coenred. He had been a loyal retainer to their father, Eorl Aelfgar, for many years before taking on the duty of the teacher to the two young boys when the eorl had died. It was a duty given to him by his lord on his deathbed and he had remained true to it until both Edwin and Morcar made it plain that they no longer valued his service. Despite the bad humour that had tinged their last parting, Coenred could not think too poorly of the young eorldermen; he had known them for too long. They had, however, acted rashly at Fulford Gate and tipped the kingdom into danger. The loss of the battle was made more lamentable because there had been no reason to fight it in the first place. Edwin and Morcar could have shut the gates of York and manned the walls with a strong fyrd, as Coenred and others had counselled, but they had chosen glory instead. In the aftermath of that fateful decision, mayhap, it was to be expected that the king might assess their worth a little less and their reliability even weaker. He had actually hinted at such a thing when he had decided to make Coenred an eorl in his own right.

It came to his mind that if they had not fought at Fulford then there may well be another 1,500 huscarls to stand here on top of this ridge and amongst them would be Hereric, his dead friend and once the mightiest of warriors that he had known.

Wyrd will have its way and it may yet come to pass that brave Hereric, and all the others who fell at Fulford Gate might yet smile down upon them today as the Saxons repelled the invading Normans and drove them back into the sea.

***

"Prepare for archers!" King Harold of England announced. The word spread quickly. Many another in the shield wall had also noticed the movement of the Norman bowmen, preparing their weapons and nocking an arrow to their bows.

All along the line of Saxons broad round wooden shields were hefted into position. At the sound of the release of the arrows, steel helmets ducked down behind the protection offered to them. A moment later and a cloud of missiles passed over their heads with only a few striking the linden wood of the protective shields. Firing uphill appeared to encourage the archers to overshoot and they failed to inflict any kind of injury with their opening volleys.

"We should have brought more archers ourselves," Osfrid offered. "They proved better at shooting uphill at Stamford Bridge than these Norman missile-men."

"Many suffered a hurt when they closed on the Norse and Theign Breme was killed. He trained them well." Harold responded.

He had seen how the Normans themselves had used archers so effectively within their own army and he had looked to exploit them more than was normal in a Saxon fyrd. At Stamford Bridge, the band of archers he had formed had fired their shots with precision and surprised the Viking enemy. Their arrows had sailed high into the air and fallen beyond the front ranks of the Norse shield wall. It was after the press had become too close that those same archers had broken heir formation and waded into the battle singularly. Theign Breme had been killed then, confronting the Vikings like a true Saxon, but his loss was missed now. Harold would have preferred the theign and his archers had remained where he had put them for then they would have had a part to play today. It was true, however, that no chieftain ever had total control over his men once the battle was joined.

"Well, we might starve the Normans of arrows at least if we don't return so many as they shoot."

The infantry advanced under the cover of more volleys of arrows. They come on from three directions, holding their kite shaped shields before them. This design had the advantage of offering protection to both their bodies and their legs. They carried fighting spears, simple swords, and axes with which to engage their foes. These soldiers were mostly men belonging to individual lords, their equipage paid for by those particular noblemen. All wore thick padded jackets over which some wore vests of chain mail. Like many a Saxon, those who lacked chain mail armour had attached patches of toughened leather or metal scales to try and give themselves extra protection. Every man also wore a conical steel helmet with a prominent noseguard. In this, they differed to the Saxons as not all of the fyrd were awarded the protection of such headgear.

They came on in a disciplined fashion with a measured step and several ranks deep. When they encountered the incline of the hill the pace of those at the front slowed appreciably and their lines compressed. The occasional arrow flew down from the hill to strike a shield or fly over their heads to visit a hurt on the archers who now stood behind their fellows. Eventually, those Norman missile-men had to stop their own firing for fear of hitting their comrades as the infantry closed on the Saxons. As soon as those bows were lowered the war-horns of the English sounded. It was a terrible sound. A blast of dragon's roar and wolf's howl that reverberated through the infantrymen's chests. They did not know what it might portend.

Like many others, Coenred moved his long fighting spear into the grasp of his left hand. All the huscarls carried at least two or three angons, short throwing spears, strapped on the reverse side of their shields. Each selected one of these. At a second blast from the trumpets, the Saxons hurled a volley of their own down the hill. Some of those behind the front line added to the barrage with large stones that were equally effective.

The throwing spears fell amongst the ranks of the Normans, drawing blood. The weapons were made with a long steel head and body riveted onto a heavy wooden shaft in the Roman manner. They were deadly missiles in the hands of trained men who could hurl them with considerable force and accuracy. Some were thrown so viciously that they pierced the wood of the kite shields and penetrated through muscle and into bone. Stones thumped into wooden shields also or clanged off steel helmets.

Still, the Normans came on, although some chose to stop and rid themselves of the heavy Saxon spears that pulled down their protective shields. The size and weight of the angons made marching or fighting difficult when they were so transfixed. Trying to remove the missiles caught fast in the shields was a mistake, however, and also the reason why the Saxons always carried more than one angon. With practised arms, the Saxons let loose a second volley of throwing spears. Anyone caught without the protection of their shield, even one already damaged by the first barrage, was left vulnerable. Many who were exposed in just such a manner died or suffered terrible injuries. The hillside began to become slippery with human blood. The screams of the injured and the dying filled the air, and the Normans had not yet closed the distance with their enemy.

***

Duke Guillaume sat immobile on his horse watching the first attack falter. Many of his supporters had derided the Saxons as peasant soldiers, not fit to make a worthy enemy of the Normans, he wondered if their opinions might have changed already. There was nothing weak or undisciplined or untrained about Harold's warband. They held a strong position and they knew it. They had practised warriors amongst them on whom they could rely to offer a stern resistance and those men would indeed do that. How strong that resistance might be would not be known until the infantry had finally closed the distance and come to sword-blows with the Saxons; if they could survive the trek up the already bloodied hill that was.

***

Another blast of the war-horns and Harold's frontline retrieved their fighting spears and put their shields back in place. The Normans continued their advance. Behind them, their lords rode to and fro, exhorting the men to the fray. They stepped over the bodies of their fallen comrades and pushed on to finally bang their kite shields into the round counterparts of their enemies.

The forces collided with a terrific impact but the defenders did not move. Prepared for the meeting the Saxon ranks initially closed to lend their weight to the heavily armoured men at the front, creating an immovable object. After the initial tremor, these same rows of men took a step back to give themselves room to strike.

The eorldermen, theigns, and huscarls ducked behind their great shields as the Normans hewed at them and from over the shoulders of these Saxons came long fighting spears, flicking forwards like the tongues of serpents. Some of these spears had backwards pointing barbs that were used to try and catch a man unawares as the weapons were pulled back by the warriors using them. The barbs removed helmets, exposing heads, or dug into shoulders and pulled a soldier off-balance. It was then that a Saxon warrior would overreach the shield wall with a large two-handed Dane-axe or a glittering sword. Their strike would deliver a death stroke or at least a serious injury to the exposed man. In this way had both the Saxons and the Vikings broken the formations of their enemies for generations, and in this way, they frustrated the hardy Normans just the same.

Robert, Count of Mortain, shook his head. "They will not move."

"No, they will not." Guillaume agreed.

"Our archers are rendered useless by the Saxons' position and the closeness of the infantry, they can exert no influence."

"So many good men made impotent by the fitfulness of war."

"What do you suggest?" Robert could not stop a tone of impatience colouring his voice.

"Why the obvious of course, wait."

"Wait?!"

Guillaume glanced at his half-brother. "You did not expect this to be over quickly did you?"

"Our men are dying before the Saxon spears and they seem to be unable to balance the account!"

"They have only just closed upon them; give them time to prove their worth!" The Duke insisted with a sterner tone.

***

Coenred breathed steadily as his training had taught him to do, but they had been fighting for some time now and tiredness was beginning to set in. Ideally, the men in the front rank would retire after 20 minutes so as to rest and recover their strength, but this depended on their being sufficient men dressed in at least equal quality armour to take their place. Today, those men were in short supply. To redress this situation the men at the front attempted to conserve their energy by employing only their shields against the enemy. They kept them held high both to protect themselves and those who stood behind them. This was tiring work also and with the press of bodies around them, there was no time to slake their thirst as the sun rose into the sky and the unseasonably warm weather sapped their strength again, as it had done at both Fulford Gate and Stamford Bridge.

Huscarls were made of stern stuff, however. Years of training as a full-time weapons man had given Coenred a body of powerful muscular strength on which he could call in such moments. His class of warrior were all rich men, at least rich enough to be able to indulge the time necessary to become experts in fighting with swords, spears, and axes. That was the obligation that came with their position. Coenred was indeed wealthier than most but he had very little free time to enjoy the benefits of his position in that respect. He left that indulgence to his younger brother and their mother who occupied his estate in the Isle of Holderness. If he survived this day, however, he would join them on that estate and be with Mildryth. That was what he would do.

If he survived this day.

***

"Cavalry!" The Duke of Normandy barked. He did not wait to hear his command communicated through the blasts of trumpets; instead, he spurred his horse forward. His personal guard was momentarily caught unawares and had to follow quickly after him.

Guillaume had spent a considerable amount of time in the rear of the army trying to get an impression as to what was happening generally. He had come to the conclusion that the Saxons were stuck like a granite boulder to the top of that wretched hill. What he did know was that the archers had failed to have any discernible impact on Harold's formation. Their arrows had sailed either aimlessly over the top of those helmeted heads or sunk harmlessly into their shields. Hardly a man up there had suffered so much as a scratch.

The infantry had not fared much better. They had lost men on the climb up the hill, cut down by those disciplined volleys of missiles. The shield wall had withstood the impact of their attack and, although Guillaume did not doubt that his men would account for some Saxon blood today, it was clearly taking too long to have any detrimental effect on the enemy's will to fight.

None of this was a surprise, however. Guillaume had had Normans in the court of King Edward for many years and he had used them to assess the military strength of the Saxons. Unlike many, he had never underestimated their tenacity or love of fighting. They were a hardy people who had fought for their lives against the Vikings for many generations. The fact that they were still here and in command of a unified country suggested that they had the mettle for the task of survival. That was what these Saxons truly were, great survivors.

His one hope was a particular military tactic that the Saxons, like their close enemies the Norse, had never mastered; the use of the horse in combat. Guillaume drew his sword and raised it into the air. It was a signal as he pushed through the ranks of horsemen who had been waiting patiently in front of him. They understood and their many trumpets announced the advance. The horseman started forward at a walk with the Duke of Normandy slightly ahead of them and quickly being surrounded by his guard. They were at the centre of the Norman line but through the use of the trumpets, both the left and right flanks were following suit.

Guillaume studied the ground closely and knew instinctively that it was not good terrain for a cavalry charge. They were beginning to traverse an incline that would stop them building momentum. No charge began at the gallop as that was where they hopefully ended. To move too quickly to the full charge was to risk the horses being blown and failing in strength or the formation becoming fragmented and losing the weight of its impact. A good commander of the horse had to know exactly when to move to the next stage of the attack. Normally, the Norman knights would plunge into the full gallop some 50 yards from the enemy lines, which was a distance that would allow them to both build up speed and retain cohesion, but that was over relatively flat ground. Charging uphill would not be so effective.

They moved to the trot, their harnesses jingled as they progressed towards the men struggling up on the hill. The trumpets sounded again but it was a different signal. The tired infantrymen heard it as a call to disengage in good order. They stepped backwards, away from the enemy but still facing them. If they hoped for the Saxons to unwittingly follow they were dismayed to see the formidable shield wall remain exactly where it was. Its position was marked now by the bodies of fallen Norman soldiers. The infantry continued their slow back step, shields and weapons directed still towards the Saxons for this was not a retreat. They understood that the cavalry was coming and that they had to give the knights room to launch their attack. They had been trained for many months in this manoeuvre, to step back in good discipline and open up their lines to allow the horsemen through. They used the ordered respite to regain their strength so that when the knights fell upon their enemy the spearmen could charge forward once again and lend their support to the attack.

***

"And now the fateful test!" King Harold observed.

"Their knights on horseback," Osfrid nodded. "We have withstood everything else so far, we can withstand this."

"We Saxons know how to fight men on foot, for that is our way also, but against men on horseback, we are mostly untried. Some may take fear at the sight."

"Any who would doubt the strength of the shield wall before the advance of a horse is not worthy to call himself a Saxon!" Osfrid insisted.

"Mayhap, my friend, but the damage would be done all the same."

"Fear thee not, My Lord, our men will stand."

"Have thee ever fought from a horse?" Thrydwulf asked in his gruff voice.

"Once, in Wales," Coenred replied. They were all of them momentarily resting, taking the unexpected chance to do so now that the disengaging Norman infantry had given them it, but also well aware of the approaching riders. "We were attacked by Welsh raiders once while heading to Hereford; they minded not that the King of Wales was in our column. There was no time to dismount and join them hand to hand, that was the way the Welsh liked to fight, sudden attacks, take their enemy by surprise."

"And how did thee find it, fighting from a horse?"

"Difficult. You are higher from the ground and your sword has not the desired reach. Also, the horses liked it not, they would move under you without warning and change direction constantly. It made using a spear all the harder."

"These Norman nags be not of the same breed as those Welsh ponies I reckon."

"Nay, they say the Normans breed these horses to war so that they will do what is asked of them, even before our bright spear points. All the same, a knight without his horse is just another warrior afoot so if you can strike at the horse and bring it down that would be the way to do it. Mayhap it will roll the rider into the dust also."

"Sound counsel!"

"I have a liking for horses," Hengist added.

"That thee may, but think not of the beast but of the man he bears on his back who wants to kill thee!" Thrydwulf barked back.

"You would do right by that," Coenred agreed.

Edwin peered over the shoulders of the huscarls in front of him and tried to spy out the movement of the men on horses. It was something to be marvelled at. He could see the Norman soldiers who had now opened a gap between themselves and the unmovable Saxons. Beyond them, he saw the mounted men, their bodies rocking in time to the gait of their horses. The sun was glinting on their armour. Some carried spears with small colourful pennants attached just below the head of the weapon.

Above the young shield-bearer fluttered the green banner of the Eorl of Holderness. It had remained untouched so far, not even pierced by an arrow. Edwin had procured the green cloth in London but it had been one of the fyrdmen who had painted the white figure upon it. For some reason just seeing the banner held aloft raised his spirits.

***

Guillaume spurred his horse to the canter and noted that it struggled at first due the gradient of the hill. He wondered for a moment if he had left the decision too late, but then dismissed the notion as there was nothing now that he could do about it. Within a couple of strides, however, the horse picked up speed. They approached the rear ranks of the infantry. Arrows flew again over their heads, hoping to catch unwary Saxons out of position. All along the front, the cavalry came, the three beats of their gait drummed out on the dry earth beneath them.

It was just before he had cleared the front ranks of the infantry that Guillaume spurred his horse one last time and drove it to the gallop. It seemed to cover the remaining ground before the impressive shield wall in a heartbeat. It actually took long enough for him to see the enemy's shields rise a little higher and for the spears to drop to a level where they could unhorse an unwary knight. He saw also the dark shadows of more throwing spears and large stones that were suddenly unleashed upon them.

Guillaume had tried to aim for the centre of the shield wall, towards the famous banner of Harold of Wessex, but his course had drifted to the left somewhat. He did not try to correct it but let his steed have its head in the final few strides. With his sword in the air and his shield hanging on his left arm, the Duke of Normandy joined the fray.

***

Coenred had nothing but his instincts to guide him in this encounter. His years of training and hard experienced and honed them to the point where he reacted to combat almost without thinking. Although he was very aware of the danger posed to him, and all the other warriors on the hill, he remained steady. He hefted his shield a little higher in anticipation of the approaching knights' attack and drew his fighting spear back, holding it overarm.

The horses came on, spurred to the gallop. Norman trumpets sounded, rough and raucous to his ears. And bright pennants flew from just below the horsemen's spearheads. It seemed as if the cavalry would just ride roughshod over the top of the shield men. As the gap closed some Saxon warriors took to shouting loudly and waving their weapons in a threatening manner. It seemed to work. At the last moment, the warhorses veered either left or right. Some even stopped suddenly. For some lucky riders, their steeds reared upon their hind legs before the many brightly painted shields and protruding spears. They kicked out with their forelegs at the obstacle before them but did little damage. For the unlucky, however, the abrupt stopping of their steeds was not so harmless. As their mounts lowered their heads and dug in their hooves they propelled any unwary riders out of their saddles. One such somersaulted over his horse's head and landed on his back on top of the enemy shields. He slid to the ground before them and was pierced by several spears before he could recover his feet. The same fate met other riders who lost their seats in a similar fashion and lay before the spears of their enemies for a frightening heartbeat before they were quickly dispatched.

Most of the horses turned sideways to the shield wall, however, and continued to run along its length. Daneaxes and spears lashed out at them but few were successful in hitting a telling mark. The Saxons simply were not prepared for this type of combat.

Coenred saw the horse in front of him rear up, the knight on its back gripping the reins with one hand, his knees closing on the saddle so as to help him maintain his seat, whilst at the same time he tried to stab downwards with his spear. With a deft lunge, the huscarl sent his own weapon forward. He had less to consider in performing this manoeuvre than the mounted Norman. He also had a bigger target to aim at. The sharp spear point cut into the horse's point of shoulder. It screamed in pain and turned on the spot before hurtling away. The knight managed to keep his seat but was forced to drop his spear. Hurting the horse did not make Coenred feel good about the incident, but he had reasoned correctly that doing so had removed an immediate danger for no cost to either himself or his men.

Standing close with a man on his left and right, and wearing his heavy steel helmet with the long cheek-guards, Coenred's peripheral vision was somewhat limited. Mayhap, it was his instincts, heightened by the rush of violence, that prompted him to turn slightly to the left and there he saw the knight racing along the shield wall. Without stopping to consider the action Coenred mentally fixed a spot just before him in open space. As the horse took another stride the huscarl sent his long fighting spear flashing forward once again.

Guillaume felt hot inside his armour. The din of combat was muffled by his helmet and the sound of his blood pumping wildly in his ears. He felt no fear, only the thrill of the moment. He had had no time to assess his position or the effectiveness of the charge or the position of the troops or anything else that did not immediately relate to keeping in his saddle and keeping his sword swinging. The Saxons to his right seem to blur into a wash of bright colours, shining steel, and dull leather, as the horse dashed past them. He exulted in it. The moment made him feel alive, mayhap even more so knowing that death was close at hand. He opened his mouth to shout again, to yell loudly and incoherently. It was an animal instinct to which he responded, not a desire to give a command or issue a challenge.

His world suddenly lost all vestige of distinction as it abruptly blurred before him. He felt a strange force take him, something violent and unthinkably swift. He was propelled forwards and upwards. An impression of more colours flew before his eyes, green, red, dirty brown. It was all too fast to make any sense out of, to form any understanding of what was happening. He was aware of something hurtling towards him. Mayhap he screamed. There was a dull collision, a moment of being aware of a pain in his face, and then everything went black.

Coenred's spear had started forward when the space before it was empty but that void had suddenly been filled by the large and powerful body of a horse. The bright steel pierced the animal at its elbow, slicing through muscle and nicking the bone of its right foreleg. Huscarls learnt to twist and withdraw their spears as soon as they felt the point pierce into muscle, otherwise, they risked the spearhead being caught in the heavy flesh. They also risked losing their weapon that way. The horse was moving much faster than a warrior on foot might normally be expected to do so, however, and though he pulled back on the shaft the animal's momentum drew the weapon sideways so that it collided with the Saxon stood to his right. Nevertheless, the spearhead came free. The horse lost its footing, its right leg collapsing just as it put its weight onto that limb. It crashed to the earth throwing its rider into the air. He arced for several feet. Then the knight came down violently face first onto the ground. Edwin led the Saxons behind Coenred in cheering their delight at the spectacle.

Henry of Rouen reacted to the fall of the duke with impressive alacrity. He had seen Guillaume's horse being speared and knew that a Saxon would step forward to end the nobleman's life with a downward swing of his axe as soon as the duke's body stopped moving. Desperately, he turned his horse, exposing its flank and himself to the deadly spears and swords of the enemy, and then covered the short distance to Guillaume's inert form. His own steed vaulted the duke's injured animal and as is it came down Henry saw a Saxon warrior was indeed raising a bright Dane-axe over the stunned nobleman. Relying on the horse's momentum Henry collided his steed with the man, who had no warning of its sudden arrival. The Saxon careened away, injured and stunned himself.

Using the animal's bulk Henry shielded the duke, turning his horse on the spot. Guillaume rose to his hands and knees, spitting earth and grass out from his mouth, blood was flowing freely from his nose.

In a moment other members of the duke's bodyguard had arrived. Young Phillip jumped to the ground and unceremoniously heaved Guillaume to his feet. With even less ceremony he pushed the heavy man up and into the saddle, which he had just vacated, and then gave the reins to one of his companions. Guillaume somehow managed to get his feet into the stirrups but lolled alarmingly on the back of the animal, his head hanging low and blood dribbling from his face.

"Get thee gone!" Phillip shouted. "Retire behind the lines!" He drew his sword and turned to face the Saxons, expecting warriors to fall upon them imminently.

It was only when the other knights arrived that Coenred realised that he had successfully struck at some important personage. They risked their own lives to save that of the fallen man like a huscarl would his lord. He was suddenly taken by the temptation to break the line and slay the man who had fallen, even as the other Normans were helping him onto the horse. Clearly, he was a nobleman of some repute. However, the horse that he had struck had fallen several yards to his right and the rider had been thrown some more yards further onwards. To leave his position in the shield wall would be to open a breach with no guarantee of either him being able to kill the fallen rider by the time he got to him or another heavily armoured man taking his place. Training and experience got the better of him. The huscarl kept his position and missed his opportunity to kill the Duke of Normandy.

***

"The duke is injured unto death!"

The word seemed to fly through the ranks of the Norman infantrymen with alarming speed. Someone had seen the pennant of the Duke of Normandy being carried amongst a huddle of several riders and there, also, they had seen a bleeding Guillaume struggling to remain in the saddle as he was led down the hill and away to the rear of the army.

The duke was injured and mayhap even dead.

The Bretons on the left flank did not continue to fall back in good order. At the news that their commander was believed to be fatally wounded, they rather turned and fled. Archers and infantrymen alike presented their backs to the Saxons and ran on tired legs towards the road that they knew led back to Hastings and the presumed safety of their wooden castle. There was no discipline or order to them, it was a route. The knights on the left flank became aware that the infantry that should have been supporting their attack was no longer present. They turned to see their men fleeing and, mayhap one or more of them, heard also the shouts that Duke Guillaume was dead. Faced with an unsupported charge against the fearsome Saxon shield wall, and one that had lost its impetus at that, the cavalry also turned and began to chase after the disappearing infantry.

Leofwine felt his spirit soar. He raised his bright sword into the air and whooped. Without hesitation, he left his position at the front of the shield wall and began to run down the hill. His bodyguard followed suit and with them came a host of young and overexcited warriors. Only the older and more experienced remained where they had been told to hold their ground.

Within several speedy strides, Leofwine found himself within a sword's reach of a tired Breton and he hacked into the man's unprotected back. The coppery smell of blood filled his nostrils as the soldier fell with a pathetic scream. The prince turned a blood spattered face onto the Saxons behind him and screamed a way cry as an encouragement for them to follow him and sink their weapons into more of their enemies.

***

"Continue the attack!"

"My Lord?" Henry of Rouen leant closer from his own horse. He had seen the duke's lips move but he had not heard what might have been said. Guillaume repeated himself, raising his head a little and looking at the other from the corner of his eyes. He realised that he was mumbling.

"Continue the attack!" He spoke louder and forced himself to sit up straighter in the saddle, pulling his head up. He spat more blood from his mouth, his teeth were stained with dirt mixed with awful scarlet. More blood ran freely from his swollen nose. He turned a terrible visage to look directly at Henry. "Keep pressing the Saxons. Don't let them recover their breath!"

"The Bretons have turned and are running!" Luc, another member of the bodyguard, shouted. He was looking back over his shoulder

"Damn them!" Guillaume cried and winced at the pain that shot through his head. His face felt numb and he had a headache, but he did not seem to have been injured in any other way. It was the shock of the fall, he told himself. The sudden impact with the ground had knocked him senseless. It was not the first time that he had had a horse killed under him. "Steady them, Henry, lead a troop forward and steady them."

"As you wish." Henry nodded his understanding.

He turned his horse and shouted for men to follow him. He did not know or care if they owed him allegiance or not. What he did understand, however, was both what the Duke of Normandy had asked of him and the significance of the proposed action. He, Henry of Rouen, had to stop the left flank from collapsing. If he allowed it to give then the battle was lost.

***

Leofwine paused where he now stood, almost half way down the hill, to rest a moment. He had reached a small hillock that protruded like a boil on the side of the ridge. Taking in several deep breaths to refresh himself after the mad charge down the incline, Leofwine glanced around to get an idea of where he was and how many of the enemy still remained to him. His sword was stained with blood and he was not alone, almost a thousand fyrdmen had followed him and they had cut and slashed at the fleeing Normans.

He would give victory to his elder brother this day and maybe then Harold would start treating him like the man he was, a warrior and a noble.

"NO!" Gyrth yelled from the top of the ridge.

He had just returned to his position, which had been nominally alongside that of his younger brother. For barely a moment, Gyrth had wandered along the lines to ensure that the shield wall was holding well, that the men were not slacking or becoming too tired. They were doing as they had been commanded to do, they were holding their line. The same could not be said for Leofwine.

Gyrth could see his brother standing on the hillock below them, somewhere about half way between the main Saxon formation and the retreating enemy, only not all of the enemy were now retreating. From his elevated position, Gyrth could see that a force of horsemen and infantry were pushing forward and trying to rally the fleeing troops. They were having some success as the disheartened men slowed their flight and responded to the calls from nobles and peasant soldiery alike.

***

The Duke of Normandy leant forward and spat bloody water onto the ground. He wiped his mouth and returned the flask to his aid. Feeling much better, despite the ache in his head, Guillaume replaced his helmet and drew his sword. His visage was grim and his intent determined. He had a battle to rescue from the cusp of despair.

It was not just the Bretons on the left that were faltering; the French on the right had also begun a retreat, although in much better order. The word had gone around that he was dead. No one would listen to the voices of desperate men trying to convince them otherwise. In part, this suggested to Guillaume that the majority of the army actually had no heart for this fight. It might even be that they almost wished him dead so that they could retire back to Normandy and their lives there. Within the boundaries of the duchy, there would be no kind of life waiting for Guillaume if he dared to return after being defeated here. He knew this to be true, without a shadow of a doubt, his enemies at home and in greater France would fall upon him without mercy.

Death would be kinder to him than defeat.

At this moment he had no idea how he might even achieve a victory, but that was not important. No, what was important was securing the resolve of the army. The only way he could do that now was to reveal to them that he was not yet dead and so he set forward, veering to the right to help Eustace, the Count of Boulogne, steady his men. The situation was serious and confusion rife. Guillaume ordered that his bannermen should ride immediately behind him. One carried a red flag with two yellow lions embroidered upon it, his ducal standard, and the other was a papal cross; the banner of Pope Alexander II. With trumpets sounding, Guillaume led his entourage through the centre to cheer his stout Normans, who had yet to take a step backwards, and then to the right flank to assist Eustace, and finally over to the left in the hope that Henry of Rouen had reversed their situation there.

With a loud cry, Guillaume set forward again. His heart remained untouched by fear and his voice called to one and all to hear him, to see him, to know that he still commanded the army this day.

***

In their tight formation of the shield wall the Saxons appeared to be invulnerable but out here, on the side of the hill, formed up loosely and with no knowledge of how to defend themselves against armoured knights carrying long spears on fast moving horses, the fyrdmen were there for the slaughtering.

Henry of Rouen led his men into their ranks as the Saxons attempted to climb the hill again. It seemed that they had already killed more of the English in these brief few minutes than the entire army had since the battle had commenced at nine in the morning. The cavalry wheeled and dashed amongst the fleeing men, stabbing with their spears or slashing down with their swords. Some of the fyrdmen turned to fight, they were brave souls, there was no doubt about that, but to do so was also a mistake. As they concentrated on avoiding the knights many failed to see the spearmen following close behind the cavalry. They were surrounded and cut down without mercy.

Eorl Leofwine called the men to him and they came as well as they could, harried as they were. Together they formed a circle on the hillock but their numbers were pitifully few now.

Gyrth could sense the disaster about to be enacted before them, even as he led a small relief force down the hillside. His instinct told him that this was a mistake, but his mind was overwhelmed by his sense of duty. Leofwine was his brother when all was said and done. He was hot-headed, rash, not the brightest of Godwinson's mayhap, but a brother all the same. Gyrth could not surrender him to the fate that wyrd appeared to have decreed. He doubted very much that Harold could have done so either. And so here he was with two hundred huscarls of his own bodyguard, plunging down the hill in what seemed like a vain attempt to rescue Leofwine. He could have brought the whole of the right flank with him but Harold had been adamant; stay and hold.

Stay and hold.

Mounted knights dashed by on all sides it seemed, their spears jabbing, swords slashing, pennants fluttering. The hooves of the horses beat out a merciless refrain. Spurs jingled. Steel clanged against steel or thudded into wood or bit into flesh. Men cried in anger and in pain and in dismay. Blood made the footing treacherous and the stench of split bowels and spilt intestines filled the air. Red and brown stained the hillside; the poets called this glory.

Eorl Leofwine shouted for his men to form a shield wall again and again, but he was aware that this was futile. They were too few in numbers and the enemy too many. Still, he encouraged his Saxons to fight. For a brief moment, amongst the chaos of battle, he found an instance of lucidity and into it sprang the half-remembered face of his youngest brother, Wulfnoth, kidnapped by the Normans so many years ago. Why he thought of him, Leofwine would not have been able to explain at any time either during or after the battle. He did not care to ponder upon it but just smiled to himself because he missed his younger brother and always had. Wulfnoth had been given as a hostage, an assurance of obedience, by their father, Eorl Godwin, to King Edward. A Norman priest had spirited the boy away from the court and over to Normandy where he had remained, treated like royalty but a prisoner all the same.

Leofwine never saw the sword that struck the side of his head. It was like a flash of light against a dark cloud of a shape that shot past, all blurred and indistinct. The helmet protected his head, as it was designed to do, but his vision blurred and he lost his sense of balance. Instinctively, holding onto his gold embellished sword, Leofwine staggered forward and tottered through the thin ranks of men before him. A roar filled his ears, like the sea on a windy day, but rougher and yet duller at the same time, as if it was angry and yet far away. A movement, all blurry as if he were looking through tears, caught his attention. He saw a young face, bright eyes, and felt a fire suddenly leap into his stomach.

It was a curious feeling. His head was ringing still and his abdomen was full of pain. He remembered feeling hot, but a moment ago, yet now he felt cold. He looked down at the spear that pierced his coat of mail. Leofwine felt far removed from the sensations of his body as if they were happening to someone else. The young Breton pulled on his spear and was shocked to see the Saxon warrior stumble towards him, the large round shield still on his left arm, the sword hanging limply from his fingers. As if he were faced with something hideous the boy pushed again with the spear and then let go of the weapon. Leofwine staggered back a step or two and then collapsed to the ground. He rolled onto his left side, pulled by the weight of the shield that was still fastened in his grip. His head lolled and his eyes were open but there was no light in them anymore.

There were very few of the men left who had followed Leofwine when Gyrth reached the hillock. He had known that would be the situation anyway, but some perverse desire to spite wyrd was driving him forward. It was as if he knew that he was going to die here and yet did not care. A reckless foolishness. This was not Gyrth's usual demeanour. He was a man who knew and appreciated his position in life and loved it all the more because of that understanding. He loved his wife and children as well, and the lovers who were not formally bound to him but had given him children all the same.

"Get back!" He shouted to the men behind him.

"My Lord, let us form up!" A huscarl replied.

"Form close but retreat also."

The warriors closed ranks into a semicircle, presenting their spears and shields to the enemy, the many Breton infantrymen, archers, and horsemen that seemingly filled the field before them. The Saxons were all heavily armoured and sure of their strength, but they knew themselves to be exposed. Slowly, very slowly, they edged their way back towards their fellows in the stout shield wall, who even now shouted their encouragements.

Coenred lent his voice to the calls even though he knew that the men before them, so tantalisingly close, were also too far from their brothers to be offered help. He liked the Eorl of East Anglia and willed for the man to return safely to their ranks, but he also knew that there was scant chance of that happening.

"The eorl will make it!" Edwin enthused. Coenred chose not to oppose his opinion. What he saw reminded him of Hereric's brave stand against the Vikings at Fulford Gate. Five hundred huscarls then had not proven to be enough.

Gyrth chose to remain in the front rank as befitted an eorlderman. He was a Godwin and proud of his family. Aethelings were the best of men, a fact that they had to prove with actions and not just with words. Their rank gave them obligation as well as privilege. Eorl Gyrth had never shirked his responsibilities and he would not do so now, even when faced with several thousand of the enemy and only a couple of hundred men at his own command.

The Normans prodded and probed the Saxon formation but they were themselves much tired by the running that they had done, both away from and then back towards their enemy again. The fighting had also taken its toll on all of them. Even the horses of the knights were blown and showed no interest in moving any faster than a slow trot. Everyone was exhausted and so no one felt like putting themselves to the trial of combat again so readily.

And then the arrow hit.

Gyrth felt the blow before the pain. Shot from close range the archer, whether by design or by luck, missed the broad wooden shield and pierced the mail vest of the Saxon noblemen. A second later and Gyrth fell backwards, all of his great strength left him in an instant. His huscarls caught him as he collapsed and covered his body with theirs, his place in the wall instantly taken by another. They laid him gently upon the soiled earth but he was already dead before they had finished making him comfortable.

In battle, it seemed that the invisible spoke and broached the news abroad before any mortal could possibly know of the event. It had happened at Stamford Bridge when the King of Norway, the War Wolf himself, had been slain, also by a single arrow. All had known in an instant that a champion had fallen. Then, the Saxons had stepped back and let the Norse take the body of their king. They had taken the chance to recover their breath and offer a truce. Today, it seemed that the spirits were against the Saxons for the Normans received the news of the death of Eorl Gyrth as if it were an incitement to more blood-letting. They did not step back and give space and time in acknowledgement of a fallen hero, they came on instead all the bloodier and more determined to kill their enemies.

A huscarl would give his life to protect his lord, but if that lord should die on the field of battle then the huscarl would remain until either he or all of his lord's enemies were dead also. The huscarls remained.

From up on top of the hill thousands of Saxons' eyes watched as a few hundred men turned on several thousand, each like a wolf before a pack of hounds. All knew the futility of the fight. All knew the outcome before the first Saxon sword fell on a Norman's head, but they all knew also that every huscarl would make a fine account in blood before his own life was taken.

***

"So many men have fallen," Bishop Odo insisted, "it is a Christian act to allow for their bodies to be recovered. My priests will perform the last rites, bathe their battered limbs, and account for each man of quality that has given his life for you this day."

"And let the Saxons on their accursed hill recover their strength?" Robert de Vitot countered passionately. Like everyone else, his armour and surcoat were spoiled by the battle.

"I would wager that we are the more tired," the Count of Mortain replied. "The cessation would profit us far more than Saxons who refuse to move from their ridge. They are not the ones that have marched up and down the damned thing!"

"And to think," Guillaume added. "We need time to think."

"Think on what?" de Vitot asked.

"On how to win this battle!" Guillaume's temper rose to the fore. "In case any of you had failed to see it, King Harold's flag still flies from that accursed ridge and we have moved him not a foot. Odo, send an embassy of your priests to the Saxons and tell them that we will collect the bodies of our fallen lords under the protection of a truce, they are to do the same without hindrance. While that is happening I want my war council to ponder the problem before us."

***

A scattered row of priests may have seemed like an incongruous means of enforcing a respite in the fighting, but it was one to which both the Normans and the Saxons gave nothing but respect. The Norman priests wandered in a somewhat disconsolate manner as men from both sides came to claim their dead, or at least the bodies of people who had enjoyed some renown and importance whilst alive. As both sides were Christian the priests also gave blessings to those who were injured or close to death or both. In their own way, they brought what little relief they could and their presence dulled the intent for violence that the two armies harboured for one another.

"This is a sad turn," Osfrid said, voicing the thoughts of many.

He looked down on the bodies of both Gyrth and Leofwine. He had liked the Eorl of East Anglia particularly, most men who had met him in life had. Gyrth had been a man under no illusions concerning himself. He had been one of Eorl Godwin's many sons, with no particular claim to anything other than the earldom he had been granted. Sound in counsel, wise beyond his years even, brave in combat, and a proven loyal supporter of his elder brother, Harold. There had been much to admire about Gyrth Godwinson. All they had now was his bloodied corpse.

Osfrid had not known Leofwine nearly as well, but the man was of a different age. There had not been anything particularly remarkable about him, either good or bad, concerning his character at least. The worst that could be said about the young eorl was that he had often tried too hard to impress his elder siblings. The best was that he had proven loyal to his heritage.

"Tostig's death I could bear, he turned upon his own in his anger and poison, but this is more than any man should be asked to endure!" Harold said in a cold voice. "Three brothers have I lost in but a month, one a nithing, true, but Godwin blood all the same. You say Leofwine left the ridge?"

"Aye, so I am told. He thought he saw a chance to plunge his sword in the backs of the Normans, they were fleeing, it is true, but they rallied and turned on him."

"Eorl Leofwine believed that the battle was to be won in but a moment when the Normans did indeed turn and run from the field," Coenred added. "There were some lords amongst the Normans, however, who turned their men and rejoined the fight. Eorl Leofwine misjudged the situation."

"And Gyrth?"

"Went to try and rescue Leofwine. By the time had reached his brother he was already dead. He stayed to protect his body." Coenred told them all.

"A gesture as noble as it was pointless."

"What would you have us do?" A Royal Companion asked.

"What would I have you do?!" Harold's voice rose. "I would have you avenge my brothers here!"

"There is an opportunity to parley with the Normans." The man continued as if he could not hear the anger in his king's voice.

"Why would I want to talk to them?" Harold's face was almost white with anger.

"Because that is what kings and other aethelings do," Osfrid said simply, facing Harold without any trepidation. Of all those present he was, mayhap, the only one who truly did not fear his lord.

"Guillaume is not an aetheling, a Norman duke, nothing more."

"But he has us pinned upon this hill."

"And we have him pinned at the foot of it. He can go no further into England."

"He might not wish to if you could come to terms."

"You forget; I tried that already. He is headstrong and twisted by his desire for the crown; my crown."

"I agree, My Lord, but there is something to consider." Coenred stepped forward a pace.

"What?!" Harold spat back.

"We thought the Normans were coming with some great power to take the crown by force but, what they show us here today is a fyrd no larger than that which we have hastily called to your banner. Given time we could swell these ranks of ours. Men would come knowing that you have stopped the Normans here, that their vaunted prowess in battle can be bettered by Saxons."

Harold opened his mouth to speak but suddenly thought better of it. He turned away from his Royal Companions and looked once more on the bodies of his brothers. He knew that there were more corpses, men not as notable as an eorl, left out there on the hillside where they had fallen. He could spare more lives if he followed the counsel given to him and he could even see some merit in what had been said. If the battle were ended this day then talks might recommence again. In the time given to do the talking, mayhap more Saxon spears would come to his aid while his fleet denied the Normans the same opportunity to resupply their own hurt numbers. He would grow stronger while Guillaume would grow weaker, but Guillaume was not a fool. Harold knew this to be true.

The King of England had seen closely how Guillaume operated in a dangerous political world. Thanks to his own failed adventure to ransom his younger brother, Wulfnoth. The duke was far too experienced to fall for such an obvious subterfuge as Osfrid and Coenred were suggesting to him, he believed.

Besides, in the several hours of fighting the Normans had inflicted no great hurt upon them. Gyrth and Leofwine were dead because they had ignored his orders to remain at the top of the hill. Gyrth he could forgive because his disobedience had been provoked by family loyalty. Leofwine he would take longer to absolve as his actions had led to the death of Gyrth, but in time he would make peace with his younger brother's spirit. This was really the sum total of all that was lost, two eorls and maybe two thousand men. Thousands more remained to him and their position on the hill had not weakened. The Normans had made no headway against them and they seemed to lack any idea how to do so. Indeed, as both Osfrid and Coenred had told him, Leofwine had been prompted by the sight of the Norman soldiers retreating, fleeing the field in fear of the Saxons.

He thought some more on that. The Normans had come close to surrendering the battle once already. If the Saxons continued their resistance and, mayhap, even claim the life of one of their nobles in turn, then victory could still be theirs.

"We stay!" Harold announced to his companions. Osfrid nodded his understanding and said no more. "We stay on this hill until the Normans are defeated. Let the men eat and drink and rest as they are wont to do. Let the Normans claim their dead unhindered. We will wait until they are finished and are ready to resume the fight again but spread this word, Osfrid, and all of you here, tell the eorls and the theigns; no one is to leave the hill again. This is where we stand and this is where we die if that is what God wills, but no one sets foot beyond the shield wall!"

***

"Is this all that you have to offer me?" Guillaume snarled at his war council. He looked around at their faces, stained with sweat and dirt and a little blood. They all looked tired, resigned even; resigned to defeat that was. That was the thing that galled him the most. He was tired and hurt as well, but he was not yet ready to surrender the day. It was too soon for that.

"They may as well be in a castle on top of that hill, their shields hold like a wall!" Robert de Vitot complained.

"Then we break them like castle walls!"

"How? We have no siege engines!"

"Our archers make no impact, our infantry cannot overcome them, and our knights lack the mobility before their spears to ride them down. We can find no way past this obstacle." The Count of Evreux asserted to common consent.

"Our runners did!" Alan the Red observed.

"Runners! What means you, runners?" Guillaume demanded of him.

"My men, though it shames me to admit it. Like all others on this field, they failed before the Saxon shields and they will continue to do so as long as these obstinate English stick to their hill, but then, when they began to run, when they turned thinking that you were dead, My Lord, the Saxons followed."

"And we cut them down where they stood!" Henry of Rouen added with a note of energy that was sadly missing from everyone else, or so it appeared.

"Yes," Alan nodded, "once out of their formation they proved easy to overcome."

"What you suggest will not be so easy to do again, when men are seen to run from a battle fear can fly faster than an arrow and cause others to flee also." The Count of Mortain observed. "We saw only a moment ago how the news of your presumed death weakened the resolve of many a man on that field."

"And yet there is some truth in what Alan the Red says," Guillaume countered.

"Yes, My Lord, but some danger also."

"We are fighting for our lives, danger cannot be escaped!"

"I meant only that the men are not trained to do this thing that I believe Alan the Red is suggesting."

"Our situation is simple," Robert, Count of Mortain, spoke up once more, "either we spill our blood needlessly on the tips of Saxon spears or we bring them down from their stronghold and spill their blood at our feet. The Bretons momentarily lost their nerve and fled the field-" Alan's face coloured to match his hair but Robert pressed on so as to deny him the opportunity to speak "-and drew some Saxons down upon them. Lord Henry was able to turn those same Bretons back on our enemy and inflict a hurt of kinds. Nothing else has worked, but if we do this thing again, and mayhap even again after that, then the Saxon shield wall might weaken enough for our knights to break through it!" Robert raised his voice as he finished speaking, giving his words some dramatic effect. It did not take too much perception to realise that the resolve of these men was bending and may give without so much as a moment's notice.

A heavy silence descended upon the impromptu council of war. Each noble was suddenly consumed by his own thoughts, but the Duke of Normandy did not like this situation. It seemed to him that they had already spent many months in councils, debating the same points over and over, and all that talk had brought them to was this; more talking. No one had any other form of action, no clever ruse or tactic, to offer; nothing useful. There was a time to talk and there was a time to act; clearly talking would not achieve anything now. Harold would remain where he was on that damned hill, knowing full well that just in doing so he was frustrating Guillaume's plans. He had bent everything to bring Godwinson to battle, understanding that only in defeating the Saxon King could he lay a proper claim to the throne, and that success would not be achieved by either talking or thinking.

"We will do it!" He announced his decision firmly and loudly. "Instruct your men, all of you, on all three sides, engage the Saxons, fight them, then turn and run. Lure them out and then, when the knights strike, turn and support them. Do this thing if you still wish to claim a prize this day."

"My Lord-" Robert de Vitot began to complain but the duke turned on him swiftly.

"You have something better to offer?" Guillaume demanded in his most authoritative tone.

"No-"

"Then hold your tongue and do as I command of you!" He roared like a lion. "All of you. Commit to this plan and save our day, for if you fail me in this thing then you had better hope that it is a Saxon spear that finds you before I do!"

***

"The princes are dead!" Hengist repeated again.

"Men die in battles, even princes," Thrydwul told him from where he still stood in the shield wall. His great round shield was resting on the ground, the top of the rim leaning against his legs. He held his tall fighting spear with two hands and leaned on it absently.

"Eorl Leofwine was young and misread the action of the enemy, he thought that they were fleeing," Coenred added.

"They were fleeing," the youngest of the huscarls insisted.

"Yes, but not all of them. Those that still held their ground were the ones who turned the tide, this is why fyrdmen should not move until commanded to do so."

"Eorl Leofwine commanded them."

"And King Harold commanded his brother," Thrydwulf growled.

"True enough!" Coenred nodded. He glanced at Aethelmaer who seemed to be staring into the sky and who had yet to speak. "Did you see Eorl Gyrth fall?"

"Aye, it was both noble and foolhardy, if you will forgive me for speaking such of an eorlderman."

"We are huscarls, not peasants!" Thrydwulf spat at the ground beneath his leather soles.

"He went to rescue his brother," Aethelmaer added. "It was a brave death, but I feel it injures us more than any."

"King Harold is still safe and the army is intact. We have lost some good men but not as many as the Normans would wish for and we still stand strong upon this hill."

"That would be it then, to stay on the hill?" Hengist asked.

"Aye lad, we stay where the king put us, on this hill. Do not follow the dead aethelings' example and presume the enemy to be consumed by fear simply because they turn their backs to you. Stand and fight as instructed and if the enemy does break off to run down the hill stay and catch your breath. Sigbert always said he hated running." Thrydwul smiled.

"His belly has grown some in the past year or two; he carries much more weight now!" Aethelmaer brightened at the memory of their absent brother.

"Sigbert will rue missing this day and I tell you this after this foreign duke has been cut down from his horse, we will all of us get a chance to build bellies as round as Sigbert's." Coenred was glad to find a way to lift their spirits.

They had all of them met Eorl Gyrth when he had ridden ahead of the Saxon army come to liberate York from Viking rule and, like many another, they had thought fondly of the man. They knew little if anything about Eorl Leofwine, but one point that they were sure of was that the death of the Eorl of East Anglia would pain their king.

"So we are clear?" Thrydwulf stood straighter and looked around at all of them. "We stay on the hill no matter what. We defend

Coenred who in his turn, as the Eorl of Holderness, defends the king; that is our duty. That is our sworn oath."

"AYE!" Their mixed voices announced their grim intent with a roar.

Coenred felt a moment of discomfort at these words, however. He realised that Thrydwulf had assumed the position of captain of huscarls, a place that had been his in the House of Aelfgar for many years. Thrydulf was a coarse man of peasant stock who had earned his right to wield a huscarl's sword through his strength and bravery. What he lacked in the way of an education, or the kind of manners that might be expected of an eorl's man, he more than made up for with his personal courage, skill as a weapons man, and experience of what it was to be a huscarl. It was clear that both Athelmaer and Hengist were happy with this arrangement also. When they returned to Holderness Coenred would set about acquiring some more men of quality to become huscarls and he would give their training over to Thrydwulf, his captain.

"Is the battle nearly done, My Lord?" Edwin enquired. He looked tired and somewhat haunted. This was only his second battle and the first, the bloody encounter at Stamford Bridge, had robbed him of all notions of glory and heroism before the swords of the enemy.

"No." Coenred shook his head.

"Then why do we wait like this?"

"This is but a respite for both sides. I doubt not that the Normans will be trying to think of some new way to bring us down from this ridge so that their warriors on horseback can wreck their ruin upon us, but we shall not let that happen."

"As if this day filled with death has not been long enough already!"

"'Tis the way of eorldermen to stretch out the day of dying when it's the likes of thee that do the dying!" Thrydwulf told him with a grim smile.

"The banner!" Hengist pointed westwards, over their heads. All turned to see the famous fighting man banner of King Harold moving. The man who had the honour to carry the flag was waving it slowly in the wind so that it could be seen by one and all.

"I would hazard a guess that the time for rest has come to an end." Coenred glanced over the top of the front rows of the shield wall to where he could see the Normans beginning to approach the hill again. "They come. On with your helmets, raise your shields high, and save your strength, but when you get the chance to strike may your aim be true!"

***

The battle recommenced in exactly the same fashion as it had begun in the morning. The archers strode forward and loosed several volleys of arrows into the massed ranks of the Saxons, doing very little hurt in the process. As they fired the infantrymen, armed with spears and swords, for the most part, marched up the hill. Once again they were met with a volley of Saxon missiles. Many of these weapons had been covertly recovered under the guise of removing bodies from the battlefield. The cries of the Bretons, the French, and the Normans rang out once more, quickly followed by battle shouts and foul oaths, and the foreign infantrymen flung themselves onto the shield wall yet again.

The fighting ranged all along the length of the ridge top with seemingly new and more terrible intent. Banners waved and trumpets blew. Swords and spears struck shields and armour and also each other. Arrows sailed overhead, attempting to reach those who stood further back from the front ranks.

How long the struggle raged no one could tell but suddenly, on the Saxons' left flank, the Norman forces began to give way. Their movement followed yet another failed charge by the mounted knights, their leader, spinning his horse on the spot, shouted at his men to retreat with alarm. If anyone noted that he did this in heavily accented English then they did not mark it. They heard what they hoped to hear and saw what they wished to see. The cavalry set off at a gallop down the hill showing no more intent to engage in combat. The infantry hesitated for they were within a spear's thrust of their enemy, but their bodies gave away their failing courage. With tell-tale glances, they looked back to their noble leaders behind them, the men on horses, and stepped backwards away from the fight. When they judged that they had put a reasonably safe distance between themselves and the Saxons the French and the men of Boulogne turned and ran once more. The archers too lowered their bows and began to follow the example set by their betters.

The fyrdmen could not resist. Middle theigns rose to be high theigns by distinguishing themselves in one form or another and the battlefield was the preferred place of many. The same held true for lower theigns and peasants who also hungered for recognition, promotion, and greater wealth. It was the way of the Saxon world, a way that rewarded the man of ability if only he should seize the moment when wyrd offered it to him.

The cautious were never recognised as heroes.

A sudden surge of men carried the front ranks forwards several steps. The more experienced warriors, mostly those holding the front line, tried to resist, but the impetus was too great. The fyrdmen pushed in between their betters and launched themselves down the hill in pursuit of their enemy. They came down with reckless abandon, like wolves on fleeing sheep. They shouted and screamed, waving their weapons in the air, all the time totally heedless to the calls of the men behind them who had remained on the hill and now urged the several thousand warriors to return to the shield wall with impassioned pleas.

When realisation dawned upon the brave but foolhardy fyrdmen it was already too late. They reached the bottom of the rise to be met by a disciplined volley of arrows that pierced their coats of leather and bit into their flesh. As the archers stood in their serried ranks, loosed more volleys the spearman marched forward once more; marched, not ran. They looked firm and determined and unafraid. Their advance was disciplined and directed.

The fyrdmen tried to organise themselves into a formation that could meet the Norman spears but many were out of breath. Some were looking back to the top of the hill as if wishing their fellows would come to their aid. Still, others were attempting to climb up that incline and return to safety, but their backs presented welcome targets to the Norman archers. Even so, the Saxon formation began to take shape, with the heavier armoured warriors pushing their way to the front, but it was too little too late. Before the infantry reached them two groups of knights did, coming from the flanks and just behind the Saxons. They rode into the massed ranks and continued through them, cutting with the steel of their swords and pushing men away with the bodies of their horses. The formation was shattered, men bodily ridden down or hacked from behind. The Norman soldiers fell upon the broken Saxons and cut them down like wheat before the scythe.

Alan the Red enjoyed similar results when he performed the same tactic on the Saxon's right. Guillaume repeated them in the centre with similar results. They lured the warriors out and down the hill to be met with destruction. Despite their several successes, the Duke of Normandy noted that the best of Harold's men, the high-theigns, eorldermen, and the huscarls, remained on the hill. He wondered for a moment if Harold had reserves of troops hidden on the reverse of the slope, troops from which he could make up the men that he had lost, many thousands now to Guillaume's reckoning. The thought momentarily disturbed him as he sat astride his horse at the bottom of the hill, resting from having cut down his own count of Saxon warriors.

If Harold did indeed have reserves hidden away then their task was hopeless. Guillaume simply lacked the numbers to shift the obstinate Saxons from the hill and that was the only way that he could succeed today. All other eventualities would lead only to defeat.

He glanced around him and saw the tired faces of his men. They had been fighting for hours with only one brief break to rest and drink and feed. The Saxons had seemingly not weakened once following each attack. If they had more men up there than his scouts had been able to discover then the Norman's situation was impossible and his choices were simple; attack once more and probably see his army smashed on those thick shields and deadly spears or retreat to Hastings and, mayhap, take ship back to Normandy. To do that would be as good as surrendering his life to his enemies there. He would die, but no more of his men would needlessly do so. But he would die and it would be ignominious. He knew not what to do.

***

"My Lord!" Aethelmaer called out.

He had retired from the front rank after the last attack had ended to slake his thirst. When Edwin had not approached with the water flask, as he had been instructed to do, Aethelmaer had looked for him. He was shocked by what he had seen almost immediately.

Edwin was sat on the floor behind his companions, his face pale and drained. An arrow protruded from the right side of his chest.

Coenred turned and saw the wounded boy. He went to him and knelt down in front of his servant.

"Edwin, can you hear me?" He asked.

"It hurts!" Edwin gasped.

"So few have been hit by arrows this day I did not expect one of us to be so dealt with," Aethelmaer said. "Is it deep?"

"I will see." Coenred removed his helmet so that his sight would not be obstructed. He took hold of the arrow and gently moved it. Edwin cried out and a little blood dribbled onto his chain mail byrnie.

"It moves!" Aethelmaer observed.

"It is not stuck so deep. I will remove it."

"My Lord, no!" Edwin sounded afeard.

"It is the way of it," Aethelmaer told him. "Once the arrow is out we will know how badly hurt you are. I can place a poultice on the wound."

"We can seal it with a hot iron!" Thrydwulf told them.

"Aye, it were best done so." Hengist agreed.

"It will hurt me!"

"It will, but not so much if I do it the huscarl way." Coenred looked meaningfully at Aethelmaer.

The young huscarl rose and made his way over the reverse side of the slope. There he found a fire in which several pieces of metal had been thrust. Many such fires were dotted along the line of the ridge for they were used to cook food and heat tea, as well as irons for the sealing of wounds.

"What is the huscarl way?" Edwin asked between clenched teeth.

Coenred glanced up and saw Aethelmaer trotting back holding an iron that glowed orange at one end. "Quickly!" He said and forcefully pulled the arrow from the boy's chest.

Edwin cried out in pain. Knowing full well what to do Thrydwulf and Hengist jumped to help Coenred. In a moment they had the boy's byrnie off over his head. Then came the padded jacket and finally his shirt. The two huscarls grabbed an arm each and held Edwin down. Aethelmaer passed the glowing iron to Coenred.

"We do this to save your life!" The Eorl of Holderness said. He pressed the hot steel to the wound and the immediate air was filled with the stench of burning flesh.

Edwin screamed louder, but then his voice trailed away. He had pushed forcefully against the hands that held him until his strength ebbed and he fell back against the earth. Coenred raised the hot iron and inspected the blackened site of the arrow wound. There was no fresh blood.

"You have yourself a war wound, boy!" Thrydwulf declared with macabre humour.

"Likely as not it will heal well," Coenred told him.

"Am I not yet dead?" Edwin breathed with his eyes tightly shut.

"You may not know it for such, but this was a kind deed," Aethelmaer told him. "A wound left open often festers."

"What will become of me?"

"It will be a great shame, but you will live," Hengist grinned. "The burn will be sore for many a day, but the arrow did not go too deep, thanks to your armour."

"And you lost hardly any blood!" Thrydwulf enthused.

"But your war-work is done this day," Coenred added.

"My Lord?"

"Edwin, you took an arrow, you cannot fight anymore."

"But you are still here? All of you!" He propped himself up on his elbows.

"We know how to dodge arrows," Hengist said.

"Hengist, will you help Edwin to the rear?" Coenred glanced at the youngest huscarl. He nodded his understanding.

"I can still fight!" Edwin insisted with characteristic bravado.

"Only a fool would choose not to acknowledge the workings of wyrd," Aethemaer told him. "Go you to the camp and fix us an evening meal. Even with an arrow wound, you can do that much for us!"

"My Lord?!" Edwin looked directly at Coenred. The Eorl of Holderness reached out and touselled the boy's hair in a surprisingly affectionate manner.

"Edwin son of Octa, your war-work is done, but your duties to me are not. Go with Hengist to the camp and fix us a meal, as Aethelmaer suggests. Rest your hurt if you have a will to. I would not ask Eanfrid to fight after taking such a hurt and I will not ask it of you. We still have work here to do, but yours is finished. Go and be useful away from the danger here, my friend."

"Come, I will take you!" They all helped Edwin to his feet and gathered up his war-gear for him. He followed the youngest huscarl without another word or backwards glance.

"And we have lost one more of our number," Thrydwulf observed as they returned their attention to the shield wall once more.

"We have lost too many of our number," Aethelmaer remarked.

"The damage is done and we cannot undo it. Best we prepare to receive the enemy once more."

"As you command, My Lord, but what is it that you want of us?" Thrydwulf already had a good idea of what the response would be.

Coenred took only a moment to consider what had come to pass and it filled him with a new fire. He was resolved not to let it happen again.

"Spread the ranks!" He commanded hotly.

"We will stand too thin!" Thrydwul pointed out unnecessarily.

"What else would you have me do?" The huscarl did not flinch before the hot words. He knew that they were neither inspired by nor directed at, himself.

Coenred was angry, like so many other experienced warriors were, at the stupidity of the fyrdmen who had fallen once more for the Norman's ploy of appearing to run for their lives. It was a trick, they all knew it now, but mayhap it might prove to be too late in the day. Several thousand Saxons had run to their deaths down there, but the chief concern of those that remained on the hill was to maintain the shield wall. To do this they had to thin their ranks from five to only three. This was the only way that they could keep the full width of the formation intact, but three ranks may prove pitifully weak when hard pressed by another attack.

The men shuffled sideways so as to make room for the newcomers in the front ranks, men who lacked fine armour and good quality swords. These were warriors would be more vulnerable to enemy spear thrusts and sword strokes. So scant were their numbers that those who blew the war-horns or waved their lord's' banners were told to draw their weapons and take their place in the diminished lines.

"NO MORE MEN SHALL LEAVE THIS PLACE OF STAND!" Coenred shouted for all to hear as he marched back and forth behind them. "Know this, any man who sets one foot forward without being told to do so dooms his brothers to death. This shield wall still stands because all those in it stand together. Leave it and die. Leave it and bring death on us all. NO MORE MEN SHALL LEAVE THIS PLACE OF STAND!"

***

The thought of retreat had never seemed more welcome than it did in that moment. Guillaume was resigned to it. He had gambled everything and lost, that much was clear to him, or so he thought until his eye was captured by a movement. He raised his hand and an aide approached, but the duke did not speak; instead, he watched. He observed and a new understanding dawned on him. All thoughts of retreat suddenly disappeared and instead, like a light in the gloom, a new resolution formed in his mind.

"Call the chief commanders to me, but them only," he told his aide sternly. "Ride quickly, as our very lives depend upon this moment!"

***

"What hour is it?" Harold demanded of anyone who was in earshot.

"By the sun I'd wager somewhere between three and four of the afternoon. The sun will set soon." Osfrid informed him.

"We have been fighting for six hours?" Harold looked incredulous. "That is too long a time for men to be hazarding their lives."

"It gives us hope though."

"Aye, if we can hold until sunset the fighting will cease. Guillaume will be held on the road to London and we will remain in a position of strength."

"It would be wise to send riders now to call for fresh men."

"Our ranks are thin enough!"

"Aye, but there are men who are carrying hurts, they are not hale and hearty enough to hold a shield mayhap, but whole enough to ride a horse; send them!"

Harold nodded. He liked the idea. Injured men could be sent in several directions to encourage local lords and theigns to come with their fyrdmen, even upon the morrow. The news that he had successfully held the Normans here, the much vaunted and much-feared foreigners, would add extra inducement to the words that he would send. The Saxons were practised in the art of defence. They had spent many generations defending themselves successfully against the Norse. When these men he called out to discovered that they had defended their position well against even the Normans then they would come knowing that it was not a lost cause. They would come hoping to be counted amongst the victorious.

"Send the riders, all that we can spare!" Harold commanded. Osfrid stalked off to find someone to give this worthy task to.

The King of England took in a deep breath and stretched his aching limbs. He looked out yet again over the heads of his valiant warriors. They had fought so long for him on this day and still remained stout and true, disdaining the violence of the Normans. He felt proud of them. He also felt regret for those fools who had fallen for the Normans' ploy and had been slain before their countrymen at the base of the hill. That simple trick had robbed him of many men. He hoped that now all those who remained to him would not be persuaded to abandon their place in the false hope of chasing a running Norman to ground. The foreigners would retreat, he was sure of that, but not until their numbers had been shattered upon the Saxon shield wall one last time.

***

"It all comes down to this," Guillaume insisted with a strong voice and a confident air.

"They remain strong," Henry of Rouen insisted. Even his energy and enthusiasm were sapping.

"No. Only seemingly so. Our ruse has thinned their numbers; I saw them rearranging their men. They are no longer as strong as they were."

"But still formidable, we cannot break their shield wall." Count Eustace observed.

"No, we cannot if we go about it in the same way that we have been doing all day," Guillaume accepted. "Indeed, we have been half-wits and I the greatest of them all!" The Duke smiled grimly at them. He noticed that his humour confounded them and that made him smile more warmly. "When we use siege engines do we attack all along the formidable walls of our enemy's stronghold?"

"No, we find the weak point and concentrate our power there," Robert of Mortain replied.

"Exactly!"

"But today, all we have done is strike the Saxons all along their shield wall," Alan the Red observed.

"And been repulsed with many dead for our efforts."

"They will not sally forth to chases us from the field again, I wager!"

"I do not want them to. What we will do is range the archers against them but this will be a feint-" Guillaume spoke forcefully so as to deny his men a chance to interrupt him, "they will keep those Saxons heads down while a thin screen of infantry advances along the width of their position once more, but we will concentrate our cavalry into three massed formations, each one striking its own point in that same shield wall. The remaining infantry will follow and add their weight to the attack. Instead of breaking the Saxons down en-mass, we will puncture them like an arrow through chain mail." Guillaume searched their tired and dirty faces for understanding.

"This has merit!" Count Eustace insisted.

"They may have the strength to resist us even now?"

"You were fooled, as was I," Guillaume answered. "I too thought that Harold might have more men behind the hill from which he was renewing the numbers of those fallen, those fools that we drew down the hill, but the truth is that he has not. Harold has thinned his ranks to maintain his shield wall's full breadth, but it is now lacking in depth. I believe that one or more determined blows, struck like a hammer-fall at weak points, will break their formation and grant us victory!"

Robert, Count of Mortain, looked at his half-brother as if he did not quite know him. Certainly, he had never heard his brother admit to so many faults at any one time before. He wondered if this were some political tactic to keep the nobles on his side, but he could see in Guillaume's eyes a new fire, an excitement almost. He had realised a means of mayhap winning this encounter with the most truculent and obstinate foe that they had yet encountered. His honesty was genuine and his self-deprecation refreshing. He was blaming no one but himself and this attitude was strangely endearing him to the men who often seemed to fear or loathe him.

"This can be done!" Alan the Red agreed.

"Then let's to it. The afternoon wanes and night marches forth upon the hour I wager. Do not let the eventide overtake us while our enemy still stands for we will suffer for it on the morrow. March, my friends, march for our victory and all that that will bring to us, one and all!"

***

"Eorl Coenred!" It was only when King Harold repeated himself that Coenred realised that he was being addressed. To date, he was the only person of significance to really have used his new title.

"My Lord?"

"How goes it here?"

"Tiresome, but the men hold their place of stand." Coenred could not help but notice how tired the king looked. More than that he perceived a shadow behind his eyes, there was a deep sorrow there that was being held in check. This was not the time for personal grief, however. That would come after the battle was done.

"There is not much of the day left, mayhap the Normans will retire before the sun sets?" Harold did not believe the words he spoke himself, but he felt a need to offer even a small crumb of comfort to the men who had fought so hard for him.

Glancing into the sky Coenred saw the first signs of the sun beginning to sink into the west; it would be complete within an hour and totally dark within two. The end was in sight, or so it seemed.

"There is a place to the north of here that some call Malfosse, an old fortification that some of the men have built dykes about to strengthen. I will retire there tonight and I wish that all of my eorldermen attend upon me."

"The evil ditch?"

"Are you superstitious?"

"Not overly."

"Good. If we must remain with the enemy still in the field then there I will hold my council of war, and I want you present to give us the benefit of your experience." As Coenred began to speak Harold held up a hand to stop him. "I know what you would say, that you are but a huscarl despite your recent promotion to eorl, but I have lost so many men of experience and good counsel, I must call all those remaining to me to gather this night. I hold you very much as one of those men, Coenred."

"Yes, My Lord, but I would ask only one thing of you?"

"Which is?" Harold looked a little surprised.

"That I do not come until my men are settled and as comfortable as they may be."

"It is one thing to have the rank of nobility, my friend, it is quite another to act with nobility. Of course, come after you have seen to your men and I will tell the others to follow your good example." With that Harold clapped him on the shoulder, a gesture usually reserved only for the closest of his companions and then turned to wander back to his position.

"You have the goodwill of a king," Thrydwul observed, "may he have the goodwill of God and then we all may be saved!"

***

It was one last throw of the die, Guillaume was well aware of that. He wondered what the nobles who had scoffed at the Saxons as a peasant army now thought of their obstinate enemy. It had been easy for them to talk boldly when they were in Normandy and far from the points of the sharp Saxon spears, the same weapons now dipped deep in Norman blood. The ability of the Saxons to withstand every attack that Guillaume had thrown upon them marked these men out as a hardy folk indeed. He had never underestimated them, at least so he told himself now. The duke had always known that they would make a most difficult foe, but then, when they had sailed from Normandy, he had also believed that he had considered every eventuality; it was clear now that he had not.

Once again he was considering defeat. Before the council, he had seemed full of confidence and had even gilded his words with uncharacteristic references to his own failings. He had done that because he had needed to be the opposite of what he was at this very moment, which was full of doubt.

The thinning of the Saxons ranks to maintain the breadth of their formation offered them a chance, but that was all it was; a chance. Nothing was certain except for the tiredness of his men and the waning of the sun. He understood full well that if this charge did not work then the next retreat would not be feigned. Tired men lost heart much more quickly than those who still had the strength of their limbs. If those same tired men saw their leaders tumbled from their horses once more, if they did not feel the Saxon wall give even an inch, then they would flee from the field. In a way he could not blame them, the day had been long and bloody, but he knew that he could not survive defeat. For that reason, Guillaume took the lead of the centre formation. He waved away objections from his bodyguards and put himself at the point of the horsemen. In his mind it was decided, he would expose himself to the same danger that he had asked everyone else to do. If he died in the attempt then, he reasoned, that would be better than to survive and see his power broken.

This was not a death wish, for he had not yet given up all hope. He believed most earnestly that this stratagem would work if executed properly. Like a stone flung from a siege engine, they had to hit the Saxon wall at a particular point and hit it hard. A breach made would be difficult to defend against. His trumpeters would announce the success wherever it occurred along the line and the cavalry would ride into it as the infantry pressed the Saxon weapons men so as not to give them leave to fill the hole. This is how it would happen or else the Duke of Normandy would die this day on an English field.

"For Matilda!" He spoke of his wife and smiled as he spurred his horse to the walk.

In front of him, the archers also walked. They made their way to the base of the hill from where they would launch their final volleys of arrows, before drawing their swords or clubs to join with the infantry in the last foray. That same infantry, thinned also by both combat and Guillaume's decision to have some of them follow the knights, walked patiently but without relish, if he was honest, behind the missile men.

Drums sounded and trumpets blew their encouragement. Banners were waved and there was much shouting as officers compelled their men to the fight once more. And they were compelled for they were not running with a savage lust for violence in their hearts. It had come to this, like the slave armies of Persia when they had met the famous Spartans at Thermopylae. Against free men, the Persians had to be whipped to take up the sword. The English were free and so many of his own men were not. He had used fear in the taking of hostages to buy allegiance from both those who owed him fealty or those who professed friendship. As his horse stepped forward under the darkening sky, Guillaume found himself wondering if he were indeed the Persian King Xerxes and Harold the mighty Leonidas. The latter had died gloriously, a hero to his people, the former achieved only one thing of note; he had won.

He had won the battle but he had lost the war.

Dispelling all other thoughts the Duke of Normandy kept that one truth, that Xerxes had won the battle, in his mind as his horse moved to the trot. A glorious death was the prize of those who fell in battle, which meant it belonged to the defeated. Guillaume would be a Xerxes this day, not a Leonidas.

***

The shock of impact came close to where King Harold's banner was waving in the grey light. Like Thunor's hammer, the charge of the cavalry struck the shield wall as this time the riders did not turn their steeds, or allow them to be turned, at the last moment. If the beasts tried to shy away from the hedge of spears their riders proved too strong and kept them on their course, straight to destruction. Long spears impaled horse and rider alike but therein lay the undoing of the close formation. A wounded horse reared, its forelegs kicking ineffectually at the air before it, as it screamed its pain and fear, and then the animal pitched forward as its strength bled out with its arterial blood. Over a thousand pounds of dying horse collapsed on the front row of the Saxons. The second row pushed backwards to avoid the same fate as those men before them, who were crushed under the beast. In doing so they forced the third row back as well. Almost immediately the knights rode their animals over the bodies of the fallen and into the breach.

King Harold saw the fall of the horses upon his men and knew that even the best of armour would not protect his brave theigns who had held that part of the wall. He watched, momentarily captivated by the scene, as several knights pushed into the opening. One fell from a spear thrust but two more deflected similar attacks with their swords and spurred their horses through the ranks so that they would be behind the fyrdmen and with more room to move. And more followed them.

It was the end of days.

He had no reserves on which to call to block the breach. Every available man had been pressed to the wall. Guillaume had found their one weakness; God had allowed him to do it.

***

At the last moment, Aethelmaer raised his shield and ducked his head behind it. His spear was snatched out of his hand by some force of unimaginable strength. The weapon had pierced the animal obliquely in the chest and exited behind the left elbow. The horse reared and spun to the left, careering into another animal, both riders desperately trying to keep their seats on their mounts. The collision forced the unbalanced horse back towards the shield wall onto which it began to topple. Instinctively the men attempted to backtrack but were resisted by the two rows behind them who, due to their many hours of training, were pushing forward to maintain the resistance of the wall.

Aethelmaer glanced over his shield to see the horse coming down before him and pushed backwards more urgently. The animal caught his shield with its head, a surprisingly heavy weight coming down at speed. It staggered him. A flailing forelimb caught the man to his right on the shoulder, but he did not fall.

The shield wall surged forward again but the presence of the horse's body forced a concave shape in the formation. More knights stormed forward, their trumpets braying the call of their success. Coming at the full gallop they leapt the fallen bodies before them and the weight of the horses was thrown heavily against the stretched Saxons.

The shield wall broke.

A wedge of mounted men broke through the thinned ranks and separated the centre of King Harold's army from the right flank. The men of Holderness found themselves being pushed back by the Norman incursion. A foreign body drove them from their king. Behind the mounted knights came many foot soldiers adding the weight of their numbers to maintain the breach.

"Push forward!" Coenred commanded.

The Saxons recovered and attempted to push back against their enemy. The knights had continued forward to get behind the lines and now they turned and came back upon them from the rear. Coenred realised that they were now fighting on two fronts and that was an impossible contest for a shield wall to enter into. There were fewer knights than infantry, however. Coenred commanded Cudbert to hold the line in front with his fyrdmen while he called Aethelmaer and Hengist to him. He could not see Thrydwulf.

"We must protect their backs. Kill the knights!" He told the younger huscarls.

They turned to meet the new threat. The Norman knights were disorganised and their horses were blown. For the moment they did not seem to represent a real threat, but that would be fleeting. With Aethelmaer and Hengist flanking him Coenred approached five horsemen who were pulling their horses around and preparing to attack the rear of the Saxon lines.

The three huscarls stood together but not as close as they would in a shield wall proper. With fighting-spears levelled they closed on the knights. The first one was having a problem with his mount. The rider could not see that the animal was pierced by a spear, the shaft had broken off but a significant part still protruding from its ribs just behind his right leg. The beast was dying and refused to move. Coenred sent his spear forward and stabbed the man in his chest. It was not a killing wound, however, the advantage of height helped put too great a distance between the rider and the Saxon. Despite the attack, the man remained in the saddle and dug his spurs into the horse. Coenred stabbed again and, having closed the distance, was able to achieve a greater impact. The horse suddenly shuddered and fell to the ground, but its master was dead before it.

The remaining four horsemen lacked the problems of their now dead companion. One of them held a spear, still intact, but the other three were reliant upon their swords. Two of them moved to the left and two to the right as they tried to outflank the huscarls. Wood and metal met as blows were traded, but no one gained an advantage.

The knight with the spear rode in close and thrust at Coenred, who ducked under the weapon. He rose up and lunged forward. The man had moved on, however, but then another appeared going in the opposite direction. Coenred continued forward, gripping his spear in two hands, his shield hanging from his arm. He drove the point into the flank of the horse. The horse fell onto its right side, the motion dragging the spear shaft out of Coenred's hands. Seeing an opportunity a Norman rode up behind the eorl and slashed at his head with his sword. Coenred fell to the ground.

"Coenred!" Aethelmaer saw his lord fall. He swapped a flurry of blows with his own protagonist and managed to drive the horse away. Quickly he went to Coenred's prone body.

Hengist glanced in their direction. He was forced to return to the fray as the knight pressing him landed a heavy sword blow that fell partly on his shield and partly on the top of his armoured shoulder. The young warrior thrust back and slashed the man's upper thigh. The Norman screamed out in both fear and pain, then wheeled his horse away. It would prove a debilitating wound.

Turning to see what had happened to Coenred, Hengist did not see the knight with the spear coming from his left and behind him. The man made the most of his advantage and drove the spear into the unprotected back of the huscarl.

Aethelmaer glanced over his shoulder in time to see Hengist fall to his knees. The young warrior's mouth was open and his eyes wide from the shock of the blow. The fall continued. Forward onto his face he went, his sword released from once strong fingers.

Aethelmaer rose and charged forward. The knight was looking down at Hengist from his now stationary horse, a grin of satisfaction on his dirty face. He was raising the spear point and the Norman's eyes moved to look at the blood that stained the weapon. Too late he saw the advance of the Saxon. With all the strength that remained to him, Aethelmaer flung himself bodily at the Norman. He leapt into the air with his sword held over his head, the point hanging in the air. As a result of his prodigious leap, he was able to bring the clear steel down in two hands and plunge it deep into the man's chest.

The huscarl collided with the horse, which staggered under the weight of the armoured warrior. He rebounded and fell backwards. The animal moved in the opposite direction, but its rider was still transfixed upon the sword and he followed Aethelmaer to the ground.

There was only one knight left. He looked down at where Aethelmaer fought to rid himself of the body of the Norman who now pinned him to the ground, having fallen on top of him. The knight had only his sword, which was not long enough to reach a man laid out in this fashion, and he did not relish leaving his mount to walk on foot behind the Saxon lines. Instead, he decided to let his horse finish the warrior off. He motioned it forward towards where Aethelmaer was rolling the body of the dead knight from off on top of himself.

Aethelmaer recovered his sword and succeeded in moving into a crouch, his shield hanging heavy on his left arm. The horse reared up above him, the knight driving his spurs into its flanks. The forehooves came down very close to the huscarl who quickly backpeddled away.

A motion to his left caught his eye. The Norman did not see it. His eyes were fixed on Aethelmaer as he tried to get his horse to rear up again. His first inclination that he was unguarded was also his last. A strong hand grabbed his belt and heaved him out of the saddle. He crashed down heavily onto his back and found himself looking up into a grim and bloodied visage.

Coenred drove his sword into the man's neck without a moment's hesitation.

"Coenred?!" Aethelmaer crossed quickly to his side.

"A wound, no more, but it knocked me senseless." He told him.

"We are all but dead. Hengist has fallen and I know not where Thrydwulf might be. I think that he has fallen also. They are all dead!"

"Then let us die fighting like huscarls!" Coenred growled.

The gap between the centre and the right had been pushed ever wider. As Thrydwulf had feared, and as Coenred had known, their ranks had been too thinly stretched. The Saxons now lacked the weight to push back and close the gap as the Norman infantry pushed and fought their way through the opening, just as they did elsewhere on the battlefield.

Coenred marched forward towards the end of the Saxon wall that was getting pushed back upon itself. He had only one intention now, to reach King Harold by whatever means he could. If that meant hacking his way through hundreds of enemy soldiers then he would do so. He knew also that Aethelmaer would not leave his side until his last breath had escaped.

Together they plunged into the fight once more. They fought the hardy soldiers of the Duke of Normandy. Several such men now stood before them. Aethelmaer was a young man but greatly experienced in war already. He knew that the battle had passed the critical stage and that they were not likely to survive it. If they were to live then something extraordinary was called for.

A spear shot forward and the young huscarl deflected it with his sword. A second caught him on the upper arm, bursting the links of his steel shirt, but not reaching the flesh beneath. A third Norman leapt forward with his spear held high, the point aiming for Aethelmaer's heart.

Coenred retrieved a fallen fighting spear and moved in front of Aethelmaer. The Norman was still in midair when the spear caught him in the stomach. Holding the spear with both hands Coenred heaved the fellow away to the right. The man was screaming in horror, but he was only one of many. Bunching his powerful muscles Coenred thrust the spear from him and saw it and the man it held pitched back into the ranks of the Normans.

In a fluid motion, Coenred drew his sword and moved forward, onto the body of a dead horse that lay before them. Another of the soldiers stabbed at him with his spear but the Eorl of Holderness caught the point on his shield and pushed the man violently back. The Norman had been standing on the body of a dead knight and he lost his footing. He fell heavily out of sight.

Several horses and men had fallen at this point, but their bodies were now creating a kind of bulwark. More knights ranged about, however, their charge had lost impetus. They were hacking and hewing at what was left of the shield wall here on the right. They were enjoying similar results as with their previous attacks, head on to the hedge of spears, but it would not be long before more of them got around the back of the tight formation. From the front came the foreign infantry and they now posed the greatest danger. The soldiers were coming forwards in numbers and they could, as they had already shown, climb over any obstacle before them.

Without waiting for men to follow him Coenred stepped forward and down from the body of the horse. He was his old self once more; the huscarl. With a cold grimness, he took to the fight without a moment's hesitation. His sword deflected blows and cut through flesh. His shield endured countless attacks. The golden dragon of Mercia painted onto a black background slowly becoming disfigured under the many hews of the enemy blades. Bodies began to surround the place where he stood, where he fought like a titan.

Aethelmaer joined him on his left. They found themselves in a maelstrom of moving bodies, flashing weapons, and dark shadows. Men's voices became indistinct. The banner of the Eorl of Holderness appeared behind them. Cudberct, Captain of Fyrdmen, with his sword arm hanging broken and limp at his side, climbed onto the dead horse now behind the huscarls. He held the pole with one hand, roaring at his enemies.

Coenred was breathing heavy. He knew that this was a fight that he could no longer win. The enemy seemed to be all around him now. They were on every side, or so it seemed, their tireless weapons stabbing at him, hitting him, opening up old wounds as well as new ones, and yet still he fought. He was cold to the pain that he felt in his limbs and his chest. Cold to the wounds that now bled and stained the once bright armour that he wore. His vision was blurred, but not from a hurt, sweat was running into his eyes from beneath the battered helmet that he wore.

Two Norman footmen appeared before him. One waved a club at him, a simple piece of wood with a large iron ball riveted at one end. Coenred dodged one fellow and stepped into the club wielder on his left, his sword describing an arc in the air. The fine Saxon steel cut through skin and flesh and then bone. Both club and hand fell to the bloodied floor and the man wheeled away with a scream.

The second of them swung a sword horizontally, held with two hands, aiming to catch the Saxon in the side. Coenred was quicker, much quicker. He allowed his sword to complete its arc, stepping into the swing and using the momentum to turn his body around on the spot. He accepted the Norman sword with his own. Then he lifted the blade up with the other's still resting on the top. He pushed that weapon away and then the man stood before him, defenceless. Without a moment's thought, Coenred thrust forward and sank the tip of his bright steel into the man's gut. He pushed, twisted, and then pulled the blade clear, using his foot to kick the dying Norman away.

He was lost in the battle. Lost in the fight. The red mist had descended and claimed him so that only the next foe held his attention. His next foe was an armoured man on a horse. The light was failing as evening came and so he looked like a dark shadow riding out of a sea of bodies.

The knight swung down with his sword but his reach was too short and Coenred dodged it easily. He thrust back himself, aiming for the horse, but the knight spun the beast expertly on the spot. Its rear caught him on the left, his much-battered shield taking the impact, but it staggered the Saxon. Again the sword came down from on high and Coenred had to parry it this time. Once, twice, three times more. The Norman was throwing everything into the downward stroke, trying to drive his enemy to the ground.

Coenred thrust himself forward. He took another blow on his shield but stabbed with his sword at the knights exposed thigh. The man pulled back on the reins, making the horse rear on its hind legs. Coenred moved to his right, ducking under the flailing hooves and slashed the animal across its belly. It screamed and staggered forward, knocking into the Saxon. Stumbling backwards Coenred attempted to right himself. He looked up and saw the horse right above him. It was a large black shape in the grey light. It loomed over him, seemingly growing bigger and yet hanging in the air as if it had not yet begun its downwards traverse.

And then it came.

Aethelmaer saw the fatally wounded horse fall on top of Coenred. He moved towards it. The rider lay on his side, his leg trapped under the beast. Aethelmaer slew him where he lay without any hesitation. Then he moved around to the front of the dead horse to see if, somehow, Coenred had escaped being trapped. All he could see was the body of a huscarl, his head still bound by a helmet, but the face turned away from him.

Before Aethelmaer could move again his body jerked involuntarily and a bloodied spear point protruded from out of his chest.

The banner of the Eorl of Holderness began to fall as several arrows pierced Cudberct. The weight of the pole proved too much for him to hold aloft but his hand never lost touch with the wood of the smooth shaft. Together they fell, no more to rise.

***

Thrydwulf knew that the battle was lost. His instinct never lied and he had lived by it for many years. This was not the situation that had looked most likely only a few moments before, but then the Normans had changed their tactics in a very subtle way. Instead of throwing all of their strength at the breadth of the wall they had concentrated it at particular points and forced openings. It was what enemies looked to do when faced with such defences.

The next logical thing to do would be to throw the reserves at the places that had been opened and plug them, but they had no such spare manpower. Only one more stratagem remained to them and it was one that seldom worked. The Saxons at Fulford Gate had tried it and had been almost annihilated. The Vikings had also attempted it at Stamford Bridge and they too had suffered grievously. There was no alternative, however, other than to flee blindly from the field, a thing no huscarl could ever consider doing.

"STEP BACK!" Thrydwulf called out in a loud, steady, and commanding voice.

Thrydwulf repeated the order, knowing full well what was intended and why. As expected the huscarls, theigns, and experienced frydmen acted on the command and repeated it to their fellows stood hard by them. Still presenting their shields and weapons to the enemy they stepped back a pace and drew a little closer together.

Their aim was to preserve the strength of the immediate shield wall, of which they were a part, and so preserve their lives. The problem with this tactic was, however, that the once single shield wall had become fractured into many smaller walls, none of which would be as effective.

In all the generations of Saxon history, no one had come up with a better response to the breaking of the shield wall, however. Some would die, that was beyond doubt, but some might survive.

Thrydwul thought about Coenred. He could not see his friend. He could not see Aethelmaer or Hengist either. They had been pushed apart by the press of bodies. The huscarl had become separated from his lord. He wanted to fight his way to him, to defend him, to do the duty of a huscarl, but he did not know where the man might be. It surprised Thrydwulf that it was not anger but a cold determination to do something to preserve life that now filled his mind.

"STEP BACK!" He shouted again knowing that he would have to repeat this command many times before they knew their fate.

***

King Harold slew the Norman soldier with a single stroke that pushed the man's spear aside and cut into the side of his neck. A second soldier came at him but Osfrid stepped forward and buried his Dane-axe into the man's left shoulder, destroying his arm and sending him to the bloodied earth.

"Osfrid!" Harold clapped him on the shoulder and the Royal Companion turned and grinned at him. It was like looking into the eyes of a wild beast. The red mist had descended upon loyal Osfrid, even as he knew that the battle had now gone against them. He was committed to his death oath; he would defend his king to the end.

Without a word, Osfrid returned his gaze to the struggling lines before them. He never saw the arrow that pierced his eye and went into his brain, killing him instantly. Harold saw it and stepped forward to catch his friend's falling body. In the midst of the struggle, it was a mistake, but as instinctive as any fighting manoeuvre that he might make. Osfrid was an old friend and trusted companion, he could not allow him to fall ignominiously into the blood stained mud beneath their feet. In clasping the brave warrior's body with both hands, however, Harold was unable to make any defence. He saw the horse's hooves and glanced up to see a Norman knight glaring back down. The man's sword flashed in the darkening light and Harold felt a pain on his neck and left collarbone.

He dropped Osfrid unceremoniously, his mind quietly regretting it even as he looked to defend his life. His left arm felt numb, unresponsive, but he swung his torso to the right and pushed with the great round shield that still hung from his damaged arm into the horse's face. As he expected the animal backed away, startled. The knight momentarily lost his balance and had to lower his sword arm to regain control of his steed. In that brief moment of respite, Harold struck back and inflicted a wound in the man's exposed leg.

Given the opportunity, the king might have done more damage, but a second knight, striding on foot having lost his horse to Saxon spears, came at him from the right. Another circled around behind him. Gallantly, like the son of Godwin that he was, Harold fought them but he could not defend himself from three directions. The links to his mail coat burst and cold steel cut into his flesh. The knights hacked and hacked at him as he fell to the floor, his bejewelled sword falling from his grasp. Still, they hacked, even after the life had left the body of the King of England. The sullied steel of the Normans butchered the majesty out of the fallen Harold.

***

There was but a moment of respite when Thrydwulf's men passed over the ridge top and onto the reverse slope. He estimated that he had some two thousand souls, mostly fyrdmen but also a few theigns. Many had been forced under his command with the splintering of the shield wall and knew him not but responded to his voice of authority all the same. Together they backed down the hill but continued to face the enemy even though, for the moment at least, they could not actually see them.

"Who are you, man?" A large theign asked of him.

"Thrydwulf, huscarl to the Eorl of Holderness." He growled back as they continued to walk slowly down the reverse slope.

"Your lord is dead I believe!"

"I do not doubt thee."

"We must get us to a place of safety."

"Mayhap I should return and defend his body?"

"To what end?"

"I am a huscarl, I cannot be robbed of my honour in this fashion!"

"You have your death-oath, that is true, but wyrd has taken you from your lord and placed you here, with a great number of men still breathing, think you not your honour would be better served by seeing these men moved safely from the slaughter?"

Thrydwulf felt a surge of conflicting emotions. He was a rough and ready man, peasant born and not given to airs and graces, but being what he was, a huscarl, a man of honour, meant more to him than he could ever express in words. Coenred had been his friend for much longer than he had been his lord. Theirs had not been an effusive relationship for that was not Thrydwulf's way. He lacked the finer manners of the others, so he spoke little in their company, but always he had been proud of being one of them.

Now, he was no longer a huscarl and probably the only one of them to still draw breath. The thought rocked him. He was not fired with anger to seek revenge but rather he became numb to the madness that surrounded them.

Without another word they continued to make their way from the ridge, even turning now to face the direction that they were taking, northwards towards Malfosse.

***

The Duke of Normandy sat on a stool that had been brought by a servant and he drank deeply from a flask containing weak beer. He was surrounded by his bodyguard, somewhat less in numbers than he liked to see, but still looking formidable. His half-brother Robert was there also, his face stern. Robert took no joy in killing, for him fighting was a necessary thing, but not for enjoyment. Guillaume believed that this was one of the aspects of his brother's character that helped make him so cool-headed in stressful situations; he rarely let his passions get control of him.

"HAROLD IS DEAD!"

The shout came sudden and was repeated several times before four men appeared before the duke. Two were on foot and two on horseback. Guillaume recognised Walter Giffard, one of his trusted servants, still seated on his horse, but the other three escaped his recall initially. They stood covered in blood and sweat, their eyes wild and their manner, like their appearance, unkempt and undisciplined.

"It is true, My Lord," Giffard said.

"How did he die?" Guillaume asked in a tone of voice that was far from jubilant.

"We hacked him down!" One of the knights on foot shouted, he raised a bloodied object into the air as a trophy of his prowess. It took Guillaume a moment to realise that the man was holding up the severed genitalia of a fallen enemy.

"He was holding his companion who was shot in the face with an arrow and he cut him to the quick!" The other foot soldier added with a grin. "Even his wife won't recognise his face after this day!" He laughed heartily.

"Where is he?" The duke's face darkened.

"We left him a bloodied corpse where he fell," the laughing warrior replied, "though we cut his flesh so many times that he verily floats in a lake of his own blood!" The other three laughed uproariously.

Robert, Count of Mortain, wondered, as he had many times previously, how men could not read his brother's face and know the danger that they were about to bring upon themselves. Guillaume rose suddenly from his seated position and glared at the four knights.

"HE WAS A KING!" The Duke of Normandy roared at them.

"He was your enemy!" Walter Giffard said in a quieter voice, all of them suddenly becoming aware that the duke's response was not what they had initially expected.

"An enemy is deserving of respect and an enemy king even more so. I will not have soldiers of fortune treat a royal personage in such a manner. Giffard, you saw the body?"

"Aye, My Lord, it as they say. They hacked his body even when he was dead." One of the men afoot shot him a baleful glance but the man on the horse paid him no heed.

"Can you find Harold again?"

"Aye, My Lord."

"Then do so and recover his body and place it under my protection."

"What of the remaining three, My Lord?"

"You will surrender your swords to the Count of Mortain and consider yourselves under arrest until I have the leisure to decide your fate." Guillaume turned away from them and stood with his hands balled into fists and placed on his hips as if he had to occupy them with something other than the necks of the knights.

"My Lord-!" One of the confused knights called out and started forward towards Guillaume but Robert spurred his horse forward and placed it between the men and his brother.

"You have heard the command. You are under arrest on your own cognizance, surrender your swords and report to the commander of the rearguard!" Robert spoke tersely to them.

The three knights looked at first mystified and then crestfallen. Sullenly they handed over their swords, the badge of their rank, to one of Robert's men, who also took the bloody prize, and they then stomped away under a cloud. Giffard turned his horse and with four spearmen in attendance headed back to where he believed the body of King Harold still lay.

"Was that necessary?" Robert asked when the others had put some distance between them.

"Do you know why I did it?"

"I know that you were fond of Harold Godwinson when he was at your court, he was a man of some merit."

"And he was a king, properly crowned."

"He wore a crown that you coveted."

"Which is why I cannot allow for those who killed him to remain near me." Guillaume turned and relaxed somewhat. "Yes, I liked Harold, he was a man after my own heart. If he had not taken the crown then verily he and I would have become great friends, I believe."

"But he did and now he's dead and the crown is yours."

"Yes, I took his crown and might it not seem in the minds of some a most simple task to accomplish?"

"To those who hacked down a man over-matched by numbers, yes, I could see how it might." Robert smiled grimly. "They did it once, they might be moved to do it again."

"Yes, mayhap not by their own ambition but by someone else's."

"This was always a risk, in the heat of a victorious battle someone was likely to kill Harold Godwinson if not yourself."

"I'd rather it had been me, at least then it would give Harold's death some legitimacy. This despoiling of his body though, it could provoke an even more violent response from the rest of the Saxons that still reside in this country. Harold was popular after all."

"They would make a martyr out of him."

"Unless God chose for him to die this day."

"One could argue that but it would be difficult to prove."

"Would it?" Guillaume looked directly at Robert. "Did they not say that Harold was holding a companion who had been shot in the face?"

"Yes, they did."

"And that Harold himself could not be known by his face alone?"

"Again, yes they did."

"Then have it put about that Harold died from an arrow to the eye, as God ordained. We will not allow him to become a martyr for they will ring their opposition to us around his death otherwise. Make safe the body also, I will have it buried somewhere secret. Mayhap those reckless knights might do is a good service after all."

"What will you do with them?"

"They will be exiled from England, but they will not go without some reward."

"They may not go quietly, talk of killing the English king would rescue their names from obscurity."

"Obscurity is exactly where they are destined to be, but not without a little recompense I suppose."

"My Lord!" Eustace, Count of Boulogne, rode up with a large body of horsemen following.

"Eustace, I rejoice to see thee unwounded!" Guillaume changed his attitude and expression, a broad grin erupting across his face.

"And I thee friend, but the day is not done, a large number of Saxons has taken up a position north of the ridge, they may form some kind of resistance still."

"They will be dealt with," Guillaume assured him.

"Give me the honour?" Eustace insisted.

"You have not done enough this day?" Robert asked.

"The Saxons are dying all over the field, but if there is one thing that they have taught me it is that they are an obstinate people. If they can gather enough numbers to them then they might still deny us a safe road to London!"

"Eustace is right," Guillaume told his brother. He turned to the nobleman. "Do you have enough spears for the task?"

"I will take all that I can with me."

"Then God grant that you clear the Saxons from their position. Go with my blessings, friend!"

***

It was, mayhap, a little too late in life but Thrydwulf realised that he was sick of fighting. They had reached the place that local men called Malfosse without incident, but some Normans had followed them at a distance so they knew that their movements had not gone unnoticed. It seemed, however, that the Normans on foot were in no hurry to encounter Saxon spears again, for they kept themselves beyond the range of an arrow.

The Malfosse presented nothing particular about it with the exception that someone had dug some half-hearted earth-works on either flank. An embankment of sorts had been begun and a few sharpened steaks inserted to make it look more formidable. The true genius of the place lay in the dyke that was now between the Saxons and the ridge. The dyke was some five foot wide and four foot deep but tall grass was growing in it, the water having run dry due to the exceptional summer. Even as they had approached the place the men who had no knowledge of the location had almost fallen foul of the invisible and sudden drop in the ground.

"What do we here?" The theign asked.

"Nothing," Thrydwulf told him.

"Nothing?"

"Friend, this is not Tadcaster. King Harold will not be sending a fyrd this way. King Harold is likely dead, just like my lord." Thrydwul had no wish to be hard on these tired men but he already knew that their world had come to an end.

"Then we should make our way north." A fyrdman suggested.

"There are others." The theign insisted. "Others will fight!"

"I doubt it. All the greatest of the eorldermen and aethelings stood with us this day, some, like us, may have escaped but many, I fear, were cut to the ground." In the dying light of the day Thrydwulf's face looked indescribably sad. "There is no one to take the place of the king, his sons are just boys."

"Evening casts a cloak over us, we should use it to depart these lands," the fyrdman suggested.

"HORSEMEN!" The call came from another fyrdman. They looked south and saw a large body of mounted knights coming towards them at a trot.

"These Normans will give us no peace!" The theign complained.

"Good, I want none!" Thrydwulf retorted. The sight of the horsemen sparked a new flame inside of him. If the huscarl had taken the trouble to examine his feelings he might have realised that though but a moment ago he had believed himself sick of the fight his instincts got the better of him. However, he told himself that this was a fight that they could not win. He did not care. There was a dark thought deep within the cave of his skull; mayhap these Normans would allow him to quit this world like a true huscarl, bloodied and fighting still. He hefted his shield back into position and drew his sword. "Loose formation!" He told them.

"What, no shield wall?"

"No shield wall," Thrydwulf repeated himself in a louder voice so all the men could hear. "We have no need of a shield wall here."

Eustace expected the Saxons to form up in their customary defensive shield wall and was momentarily perplexed that they remained scattered behind the incomplete fortifications. A few of them were gesticulating and shouting at the Norman horsemen, but most looked decidedly disinterested, at least from where he sat atop his trotting horse.

"The fight has gone out of them!" Robert de Vitot Declared.

"Mayhap, or else they are so tired from the day's work that they can no longer muster a defence?"

"What matters it to us, a few more dead Saxons is fewer swords to worry about!"

"Aye, let's to it."

As they closed the distance to the Saxons Eustace settled his mind to the task. He had come here as an ally of the Duke of Normandy, but he expected to be suitably rewarded for his efforts. His men had fought well on the right flank, he deserved some recognition for the fact. Finishing off these last fyrdmen would only strengthen his claim on Guillaume, a man known to resist parting with his money.

Eustace drew his sword once more and raised it into the air as the signal to advance to the canter. The earth trembled to the impact of so many hooves as the knights advanced. Very few of them now carried spears as they had become broken in the extended fighting of the day, but they had all been replaced with the sharp steel of their swords.

Thrydwulf watched them come, leaning on his spear in an uncharacteristically reclined manner. He appeared relaxed, even accepting of their apparent fate. Such was not the truth, however. He could feel no desire to kill again this day, but he knew also that these Normans would not let them be. This fight had to be done and it seemed to him that it be done in the quickest manner possible and so he set the trap.

When the horses accelerated to the gallop Thrydwulf changed his stance, raising the shield on his left hand and moving his fighting spear into an overhand position. All the Saxons prepared to meet their enemy, but still, they stood separately.

Eustace of Boulogne banished his confusion at the abject stupidity of the Saxons to respond properly to a cavalry charge, all it meant was that they would slaughter them where they stood.

Beneath his leather shoes, Thrydwulf could feel the tremors in the ground caused by the approaching horses. He regretted that the animals would suffer so because he had always had a fondness for them. He reminded himself, however, that huscarls had the sense not to put such as horses in harm's way unnecessarily; they used horses to get to the battlefield, not to fight from upon them.

The knights roared their various war cries, their trumpets blew, and small pennants fluttered from the few spear shafts that remained intact. They came like a wave of irresistible force, crashing down to sweep away all Saxon resistance. Robert de Vitot rode immediately behind Eustace, he could see the nobleman's back, smell his horse, and occasionally catch a glance of the enemy on whom they were now closing so fast. He held his sword at the ready, away from his body. His heart pounded with the thrill of the charge and even though his muscles ached from the day's long toil he remained hungry for more blood. What Robert did not expect was for Eustace to suddenly disappear right before his eyes. He got a sudden, clear, and unobstructed view of the Saxons, loosely arranged in front of him, before his world became a sudden maelstrom of sound, blurred vision, movement, dull pain, and sudden darkness.

The front third of the Count of Boulogne's force disappeared into the hidden dyke at the gallop and without any warning. The bones of men and horses alike were broken like twigs under the impetus of their forward charge, sudden fall, and the weight of quickly descending bodies. The middle third could not halt their own advance and rode over the fallen, hooves crushing man and animal alike. These horses stumbled and fell, throwing riders down to the waiting Saxons who, in their turn, pounced upon them eagerly. The final third of the horsemen also came on, but they had managed to slow their steeds if not actually stop them. It did not matter, the Saxons sprang over the bodies in the dyke, inert or flailing, and attacked the stunned riders with a savage vengeance. The power of the charge was dissipated long before it reached its objective.

As soon as he could Thrydwulf stepped back from the killing. He had no stomach for it now and besides, there were no fighting men left to match himself against. Most had either been dragged from their horses and hacked to death or, barely a handful of them, had managed to turn their beasts and beat a hasty retreat.

"This day is done!" Thrydwulf announced to no one in particular.

"What now?" The theign asked of him.

"Whatever thy wish!" The huscarl answered.

"I am for the north." Thrydwulf nodded his understanding. "You can come too, there will be a need for a good captain of huscarls."

"Think you so?" The warrior gazed at the carnage before them. "The Normans have won haven't they?"

"I believe it to be so."

"Harold is dead along with most of his kin. His enemies will flock to the Norman banners and sell us to them for estates and titles that they ill deserve."

"I remain a high-theign!"

"Aye, I know, but you will have a Norman overlord and he may not like a man such as I, a killer of his kind, standing at your side. Besides..." Thrydwulf turned and looked eastwards into the distance.

"Besides what?"

"Besides, I have a longing to walk the earth, like other Saxons before me." He turned to look the theign in the face. A rough man of peasant birth who had risen through his unrivalled prowess as a weapons man to become a huscarl, a man of honour, wealth, and station. They were the elite of their kind and dangerous, for that much alone the Normans would not welcome them.

"Where will you go?"

"Norway. We killed many of their warriors at Stamford Bridge; mayhap they will be in need of one who proved himself better than their own?" Thrydwulf managed a tired smile.

"May wyrd be kind with you."

"Wyrd will do as it likes and I pray to no gods, but all the same, friend, may favour find you wherever it is you go. We were once members of a great brotherhood, Coenred, Hereric, Sigbert, and I.

The best huscarls that any lord ever assembled if only Edwin had been deserving of us?"

"Never forget that friend, wherever your wanderings take you remember all of your brothers; living and dead."

"Living and dead." Thrydwulf heaved his sword and turned to leave but then suddenly stopped. "What manner of huscarl am I? I swore my death-oath to my lord and friend. He lies dead upon the field of battle while I still live!"

"Wyrd will have its way, friend."

"There is no honour in this."

"Huscarl, I fear our world is ended, as are our days. Mayhap you are right and the Normans will let me live as a theign with one of them as my overlord, but if you are right in this thinking then they will not permit me to have many swords at my call, least of all a champion as formidable as yourself."

"A champion? Even in this dark hour, you find a reason to jest!"

"If I jest it is to make your parting a little easier for we will not see one another again in this life and it has been an honour to know you brother, even for so short a time."

"And I you, brother." This time Thrydwulf did turn on his heel and stalked off into the darkness.

***

Edwin crept through the dark leading the horse. Senlatche Ridge was an eerie place now after the battle. The Normans had placed men around the site to keep the scavengers away. Much of their army had returned to Hastings to recover from their exertions and the toll of the encounter. He was still nursing the wound in his shoulder. Feeling sorry for himself at his forced departure from the battle the first inclination that wyrd had turned against the Saxons had reached them. Around a small fire, he had sat with other wounded men and the boys employed to fetch and carry water and food for the warriors. A dark fatality had descended upon them all. Those men who could had begun to leave, which only seemed to add to the despondency. No one had spoken very much. Further down the hill, the horses had been pegged and it seemed that many a man decided that the owners of these beasts now lay dead on the other side of the ridge. They took whichever they came to first without a challenge.

For some reason, this open theft annoyed Edwin. His horse was down there along with Coenred's and the pack horse. He was inspired to defend it and so he had jumped to his feet, gripped his langseax, and determined to protect his master's belongings. He did not know if Coenred was indeed dead, but even if that was what had become of him Edwin was decided not return to Holderness alone and he would need at least one horse to carry them both. The rush for the horses had not been that great, however, someone was showing an interest in Coenred's saddle.

"Oi! Be off, that be my masters!" Edwin had yelled at him as he came down the hill.

The man turned and looked at him. He was a fyrdman. A dirty and blood stained bandage was wrapped around his head. "I reckon your master won't be needing this anymore lad, but there are plenty to choose from so don't get riled. No one's interested in fighting anymore!" He scowled at the boy and then turned on his heel to pick out another steed.

Edwin felt like there was a stone in his stomach. He knew that the man was probably telling the truth. Coenred was likely dead, along with Thrydwulf, Aethelmaer, and Hengist, and all their fyrdmen as well. He could not summon his customary optimism to lift his own spirits.

Once he reached the horses he put the langseax away and stroked each one of them in turn. They seemed skittish. More people were coming down the hill now, every one of them intent on escaping the closing of the battle, which would account for many more lives.

"You should get thee gone!"

Edwin turned to look at the man. He was dressed in reasonably good quality armour, stained by the day's work. He judged him to be a theign of middle rank.

"I would stay and fight if not for this hurt," he told him.

"Aye, so would many such, and die as likely as not." He steadied his horse. "The battle's done and your master probably dead like, get thee gone."

"I won't leave him!" Anger tinged his voice.

"A noble sentiment, was he a lord? A theign maybe or a huscarl?"

"Yes, a huscarl, but an eorl now."

"There is no rank recognised by the dead, boy. They are all just the dead. However, if you would look to recover your master's body then get thee to a place of concealment. Take as many horses as you need or can manage. Wait until the witching hour and then return to his last place of stand, mayhap you will find him there."

"You do not stay to fight?"

"I have kith and kin to tend to. My lord is dead, I saw him fall, and I am no huscarl but a theign. I have no death oath to keep me here. It's each for themselves now, for the likes of thee and me."

"I will stay."

"Aye, but not to fight. Do as I say and wyrd might smile enough on you that you find his body and take it home with thee. Fare thee well, boy. Fare thee well."

Edwin had done as the man had said. Taking all three horses he had moved into the woodland nearby and tethered them in a small clearing, screened by bushes and trees. Then he had waited for the longest time of his life. In those hours he had thought of Coenred and their chance meeting in York. Edwin had been orphaned when raiders had burned down the family farm in the middle of the night. Only the call of nature had saved him. Afterwards, he had become destitute and close to giving himself as a bondsman to anyone who would take him in. Instead, Coenred had taken him as his shield-bearer. He had been a hard master, but only in the sense that he was a warrior and his trade required him to be a hard man. Never had he struck or berated Edwin. He had seen other servants used that way and worse, even in public. Coenred had been good to him. That was a strong enough reason for taking his master's body home to Holderness. Better that such a noble man was buried on his own land then left down here to be spoiled by foreigners.

He left the horse at the top of the ridge, using a broken spear thrust into the hard ground as a tethering post.

The king's standard had gone, taken no doubt as a trophy. Remembering where they had first stood in the morning Edwin veered to the right of the centre of the ridge. Bodies were scattered everywhere and it was probably a small mercy that they were not completely visible in the moonlight. The Saxons had learnt that the Normans tended towards cruel atrocities and, as if in proof of this, many a brave warrior had been hacked severely, even after they had fallen, and their remains hardly suggested that they had been people at all when they had lived.

It was not too difficult in the light of a new moon for Edwin to discover that there were dead horses lying amongst the dead men. This saddened him. He had a liking for horses. The men who had fallen here had had a choice in their fate, the horses had not. Nevertheless, he had to move amongst their grisly remains to achieve his own goal. The first indication that he was in the right place was the discovery of the pennant for the Eorl of Holderness. The white line drawing of the huscarl on the green cloth seemed to shine in the moonlight. Edwin scurried over to it and recognised the pierced body of Cudberct, the captain of the fyrdmen. There was nothing that Edwin could do for the man now, but he withdrew his knife and cut the banner from the pole. It seemed right that this emblem did not fall into the hands of the enemy.

It occurred to Edwin that Coenred would lie somewhere in this vicinity, surrounded by his friends, his warriors. It would be grisly work, but he was determined to accomplish the task that he had set himself. In a low crouch, he began to circle the area around Cudberct. In this manner, he came across young Hengist and then Aethelmaer. Although he had not been a huscarl himself the two younger warriors had always treated him well, mayhap finding some kinship in their shared youth. Seeing their dead faces both saddened him further and yet also made him all the more determined to find Coenred.

And find him he did.

He had come across yet another horse. There were bodies lying around it, curiously mainly Normans. When he made his way round to the front of the animal he discovered his master. The dead horse was laid on top of him with most of his body under the carcass. It was the helmet that signalled the dead warrior to be Coenred. It had a distinctive long nose guard and equally long cheek guards as well. Edwin knew that steel helmet well as he had had to care for it when his master was not wearing it.

A flame of elation ignited within him but it was quickly doused by the sudden realisation that Coenred was pinned to the ground by a dead horse that had to be removed before he could pull his body free. For a while, he simply sat and stared at the problem before him and wondered how he was going to achieve this task. First, he tried to lever the animal away using a broken fighting spear that was still long enough to work effectively for the task, but the dead weight of the horse would not move. The injury in his shoulder also stopped Edwin from exerting all of his stocky strength as well. Next, he thought of butchering the beast so as to lessen its weight, but he realised that this would be both a lengthy and noisy task. Eventually, it occurred to him that he could use the horse he had brought to drag Coenred out from under dead steed.

A moment later and he returned with the pack horse. It clearly did not like being there, no doubt spooked by the smell of death that was everywhere. As part of the equipment that they had brought with them on the journey down from York, there was a generous length of rope. Coenred, like many who travelled frequently, had often said that a length of rope was indispensable and so it had proven on more than one occasion. Edwin was glad for the wisdom of huscarls.

It took some struggling but eventually, Edwin was able to thread the rope under his master's arms and over his chest. He apologised in a quiet voice when he had to be rough to prise the body up so as to pass the rope underneath it. Finally, he was able to tie the rope off at this end and then tie the other to the pack horse's harness. When he was ready Edwin took hold of the bridle and encouraged the animal to pull. There was a moment when he wondered if he might cause Coenred more harm in doing this, but then he berated himself for being a fool; the man was already dead and therefore beyond all further harm. The horse stumbled amongst the dead and slowly made forward over the grisly ground. Suddenly its pace quickened and Edwin stopped it immediately.

He returned to Coenred. In the weak moonlight, he could see his master quite well. There was dried blood on his face and all over his fine armour. It was impossible to tell what might have been his own and what had come from the dead horse. Edwin tried to lift him but the weight was too much, even for his broad shoulders. He looked over the fallen warrior and decided what must be done. Working quickly, but also as quietly as he could, Edwin removed Coenred's war harness. He put the sword, which was still in his hand, to one side and removed Mildryth's scramseax from the heavy leather belt that he also unfastened. He glanced at the knife appreciatively in the moon light and then tucked it inside his own tunic. Removing the coat of mail was difficult and took much longer than Edwin would have liked but eventually, it was done. He would have preferred to have been able to carry such a valuable item with him, but he knew that it was too desirable and would attract the attention of others. He tried to lift Coenred again, putting his hands under the warrior's arms and around his chest. This time he had more luck.

Edwin was shorter than Coenred but he had grown up on a farm and was used to physical work. His back was broad and his own strength impressive. He dragged the huscarl over to the pack horse and heaved him upright. Gritting his teeth he first leaned the man's body against the side of the horse, which moved but not enough to allow the body to fall, and then heaved him up so that he lay face down on its back. The animal took several steps away but protested no more than that and Coenred did not fall. Edwin took a moment to bite his lip as pain surged across this shoulder. He feared that he might have re-opened the wound. He put his hand into his tunic but he could not feel any blood.

Slowly he led the pack horse, with the former huscarl on its back, towards the forest where he had waited for so long. Back there, where the other two horses still patiently waited, he had passed the time by making a litter to help carry Coenred's body. He had reasoned that the litter would only hinder his movement amongst the bodies that covered the battlefield. As he walked the horse, giving occasional glances at the body to be reassured that it was not in danger of falling off, he congratulated himself with this piece of reasoning.

When they reached the small clearing Edwin took Coenred down from the pack horse and laid him carefully on the litter that was already fastened to his own horse. He placed his master's sword beneath him and then wrapped him in his cloak. He used a length of rope to fasten him onto the litter. Glancing back he wondered what would befall the bodies of his master's former companions, but he was just one man and he could not rescue them all no matter how much he wished to do so.

There was nothing left to do now but to leave the area. Edwin tied the pack horse to Coenred's and took its reins after mounting his own in his left hand. Together they headed out of the forest and skirted the north of the ridge and then started walking down the northern road accompanied by the sound of the litter scraping against the earth. He had not gone very far when an armoured figure suddenly stepped from out of the shadows at the side of the road and spoke to him in a foreign accent. Edwin stopped his horse and waited. He wore his langseax still, hanging at his side, but he felt too weary to draw the weapon. He was not here to fight.

The Norman soldier advanced with his spear levelled. He was nervous, being left to guard this area on his own at night in a hostile land. He was also tired and bruised. He looked at the horses and then quickly assessed the young man riding the lead animal. There was nothing threatening in his demeanour, he decided. In fact, the Saxon looked very much how he also felt.

"What do you here?" The Norman demanded in a heavy accent.

"My Lord!" Edwin waved behind him, towards the litter. "He died in the battle. I am taking him home."

The Norman advanced cautiously and circled around so that he could see what was on the litter. There was no doubting the shape of the body. "Dead?" He asked.

"Dead." Edwin agreed sadly.

The soldier moved closer and prodded the body with the butt of his spear. There was neither movement nor sound. He relaxed somewhat and turned to Edwin.

"What do you do with it?"

"I'm taking him home. Up north." Edwin waved absently northwards. The soldier looked him over again.

"Weapons?" Edwin showed him the langseax hanging from his belt but made no effort to remove it.

"To keep away robbers." He said in explanation. It was obvious to the soldier that the langseax was not a sword of note and, therefore, not of any real value.

"You go north?" Edwin nodded in reply.

The soldier stopped to think. His orders were to chase away the body robbers who descended upon such sites after a battle. He could see that there was no fight left in this Saxon, just an admirable loyalty to his fallen lord. He had served in England previously as an attendant of one of King Edward's Norman advisors and he did not share the insulting assessment of the Saxon's character that many in the army seemed to have. If this boy was taking a dead body north to bury then he could see no harm in it.

"Gold?" The thought came to him late, perhaps due to his own tiredness. Again Edwin nodded and held out Coenred's purse. He was not in the habit of carrying lots of money on him, but there was enough in the bag to make it worth having. The soldier received the purse and weighed it speculatively in his hand; he liked the feel of it. "You go north and do not stop until home." He decided. "Keep sword for protection and I wish you a safe journey. I have never seen you nor you me!"

"Agreed!" Edwin said without emotion.

The young Saxon prompted his horse forward again and started once more northward. The Norman soldier stood and watched him leave. In truth he was sick of fighting and killing and somehow allowing this man to take the body of his lord home from the field made him feel a little better. The money in the purse would also help warm him against the coming of what would probably prove to be an unfriendly winter.

Thursday, 25th October 1066

Coenred's Estate in the Isle of Holderness

Mildryth stepped into the morning sunlight and pulled her woollen cloak more tightly around her. There had been a heavy frost and her breath misted before her eyes. She sighed deeply. Eanfrid had told her that none of the men of this family had died away from the estate. She had wished for that to be true.

It was barely the eighth hour of the morning and the sky was still dark. The sun was rising, however, but it would lie low on the horizon and its light would be weak. This was the time of the days growing shorter and the nights longer. Traditionally people stayed close to their hearths where it was warm and where they would have company. Mildryth longed for a day when she did not sit all alone by her hearth.

Edwin appeared, riding his horse. He waved when he saw her and it seemed to Mildryth that a certain light had gone out of the young man since his return from the south. He appeared to spend a lot of time with his horse as if it were the only friend that he had in this turning world. Although Osred had had a house built for him, so that he could stay on the estate, Edwin had shown no interest in either working the land or tending to the sheep. The only person that he had time for was Eanfrid and from what Cynwise told her all they did was talk about Coenred. Together they would sit and swap stories. Eanfrid had more to tell but he was eager to learn what his former master had done in the battles that he had missed. It seemed, now, that the two of them lived in a world that existed only in the past.

It was not in Mildryth's nature to live that way. There was too much sorrow for her there and so she looked to the future and that brought a small smile to her chilled face. Absently she held her stomach and her smile became more knowing. Coenred had given her a gift.

She was a woman of the world. Lying with Coenred had not been done in innocence; always she had understood the likeliest outcome of that love. There was even some joy in the knowledge that she was not too old yet to be without such a reason to live. Godgifu had told her that Abbe was overjoyed that her eldest son had at last fathered a child, even if it was out of wedlock. She was barely three months into the pregnancy and not even showing as yet, but the wily old woman had read the signs expertly and knew of Mildryth's condition. It was a secret that she had shared only with her younger son's wife.

That made Mildryth smile again. It was a sign of acceptance if nothing else. Coenred's mother had a fierce love for her grandchildren. There would always be a home for them here, in Holderness. Boy or girl, it would not matter.

The weak light of the sun glinted on the slow moving river to the south. Beyond its dark waters, she could see the far hills of Lyndsey, dusted with snow and shining gently. She felt cold and shivered. As if in full understanding of this an arm wrapped around her and pulled her gently backwards. She felt the soft collision of their bodies.

"It is cold," was all he said.

"But the air is fresh."

"You are cold also."

"My cloak is thick and warm, but where is yours?" She turned to face him.

"I am man enough still to stand a little cold air." He smiled at her and she saw a similar sadness in his eyes as Edwin carried, only it was much deeper. "I will fetch some more wood for the fire today."

"You cannot, your wounds-"

"Are mended, but my strength will not return to me if I spend all of my time sat beside the hearth, no matter how warm it is or how delightful the company. I must swing an axe from time to time."

"Coenred." She laid her head against his chest, covered as it was only in a linen shirt. He encompassed her with both his arms and laid his cheek on her soft hair.

"It will not be in anger; my war-work is done."

"What is to become of us?"

"I know not. Mayhap some Norman lord will take this land for his own and make us work for him, or mayhap all the eorls that still live will be called to the court of the Normans and made to swear an oath of fealty so that they may keep their lands and titles."

"Will you swear such an oath?"

"To keep Holderness? Yes, I would. If doing so meant that all who still reside here can keep their living and their homes then that will be the way of it."

"You will not join the others who call for the Saxons of the north to rise up?"

"All the aethelings are dead; there are none to lead us. In this Edwin and Morcar are right, for once, mayhap."

"Some ask for you to lead them."

"I am not that man, even as the Eorl of Holderness. I have put up my sword and my shield, as I swore to do. You may have no fear on that score, Mildryth."

She looked up into his damaged face and was pleased to see that he was smiling. There was a little light in his eyes now and a warmth about him that she found reassuring.

"I have something for you." He released her and stepped back a pace. From behind his back, he took something and covered it with both hands so that she might not see it too soon. "Here!"

"What is it?"

"Hold out your hands." She did as he asked and felt something heavy drop onto her palms. When he withdrew his own hands she saw her scramseax, once again. "You told me to return this to you when the argument of the day was settled and such as we meant nothing to the great men of our day. Today is such a day."

"I had never thought to see this again!" Mildryth declared. Slowly she drew the blade from its sheath and saw her name engraved there.

"I kept it always as a token of the bargain we made that day in the longhouse of York. It never left my side, not once." He stroked her hair with a finger. "Well, except once, when Edwin took it."

"Edwin is not to be blamed for that!"

"No, I don't look to admonish him for it either. I owe that man my life."

"Even though he thought you dead?"

"He had no reason to know that I still lived. I was senseless to the world. It was only when he stopped at the priory and the priest there offered to clean me, to make me fit for burial, that it was revealed that I had not died. The priest was a healer, the second such that I have encountered. He delayed our journey home somewhat."

"I do not complain, for Edwin brought you home alive."

"And with your scramseax."

"It kept you safe, I knew that it would."

"It kept me bound to you."

"Then it is only right that I give you something in return." Her smile became more expansive.

"Mildryth, there is nothing that you can give me that is more than what you already have." He looked a little confused and it almost made her laugh. Men knew so little about women.

"There is one thing that I can give you that you have not guessed at, my love. We will have a child this summer!"

She looked expectantly into his face. At first, the confusion remained, but then it gave way to realisation and that, in its turn, gave way to joy.

"I am to be a father?"

"Yes!"

He hugged her then with unrestrained enthusiasm and her own joy was complete. Whatever the future days might bring under the reign of the foreign king she knew that she would have Coenred in her life to help her face those days. He would be here for her and their child, and for all the people who lived on the estate. He may no longer look to go to war but she knew that the warrior in him would always be there to fight for them and to defend them against come what may.

"Come back inside and sit with me before the hearth and let us talk of many things that we may have yet come to pass."

"Yes."

He held her fingers as he turned and made for the house that was just a little ways behind them and she let him lead her across the threshold. She would be a wife and a mother again, only this time she knew how fragile life could be. It was a second chance at happiness and so Mildryth determined to live each day to its fullest.

Rome, Italy. 1087

The way of wyrd is beyond the understanding of any man. My Lord, King Harold Godwinson of England, commanded me to London before he joined battle with the Bastard of Normandy. At Senlatche Ridge he stood and fell with all of his proud Saxon warriors and a thief was made a king. I could no longer reside in the land of my fathers for I would not serve one who was so much less than the man he had murdered.

There were many who called for the Saxons to rise up and destroy the invaders but they were men who had tarried when called to the banners of their king. There was not one amongst their number who could command the way that Harold had. I would have nothing to do with those who, in my estimation, had failed their king so completely. They deserved their fate under the heels of their new masters.

And wyrd plays a new trick by bringing me to Rome, the seat of the church that I refuse to acknowledge. I am called a heathen here but my skill with words saves me from any true persecution. I serve a new lord who has need of men who can write and speak in various tongues. It serves me to serve him for here I learn much merely by listening. It is in this capacity that I learned of something that put a little joy into my later years; the thieving king is dead!

I have spoken with one come directly from the Ducal Court of Normandy to inform the papacy of what has transpired. Of course, there is no pope to be found here in Rome, only turmoil following the death of Pope Victor III. The manner in which these Christians go about choosing their leaders both mystifies and entertains me. The Witan was by far a more preferable way by which to choose a leader. It is said that it will not be until next year before a new pope succeeds the previous one, who managed to reign for a little more than a year. There is even one here known as the *antipapa*, a man called Clement III, who claims to be the legitimate pope and rules Rome accordingly. If it was not for the great lords of the many courts who regard themselves as Christian, as my lord King Harold did, then I would fail to see how this religion of theirs' would survive. Regardless of the chaos that now ensues the lords here hunger for such accounts for, as they like to say, when a mighty tree falls it creates openings within the forest and this was one large and corpulent tree.

The life of Guillaume of Normandy knew little in the way of peace and it was while campaigning, defeating the French at a town called Mantes, that his end was begun. A stray ember, I am told, frightened his horse, which bolted suddenly. The fat duke was thrown against the pommel of his saddle and his gut burst within him. He took five weeks to die, residing all that time in the Priory of St. Gervase at Rouen. It seems that guilt settled upon his head for I am told that he pardoned those he had imprisoned at that time, including his brother Odo who so believed that his god had granted them victory over the Saxons.

Guillaume began to dispose of his wealth to the church and the poor both. Of his possessions, he granted Normandy to his errant son, Robert, and the Crown of England to William Rufus. Neither stayed long after the bequest was made and it is for certain that neither son was there on the day that their father died. No, on Thursday 9th September, Guillaume lay in his cell, surrounded by lords and bishops who thought only to retire to their own lands to safeguard their possessions. Like carrion eaters, they waited upon Guillaume to expire. The servant of the Norman Court told me that the duke's last breath was expended in asking God to forgive him for taking what was not his to possess. He died with the remorse of a true thief upon his tongue.

And he was thereafter treated like a thief. Upon realising that he was dead the lords and bishops quit that place in all haste, leaving the body of their duke to be tended by his servants, who quickly stripped it naked and left it lying on the cold stone floor. It fell to a poor knight to undertake the funeral honours of this once supposed king. I am told that when it came to laying him in his coffin they could not close the lid, so large had his stomach become in later life, and when it was forced shut his guts burst. So passes in suitable glory the king of thieves and the murderer of the Saxon people.

I will live out my life here in Rome and when I die I expect to be laid out in an unremarkable grave, one befitting an honest and loyal man. I have made no claim to greatness but I have had the pleasure of knowing some great men. Harold Godwinson was not a man without faults, as no man can claim to be, but he would have better served his people than the foreigner did. Harold had no aspirations to leave the shores of England, unlike the absent Norman. I would have been an eorl myself if wyrd had chosen a different path for my people, so I remain a simple man of letters. It gives me pleasure, however, knowing that I have seen the end of the Bastard of Normandy before my time comes to quit this turning earth. I will go to the hall of my ancestors and there we will sing the sorrow song of our people.

Grendel of Wessex

Known also as Half-foot.

Author's Notes

And so the Sorrow Song Trilogy comes to a close. I have tried to suggest through this account a more realistic account of what happened at the Battle of Hastings than that which was told to me when I was at school. The Norman's were never in a superior position and their victory was never unquestioned. More recent research on this famous battle has revealed exactly what a gamble it proved to be for Guillaume of Normandy. It has also shown that the actual outcome of the battle depended more upon luck than tactical genius, but that is so often the case in such encounters. Of course, the Normans wanted to paint a different picture when they were faced with ruling a hostile country and Guillaume was very aware that to give his rule some legitimacy a claim that God had chosen Harold to die would not harm his prospects.

I have thoroughly enjoyed writing this series of books but I doubt that I will be returning to the genre of historical fiction anytime soon. I have other projects underway that will take me in very different directions. That said, I am very proud of these books and the tale that has been woven through them. I hope that you, as a reader, have found them enjoyable as well.

Also by Peter C Whitaker

The Sorrow Song Trilogy
The War Wolf
For Rapture of Ravens
The Blade's Fell Blow

Alternate History
Eugenica

Historical Personages

King Edward the Confessor.

Born 1003 and died in January 1066. He spent his early years in exile in Normandy before returning to England as the recognised heir of King Harthacnut and ascended to the throne in 1042. He married Edith of Wessex, daughter of the powerful Eorl Godwin, in 1045. This union failed to produce an heir, which in turn plunged Anglo-Saxon England into crisis upon the death of Edward.

Harold Godwinson.

Born the second son of Eorl Godwin of Wessex in 1022, Harold succeeded his father as Eorl of Wessex following the latter's death in 1053. Prior to this he had handfasted to Ealdgyth Swannesha who gave him at least 6 children. Harold met Guillaume of Normandy in 1064 after being shipwrecked. The two seem to have formed a deep respect for each other. On the death of King Edward in 1066 Harold Godwinson claimed the throne. In the same year he divorced his common-law wife and married Ealdgyth of Mercia, possibly a political move to try and unite the kingdom. Harold was killed in battle at Senlatche Ridge near Hastings in 1066.

Tostig Godwinson.

Born in 1026 as the third son of Eorl Godwin Tostig was promoted to the Eorldom Northumbria in 1055. His rule there was considered harsh. He was implicated in the murder of several theigns who were nominally under his protection when visiting the eorl at his request in 1064. In the following year Northumbria revolted while Tostig was away hunting with King Edward and elected Morcar of Mercia as his replacement. His brother, Eorl Harold, chose to support the rebellion and King Edward exiled Tostig as a result, an act that created a fatal schism in the Godwin family. Tostig made several attempts to return to England but they all failed until he allied himself with King Hardrada of Norway. He died at Stamford Bridge in 1066.

Eorl Edwin of Mercia and Eorl Morcar of Northumbria.

Edwin was born around 1046 and Morcar around 1049. Their father was Eorl Aelfgar of Mercia, a powerful and active rival of the Godwins of Wessex. Edwin was promoted to the Eorldom of Mercia following his father's death in 1062 and 3 years later Morcar became the Eorl of Northumbria, succeeding the banished Tostig Godwinson. The brothers continued their father's rivalry with Wessex, an ambition that was not altered by the marriage of their elder sister, Ealdgyth of Mercia, to King Harold Godwinson. Edwin survived the Norman Conquest but died as a traitor in 1071 after attempting a rebellion against King Guillaume. Morcar survived this rebellion as an exile but was imprisoned for several years during which time he appears to have died.

King Harald Hardrada of Norway.

Born in 1015 King Harald lived to become the greatest Viking of his day. He was exiled early in his life and lived successfully as a mercenary abroad, even attaining the captaincy of the Emperor of Byzantium's Varangian Guard. He returned to Norway and in 1047 forcibly took the throne. It is said that he dealt with opposition violently and so earned the name Hardrada or hard rule. He began his long and fruitless war against Denmark almost immediately and it was this that led him to form an alliance with Tostig Godwinson when he looked to restore his wealth and reputation by making good a weak claim to King Edward of England's crown. By all accounts Harald was a very tall man, easily exceeding 6 foot. Throughout his long military career he went undefeated until he encountered King Harold of England at Stamford Bridge in 1066 where he died.

Duke Guillaume of Normandy.

Guillaume would become more popularly known as William as the English found his French name too difficult to pronounce. He was born in 1028 as the illegitimate son of Robert, Duke of Normandy. In 1035 Guillaume became the Duke of Normandy following the death of his father. His transition was not easy and it was not until 1047 before Guillaume was able to consolidate power within his duchy. Even then it was not until 1060 before Normandy itself was free from external threats as represented by the King of France who frequently changed his allegiances. Guillaume's claim to the English throne is founded mostly upon a promise made in 1051 by King Edward of England to choose Guillaume of Normandy as his heir as he was the grandson of Edward's maternal uncle, Richard II of Normandy. When Harold Godwinson declared himself King of England the Duke of Normandy set about his plans to make good his own claim. In 1066 he succeeded Harold. King William reigned until 1087.

Anglo-Saxon and Viking Lexicon

Aethelings	highest branch of the aristocracy including the immediate royal family
Angon	throwing spear
Bondsman	a freeman who has surrendered his freedom for a fixed period due to debt or poverty
Burh	stronghold, later known as 'borough'.
Butescarl	mercenary soldier
Byrnie	coat of steel mail or toughened leather
Ceorl	the peasant class of freemen who owed fealty to their appointed theigns
Dane-axe	large two handed war axe popular with both Vikings and Saxon warriors
Danelaw	that part of England ruled by Vikings between 884 to 954, including large parts of Northumbria
Drekkar	Norse longship, typical Viking warship
Eoldermen	the highest rank of the aristocracy beneath the aethelings.

Eorl	an eolderman, the modern day equivalent is an earl
Fyrd	the Saxon army
Fyrdman	a freeman who fulfils his settlements obligation to provide warriors for military service
Gambeson	a padded jacket worn under a byrnie
Gebur	the third and lowest class of free peasant
Geneatas	the first and highest class of free peasant
Gesipas	king's companion in a military capacity
Grims' By	Viking name for the town of Grimsby, Lincolnshire
Hadseax	small knife, usually a domestic utensil
Handfast	traditional marriage system predating the Christian church
Hide	unit of measurement, 1 hide considered sufficient land to feed 1 family
Hloth	troop, band, gang, often applied to thieves and robbers
Horsbegen	Horse warden

Huscarl	professional elite warriors recruited by the king and later by those lords who could afford them.
Inderawuda	the market town of Beverley, East Yorkshire
Jarl	Nordic equivalent of the Saxon eorl
Jorvik	Viking name for York
Kotsetla	second and middle class of freeman peasant
Langseax	larger variant of the scramseax knife used for heavy work and also as a sword by fyrdmen
League	unit of measurement, 1 league = 3 miles
Lithsman	sailor
Mercia	Former Anglo-Saxon kingdom bordering Wales and extending over what is now the midlands of modern day England
Michaelmas	church festival held on 29th September
Midden	dunghill, refuse tip
Natural foot	unit of measurement, 1 natural foot = 9.8 inches
Nithing	man without honour

Northumbria	former Anglo-Saxon kingdom extending from the River Humber up to Scotland's southern border.
Rod	unit of measurement, 1 rod = 5.5 metres
Rus	Russia
Sandwic	the town of Sandwich, Kent
Scop	poet, story-teller
Scramseax	knife ranging in size from 3 to 30 inches
Skaroaborg	Viking name for the town of Scarborough, North Yorkshire
Snekke	Viking ship similar to the larger longship but commomly used to carry supplies as well as smaller numbers of warriors
Span	unit of measurement, 1 span = 9 inches
St. Peter's Burgh	Saxon name for Peterborough
Theign	members of the warrior class granted a minimum of 5 hides of land by the king or an eolderman, divided into lower, middling and higher classes, responsible for imposing the king's law on the peasant classes
Theow	slave, usually captured in war, or a bondsman

Wergel	Anglo-Saxon system of compensation for the death or injury of a free person
Wessex	former Anglo-Saxon kigndom bordering Cornwall in the west and Kent in the east
Witan	council of leaders constituted from the athelings, eoldermen and bishops

Printed in Great Britain
by Amazon